A LIFE WORTH LIVING

A LIFE WORTH LIVING

by Lorrie Kruse

STORYTELLER
A Publisher of Quality Fiction

Copyright © 2011 by Lorrie Kruse

All rights reserved. No part of this book may be reproduced in any form, by any electronic or mechanical means, including photocopying, recording, or information storage and retrieval, without permission in writing from the author.

ISBN-13: 978-0-9847254-3-4

Book Website
www.LorrieKruse.com

Give feedback to:
for_teddy@arczip.com

A LIFE WORTH LIVING is a work of fiction. Apart from the well-known actual people, events and locales that figure in the narative, all names, characters, places and incidents are the product of the author's imagination or are used fictitiously. Any resemblance to current events or locales, or to living persons, is entirely coincidental.

Cover art by Kathey Amaral
kattnboys.deviantart.com

Storyteller Publishing
www.storytellerpublishing.com
Email: info@storytellerpublishing.com

Printed in U.S.A

ACKNOWLEDGEMENTS

First and foremost, I thank God for giving me the talent to string words together to form coherent sentences and to link them together into an entire story. I thank You for all the blessings You've given me.

Thanks to Storyteller Publishing for liking my book enough to publish it, and to my editor for fixing the passive phrases and making them sing. You rock! Thanks to the wonderful cover artist, Kathey, who made an absolutely beautiful cover. Thanks also to models David and Cassandra for becoming Matt and Abby.

I thank my husband, Brian, for believing in me, for encouraging me every step of the way in getting this book published, and for never allowing me to feel I was wasting time writing. Thanks to my son Tyler for being understanding when writing got in the way of life.

I thank my sister Bonnie Husnick and my friends Peg Rosin and Laurel Bradley for being such wonderful cheerleaders.

Thank you Central Wisconsin Creative Writers' Group. Without you, I might have forever believed my rudimentary writing was the best ever. Because of you I keep raising the bar, pushing to write a great story instead of an okay-story, and for pushing it in directions I hadn't thought of. We make a fabulous team.

And, I especially thank all of the people who have helped me with researching this story. Without your help this book would lack the realism of Matt's and Abby's worlds. I thank Jeff Mattmiller and Pamela Sobkowiak for allowing me to interview them about the real life of a paralyzed person (and Pam for reading an early incarnation of this book). Thanks to the administrative staff of Saint Joseph's Hospital in Marshfield, WI, for allowing me access to their personnel for medical research. I thank Alice Werner for assisting me on the trauma end of Matt's world (and for reading early vesions of this book) and Jamy Yohn for her expertise in physical therapy. There are many others who have helped me, and I thank you all as well.

DEDICATION

I dedicate this book to all the people who live through adversity daily and refuse to let it hold them back. You are an inspiration.

To those of you tempted to let crisis do you in, please give life another chance. What looks bleak and hopeless today truly will take on a whole new look tomorrow. Just ask Matt who thought a happy ending wasn't possible. Overall, it truly is A Life Worth Living.

"If you're going through hell, keep going."
Sir Winston Churchill

CHAPTER ONE

Matthew Huntz awoke with the groggy sensation of a mid-day nap. Teetering on the edge of asleep and awake, he longed to give in to sleep. A sense of wrongness pulled him in the other direction.

His tongue felt thick, like it'd been sprayed with drywall paste. An overly clean scent of Lysol stung his nose—too clean for his house. The pillow beneath his head was too crisp.

Giving up on sleep, he opened his eyes. A hospital bed guardrail stretched out just inches from his face. His heart did a weird thump flutter that would have been okay had he been looking at a pretty girl and not the pebbly texture of the plastic rail.

Damn. His attention shifted to the IV needle that pierced his hand. His skin puckered beneath the tightly-pulled tape.

How the hell had he ended up in the hospital? Accident? No. He distinctly remembered getting home. Actually, what he remembered was breaking into his house—again. One of these days he'd learn to keep track of his keys. The point was, he'd gotten home.

Footsteps pattered outside his door. "Hello," he called out. His voice was gravelly, barely carrying past the bed. The sound of the footsteps moved into his room anyhow. He relaxed at the sight of his father. Which was silly. At twenty-six, Matt knew his father wasn't some mystical being who could make the world perfect just by his mere presence. Still, he felt better.

His mother followed closely behind his father. She looked tired and her clothes were rumpled. She was still beautiful, regal, with her back straight and her head held high, as though balancing a book on her head.

His father sank into a chair while his mother stepped

up to the bed. Lying on his side, Matt tried to look up at her, but his head wouldn't move. All reason fled as a panicky sensation deep in his stomach took over. He almost whimpered, a wimpy-girl noise, but the sound got stuck somewhere between his brain and his too-dry tongue. Thank heavens it had. Bad enough he was stuck in a hospital bed without knowing why without adding insult to injury by crying out in front of his father. Besides, as quickly as the cry had formulated in his brain, he'd noticed the rigid edge of the plastic collar pressing into his chin, holding his head in place.

"Matthew," his mother said, her voice raised. Her eyes remained riveted on her son as she reached behind her, patting the air until she found his dad. "Look, Carl. Matthew's awake."

Matthew. His given name. The one they used whenever he'd gotten into trouble as a kid. Or when they were worried. Either way, trouble or worry, nothing good ever came with that extra syllable.

He looked past his parents to where he figured his fiancée should be. He saw nothing but a patch of light blue wall. His parents were here. Shouldn't Crystal be here as well?

"You gave us a scare," his father said. "How do you feel?"

Where are you, babe?

His father put a hand on Matt's arm.

Matt stared at the wall another second and then turned his attention to his father. "Like I fell off a roof." The words squeezed out slowly. Had he fallen at one of the houses they were working on? No. He'd gotten home.

"I'll bet you do. You've got one heck of a goose egg where you hit the side window."

Side window? "Can't remember."

"The doctor said you probably wouldn't. He called it protective amnesia, or some nonsense like that. He said it was a good thing, that it would keep you from reliving the accident."

"Accident?"

"On Highway A, near the gravel pit. You hit a tree."

He tried to force a memory but none came. The Hideout was on Highway A. Wednesday wasn't pool night, though. Had he made plans to meet Crystal there after work? An uneasy feeling pestered him. He wouldn't have gone out there on a whim. Not with fifteen miles of ice-glazed, backwoods Wisconsin roads leading the way. The roads *had* been icy. That much he did remember.

His thoughts went back to Crystal. His father hadn't said he'd been alone. He stared at the robin egg blue patch of wall where he'd earlier expected to find his fiancée standing. He pictured her comatose in a bed like his own. The panicky feeling hit full force. "Where's Crystal?" He reached out and grabbed the guardrail. "Was she with me? Tell me she's okay."

"She wasn't with you. She's fine."

He searched his father's eyes. If his fiancée truly was okay, wouldn't she be here at his side? "Where is she? I want to see her."

His father looked up at Matt's mom. An entire conversation passed between them in an instant without spoken words. The same connection of thoughts he and Crystal had yet to achieve.

"She had to go back to work," his father said. "She's already missed two days."

Two days? Matt worked through a mental calendar. The accident must have happened Wednesday night. Thursday. Friday. Crystal didn't work on Saturday. "What day is it?"

"Monday."

Five days gone. His dad wouldn't abandon their jobsites that long unless there was good reason. That same good reason would have Crystal at his side. She had to be in the hospital somewhere, confined to a bed.

"I have to find her." He pushed back the covers to get up. His legs wouldn't move. Another wave of panic built. *It's okay. Nothing's wrong. It'll be like when I tried to move my head.*

His mother just stood there with one hand pressed to

her mouth and her other arm wrapped around her waist, trying not to cry. Something she didn't do easily.

Matt tried to ignore the way his heart slammed against his ribcage. He touched his thigh. His fingers dug into muscle. The only sensation he felt was the gown's soft cotton weave against his fingertips. He moved his hand to his hip, to his stomach. Nothing.

His father stood and captured his wrist. "Son."

"What's going on?" Matt asked.

"We should let the doctor explain."

"Will it sound better from him?"

His mother lowered her hand. She stood straight. "Honey, you broke a bone in your back." Her voice was soft, as if hoping to lessen the impact of her words.

A broken bone. Broken bones could be mended.

With a pat on Matt's arm, his father said, "I'll go find Dr. Meyer."

Matt looked up at his mother, wanting her assurance that everything would be okay. *Everything* was rather broad. So he narrowed it down. "Crystal's really okay?"

"Yes, honey. She's just fine." She smoothed her fingers over his hair, her touch light.

He wanted to believe her. Really, really wanted to. But he had a hard time believing Crystal would be sitting at her desk at the office while he was unconscious in a hospital bed.

His father came back and stood behind his wife. His arms enveloped her in a loving way, like always. Matt prayed he and Crystal would be like them thirty-some years from now.

A man stepped into the room seconds later. He looked youthful, even with gray around his temples. His blue jeans and Hawaiian shirt contrasted with the stethoscope draped around his neck. "I'm Dr. James Meyer. Do you know why you're here?"

"Mix-up with a crappy travel agent?"

Instead of laughing, his father rolled his eyes and shook his head. Not even a hint of a smile. Matt looked back at Dr. Meyer who, unlike his father, was smiling.

"Dad said I had an accident. Broke something."

"Yes, the T1 vertebra." Dr. Meyer sat in the chair by the bed. He opened Matt's chart and held up an illustration of the spine. Pointing to a bone high in the back, he said, "This one."

"I can't feel my legs."

"Your chart says you're in construction. I assume you understand how electrical wiring works?"

"Yeah?"

"Imagine your spinal cord is a main electric line and your nerves are wires branching off the main. Your vertebra is pressing against the main wire, preventing the electrical impulses from passing that point. The swelling should be down enough by tomorrow to allow us to operate."

"Fixing the main line, right?"

"It will fix the fracture."

"Which will fix everything else."

"It's not that simple. If there's damage to your spine—"

"No." Blood pulsed behind Matt's ears. "It's going to fix everything." He looked to his father. *Tell him, Dad. Tell him it's going to fix it.*

His father stubbornly remained silent.

Dr. Meyer sat motionless for a moment and then nodded. "Do you have any questions?"

He did, but he doubted the doctor could answer why this happened to him. Or what he was supposed to do if he didn't get better. No. *Until* he got better. Not *if*. Definitely not *if*. He tried to shake his head. The collar stopped him. "No."

"If you think of anything, have the nurse call me. Otherwise, I'll check in later."

Within seconds after Dr. Meyer left, someone else entered the room. Soft-soled shoes whispered across the floor. Too soft to be Crystal's dress shoes. A nurse came into view. Smiley faces covered her blue smock. Probably meant to cheer up the patients. Wasn't working.

"Sorry to do this to you," she said, "but I've got to kick you out."

He wished the nurse had been referring to him. He'd love nothing more than to leave. Just get out of bed and walk out of here. Even if it meant having his naked ass hanging out the back of the faded gown.

"Can't we stay just a bit longer?" his mother asked.

"I wish I could let you, but your son needs his rest. Two people can come back in forty-five minutes."

"But he just woke up."

Matt forced a smile to reassure his mother. "Don't worry, Ma. I'm not going anywhere." With or without the ugly gown. Not anytime soon, anyhow. He had to work hard to keep the smile in place.

His father squeezed Matt's shoulder. "We'll talk more later, okay? For now, do as the nurse says and get some rest."

His mother leaned over to kiss his cheek. He couldn't feel her hand even though he was certain she was touching his back.

"Ready for a change of scenery?" the nurse asked as another nurse joined her.

Matt watched his parents leave. "An ocean view would be nice." Walking barefoot on a sandy beach with Crystal at his side, this mess behind them.

A sudden, sharp ache in his chest competed with the throbbing at his temples. Why was Crystal at work when she should be here with him?

"Somewhere warm," the second nurse said. "Aruba, maybe." They pulled the covers away and gathered up stacks of pillows he hadn't been aware of.

"On three, we're going to roll you," the first nurse said. "One. Two. Three." Pain rocketed through his neck when they moved him onto his back.

"Nice ceiling," he said, riding out the wave of pain. "The ocean would be better."

Both nurses grabbed the sheet and pulled him toward the left edge of the bed. As soon as he realized he was about to be rolled again, he reached for the guardrail. "Really." His voice rose like a sissy's. Thank heavens his father wasn't here right now. "The ceiling is fine."

The guardrail slipped from his fingers. He clenched his teeth and groaned as they rolled him onto his right side.

"Sorry." The first nurse picked up a pillow and pressed it to his stomach while the other nurse left the room in a flurry of quiet footsteps. Probably rushing off to politely inflict pain on some other poor soul. "It's best you lay on your side. Helps you breathe more deeply so you don't get a buildup of fluid in your lungs."

He willed himself to feel the next pillow. It may as well have been air.

She pulled the covers back into place and then grabbed a corded control, placing it in his hand. "You've got a steady dose of morphine through the IV. However, this button will give you an extra dose. Is there anything you need?"

Crystal. Here. With me. "No."

"Okay. Push the call button if you need me."

He closed his eyes and listened to the sound of the nurse's footsteps as she left the room. Such a simple sound. One he wondered if he'd ever make again. No, damn it. When. When would he make that sound again?

What if it's never?

Not wanting to go down that road, he shook his head the little bit the collar allowed. The throbbing at his temple screamed. He rubbed his thumb across the button on the morphine control. No. He couldn't. He didn't want to be asleep when Crystal came. Because she would come. As soon as she knew he was awake, she'd come.

Hoping to ease the headache, he massaged his forehead. Fresh pain shot from the sutured wound he grazed. He didn't want to think anymore. Not about Crystal. Not about his injuries. Not about anything. Besides, everything would be fine after the surgery. It had to be.

He gave in and pushed the button.

CHAPTER TWO

"Matthew, wake up." A female voice drifted through to his consciousness. "The surgery is over."

Sludge filled his head. The task of opening his eyes too complicated, he left them closed. The woman had said something. He couldn't remember what. Something important? He didn't know or care. He just wanted to burrow under a thick layer of blankets and sleep for forty years.

"Matthew, come on. Wake up."

He opened his eyes to thin slits. Why was she pestering him?

"That's right. Keep opening them. Let me see those brown eyes of yours."

He moved his head, bringing her into sight, prepared to tell her to leave him alone. It took him a moment to realize the collar was gone. He touched his neck. Skin. Nothing but skin. What she'd said finally sank in. The surgery was over. With Christmas-morning expectation, he touched his hip and then moved as far down his leg as he could reach and back up again. His heart thudded. Nothing. He must have misunderstood. She must have said he was going into surgery.

"We'll have you settled back in your bed soon," she said as she stepped out of view. The gurney moved.

No. They still had to operate. Fix that main line, which would fix everything else. He reached out with awkward movements. He couldn't find anything solid to grab on to. Blinding pain shot down his neck when he moved his head. He reached up to massage away the pain. A layer of gauze covered the back of his neck. His breaths came hard and fast.

They had operated.

He closed his eyes and willed the pain to go away—

the physical and the emotional. The nurse pushed him through a set of swinging doors. The cart swayed gently as they moved down the corridor. The lights above him took on a strobe-like quality. His breathing slowed, and the sludge coating seeped around his brain again. His last conscious thought was that this had to be a dream. A horrible nightmare. Because stuff like this happened to other people, not to him.

He was only half aware as people came and went throughout the day—nurses, his parents, his brother Brad and his wife Jenny, his best friend Derrick...and Crystal...finally. She was with him now, her fingers woven through his. He knew it was her by the fit of their hands. He tried to focus on her touch, but what he couldn't feel stood out more.

The dream wasn't a dream.

A tight band squeezed his heart. Tears burned his eyes. His father wouldn't give in to the tears. Neither would he.

Crystal's fingers tightened around his. She sniffed loudly. Her pain became more important than his own. He opened his eyes. The room was dimly lit, but he couldn't miss the fresh tears that crept down her cheeks. Damn, he hated seeing her hurting like this. He gave her hand a tug until she looked at him. Just like his mother, she was beautiful, as always—even with the red-rimmed eyes and a pink nose contrasting with her emerald green silk blouse. Leave it to Crystal to wear silk to the hospital. He twisted his mouth into a grin, hoping to calm her. "Better call a plumber, babe. Your face is leaking."

She swiped her fingers across her cheeks. Somehow, her makeup remained intact. He wanted to wrap her in his arms and hold her close. Take away the pain that had her crying. He did the next best thing. He brought her hand to his lips. Thank heavens she hadn't been in the truck with him. If she'd been injured, or—

No, he refused to let his mind go there.

She edged closer. Not a strand of her short, blonde hair swayed with the movement. Of course, that would be a difficult feat considering how teased it was. "Fluffing," she called it.

"How are you?" she asked.

He rubbed his thumb over the back of her hand. "Thankful you weren't with me in the truck. Dad said I had the accident by the gravel pit. Did we have plans?"

She shook her head before looking away.

"Did I call?" he asked.

"No." Her gaze locked on to his. "You didn't call."

He hated not being able to remember. He kept digging, needing to know what happened. "You know why I was out there?"

Her lip trembled. Tears flooded the corners of her eyes. Her, crying. The very thing he never wanted to be responsible for. He held out his arm. She stood and then leaned close to him, jarring his neck in a burst of pain. For a brief second he thought about giving himself a dose of morphine. But only for a second. Right up until he realized he'd be sleeping through his time with Crystal, now that she was finally here.

He buried his face in her hair and breathed deeply, willing the pain away. Her hairspray's sweet scent made his nose twitch and he hoped he wouldn't sneeze. He focused on her filling his arms and the weight of her against him as he pressed kisses to her head. "I love you, babe."

Her body shook. Hot tears warmed his neck.

The overhead lights came on. He lifted his lips from Crystal's hair and saw Dr. Meyer's reflection in the window surrounded by the night blackness outside. Behind Dr. Meyer was a nurse. Crystal pulled away from Matt and then stood and turned away.

Great timing. Matt struggled to not glare at Dr. Meyer. "Don't they ever let you leave?"

Beside him, Crystal wiped her face with the backs of her hands. She felt too far away. Way too far.

Dr. Meyer smiled. "I have two teen-aged boys at home. Being here keeps me out of the war zone." He opened Matt's chart, scanned the pages, and then looked up. "On a scale of one to ten, ten being unmanageable, how would you rate your pain?"

Matt looked at Crystal. The distance between them kicked the emotional pain scale up to around twenty. He wished he knew exactly what she was thinking.

"Matthew?" Dr. Meyer prompted.

His neck hurt like a bitch, but he wasn't about to admit it. "About a three. Two, maybe."

Dr. Meyer made a notation in the chart and then turned his attention on Crystal. "I'm going to test Matthew's sensation. Perhaps you'd like to step out of the room until we're done."

Crystal nodded and then slipped from view.

Matt couldn't stand the sound of her footsteps carrying her away. "Crystal, stop."

She leaned back into his field of vision.

"Stay."

She hovered by the end of the bed. She seemed nervous, like he'd asked her to do something illegal. He held out his hand. Time stretched. His arm grew heavy hanging in the air. Why couldn't she just come to him? He tried to keep his face impassive. Finally, she stepped forward. Her hand meshed with his. He tightened his fingers around hers. Everything was going to be okay.

Although he wasn't surprised when the testing revealed he had no return of sensation, bitter disappointment accompanied each poke of Dr. Meyer's mangled paperclip. Each "no" response felt like a piece of his soul being ripped away.

He'd get through this, he told himself as the nurse pulled the covers back into place. "This is just temporary."

Dr. Meyer pulled a chair close to the bed and sat. "I'm going to be straight with you. You had no areas of sensation below your injury. That typically indicates a complete injury."

"Which means?"

The room was silent for a moment. With his eyes locked on his patient's, Dr. Meyer said, "Complete injuries are permanent, with no chance of recovery."

An ocean roared in Matt's ears.
No chance of recovery.
Permanent.
Matt saw his future slipping away. "So you're saying I get the good parking spots now?"

"Not yet. The only conclusive indication of a complete injury is a severed or severely damaged spinal cord, neither of which you have. Therefore, your injury could very well be incomplete, which means you may recover some or most of your sensation and, or mobility."

But not all?

Crystal rubbed his shoulder. "It'll be okay, honey. You'll walk again. I know you will."

He put his hand over hers. "Like she said, I'm going to walk again. So tell me what I need to do to make that happen."

The doctor shook his head. "There isn't anything you can do except give your spinal cord a chance to heal."

"How long will that take?" Crystal asked. "A week or so?"

Yeah. A week or so. It'd be hard, but he could put up with being stuck in bed for that long.

"Every injury is different. It could come back right away. It might return slowly. However, a recovery after eighteen months is rare."

"Eighteen months," Crystal echoed.

The amount of time seemed like a lifetime while also feeling no longer than a blink of an eye.

Crystal pulled her hand from beneath his. "But it probably won't take that long, will it? I mean, you're just saying eighteen months as a precaution, right? Matt can't possibly be stuck this way that long."

Nothing wrong in what she'd said, but Matt heard something else. He heard her saying she couldn't possibly be stuck with him this way for that long.

"Matt's got a very physical job," she said. "One he loves."

He let go of the breath of air he'd worked up. Of course, her concern had been for him. Something he never should have doubted.

"Normally, any recovery that will happen comes soon after the injury, but some recovery later is not unheard of."

Matt chose to blank out the words "any" and "some" and focused instead on "soon." He liked soon. The quicker he was back on his feet, the better.

"Will Matt—" Crystal covered her mouth and looked up toward the ceiling. He expected the tears to start up, but her eyes remained dry, which left him wondering why she'd quit talking.

"Yes?" Dr. Meyer asked.

She lowered her hand. Her gaze fell on Matt for just a second before she looked away. If the question was that hard, he didn't want to hear it. He found himself mentally leaning forward, anyhow, virtually on the edge of his seat, waiting.

"Will he get his memory back?"

Matt frowned. *That* was the question she couldn't ask?

"It's not likely..."

Crystal nodded while Dr. Meyer went on to say something about head injuries and the mind being like an erased tape, stuff Matt paid little attention to as his thoughts fixated on Crystal's reaction. Why the hell had she needed to work up the courage to ask such a thing? Why had the question even come up? If he ever figured her out, it'd be a miracle.

"Matthew?"

"Huh?" Matt grunted as he looked away from his fiancée and back at the doctor.

"I asked if you had any questions."

He thought for a moment. "How long am I going to be here?"

"Six to eight weeks for physical, recreational, and occupational therapy."

Six to eight weeks? Hadn't the doctor said his recovery would happen quickly? Six to eight weeks didn't sound very damn quick. It sounded like valuable time wasting away when his father needed a full crew. Clearing up their current contracts was crucial. Once the frost lifted, the four men of Huntz & Sons Construction had to devote all of their time to the group home, or they'd never get it done before the deadline. "I can't miss that much work."

"Your dad will make do without you," Crystal said.

Only if his father hired another crewmember, which would never happen. Huntz & Sons was just that—Carl Huntz and his sons, the two natural-born and the one honorary son. Matt's friend Derrick might not have Huntz blood running through him, but he was as much a son as either Matt or Brad.

"I know eight weeks sounds like a long time," Dr. Meyer said, "but there's a lot that needs to be accomplished. You'll need to learn how to sit on your own, how to roll over, how—"

"Stop," Matt said. He didn't want to hear about the things he had to learn all over again, things he'd been doing successfully on his own for most of his life. Successful. The word stood out. All his life, he'd tried to be the best at everything he'd done in an attempt to make his dad proud, but he always fell short. He wouldn't fail this time. He squeezed Crystal's hand. He *would* walk again, and he'd be doing it in time to save the group home contract.

§

The sun had barely broken the horizon the next morning when the nurses moved Matt out of ICU. He had a new room, but nothing had changed. He was still stuck in bed, dependent on others for his every need.

"Nice room," his mother said as she turned in a circle while his father sank into a faux-leather chair.

"I'd prefer the Holiday Inn," Matt said. "They don't wake you up every couple hours. Room service is better, too." He looked at the doorway, expecting to see his fiancée. Nothing but empty hallway.

"Can't speak for the room service," his father said, "but I can guarantee you this place is quieter than the Super 8. Kids running up and down the hall at all hours of the night. I should have saved my money and camped out in the waiting room, like we did the first night."

"You should have just gone home and slept in your own bed," Matt said, although he was happy his parents had stuck around.

"And screw up your mother's vacation?" his father asked.

Matt's mother nuzzled her cheek to his father's. "Don't think this gets you out of taking me to Hawaii someday."

Still watching the doorway, Matt asked, "What day is it? Saturday? Sunday?"

"Not even close, honey," his mother said. "Today's Wednesday."

Workday. Matt sank into the pillow. No sense watching for Crystal. His gaze shifted to his father, who'd picked up the remote control and seemed content flipping through the channels. His father, with deadlines to meet. Matt felt a tug deep inside. The people you loved came first. So why wasn't Crystal here instead of at work?

Someone stepped into the room. Matt looked to the doorway with expectation that quickly turned to disappointment. A nurse in a fluorescent pink uniform walked toward him with a tray. "Ready for breakfast? Cheerios and apple juice."

"What happened to the three cheese omelet and sausages I ordered?" Actually, he wanted a Coke and a pack of Pop-Tarts. He wanted to have his breakfast in his truck on the way to a jobsite. He wanted there to be a purpose to his day. A day's hard work he could be proud of.

"You mean I mixed up yet another order?" She set his breakfast on the over-bed table. He caught a glimpse of her name as her ID tag twisted and swayed. Becky something.

"Just like I said, Holiday Inn has better room service."

Becky arched her eyebrows. "But will anyone at Holiday Inn give you a sponge bath? I think not."

"She's got a point," his father said.

Becky gave a fake pout. "Since you don't like my service, I'm leaving."

When she stepped away from the bed, Matt said,

"Hey, wait. Aren't you going to get me up so I can eat this gourmet breakfast?"

"Sorry. You'll have to eat lying down. My orders are to keep an eye on you for a while before we try to get you up."

"At Holiday Inn, they'd let me sit up."

She shrugged. "Buzz me if you need anything."

Someone hiding behind a giant Garfield balloon blocked the doorway. Only the person's legs were visible, but he could have picked those legs out of a lineup.

"Babe, you're here." A light-hearted sensation filled him, buoying him much like the helium balloon tethered to the orange ribbon.

Crystal peeked beneath the balloon and smiled. "Yes. I'm here. You're here. Your parents are here. And so is this poor nurse, who is trying to leave." She stepped to the side. Garfield hung in the doorway a second before bobbing out of the way.

He let his eyes travel the length of her legs. "If I haven't said it recently, your legs are sexy as hell."

Crystal's smile faded. Her gaze settled on Matt's blanket-covered legs for just a second before shooting away. "Speaking of legs, how are yours?"

He knew what she was asking, and he hated to disappoint her. He put on a smile and yanked the covers back, intending on revealing hair-covered legs. "Ma, what's your opinion? Are these sexy?"

His mother's cheeks colored and she looked away. "I'm sure your legs are just fine."

Garfield bounced as Crystal made a quick turn. She crouched by the folding chair and busied herself with tying down the balloon.

His father burst out laughing.

"What?" Matt asked.

His father was still chuckling as he got out of the chair and adjusted the blankets. "It's safe, girls."

"What?" Matt asked again.

"You were just showing off more than your legs, Son."

Great. Chalk up one more for Matt, the screw-up.

Crystal was still crouched with her back to him, fiddling with the balloon's ribbon as though she hadn't heard that the coast was clear.

"Do you want to eat?" his mother asked as she rattled the Cheerio package.

His gaze lingered on Crystal. "Sure. Don't want that fancy breakfast to get cold."

His father's cell phone rang out the tune of We Are the Champions.

His mother waved the opened Cheerios at his father. "Carl, you know you're not supposed to use your cell phone here."

His father motioned her away and brought the phone to his ear. "Huntz & Sons Construction."

With a shake of her head, his mother handed Matt the cereal container.

He looked away from Crystal and eyed the dry cereal. "Aren't you forgetting something?" When his mother answered with a blank stare, he added, "The milk."

His father stood and moved out of view.

"I figured it would be easier for you to eat it dry," his mother said.

"You mean like Kaylee eats it?" he said, thinking of his niece. "I don't think so. I'm twenty-six, not two."

His mother poured some milk from his cup into the plastic bowl.

He made a grab for the spoon, but his mother was quicker. "I can feed myself," he said.

"You'd best let me help if you insist on having milk on it." His mother dipped the spoon into the bowl.

No way was he going to let his mother feed him like a little kid, not when he'd spent the last ten years trying to prove he was every bit the man his father was. "Ma, I can do it. I've been feeding myself for years."

"Not lying on your side, you haven't."

Crystal was sitting now. She pulled on Garfield's string and let go. The balloon bounced. "Babe," he said. "Tell her I can do it."

Crystal looked up. "How many sweatshirts do you

have with spaghetti sauce stains?"

"Thanks for the help." He looked back at his mom. "I can do it."

His mother rolled her eyes but handed over the spoon. Milk splashed onto the crisp sheet as he navigated the spoon closer. One Cheerio made it to his mouth. He glanced at Crystal who looked away.

"I can do this," he said when his mother reached for the spoon. For crying out loud, this wasn't rocket science and he wasn't incompetent. He concentrated on keeping his hand steady. Only a drop of milk spilled.

"Yes, that is wonderful news," his father said into the phone. His voice held all the excitement of someone setting up a root canal appointment. "I'll send my son Brad over later to pick up the blueprints."

Matt slanted the spoon once it reached his mouth. Milk-soaked Cheerios slid down his cheek.

"Who was that?" Matt's mom asked as she dabbed his cheek with a wadded napkin. At least she hadn't spit on it first.

"Rex Johnson."

Matt's ears perked up when he heard the group home developer's name.

"He's already got all the rooms filled for the group home, and it's not even built yet. He's thinking of building another home next summer. As long as we don't go over budget and we're on time with this build, the contract's ours."

Matt did a mental high five.

"That's wonderful," his mother said.

"Yeah. Wonderful." His father dropped into his chair.

Matt's high took a nosedive. His father had said the job was too big for four men. Matt had insisted they bid on it, anyway, thinking he could prove his worth if he could grow his father's business into one that could compete with the larger crews. The bid had been tight with four men. It would be impossible with only three.

Conscious of his father just six feet away, he dug into his cereal with determination. He'd work so damn hard to get better that a colony of worker ants would look like slackers in comparison.

Milk dripped from the spoon.

His mother hovered beside the bed, poised to take over feeding him at the first sign of failure. He tightened his jaw. She may as well put her sweet ass in a chair and relax because he wasn't going to fail. Not at feeding himself. Not at getting better.

More milk dripped onto the crisp, white sheet. By the time the spoon reached his mouth, only one damp cereal O remained.

His mother moved closer as he shoved his spoon into the bowl again. Milk splashed onto the table. A trail of cereal littered a path to his mouth.

Even his two-year-old niece managed better at feeding herself than he was doing. If he couldn't do something simple enough for a two-year-old to master, how would he ever keep his dad from going over on the build? Why the hell would Crystal want to marry him now, with him like this?

Stop it.

He would not fail.

Milk-soaked cereal splattered the tabletop. He shoveled up another spoonful and lost his load two inches from the bowl.

"Matthew, let me help," his mother said.

"No," he spat.

The harder he tried, the more uncoordinated he became. He threw the spoon. It bounced off the edge of the bowl and then clattered onto the table. He closed his eyes and took deep breaths.

A soft hand touched his arm. "Look at me," Crystal said.

She had a dampened Cheerio stuck to the end of her nose. "Would you like me to help you eat? I'm quite good at it."

Despite his mood, he laughed. He tapped the Cheerio stuck to her nose. It fell and joined the ones on his mattress. "That you are, babe. And that's why I love you."

CHAPTER THREE

In Matt's dream, he knelt on Rex Johnson's roof and hammered a shingle into place. Crystal sat beside him, looking regal on a simple folding chair. The diamonds in her many pieces of jewelry complemented her silk, floor-length dress, each jewel glistening from the light that reflected off a giant hourglass. Sand filtered from its top chamber at a lazy pace.

"We need to get this job done before the sand is gone." His father handed Matt another shingle from their last bundle.

"Plenty of time," Matt said.

"This is an important job." His father handed him another shingle. "I'm depending on you, Son."

"This diamond isn't big enough." Crystal held out her left hand, displaying the two-carat jewel in her engagement ring.

The shingle he'd just nailed down came loose and went sailing through the air. "What?" he asked, wondering what had happened to his shingle.

"If you work harder, I can have bigger diamonds. And more silk. Silk panties and silk stockings. Silk carpets and silk walls. I want silk all around me."

Another shingle lifted free and flew away.

"Quick," his father said as he handed Matt a new shingle. "Hurry. I'm depending on you."

"A silk car with diamond wheels."

The sand in the hourglass swirled like a whirlpool and poured into the bottom chamber. Every shingle curled away from the roof and took flight.

Matt awoke with a start. Silence surrounded him. The room was cast in shadows as if the afternoon sun wasn't strong enough to penetrate the windows behind him. Crystal's folding chair, which was cocked at an angle to the bed, was deserted. The other two chairs were equally abandoned. With no more proof than three empty chairs, he knew they'd left. They'd headed home while he'd been sleeping. No goodbyes.

A vague memory of the dream clung to him as he stared at Crystal's empty chair. He was letting her down. His father, too. Every second he spent stuck in this bed with boat anchors for legs was yet another failure.

Matt's pity party was interrupted when someone knocked on his open door. "Mr. Huntz?"

A woman in a wheelchair rolled toward him. The ID pinned to her shirt identified her as a hospital employee. She smiled and held out her hand. "Hello, Matt. I'm Deborah Stryker, the social worker assigned to your case."

Matt grunted as he accepted her handshake. Why the hell did he need a social worker?

"You'll be starting therapy soon, so we need to decide where you'll go for rehabilitation. We also need to fill out the forms to apply for Social Security disability benefits."

The last four words echoed in his head. He wasn't disabled. Temporarily broken maybe but not disabled. "I don't need disability."

"I didn't want to file for disability, either. Flat out refused because I was going to walk again. By the time I realized I needed it, I was so far in debt I lost my house."

His house. A duplicate to the one he'd grown up in. All the work he'd put into it, making it into a home for a family of his own. Hours and hours of remodeling after twelve-hour days working on other people's homes. No way would he let the bank foreclose on his loan.

Would it hurt to at least consider applying for disability? He opened his mouth. An irrational fear overtook him. If he filed for disability, it'd be like saying he was okay with being paralyzed and then he'd never walk again. Irrational or not, he couldn't take the chance. "I said, I don't need disability."

"Tell you what. I already filled out the form with what I could find in your file. I'll just leave the papers with you. If you change your mind, you can finish filling it out." She set the paper on his over-bed table.

He couldn't see the form, but he could feel its magnetic pull. Slowly sucking away whatever hope he had of walking again.

"Even though you don't need the disability benefits, you might want to send the form in anyhow." She flashed a smile. "Sort of like a Murphy's Law insurance policy. Better to file and not need it than to file at the last minute and then wait five months for your first payment."

"Five months? You're joking, right?"

"Not at all."

He rubbed his leg, searching for proof he didn't need her stupid form. All he felt was the slick nylon fabric of the running pants some nurse had dressed him in. Didn't matter. He was *not* going to file for disability. He'd call the bank and ask for an extension, if he had to. Maybe make interest-only payments for a while. Anything to keep from filing for disability. "I'll think on it." He'd rip up the form as soon as she left.

"Fair enough. Next, we need to decide where you'll have your therapy."

His parents stepped through the doorway. Crystal was a step behind. A sense of peace settled over him at the sight of them, but he couldn't help wondering why Crystal hung back.

He was filled with the urge to go to her, to cover her with kisses, to wrap her in his arms and never let go. But his legs remained weighted into place, chaining him down. "Babe, you're still here."

Her smile set his heart soaring. "Do we have to go through this every time I step through the door? Yes, I'm here. Your parents are here. Somebody I've never met before is here."

He held out his hand. "Stop being such a smart ass and get over here."

She stepped forward and sat lightly on the edge of the bed. He slid his hand into hers.

Ms. Stryker cleared her throat. "If you'd like, I can come back later."

"Sorry. Now is fine. In fact, better than fine." He tightened his fingers around Crystal's. "This is something that's going to affect us all."

"We were discussing where Matthew is going to have his rehabilitation." Deborah Stryker laid some glossy pamphlets on his bed. "There's a rehabilitation center right here at St. Luke's. Or there are specialty rehab centers that deal strictly with spinal cord injuries and head trauma."

He let go of Crystal's hand and picked up one of the brochures. The picture on the cover showed a man gripping parallel bars, his legs held straight with braces. Standing. Exactly what Matt wanted, but without the braces. The brochure was for a specialty rehabilitation center in Colorado. Too far away. He set down the leaflet and grabbed a new one. This one showed a woman wheeling up a ramp. The image of the standing man stuck in his head.

Crystal leaned forward and grabbed the discarded brochure. She put her hand on Matt's leg and then yanked it back as though she'd been burned.

Tension knotted his shoulders. He stared at the woman's picture. What he saw was Crystal's hand ricocheting off his leg. Didn't she know he wouldn't break? That his paralysis wasn't contagious? That he needed her touch where he couldn't feel it as much as where he could?

"Are you done looking at that one?" his father asked.

"One sec." Pretending Crystal's reaction didn't hurt, he opened the leaflet for St. Luke's rehabilitation center. Three photos depicted more patients in wheelchairs. He turned to the back. Not a single picture of any patients standing.

Unimpressed, he handed the St. Luke's pamphlet to his father and then flipped through the other brochures. He stopped when he saw another man in braces who was standing with crutches. *Milwaukee Spine Care Center.* Milwaukee wasn't as close to home as St. Luke's, but it was a hell of a lot closer than Colorado.

He scanned the rest of the brochures, comparing the hospitals to the specialty centers. The hospitals seemed to concentrate on teaching skills to adapt to life in a wheelchair. The leaflets for the rehab centers implied a guarantee of resuming a life as close as possible to what he'd had before the accident. What he wanted was a life *exactly* like what he'd had before the accident, but there didn't seem to be a rehab center for that. He went back to the brochure for Milwaukee Spine Care Center.

Milwaukee was two hundred miles from Fuller Lake. Too far for Crystal and his parents to come during the workweek. He'd only get to see them on weekends, and he couldn't expect them to come every weekend.

"Where's the closest one of these specialty places?"

"Milwaukee."

Damn.

Matt stared at the man standing between the parallel bars and then shifted to the woman in the wheelchair on the ramp. Within a second, his focus was back on the man standing. "How long would I have to be at one of these places?"

"Six, seven, maybe eight weeks."

"Eight weeks," his mother said, her voice growing louder.

Eight weeks separated from Crystal. Eight weeks away from his family.

Or a lifetime in a wheelchair.

He didn't want to leave the people he loved, but he'd rather be without them for a short while than spend his life in a wheelchair. He stared at the standing man with crutches. He wanted to be that man.

"If you'd like, I can check to see which facilities have openings and contact your insurance carrier to find out where they'll authorize admittance."

Her last words echoed off the walls. He looked away from the standing man. "What?"

"Some insurance companies won't authorize payments to the more expensive rehabilitation centers."

Going to Milwaukee threatened to slip from his grasp.

A person couldn't get worse insurance than he had. He gripped on to one last straw of hope. "What happens if my insurance won't pay? Does that mean I'm stuck here?"

"Certainly not. As long as you can pay for your rehabilitation, they'll accept you as a patient."

Rehab that might get him walking again. Rehab that would give him a lifetime of debt, which was already maxed out, and take him away from the people he loved.

Or he could stay here, close to home. Therapy his insurance would likely pay for. Therapy that apparently would do little more than train him to adapt to his physical limitations.

The options were like offering a drowning man his choice of a child-sized life preserver or a rubber raft with a leak.

He fought against the sinking feeling. The four pairs of eyes staring at him made it harder. "And you said it'll take five months for disability to kick in, if I decide to file."

"Yes."

His father squeezed his shoulder. "You want to go to that place, we'll find a way for you to go. We'll use the house as collateral for a loan, if we have to."

"Would this be the same house you just used as collateral for a business loan?" Matt felt his last chance drifting away.

"I wouldn't be the first person to have multiple loans against their house."

"You can use the wedding money," Crystal said. "We might be out our deposits, but I can cancel the band and the banquet hall."

He eyed his fiancée. Her solution left a foul taste coating the back of his tongue. "What are you saying, Crystal? Are you saying we should cancel the wedding?"

"No." Her gaze skated away from his. "I'm just saying we don't need a big wedding. We'd be just as married if the wedding's at the courthouse with a family-only dinner afterward."

A headache formed between his eyes. He pictured Crystal's hand springing away from his leg. What if

Milwaukee Spine Care Center couldn't get him walking again? Time apart wouldn't help Crystal accept his condition. They needed to be together right now.

But it wasn't just his relationship with Crystal he had to worry about. There was the construction business. The group home contract. The promise of another contract. All of which meant a full recovery was crucial.

The headache throbbed.

He held up the brochure for Milwaukee. "This place, will it get me walking again?"

Crystal sat ramrod straight, her eyes focused on Deborah.

"The only thing that will get you walking again is if your spinal cord heals enough. However, a rehabilitation center can offer an improved level of mobility that you might not get with treatment at a hospital."

Not quite the guarantee he'd been searching for. But he didn't need a guarantee. Just hope. A glimmer of a chance. "But I'll have a greater chance of a full recovery if I go to Milwaukee than if I stay here, right?"

"A specialty hospital will increase your independence."

Why couldn't she answer the question? Didn't she know independence didn't mean squat if it didn't get the group home built? "Forget independence. I'm talking about walking. Standing. Even just moving my legs. Do I have a greater chance of any of that happening if I go to Milwaukee?"

"No."

Everything around him blurred. In his head, he saw himself far in the future, still in a wheelchair. Before he could dwell on what that meant for his job, he grabbed Crystal's hand. "We're getting married once, and only once. I want you to have the wedding we planned." He shifted his attention to Deborah. The words formed, but he had a hard time getting them past his lips. *Just say it. Get it over with.* "Sign me up to have my rehab here."

"Don't be hasty," Crystal said. "This is an important decision. You should think on it for a few days."

He laughed to stop himself from giving in to despair.

"You think a few days will make a difference? You think my insurance will magically get better? You think the money fairy's going to come along and drop a load of cash at my feet?"

"Matt, I meant it when I said we'd help out," his father said. "I'll take another mortgage on the house. I'll use every bit of equipment we own as collateral, if I have to. We'll get you the money."

Invisible hands pushed his face beneath the water. Somehow, he managed not to gasp for air. He forced a smile. "It's not a big deal, Dad. Staying here's fine."

Deborah had barely disappeared into the hallway when his mother said, "You made the right decision, honey. I'm sure the therapy department here is very good."

Then why did it feel so very wrong?

He loved his parents, but he needed time alone with Crystal. "Dad, I appreciate your taking so much time away from work to be here, but you should go back to Fuller Lake. Make sure Brad and Derrick haven't been spending their days drinking beer and watching TV instead of working."

His father squeezed Matt's shoulder.

"It's been a really long day, and I'm tired. Once I fall asleep, I'll probably be out for the night, so you guys may as well head back home instead of sitting here watching me sleep."

His mother gave him a hug. "This will be good for you. I know it."

His father nodded. "We'll see you tomorrow." He gave his son a wave before he stepped out of the room.

Crystal had her jacket on and her purse slung over her shoulder.

He patted the mattress. "Sit."

She hesitated a moment before she perched on the edge of the bed. "You should go to Milwaukee."

Even though he agreed, there was something in her tone that set him on edge. "Why? Either I'm going to walk again or I'm not. Where I have rehab isn't going to change that."

She picked up the brochure that was still lying on his bed. "Look." She tapped the paper with a manicured nail that glistened like a newly waxed car. "It says right here that their patients have a higher level of independence. You don't want to rely on your mother for the rest of your life, do you?"

The bad feeling intensified. "If I have to rely on someone, what makes you think it's going to be her? Why wouldn't it be you? Is there something I should know?"

She looked away. "You know your mother. If she can find any way to control you, she will, whether we're married or not."

He didn't like that *or not* part. He turned her face back to his, holding her chin. "Is there something I should know?"

She tried to turn away, but he held tight. She shifted her eyes.

"I'm going to ask one more time. Is there something I should know?"

Her eyes came back to him for a fraction of a second. "No."

"I love you, Crystal. You know that, don't you?"

"Sure." The same tone as whenever she said *fine* when it was anything but fine.

"I'm not going to Milwaukee. Not just because of the money but because I hate the thought of being so far away from you. Do you understand?"

She nodded again, but her bottom lip trembled. He let go of her chin and gathered her hand in his. He put as much confidence into his tone as he could manage. "Everything's going to be okay, babe."

Her eyes welled with tears. "What if it's not okay?"

What if? The exact direction he didn't want his thoughts to go. "It will be. Trust me."

Crystal did a little eye roll, one so quick he never would have noticed had he not been staring at her.

"What?" he asked.

"Nothing."

"Crystal." The single word came out as a reprimand.

She pulled her hand from his and stood. Her hands flew through the air as she paced. "You think you have control over everything, Matt, but you don't."

"I do not think I have control over everything." He tried to act like it most of the time, but he rarely felt in control of anything.

"You do, too. No matter what's wrong, Mighty Matt can fix it." She stopped her pacing and faced him. "You can't fix everything."

"What are you trying to say?"

"Just because you want a full recovery doesn't mean you can make one happen." She came back to the bed and sat. "Matt, what if you never walk again?"

He was ready to protest that he had no intention of not walking again, but he couldn't make the words form. She was right. He couldn't force his spinal cord to heal. But, God willing, his physical therapist could. He took her hand and smiled even though he felt like a lie was about to spill from his mouth. "Then I'll be Mighty Matt in a wheelchair."

§

Abby Fischner tried to hold back her excitement as she stepped into room 315. Bright late-morning sunshine illuminated the room as if to demonstrate the importance of this therapy assignment. This wasn't another hip replacement. No knee surgery this time. Unfortunately, her newest patient didn't have a brain injury either, but she wasn't about to quibble over details. If the interview she'd just had in Milwaukee was a success, she'd finally be on her way to achieving her goal of working with brain-injured patients.

Matthew Huntz lay on top of the covers, his back toward her. With the TV turned low and the gentle movement of his shoulder with each breath, he appeared to be sleeping. She gnawed on her bottom lip as she debated waking him. She took a quiet step forward and then paused at the foot of the bed, surprised to find his eyes open and his hand fisted around a clump of blankets. Turning his brown eyes her way, she caught a glimmer of worry before his face transformed into a stoic mask.

Deborah Stryker had said he was good looking. She hadn't been kidding. Thick, dark hair. Rich brown eyes. The start of a scruffy beard that made him look rugged instead of unkempt. Muscles that strained the sleeves of his sweatshirt. The type of man who probably kept a girlfriend for a month before moving on. Oh, well. She wasn't here to assess his looks or his commitment issues. She was here to plan his treatment and get him mobile. She stood straighter and put on her best professional smile. "Hi, I'm Abigail Fischner from the physical therapy department. I have a few questions I need to ask to help plan your rehab."

Although he relaxed his fingers, the blankets remained bunched beneath his hand. He gave her a smile that looked as genuine as a chip of glass in a bubblegum machine ring. "Forgive me for not getting up."

"Well, that's what we're going to work on." She pulled a chair closer and sat. A stray hair, which had worked its way free of her ponytail, brushed her cheek. She tucked it behind her ear. "What do you hope to achieve from physical therapy?"

"I need to walk again." Gripping the guardrail, he pulled himself closer, his jaw tightening with the effort. "Can you make that happen?"

His laser-beam gaze cut into her. Unable to give him the reassurances he wanted, she looked away to his fingers cinched around the plastic rail. Strong fingers she could easily envision pulling him up the side of a mountain or gripping a hammer for hours on end like his chart indicated. Being paralyzed would not be easy for a man like him.

She shifted her attention back to his face. Beneath the handsome exterior he looked vulnerable, a contrast to the independent, active man his chart described. Both Dr. Meyer and Deborah would have explained that physical therapy wouldn't cure him. She understood clinging to hope, though. She'd done her share throughout the years.

His features took on a hard edge. "Go ahead. Say it."

You can't help me walk again."

She remembered what it felt like to be a ten-year-old, unable to help as her mother clung to life with the help of a respirator. How was she supposed to tell him there was nothing she could do to force a recovery? That all she could do was help him adapt. She softened her voice. "No. I'm sorry. I can't."

"Then, what the hell good are you?" He reached behind him and grabbed on to the rail.

His words slapped at her confidence. She hadn't been able to help her mother. *Stop it. You were only ten. You might not be able to cure Mr. Huntz, but you can help him.* She held her head higher. "Good enough to be assigned as your therapist." *And good enough to get an interview at the best rehab center in Wisconsin.*

His neck muscles tightened. Although he let out a quick grunt and his breathing sped up, he kept pulling. Instinct urged her to help, but she sat back and waited. He expended an excessive amount of energy as he struggled to pull himself onto his left side. Most people would have surrendered before they'd even started. The rest would have quit halfway to their goal. Not her newest patient. Like Deborah said, he had determination. She had to give him that.

He looked like a mangled Gumby doll when he finally released the rail, his legs twisted one way, his face and chest the other.

"Show's over," he said, his voice gravelly. "You can leave now."

No way was she leaving. She wasn't going to walk out on the opportunity to work with a paralyzed patient. "If you put that kind of effort into physical therapy, you'll be mobile in no time."

"The only kind of mobile I want is me walking again."

Errrggghhh. Working with him was going to be a challenge, but she had news for him. She could be every bit as stubborn as he could be. She got up and dragged the chair to the other side of the bed and then sat. One corner of her mouth lifted. "Are you going to turn your back on me again?"

"Not if you save me the trouble and leave, instead."

Not on your life, buddy. She plunked a printed schedule onto the bed. "Here's when you're expected to be in therapy."

His eyes never left hers. "Do you work on commission or something?"

"Do you enjoy being in that bed?"

"Aren't therapists supposed to be nice to their patients?"

"The less cooperative you are, the longer it's going to take. I get paid the same salary whether you're here six weeks or sixty." She leaned back, crossed her legs, and smiled. "It's up to you."

A muscle twitched at his jaw.

She forced herself to remain still with her gaze locked on his.

"When do we start?" he asked.

Her shoulders relaxed, and she exhaled. She leaned forward and tapped the schedule. "Monday, at nine a.m."

He finally picked up the page. His eyebrows rose as he scanned the page filled with twice-daily sessions of physical therapy, dual occupational therapy sessions, and recreational therapy. Mixed in were patient activities designed to hone newly learned skills. "I guess I'm not here for a relaxing vacation, am I?"

"What would you be doing now if this were a relaxing vacation?"

He lowered the schedule, bringing his unamused face back into view. "What does it matter? I'm not on a vacation."

"Humor me."

His eyes became as pinched as his mouth.

She did the opposite, trying her best to keep her features as relaxed as possible.

He let out a sigh that could have been heard all the way to Admitting. "Can I pretend it's fall?"

"Sure. It's your vacation."

"Okay. Fine. I'd be camping in Door County. I'd spend

my days biking with my fiancée, taking in the view."

Fiancée? That bit of news surprised her. Probably one of those open-ended engagements with no real wedding in sight.

"If you've never been to Door County in the fall," he said, "you're missing out. All those orange and red leaves."

Putting her mind back to their conversation, she pictured him on a bike, his legs immobile and his arms doing all the work. "You can still do that, even without a full recovery."

He puffed out a laugh. "Sure."

"Really. There are bikes you can pedal with your hands." She made a mental note to gather up information on bikes and decided she'd also get him some information on rock climbing needs for the paralyzed. "You name it, anything you want to do, we can probably find a way for you to do it from a wheelchair."

The therapy schedule still in his hand, he crossed his arms, the paper crackling as it smashed into the nook between the mattress and his chest. "Fine. Basketball."

She held back a smile. Instead of appearing tough and challenging, which is what she assumed he was aiming for, he simply looked like he was warding off a chill. "No problem. There are wheelchair basketball teams."

"Downhill skiing."

"Very doable. ESPN had a feature about it just last night."

He held her gaze for several seconds before he smiled, punctuating the word with a raise of his eyebrows. "Kickball."

She opened her mouth and then realized she didn't have a comeback. "The point is, being paralyzed doesn't mean an end to the activities you enjoy. All we have to do is find ways to modify the equipment to fit your needs. I may not have an immediate answer, but if you give me enough time, I'll figure something out."

His gaze stabbed her. "Modify my equipment, huh?"

"That's right."

"I'm a twenty-six-year old male with a lot of *activities*

I enjoy. You really think you can modify my *equipment* to fit all my needs?"

"Of course. Like I said, if you give me enough time, I can figure something out."

"Good, because there's a certain piece of equipment I'd want to be using on that dream vacation. A lot. How do you suggest we go about modifying it?"

Not wanting to let on that she was clueless as to what he was referring to, she said, "We go at it head on—"

He nodded like he was taking it all in. His smile looked like one of those that said she was the focus of a joke.

She blundered on. "...and examine the needs closely." Then she caught on. His *equipment*. The room grew hot. She fought the urge to look away. Her instinct was to tell him that really wasn't part of her job. Was that what she planned to do if she got the job in Milwaukee? Anytime a patient brought up something she found uncomfortable, avoid the question? Resisting the urge to tug at her neckline, she said, "Many men with your level of injury find they're able to obtain an erection by direct stimulation. If that doesn't work— "

"Forget it." He looked away. His fingers formed a fist.

"I don't mind discussing this."

His eyes shot back to her. "But I do. Damn it, I'm getting married in five months."

A real wedding? The man was full of surprises.

"It's bad enough worrying about how I'm going to support my wife without wondering how I'm going to please her in bed. I don't want my equipment modified. I want everything back the way it belongs, and if you can't help me, then I want someone who can."

"No therapist can guarantee—"

"Unka Matyou," a little voice said from the doorway.

The assessment wasn't finished, but Abby didn't mind the interruption. She stayed seated, her gaze jumping from person to person. A toddler, with blonde ringlets tied up in pigtails, struggled to free herself from the grasp of a stunningly beautiful older woman who shared Matt's features, right down to the same dark hair and eyes, and the same thin nose. Beside them was a younger woman, whom Abby pegged to be just a few years older than herself. Her hair was as blonde and curly as the little girl's, although the woman was nowhere near as energetic. Her shoulders slumped with apparent exhaustion.

Matt's family.

"What are you guys doing here?" Matt asked. A smile that seemed impossible to imagine on him a moment ago lit up his face.

"Kaylee's been begging to see her uncle, so we decided to come early. Your father and Crystal will drive over later with Brad."

"Kaywe see Unka Matyou." The little girl swung her feet.

"Is that my little Kaylee bug?" Matt patted his thigh. "Come here and let me see how much you've grown."

The little girl's legs were already running before her grandmother lowered her to the ground. The second she reached the bed, she stretched her arms high. As though Kaylee shared her uncle's rock-climbing abilities, she grabbed on to a handful of blankets and pulled herself up.

"Kaylee, get down," the younger woman called, hurrying toward her daughter. "You're going to hurt Uncle Matt."

The little girl continued her climb, paying little attention as the covers slid toward her. Kaylee lunged over the edge, onto the mattress, at the same moment her mother reached out.

"She's going to be the death of me." The young woman slumped onto the bed by Matt's feet.

"You don't know how often I said that about Matthew," the older woman said. She stood behind her son with her hand on Matt's shoulder. "And I'm still saying it, aren't I dear?"

Matt rolled his eyes.

"Are you okay with her there?" the young woman asked.

Matt laughed. "She's good medicine." He held out his

hand to the little girl crawling over his legs. "Aren't you, Kaylee bug?"

A lump formed in Abby's throat as she watched Matt interact with his family. She had observed many families over the years. There were the ones who put as much space as possible between them and the patient. They rarely spoke, their attention too focused on the TV. These kinds of families were like pictures on a wall. Nice to have around but not all that useful.

There were the ones who stood halfway between the bed and the door, visiting for a few minutes before something more pressing called them away. The ones who came out of duty, for appearance's sake. Their presence set her on edge, and she never stayed long when they visited.

This family, though, was rare. The ones who clumped around the patient like the hours apart were painful. Abby blinked as emotions welled inside her. If she had her choice, she'd pick a family like this one to belong to, any day.

Matt's mother had her brown eyes trained on the stranger in the room. Gathering up her composure, Abby stood and extended her hand, reaching across Matt's bed. "I'm Abby Fischner, Matthew's physical therapist."

"I'm Matt's mother, Ruth Huntz." The older woman's hand was warm and soft, yet firm. The type of woman who would invite you into her home, cook you dinner, and make you feel like a part of the family. Abby wanted to cling to the woman, but she forced her fingers to let go.

Matt's mother gestured to the other woman. "That's Jenny, Matt's sister-in-law, the mother to this little handful."

Jenny's smile said everyone she met was a friend.

Abby looked back at the little girl. Matt had her snuggled close, his mouth pressed to the top of her head. A surge of heat spread through Abby as she watched his display of gentleness and apparent love.

"You smell like pooh," he said.

"Do not."

"Yeah, you do. Shampoo."

Abby tried to look away from Matt, but she couldn't.

"You silly, Unka Matyou." Kaylee squirmed from his arms and sat cross-legged. The toe of a pink tennis shoe dug into his ribs in a way that should have been painful yet went unnoticed.

"Tell me what you've been up to," Matt said. "You in college yet?"

A pang of sadness spread through Abby at the scattered images of her father rocking her to sleep, reading her a story, kissing a bruised knee, and then abandoning her. She pushed her father back into the dark recesses of her brain.

Matt's mother had her hand on his shoulder again. A quiet rustling issued from his sweatshirt as she rubbed her palm in a small circle. Touched by the palpable love of this family, Abby wished she could stay with them forever. She didn't belong, though.

She took a step back. "I'll see you Monday."

Matt's gaze connected with hers. "Looking forward to it."

Kaylee pushed her little fingers against his cheek, his skin dimpling as she demanded, "Look me, Unka Matyou. Look."

His attention lingered on Abby for a moment before turning to his niece. "Yeah, munchkin. What'cha want?"

"Want you tickle Kaywe."

"Like this?" he asked as he poked her ribs.

The little girl broke into giggles.

As soon as Abby cleared the door, she stepped to the side and pressed her back to the wall. Inside the room, Matt's deep laugh echoed. She closed her eyes and listened to him tease his niece. She felt the love in that room. Tears formed in her eyes. She desperately wanted to love, to be loved, to be a part of a family once again.

CHAPTER FOUR

Seated in the recliner next to his bed, Matt doodled a house design on a napkin. If he ignored the safety rails on the bed, he could almost convince himself everything was back to normal. Well, he might have to do a little more in the way of creative snow jobs, like invent a damn good reason for him to be sitting on his ass doodling at nine in the morning on a workday. That, and come up with an explanation for why he couldn't feel his ass making an impression in the padded vinyl.

He leaned his head back and closed his eyes. Bad move. He was more aware than ever of the divot his head made against the recliner back, which made him even more conscious of the fact that he couldn't feel his ass.

Tight pressure cinched a ring around his neck.

Think about something else.

Like what? The fact that, pretty soon, I'm not going to have any money to pay bills? Or, that my physical therapist looks young enough to be a high school cheerleader?

He could have gotten a real therapist, one who worked only with spinal cord injuries, but no. He'd insisted on staying here, to be close to Crystal. And now, he was stuck with a kid in charge of his therapy. Good plan.

"Bro?" a deep voice whispered.

Matt opened his eyes. His best friend, Derrick Vetter, stood just inside the door. He looked like a piece of home in his drywall-mud-splattered jeans and worn winter jacket. Such a change from the kid he'd been in second grade. The only reason Matt had asked the new kid to sit at his table at lunch was because it was the exact thing his father would have done. He hadn't expected to actually like the pasty-white geek dressed in a suit, complete with a pocket protector. He certainly hadn't expected to form a lasting friendship with him, not when he already had a pack of friends, all of whom were vying for "best friend" status.

Derrick's left hand was clenched around the rolled edge of a McDonald's bag. The scent of greasy hash browns filled the air.

Matt grinned. "I hope there's a Sausage McMuffin in there."

"If you had any sense of good taste, I would have gotten you coffee, too."

"That'll be the day, when I'm addicted to coffee like you and Crystal."

"Like I said, no sense of taste."

Matt watched his friend's legs move with fluid grace. For a fraction of a second, a bitter jealousy stirred deep in his heart. He hated Derrick for being able to walk. Hated him. He drew in a deep breath and let it trickle out, forcing the anger out, as well. It wasn't Derrick's fault Matt had the accident.

"What brings you to these parts?"

"Coming to bring you breakfast not enough of a reason, bro?" Derrick handed Matt the bag and then grabbed a chair.

"Not during working hours. I doubt Dad's letting you play hooky."

Derrick picked up Matt's work of art. "Looks like I should have brought you drawing pads instead of breakfast." He dropped the napkin back onto the table. "Our window order came in, but they can't deliver until Monday and we need it now. Brad and Pops are tied up, so that left me." Derrick leaned forward and rested his arms on his thighs. "So, how are you?"

"Great." Matt fumbled with the McMuffin's paper wrapper. The comment about Brad and his father stuck to his brain like a burr on socks. They wouldn't be so busy if Matt hadn't taken an unplanned vacation.

Derrick tipped his head and frowned. "You don't look half bad."

"Thanks, I think." He took in his friend's tired eyes and wished he could say the same.

Furrows formed between Derrick's brows. "No, I mean, I just thought since you're…"

Silence spread between them.

Matt forced a smile and made his voice light. "You can say it. Paralyzed." The last word was bitter on his tongue. "Doesn't seem possible. We were shooting hoops one night, and then the next…" Derrick's gaze fell to his clasped hands hanging between his knees. After a moment of silence, he said, "This shouldn't have happened to you."

It shouldn't have, but it had.

He and Derrick had shared a lot of secrets throughout the years, things Matt would have never given up to anyone else, not even under extreme torture. He wanted to spit out the standard lines that it was okay, that *he* was okay, but he couldn't lie to his friend. "I'm scared."

Derrick closed his eyes for a moment as he took in a deep breath. He let it out slowly. His cheeks remained puffed out until he finally sat up straight, his gaze meeting Matt's only briefly. "I'd be damn scared, myself."

"What if I don't walk again? How am I supposed to work?"

"There are plenty of jobs you can do."

"None that are going to get the group home done under budget and on time. I convinced Dad to bid on the contract, and now I've screwed it all up."

"You didn't screw up anything. This isn't your fault."

"How do you know? What if I could have avoided the accident?"

"It's true, then? That you don't remember anything about the accident?"

"Last thing I remember is crawling through my kitchen window." Wishing the whole time he'd replaced the spare house key to its hiding place outside the last time he'd used it.

"That reminds me." Derrick dug in his jacket pocket and then held up Matt's key ring. "Think these might have helped?"

"Where'd you find 'em?" Matt had searched the jobsite for at least an hour.

"Right where you'd expect them to be. In the tool trailer, behind the miter box, under the sandpaper." Derrick dug in his pocket again. This time he pulled out Matt's cell phone. "Good thing your pecker's attached."

"Where was my phone?"

"On the bathroom window ledge—outside—under a pile of snow."

Great. Matt snagged the phone, hit the power button, and said a little prayer. The start-up jingle played. Even as he muttered a thank you to the cell phone gods, something felt wrong. Before the thought could take root, Derrick distracted him.

"You know, all you'd have to do is put your stuff away when you're done with it."

"You sound like Dad."

Derrick shrugged.

Put your stuff away when you're done with it, he thought as he set the phone on the table. Such a simple concept, one he'd heard a thousand times. He had a problem with simple. He had a problem with a lot of things. Like not being able to remember leaving the house. "It's weird having a chunk of your memory missing."

"I'd think that'd feel normal to you." The dimple in Derrick's cheek showed.

"Remind me to laugh later, okay? Seriously, it's bugging me why I was out there."

Derrick picked at a lump of putty embedded in his jeans. "You decided to take a cruise. Nothing odd about that."

"I wouldn't have been out for a ride. The roads were bad."

Derrick kept his head down, but his finger paused. "You probably didn't know it was that bad."

"I remember almost hitting the garage when I got home, the driveway was so slick. There's no way I would have gone back out unless there was a good reason."

"Knowing why isn't going to change anything, is it?"

Matt shrugged.

"You should be happy you can't remember. You really

want to go through the accident over and over?" He looked back at Matt for just a second. "Trust me. It's best you don't remember."

Matt looked down at his uneaten sandwich. He'd been a hell of a lot hungrier ten minutes ago. "I can't stand that I'm letting Dad down. Crystal, too." He rubbed his forehead as the weight of all of his worries pressed down on him. "Damn, Derrick. How can I expect Crystal to stick by me? This isn't fair to her."

"Oh, come on now. You don't seriously think she'd break up with you just because you're paralyzed, do you?"

"Just because I'm paralyzed? Of course not. But it isn't going to help matters. Not when we've had more than our share of ups and downs."

"Just like the rest of the world. Nobody's got a perfect relationship."

"My parents do."

"Your parents don't air their problems in public, that's all. Crystal's not going to leave you hanging, not over this, and that's a guarantee I feel comfortable making."

Matt found himself smiling. "And I should take your word on this because you're so successful at long relationships, huh?"

"Hey, I dated Heidi for eight months."

"Her name was Holly, and you barely made it four." Like he was anyone to talk. Until he'd met Crystal, his relationships had been as short and scattered as Derrick's.

"Four months? Really? It felt longer." Derrick glanced at his watch. "Speaking of longer, wish I could stay, but I promised Pops I'd be back by eleven." Derrick stood. His gaze landed on Matt's legs for only a second before he looked away, his attention high on the wall. The lighthearted moment vanished. "I'm sorry, Matt. This never should have happened."

Before Matt could open his mouth, Derrick had left. Matt frowned at the empty doorway. He wasn't sure which was more unsettling—that Derrick had called him by his name, instead of "bro," or that it looked like his pal was about to cry.

Despite Derrick's advice, he thought back to that night. Why had he gone out? If only he could remember. Then what? He'd magically be able to walk again? Like Derrick said, maybe it was best he didn't know. Besides, trying to recall a memory that wasn't there was giving him a headache. That, and worrying about how he was going to make ends meet.

He thought again about calling the bank to ask for interest-only payments for awhile. It had been a random thought before. Working things out in his head. A random thought that might be the only way to hold on to his house.

Two phones were within reach. One attached to the bed. His cell phone, right there within reach on the over-bed table.

He closed his eyes and rubbed his temples. He saw his house superimposed on his retinas. It really was a great house. One he couldn't stand to lose.

He grabbed his cell phone, and that weird feeling hit him again. He looked at the phone from all angles. Visually, it looked the same, right down to the drywall putty embedded in the grooves and a paint-smeared thumbprint on the back. He stared at the display, and it hit him. The battery bar showed a full charge. The battery should be dead or, at the very least, well on its way.

Obviously, Derrick had charged it. Which made sense. 'Cause that's how Derrick was. Always thinking two steps ahead. Why go through the work of giving the phone back only to have it be dead? Satisfied, he punched the menu button. Instead of dialing the bank's number, he scrolled backward through his incoming call history. He was curious about what had been happening in his real life, which didn't seem to have slowed down. He'd already gotten three calls today, alone.

Ski-Doo dealer, probably with a question about the Jet Ski he'd ordered. The one he'd have to postpone until money wasn't an issue anymore. Wally, from bowling. Travis, from pool. Going back further, he saw several numbers he didn't recognize mixed in with those of friends and other common numbers. The lady who owned the duplex they were remodeling had called the day after the accident. Then the history jumped to the day before the accident with a call from Sam, from pool.

"Wait a minute," he mumbled as he scrolled back up. No calls the day of his accident? Stranger things had happened, but not this. He scrolled back down with the same results. "Piece of crap phone."

Still baffled, he dialed his bank's number. Maybe when the cell phone bill came, he'd look at the itemization pages he usually ignored. See if he'd really gone a whole day without getting any calls.

"Good morning. Fuller Lake Community Bank. How may I help you?"

Putting aside his phone's mysterious glitch, he asked for a loan officer. The man "Uh huh'd" through Matt's explanation of why he couldn't make his full payments. "So I was hoping I could make only partial payments for a while."

"A while?"

"Five months, maybe." The number had popped into his head. A nice number. Half of ten.

"On all of your loans?"

His stomach tightened as he imagined the guy laughing and asking if Matt were crazy. "If possible."

Dead silence filled the air.

Matt clenched the phone.

"All right, Mr. Huntz. I'll put a note on your file approving a five-month extension during which you can make interest-only payments."

He made arrangements for the payments to be automatically transferred from his savingsaccount each month and then hung up. Five months. Why'd he say five months? And what the hell was he supposed to do after that if he wasn't walking again? Beg the bank for another five months? Even if the bank said yes, his savings would be gone by then.

No. He couldn't think that way. He'd told Crystal things would work out, and they would. Somehow.

Five months. The same amount of time it'd take for disability to kick in. His eyes tracked over to the nightstand where the disability benefits form lay amidst the rehab center brochures.

There had to be another way.

Like what? Sell the house before the bank could foreclose on it?

Shit.

Hating himself for what he was about to do, he grabbed on to the arm of the chair and stretched toward the nightstand. He worked the form closer with his fingertips. Rehab center brochures tumbled off the nightstand as he snagged the form. The brochure for Milwaukee Spine Care Center landed on top.

He let his gaze linger for a moment and then sighed. Going to Milwaukee just wasn't in the cards. Turning his attention to the disability benefits form, he told himself this was a show of responsibility. Doing the right thing. Making a pact with the devil was what it felt like. Providing for Crystal, he reminded himself. That's what this was all about. It had nothing to do with admitting he might not be able to work. Still, signing his name felt like he was signing a contract agreeing to stay paralyzed.

Eager to be rid of the form, he dialed the extension for Deborah Stryker's office. She promised to collect it within the hour.

"Oh, by the way," she said just before he could disconnect the call. "I called your insurance company this morning. Just in case you change your mind about staying here for therapy."

He felt a smile creep into place. Maybe he could go to Milwaukee after all. A reward for signing the damn form.

The smile fell. No. Going to Milwaukee wasn't what he wanted. Still, he held his breath while he waited for her to continue.

"Your insurance won't pay the full benefits for a specialty rehab center."

He released the breath but with a sense of loss. Funny how he could feel disappointed and relieved at the same time. At least now he wouldn't have to second-guess his decision.

"However," Deborah continued, "your insurance *will* allow admittance to a specialty center and the benefits are only fifteen percent less than what they'll pay if you stay here."

Shit. Nothing like dangling a brand new laser level in front of a gadget junkie who'd sworn off buying more tools. He had to force out the words. "I already made my decision. I'm staying here."

"It's a good decision. Everyone on the therapy staff here is a highly qualified professional."

He thought of Cheerleader Abby and found Deborah's statement hard to swallow. "Where'd you have your therapy?"

"At a general hospital in Madison. My care was more than adequate. The problem was, I wasn't willing to work at it and the therapists were too busy to force me to see how badly I was screwing up my life." She paused, as if to give the words time to sink in. "It took me a long time before I was able to care for myself. At the time, it didn't matter to me. After all, I was going to be one of the few who recovered."

"You say that like there's no hope at all."

"No, I say it like it's wrong to ignore the fact that your condition might be forever. I also called Milwaukee Spine Care Center."

"And?"

"They have an open bed."

Those words stuck with him long after he'd hung up.

They have an open bed.

For you.

"Dangle that damn laser level some more, why don't you?" Despite what he wanted, he'd made his decision and it was the right one. Staying here was best.

§

As if to prove Matt's decision to stay had been the right one, his afternoon was filled with visits from friends who wouldn't have gone all the way to Milwaukee. When he saw Crystal walk in with his parents that night, any final doubts were washed away. If he were in Milwaukee, he'd be alone tonight. No Mom. No Dad.

No Crystal.

Snug in his bed, Matt put out his arm, willing Crystal to fill the open space. She set a plastic shopping bag on the bed next to him and then leaned over. Her kiss on his cheek was quick, reminding him of his mother's kisses. All too soon, she was standing beside him instead of being in his arms where he wanted her. She brushed her finger across his cheek. "Too busy to shave today, huh?"

He rubbed the bristle. "I kind of like it."

"This is just a passing phase, right?"

He'd been shaving daily since he was sixteen. With a zillion other things to occupy his time since he'd been in the hospital, he hadn't bothered. He kind of liked having one less thing to do. Besides, the beard was coming in nicely. Seemed like a shame to get rid of it. He shrugged.

Crystal sighed and shook her head. Apparently, she didn't feel the same way. But she didn't push the matter. Instead, she asked, "Any new developments today?" Her eyebrows were slightly arched, expectant.

New developments. Like, had he moved his toes? Taken a step? Anything positive in the way of a recovery. He wished they were back on the topic of his beard. But they weren't. He couldn't make himself say no, that there'd been no recovery, so he settled on distraction. "Yeah."

Her lips parted. The eyebrows rose further.

"I slept away only half my day."

Her mouth slammed closed and her eyebrows relaxed. Clearly not the news she'd been hoping for. She pushed the bag closer to him. "I brought you something to keep you busy for a while. Maybe you can stay awake even longer tomorrow."

"That's sweet." *I don't need gifts, babe, just you.* He peeked into the bag. A new personal CD player, still in its rigid plastic tomb. Two cellophane-wrapped CDs. He glanced up at Crystal when he saw the artists. *Brooks and Dunn. Toby Keith.* Music he liked that she hated.

"Figured I was safe since the CD player comes with headphones," she said, giving him a smile.

He looked back in the bag. A bundle of AA batteries. "You weren't kidding about keeping me busy, were you? It'll take hours to get through all this plastic."

"I thought you liked a good challenge."

He tucked the bag next to his pillow and said, "Thanks, babe."

"My turn, now." His mother gave him a quick hug and then handed him another plastic bag. "I brought your mail and the things you asked for."

"The picture?" Matt asked. If he had to be stuck here another six weeks or more, he wanted to make this place feel more like home. Which meant having Crystal's picture on the nightstand.

"Picture?" Crystal asked.

"Yeah, the one of you from camping." He dug through the bag until he found it. He handed it to Crystal. "Can you put this on the nightstand?"

She held it in both hands. She seemed to not breathe as she stared at the image.

"I love that picture." His eyes were drawn to the woman pressed beneath the glass. "That look in your eyes. The curve of your lips. You look so in love...and all I can think is you were looking at me."

Her gaze shifted to meet his.

"I love you so much, Crystal."

"Good God, they're going to kiss," his father said. A hint of laughter tinged his voice.

Matt kept his eyes on Crystal. "I'll spare you, Dad. Crystal and I have the rest of our lives to kiss, don't we?"

Her nod was little more than a quick jerk of her chin. He tried to dismiss the sense of rejection until he noticed a movement from the corner of his eye. Crystal, twirling her engagement ring around her finger.

His father coughed, long and hard, along with a good round of chest thumping.

"You okay?" Matt asked, looking away from Crystal's fidgeting.

"Just a little burp is all." His dad popped a handful of antacids in his mouth.

"Geeze. I'd hate to see a big one."

"It's all that greasy fast food you've been eating for lunch," Matt's mother said.

Matt's eyebrows slid together. "Fast food? You not making lunch anymore, Ma?"

"Your father said it's easier to just grab a burger and eat it on the jobsite."

"I just like a good greasy burger every now and then, that's all." His father slid the roll of Tums into his pocket and then pulled out a deck of cards. "I'm going to fall asleep if I just sit here doing nothing. Anybody want to play cards?"

"Sounds like a great idea," Matt said. *Keep Crystal's hands full of cards, she won't be able to play with the ring.* He reached behind him, grabbed the side rail, and pulled. Trying to roll onto his back, he was more than aware of his father just feet away. Against his will, he let out a soft moan as his neck muscles tightened. Damn, it hurt like a son-of-a-bitch, but at least he could feel it.

"Honey, you should ask for help," Crystal said. She rubbed his arm as he flopped onto his back.

"Sure thing, babe. As soon as I need some help, I'll ask."

His father stared at him. Matt grinned, holding the smile in place, pretending he didn't need help with most everything he did these days. He pressed the button to raise the head of the bed, more than aware he couldn't sit up on his own. Something so frigging simple a baby could do.

He looked at his legs. They were all twisted, like a rag doll that'd been tossed into the air. A tightness that was becoming all too familiar formed in his chest.

"Dummy Rummy?" his father asked as he dealt the cards.

"You can skip me," Crystal said.

Sure. Keep your hands free to fiddle with the damn ring. "It'll be fun." He gave her his winning smile while he moved the over-bed table closer, trying to camouflage his twisted legs. "I promise."

She rolled her eyes. "Fine. Deal me in."

"Thanks, babe."

With two wins in his pocket, Matt forgot his twisted legs, forgot Crystal's reminder that he couldn't do anything on his own, and forgot the helpless feeling that made him want to cry. He put his cards down and said, "Looks like I win again."

Glancing at Crystal's cards, he instantly added her damages. "Ooh, babe. Twenty-five points. Sorry." He shifted to his mom's cards. "But not as bad as that. Sixty?"

"I still don't get how you do that," his mom said. "You barely looked at my cards."

He tapped his forehead. "Powerful calculator." He shifted his attention to his dad, who was adding his cards to the running score for their third game. "You've got a total of seventy-five," Matt said. "Ma's at one fifty, Crystal's at ninety, and I'm the king at fifty-five."

His father ignored him as he added everyone's scores. After a moment, he tossed down the pencil. "Should have sent you to college to be a banker."

"Or an accountant," his mother added.

"Don't think so. I much prefer pounding nails to pounding adding machine keys." At age five, he'd wanted to be a fireman. Three months later, he wanted to be a dentist. A few months after that, a dinosaur. But from the time his father had first brought him to one of the homes he'd been remodeling, there'd been no question about what Matt was going to do when he grew up. He'd known that he'd work side-by-side with his father.

His father yawned, stretching his arms wide above his head. "Speaking of pounding nails, dawn comes mighty early."

Matt hated what was coming next, their leaving, even though he knew they couldn't stay all night.

"And the hour you get up comes even earlier." The deep creases across his mother's forehead said she didn't think kindly of how early her husband was getting up.

"Gives me more time to think about how wonderful you are," his dad said with a wink.

Crystal pushed herself off the bed. She gave Matt the kiss he'd wished for earlier.

She let her lips linger for a moment before she stepped back, allowing his mother to hug him.

Crystal had her coat on and her purse slung over her shoulder in the amount of time it took his mother to hug him. He knew it wasn't practical, but he wished Crystal would have driven separately so he could have some time alone with her.

His dad tossed Matt's mom a crowded key ring. "How about you and Crystal go start the car. I'll be just a moment."

Thanks, Dad. Thanks for sending my fiancée away even quicker.

His mom frowned for just a second before she nodded. "See you tomorrow." She waved to her son. "Sleep tight."

"You start therapy Monday," his dad said as soon as they were alone.

"Yes..."

"You can still tell that woman you want to go to one of those specialty places."

Matt refrained from rolling his eyes. "Dad, I told you, I'm okay with staying here."

"You don't need to worry about the money. I've got it all figured out."

"That's good. Use it to take Ma on a good vacation someday."

His father looked toward the ceiling. His jaw was set tight. He didn't say a word, but Matt could read his father's posture. *Damn, stubborn kid,* was what he was thinking. Matt didn't see it that way. He saw it as doing what was best for his family. Like his father would do. Why couldn't his father understand that? "Dad, really, I want to stay here."

"I thought what you *wanted* was to take over the business someday."

"I do."

"Then go to Milwaukee where you'll get the best therapy possible."

Go to Milwaukee. Rack up a pile of debt for his parents, on top of his own. With no guarantee of it making any difference. "You heard the lady. Going to Milwaukee isn't the magical cure to get me walking again."

"Staying here isn't, either."

"Talk about—" He clamped his mouth shut before the word *stubborn* could slip out. "You know, Dad, I appreciate your advice, but the decision's made. I'm staying here."

"What about money? How are you set for paying your bills?"

It'd be nice to let someone else shoulder the responsibility, but this wasn't his father's mess. He pasted on a smile. "Got it covered."

His dad didn't move.

Matt kept his smile in place. He and his brother used to have staring contests when they were little. Brad never won.

"Crystal was right when she said you should ask for help. There's nothing shameful in admitting you can't do everything."

"I said, I've got it covered."

"For how long?"

Matt looked away. He could feel his father's eyes burning holes in him. Matt let out a deep sigh and then let his eyes drift back to his dad. "I think I can make it two months. Then..." He shrugged.

"We'll work it out," his dad said with a nod. "Don't you worry about it. I've got it all figured out." He bent over and took Matt in a pair of strong arms. "Everything's going to be fine."

§

What did I do to deserve this life? Abby's shoulders slumped as she punched in the security code to the nursing home. Whatever she'd done to chase away her father, did it have to include a life-long sentence, too?

The status light changed from red to green, the lock clicking as it disengaged. She pushed open the door and entered a world that, on the surface, appeared way too similar to the one she'd just left a couple of hours ago.

There was nobody at the nurses' station. A chirping noise kept time with the blinking, white lights on the grid behind the desk. Three lights today. Three residents on this wing requiring immediate care. Three residents waiting while the overworked staff took care of other duties. As she turned down the corridor on the right, her eyes automatically sought out the light above her mother's door. Off, thank heavens.

She sidestepped Sleeping Hallway Man, the elderly man in a wheelchair who seemed to only be able to sleep in the hallway. At the end of the hall, one of the residents called out her usual mantra of "help," sounding like a wounded cat meowing. Overshadowing it all was a stale scent, like death waiting to happen.

I hate this place. I could turn around and leave. Mom would never know I hadn't visited.

She bit her lip against the stab of guilt. Her mother might not know, but Abby would.

She quickened her pace, hurrying to her mother's room.

At first glance, Helen Fischner looked like Average Jane Blow seated in a rocking chair, reading a book. But Abby knew better. Average Jane Blow would be rocking, even just the littlest bit. And Average Jane Blow wouldn't be wearing a green floral skirt and an orange plaid shirt with the buttons in the wrong holes.

"Hi, Mom," Abby said as she shrugged off her jacket.

Helen's attention didn't waiver from the book in her hands.

Abby set her coat and purse on the bed and then crouched in front of her mother. Helen's unmoving eyes stayed focused on the book. She looked like she'd been flash-frozen, forever fixed on one word. She'd stay that way for hours. Abby gently moved her mother's face away from the book. "Hi, Mom. How was your day?"

Her mother stared at her so deeply it felt as if she were staring right into Abby's soul. She wondered, if that were the case, what her mother saw in her. Hopefully, a good person, someone who'd earned the right to be loved. More likely, her mother saw a woman full of flaws, too many for any man to see her as anything other than a sexual diversion.

Helen blinked and then smiled, her face so beautiful it made Abby's heart ache. "Abby."

Abby smiled back, wishing the alert, smiling woman across from her could remain that way forever. But her mother's smile faded, along with the look of recognition, as she slipped back into her own little world where she'd stay until she had a reason to return to the here and now. Abby checked out the title of her mother's book. *A Summer's Journey.* "What are you reading today?"

"*War and Peace.*" The book she'd been reading before her accident.

As a physical therapist who wanted to work with brain-injured patients, she knew she should get her mother to acknowledge what book she was really reading, but she was too exhausted for the fight it would surely bring on. "Is it good?"

"The words ran out."

Her mother had reached the end of the page and couldn't comprehend that she needed to turn it. Tired or not, the physical therapist within jumped to action as Abby demonstrated how to turn the page. She flipped back to the page her mother had been on. A simple concept. Much easier to tackle than the correct title of the book. "Now, you do it."

Helen grabbed several pages and flipped them.

"Just one page." Abby turned back to the page her mother had been on.

Helen's fingers fumbled as she attempted to turn over just one page, grabbing several instead, as uncoordinated as a person wearing gloves.

Abby wanted to take over and turn the page, but that wouldn't help her mother. "Remember, just one page."

Helen's foot tapped the floor. The chair rocked. The paper tore and crinkled as she thumbed at the page, trying to get just one sheet. "They're..." Her beautiful face contorted as the word failed to come. The chair rocked faster. Another page ripped.

Sensing her mother about to erupt, Abby shrank back.

The book flew past Abby, so close she felt the breeze. It smacked the wall and then landed on the floor with a slap.

"You snotted the pages together so I couldn't trip them."

She could defend herself until her tongue turned to cotton, but her mother would never admit it hadn't been Abby's fault. Maybe it was her fault. She may not have glued the pages together, but she'd been the one to push her. She rubbed her mother's knee, trying to calm her.

"The pages were fine until you got here."

Just words of frustration, but they still registered within Abby, soaking into her core. "I'm sorry, Mom."

"I want to go home. When is Danny coming to get me?"

Abby mentally winced at her father's name and the same question she'd asked a thousand times herself. Ever since he'd dumped her on Aunt Norma's doorstep a month after her mother's accident. "Not tonight," she said as she sat on her mother's bed.

"Tomorrow?" Helen asked.

Only if the sky turned green and the grass turned purple. Maybe then he'd come. "I don't know, Mom."

"He said we'd be together forever."

Forever. A meaningless word. Wanting to shift her mother away from the topic, Abby asked, "Did you go to the activities room today?"

"We made chickendoodle cookies."

"Snickerdoodle?"

"Yes. Chickendoodle. Flour and sugar and butter and horse feathers."

"Horse feathers," Abby said, managing a laugh. "My favorite."

"Just like your father."

Searching for a new distraction, Abby resorted to the game she'd invented years ago to help sharpen her mother's mind. "Do you like snails?"

"More than puppy dog tails. Do you like snot?"

Abby laughed at her mother's word choice. "Yes, a whole lot. Do you like frogs?"

"Only on logs. Do you like mice?"

"I find them real nice. Do you like a girl named Franny?" Even as the name spilled from her tongue, she realized her ploy for distraction had just failed.

"Where is Danny? He said he'd come for me."

Abby groaned inside. Her father had been gone for seventeen years, yet, for her mother, it may as well have been yesterday.

She wanted to yell that he was gone and that he wasn't coming back. She wanted to beat the truth into her mother's damaged head until reality stuck. But what she wanted to do even more was put her head on her mother's shoulder and cry. If only for five minutes, she wanted her mother to be the mother so she could be the kid. She wanted her mother to say it was okay that he'd left them, that they were doing fine without him, and that they didn't need him. Most of all, she wanted her mother's assurance that the little girl Abby had been hadn't chased away her father.

Her mother stared at her, full of innocence. "Is Danny here?"

"Not tonight." She needed a new distraction, one that didn't involve talking. Feeling a little guilty, she grabbed the TV remote tethered to the bed by a cord. "How about we watch TV?"

Without argument, Helen faced the TV. Within minutes, her eyes took on a glazed appearance. Abby could easily sneak away unnoticed, long before her self-imposed two-hour visit was up. If she left early today, though, she'd easily allow herself to leave early tomorrow. Next, she'd justify coming only every other day until she stopped coming altogether. Like father, like daughter.

Worn down by dealing with her mother, the old tears easily worked their way to the surface. She bit her lip to hold them back. She didn't have as much luck stopping the memory of her father. She saw herself curled on his lap as he read to her. She could feel the softness of his old flannel shirt soft, the strength of his arms, and the comfort of his lap. And there was no other place she would rather be.

Fearing she was about to lose the battle with her tears, she pulled a paperback romance from her purse. In the world of make believe, the heroine's trivial problems would be solved within two hundred and fifty pages. Love was lasting. The hero never left the heroine. Parents didn't leave their children. And every story ended with happily-ever-after.

She held the book with one hand and pulled her pony tail loose with the other and finger-combed her shoulder-length hair. If life were a book, there'd be a man running his fingers through her hair right now, instead. They'd be stretched out in front of a crackling fire. Somewhere far, far away from this nursing home.

In the book, Chase had just told Piper he loved her when, in real life, the CNA came into the room, bringing reality with her. Sally stooped over to pick up Helen's discarded book. "Your mother's been exercising her arm again, I see."

"I made the mistake of showing her how to turn the page." Abby stashed her book back in her purse.

"Trying to teach her anything is useless, you know, but you get a gold star for trying."

Helen stared at the TV without any recognition that she was the topic of conversation. Sally put the book on the nightstand and then waved her hand in front of Abby's mother's face. "Helen, time to tell your daughter goodnight."

Helen's eyes shot to Abby. "You're leaving, already? You just got here."

"I've been here two hours, Mom."

"I know how to tell time. It's only..." She looked at the wall clock and then back at Abby. "You're messing with my mind. You changed the clock just to...nail with me." She shook her finger at her daughter. "And don't you lie to me or I'll tell your father when he gets home. Where is your father, anyhow? He should be here by now."

More than ready to make her escape, Abby gave her mother a hug and a kiss. "Goodnight, Mom. I'll see you tomorrow."

Most nights, her mother returned the hug without a fuss. Tonight, her mother clung to her. "Take me with you."

Abby's whole being tensed. "Tomorrow, okay? We'll go for a car ride. Go and get ice cream. Would you like that?"

"I want to go, now."

"Tomorrow." Feeling trapped, in more ways than one, Abby pried her mother's arms loose. She wanted to make her escape. Not just for tonight, but forever. Just step out that door and disappear.

"You're going to leave and never come back, just like Danny."

Like her mother had read her mind. She crouched and locked her gaze on her mother's beautiful blue eyes. "I'll always come back, Mom." It was the truth, but it felt like a lie. She had to force herself not to look away in guilt. "I'll always come back."

CHAPTER FIVE

Matt's hands lay limp in his lap as the CNA wheeled him to the gym on Monday morning for his first round of therapy. A man who was calm and relaxed, without a care in the world. That's what he hoped anyone looking at him would see. Act confident and you'll be confident. It usually worked. Usually. Not today.

He wanted to believe what he'd been telling everyone. Everything would be fine. Fine. As in, him, walking. But it was hard to hold on to that belief when he was on his way to learn how to adapt to a life without walking.

The CNA pushed him through a set of double doors into a room filled with blue padded tables and basic exercise equipment. Not a single set of parallel bars in sight. His shoulders slumped as the dream slipped further away.

Off to the right was a nurses' station where Abby stood behind a desk. She looked up and waved, her smile wide, as if his arrival was the highlight of her day. The cheerleader held up a finger, motioning she'd be with him in a moment. His mouth tightened in a half sneer as she all but skipped over to a file cabinet. Probably to get her pompons.

The CNA, who was old enough to be the cheerleader's mother, parked his wheelchair to the left of the doors. "I'll be back for you in forty-five minutes."

Forty-five minutes stuck with the cheerleader. He didn't think he could put up with Ms. Peppy that long. "I'll give you twenty bucks if you come back for me in thirty."

"See you in forty-five."

Across the room, a therapist worked with a man on one of the blue vinyl mats. She looked about as far away from being a cheerleader as possible. She had to be at least forty-five years old. Chubby. She looked like it'd take a jackhammer to crack the frown off her face. Sure bet there were no pompons hidden beneath her bed. The important thing was, it looked like she knew what she was doing.

There was a third therapist, also older than Abby. Much older. She'd probably been a therapist as long as Abby had been alive. Which meant she had lots of experience.

He looked back at Abby. The tightness in his shoulders stretched to the back of his neck. Why'd he have to get stuck with the cheerleader? What was it about her that got under his skin, anyway? No matter how many times he'd told himself he was being an ass when she'd been in his room, he'd found it impossible to be nice. She was fifteen feet away, and he already felt nasty crawling through his veins.

Trying to put her out of his mind, he turned his attention to the exercise and weight-lifting equipment that lined the farthest wall. He had better equipment in the workout room he'd built in his attic, back home.

"Ready to begin, Matthew?" Abby asked.

She'd managed to sneak up on him. His heart gave three quick beats before it settled into a regular pace. He looked up at Abby in her purple smock top with her hair pulled up and her lips all shiny. "Shit. You ever hear of shoes that make noise?"

"Sure have, but they're not as much fun. Speaking of fun, are you ready to start?"

His pulse jumped up another notch. "Been looking forward to it all morning."

Abby moved him to a padded exercise table and then set the wheelchair's brake. She swung the armrest out of the way before handing him a highly polished transfer board. "You want to tuck—"

"I took Wheelchair 101." Damn it. They hadn't even been together a full minute, and he was already barking at her.

She stood back and crossed her arms with a "have at it" expression.

Using the remaining armrest for balance, he leaned

sideways to tuck the board beneath his thigh. He hated relying on others to move him, and it also bothered him that he needed to grip the armrest to keep from falling over. Hopefully, the cheerleader could help with that.

When the board was in place, Abby leaned over. He rested against her shoulder like he'd been shown. Her hair smelled nice, like strawberries.

"Today, we're going to work on balance." Abby slid him across the board. She kept her hands on his shoulders once he was settled onto the mat. "Your head is your center of gravity. If you lift your hand, you'll want to move your head in the opposite direction to counterbalance. I'm going to let go in five seconds, so do whatever you feel you need to in order to stay upright."

He pressed his hands against the vinyl mat. Abby pulled her hands away. His body rushed backward, filling him with the sensation of falling. His weight settled on his arms. His breath came out in a burst, even though he was safe.

"It won't be so bad once you learn how to control your weight," Abby said.

His heart still pounding, he looked at her, really looked at her, for the first time since he'd been brought in. She wasn't in the same league as Crystal, but Abby qualified as pretty. The bright overhead lights brought out the natural golden tones in her silky, light brown hair, which was pulled back in a ponytail like Kaylee often wore. Unlike Crystal, who used makeup to its fullest, Abby wore very little. Her only indulgence seemed to be lip gloss.

"I'm taking you on your word," he said.

"You'll see." She bent those lips into a smile that would have convinced an armless man to buy gloves. "Lift your right hand, Matthew."

The last word was like nails on a chalkboard. "My name is Matt. Got it?"

"Okay, *Matt*. Lift your right hand."

It was going to be an awfully long six weeks if he couldn't control his tongue. He sighed. "I didn't mean to snap. I just hate being called Matthew. Makes me feel like

I'm being yelled at."

She flashed him another one of those buy-these-gloves smiles. "Apology accepted." She raised her hand in front of her as if to remind him of her request.

Inside his head, the motion of lifting his arm was easy. In reality, he had to concentrate on tipping his head just the right amount to counterbalance his arm. The fact that he had to concentrate so hard on something so simple renewed the resident anger to a slow simmer.

"When I was a kid, anytime I did something wrong, it was Abigail Marie Fischner. Never just Abigail. Always had to be the full gamut."

He nodded, his body wobbling with the movement. "I know what you mean. I got yelled at so much, I thought my first name was Matthewlucashuntz. It wasn't until I was in kindergarten that I realized it was three names, instead of one."

She arched her eyebrows. "You were a troublemaker?"

Troublemaker? That depended on whether you asked him or his mother. "Nah. I prefer to think I was overly inquisitive. My niece, Kaylee, is that way."

"She seems like a very sweet kid."

He furrowed his forehead for a moment until he remembered that Abby had met Kaylee. "My mom thinks Kaylee got her curiosity from me."

"A legacy from her uncle."

The muscles tightened across his shoulders, and his jaw twitched. Was that the only legacy he'd leave as his mark on the world? He'd personally shoved a mile-long tube in his dick that morning, just so he could piss. Something like that should have registered somewhere between down-right-painful and mildly-annoying. He hadn't felt a thing. Not his hand. Not the tube. Not even the pressure of needing to piss. In his estimation, that didn't say much for his future between the sheets.

"Okay, lift your left arm now," Abby said.

Back in the good old days, he'd have simply sat up straight and held up his left arm. Now, the motion required thought and patience. Once he recovered, he'd never again take for granted all the little things he'd done without thought for so many years.

"Good." She held her hand in front of him. "Touch my fingers with your right hand."

"Touch your fingers? I'm paying big bucks for therapy and that's the best you can come up with?"

Her mouth quivered as though she was trying to hold back a smile. "Okay. We'll move to phase two. Be right back."

He watched her bounce away, and his weight wavered when he twisted his neck. He pictured himself toppling forward. He kept his head perfectly still, and the sensation that he was about to fall passed. Was this the way it was always going to be? Having to think long and hard about every move he made? Fearing he would fall flat on his face? *Think confident. Be confident.* He moved his head just enough to make him sway. Mr. Confident vanished in a flash. He held his breath until he steadied.

Abby came back with a tennis ball.

"Goody. We're going to play tennis instead of work, huh?" He slowly turned his head to look straight ahead, stopping whenever he felt his body sway. The cheerleader turned tennis pro stayed silent as though she realized he needed his full concentration. It seemed to take forever before he inched his face forward again, but he made it without falling.

"Ready?" she asked.

For what, he didn't know. "Sure."

"Catch," she said as she tossed the ball.

Instinct took over. He reached out. From the corner of his eye, he noticed Ms. Bouncy lean toward him with her hands raised as if preparing to catch him. He barely cracked a confident smile before he fell over, crashing against the padded mat.

Abby put her hands on her hips. "So, do you want to do things my way? Or yours?"

He pushed himself up, conscious of her watching him. His elbow hurt, along with his ego. "I'd hate to stand in the way of the couple weeks of schooling you went through."

"Thought so. Lift both hands and reach for my finger with your right hand."

Biting his lip, he reached to touch her fingers.

"Good." She pulled her hand a half inch away. "Touch my fingers, now."

He followed all of her stupid directions until she motioned him to put his hands down. The cheerleader was a pain in the ass, but she wasn't the powder puff he'd pegged her for.

"You did well," she said. "We're going to work on rolling over, now. I'm going to have you lie down."

She leaned in toward him, preparing to help him lie down. He was about to spout off that he didn't need her help. Then, he remembered crashing onto the mat earlier. He clamped his jaw tight while she eased him backward. As soon as his head touched the vinyl, she stood and held up her hands like she was praying. "Clasp your hands, like this."

He clasped his hands. "Now I lay me down to sleep."

"You can nap when we're done. In fact, you'll probably want to."

He held back a laugh. Like rolling over was going to tire him.

She moved her hands above her right shoulder. "Swing your arms as though you're chopping wood sideways."

He linked his hands and stretched them over his head to his right side. Rapidly swinging his arms to the left, he brought his hands even with his hips, yet he remained on his back. This was supposed to help him roll over?

"Try again."

Bringing his arms into position again, he wondered how stupid he looked. He sure felt stupid. Abby stood with her attention focused on his movements. If she'd had even a hint of a smile, he would have thought this was all a joke. As if she wanted to see if he'd do this incredibly ridiculous thing, just because she'd told him to. But she was all business.

"You can do it, Matt. Just put some power behind your swing."

Sure. Easy. No problem.

He brought his arms down as hard as he could but failed to roll over. Warmth infused his cheeks. Maybe he didn't want to roll over. Maybe he'd just go through his life stuck on his back whenever he was lying down.

Shit.

He tried again. And again. He tried until his arms and shoulders ached, but there was no way he was giving up. Not until he rolled over and made the cheerleader happy. Took him seven times, but his body finally rolled to the left.

"Wonderful," Abby said with an excited tone that sounded like he'd done something truly spectacular. She was so impressed, she made him do it again. Over and over. Until he thought he was going to keel over from exhaustion. He wanted to tell her what she could do with her lessons, but he was too tired to talk.

He glanced at the door, expecting to see the CNA waiting for him. His forty-five minutes had to have been up at least twenty minutes ago.

Abby raised the table. "Now, you get to relax while I do all the work."

"About fu..." He cleared his throat.

The corner of her mouth tipped upward for just a second before she pinched her lips together. He had the feeling she was enjoying this.

She picked up his leg and rotated his hip joint. "It'll get better as you get stronger."

Before the damned accident had turned his world upside down, he'd been in the habit of working out forty minutes every morning before putting in a full day lifting lumber and sheetrock and bundles of shingles. How strong did a person have to be to sit up and roll over?

She pushed his knee toward his chest and then straightened his leg. The tension returned to his shoulders and neck. He should be able to move his own damn leg. The thing was still there, attached to his body. The nerves, the veins, the bones, the tendons. All there. Nothing missing. It seemed so wrong that he had no control over pieces of his own body. It wasn't just the lack of movement that bothered him but also the fact that he couldn't feel her hands on his leg.

Finally, Abby put his leg down one last time. He tried to ignore the helpless feeling as she transferred him into the wheelchair. Mean and nasty pulsed through his veins again, simmering beneath the surface.

"Good job, Matt," Abby said as the other woman took control of the wheelchair. "I'll see you tomorrow,"

"Can't wait."

The CNA moved at a snail's pace. He thought about pushing the wheels for her, but that required too much energy. They'd just made it to the door when Abby called out. "Oh, wait."

She came up beside them. "I forgot, I have something for you." She handed him some papers. "I gathered up some information on bikes you can pedal with your hands, like we discussed. I also found an article about a paralyzed man who rock climbs."

The top sheet showed two models of a recumbent-style bike. May as well hang a neon sign over the guy's head that glared *PARALYZED*. A panicky sensation crawled beneath his skin. He didn't want the damn bike. He didn't want to climb mountains with special equipment. What he wanted was to be normal again. To be a man. Just like his dad.

He looked away. "I'm ready to go back to my room."

§

At the end of the day, Abby settled down in the quiet gym with a stack of patient files. Marsha and Sara had already left—the reversal of cockroaches—they scattered at the sound of quiet. Abby, however, found the hours after the patients had left to be the best time to do paperwork. Of course, she didn't have a family waiting for her at home.

And they didn't have a nursing home visit waiting for them.

She opened the top file. Matthew Huntz. No. Make that *Matt* Huntz. Exhaustion settled over her like a heavy coat. And that was the effect of only one session with him. Tomorrow, that would be doubled as they added in the afternoon session. Matt Huntz thought he knew best, like *he* was the therapist.

He seemed to dislike her. Not like it really mattered. Her role was to get him mobile again—not to win a popularity contest. Their association would be over in eight weeks when he went home. Sooner, if she got the job at Milwaukee Spine Care Center.

The interview had been over a week ago. She could only assume they'd made a decision by now. Obviously, that decision didn't include her. She sucked her bottom lip in between her teeth. If she didn't get the job, so what? She could always find a job somewhere else that would allow her to work exclusively with brain-injured patients.

She looked up as the gym doors opened. An instant smile formed when she saw the doctor walking toward her. Staying at St. Luke's did have its benefits.

Paul wasn't the type who earned second glances, not with his black-rimmed glasses and his receding hairline. But he qualified as "cute." And he'd worked hard to convince her to go out on that first date. She'd finally given in. After all, anyone who'd worked that hard for a date wasn't likely to drop out of her life after a date or two. And now, after several months, she thought that possibly, just possibly, she might fall in love with him. Someday.

"I've missed you, honey bun." He spread his arms wide apart. She stood and settled comfortably into their security. His mouth settled over hers. Tight in his embrace, she had no choice but to move with him as he led her away from the desk. Not like she planned on resisting.

He pressed her against the wall beside the filing cabinets where they wouldn't be seen by anyone coming in. She ignored the stethoscope in his lab coat that jabbed her belly and concentrated on his lips, instead. With any luck, kissing would be enough for him.

Her heart skipped a beat when he slid his hand beneath her uniform top. They shouldn't be doing this here. She held back her protest. Sometimes, you had to do things you didn't want to do, and this was one of those things.

He teased her satin-covered nipple with his thumb. In spite of herself, she tipped her head back and moaned softly. Her good sense warned her that what she was doing was wrong, but she pushed it away. Something that felt this good couldn't be wrong. And he liked touching her. *Her.* Not someone else, but her.

"Skip visiting your mom tonight." He nibbled her lip. "I'll make it worth your while."

A nursing-home-free evening sounded wonderful. Especially when that evening would be spent with Paul.

"Lobster and expensive wine." Little kisses across her jaw.

She'd be happy with take-out pizza and bottled water.

His mouth moved to the tender skin below her ear. "An evening of intellectual conversation."

No fighting about how to turn the page or what time it was.

To the crook of her neck. "We can follow it up with breakfast in bed."

An entire evening with him.

He squeezed her nipple just the right amount to spread heat through her belly. If she missed one visit, her mother would never notice.

He sucked lightly on her neck. In his bed, she knew he'd suck other places. Something else he liked doing. If she kept him happy, then maybe he'd love her. She opened her mouth to say yes, that she'd skip visiting her mother tonight. But then she wondered how easily she'd agree if Paul asked her again tomorrow to skip her visit. And then, the next time, would she even pause just the slightest? "I have to visit my mother, but I can come over, after."

"It'll be too late for lobster, then."

She slid her hand around to his lower front. "But it won't be too late for this."

He leaned heavily against her. "You're killing me,

Abby. I want to take you into the supply closet and fuck you until you scream so loud they hear you in the next county."

She didn't want to be fucked. She wanted to be made love to. And the supply closet was about the last place she wanted to do it. But she was the one he wanted sex with and not someone else, and that was close enough to love to suit her. "So, do it."

"You tempt me. Surely, you do." He pulled away far enough to look in her eyes. "But I don't want it to be just about sex. I want more." With a grin, he pulled her hand off his crotch. "But if you keep that up, I'll settle for wild, animal sex."

Feeling like a tramp, she reached for him again, but he sidestepped her. "Seriously, Abby. I want this to be more than sex. I want a relationship with you. One that involves us being together longer than an hour here and an hour there."

A relationship. Something more than a quick dinner and sex. Marriage? Kids? The happily-ever-after that had escaped her for so long?

He stepped closer. "I think it's time I meet your mom."

"No." The word shot out on impulse. Which made no sense. Meeting her mother was a good thing. It showed he was serious about her. "I mean, yes, you should meet Mom. Someday. Just not tonight." *Why not?* "I need to prepare her. She doesn't take change well, not even good change."

"Well, you prepare her, then. Because I plan on being in your life for the long haul." He cupped the side of her face and stared into her eyes. "I love you, Abby."

Wrapping her arms around him, she struggled to not cling to him. Had he really said he loved her? She wanted to sing and dance. But mostly, she wanted to cry.

CHAPTER SIX

Despite wishing for independence, Matt was content to let the CNA push him down the hallway after his last therapy session on Wednesday. His third day of therapy hadn't been any easier than his second, and both of them made his first day seem like child's play. When you got right down to it, the little bit he did in the sessions amounted to close to nothing, at least compared to what he had done in a day as a construction worker. But it was the most tiring "close to nothing" he'd ever done.

He welcomed entering the doorway to his room. A nap comprised his plans for the next couple of hours. But no such luck. Here came Deborah Stryker, wheeling in right behind him.

"Matthew, how's it going? Are you working hard in therapy?"

He let out a small laugh because that was all the energy he had.

"I happened to be talking to admitting at Milwaukee Spine Care Center. They still have that open room. Just in case you care." A smile played on her lips as though she knew how much he'd wanted to go there. She gave her wheels a push. "You have yourself a nice evening."

You have a nice evening, too, you witch. How many times did he have to tell her he was fine where he was?

The picture of the man in braces flashed in his head as the nurse got him settled into bed. He was about as far away from being that man as he could get. He forced away the image. It had only been a few days. He couldn't expect to be doing wheelchair and bed transfers all on his own, already.

He closed his eyes. His thoughts went to the rehab center in Milwaukee, and he wished he were there. *Damn it, stop it. You made your decision. Stop wishing for what's not going to be.*

As tired as he was, sleep was slow in coming. He'd barely drifted off when his cell phone rang. His heart raced as he opened his eyes. He grabbed the phone and mumbled, "Hello."

"Mr. Huntz? This is Rose, at Fuller Lake Community Bank. I was just getting ready to transfer your loan payments when I noticed they have already been made. I wanted to be sure I didn't have down the wrong information."

His heart still raced from the sudden awakening. "What do you mean, my payments have been made?"

"Just that. The payments were already made. On all of your loans."

"You sure you've got the right accounts? Matthew Huntz. H. U. N. T. Z. My base account is 198362."

"That's what I have."

His gaze skated around the room. This had to be a prank. When no laugh came, he asked, "Can you tell who made the payments?"

"I'm sorry. There's no way to track the source. The payments were made in cash."

"Great." How lucky for him.

"We'll transfer your interest payments from your savings account next month, like you arranged. Have a good day."

He flipped his phone closed. All remnants of sleep had vanished. Who the hell would have paid his loans?

His father? He'd said he would help. No. Matt had told his dad he was good for a few months. That should have satisfied his father. And his father never would have paid the loans without telling Matt first. Would he? Of course not.

His brother? No. Brad's money was tighter than his own.

Crystal? No way.

Derrick? He dismissed him almost as fast as his name had come to mind. Sure, they were closer than friends, but this was a lot different than lending someone fifty bucks until payday.

Which brought him back to his father.

He flipped his phone open and pressed the number "2" to speed dial his father's cell. It seemed to take forever before his father answered, and when he did, his words were rushed between labored breaths. "Can this wait? I'm in the middle of something."

It'd only take a few seconds to ask. A couple of seconds for the answer.

Through the phone, he heard a distant voice. "Mr. Huntz, I don't have all day."

Just a second. That's all he needed. "I was just wondering if—"

"Mr. Huntz!"

"I'm sorry, Matt, I've really got to go. See you later." His father disconnected the call.

"...you paid my loans," Matt said to the dead phone. He wanted to call back, but he closed his phone instead.

CHAPTER SEVEN

With the gym resembling a ghost town on Wednesday afternoon, Abby settled in at the desk with her patient files. The telephone interrupted her before she even had a chance to open the top file. Paul, she thought, smiling as she snagged the phone. Calling to say he loved her.

Love. Her smile vanished. Why was it that the more serious a relationship got, the more fragile it became?

"Therapy department, Abigail Fischner."

"Hello, Ms. Fischner. This is Kyle Jones from Milwaukee Spine Care Center."

Her breath held suspended. It wasn't Paul, but this call was just as good. Better in fact...she hoped. She tried to read his voice, but his tone was neutral. Surely she'd gotten the job. Rejections usually came in letters, not personal phone calls.

"I hope it's all right for me to call you at work."

"Yes." Her chest barely moved. *Please say I got the job. Please, please.*

"I'd like to offer you the position."

Her feet wiggled while her lips formed a yes around a smile. Before the word could spill from her mouth, Paul pushed into her thoughts. He'd said he loved her. What if they weren't just words like they had been with Jovan? What if it was real this time? And there was her mother to think about. Moving her mother was going to be a challenge.

"Ms. Fischner?"

"I'm sorry. I'm just a bit...stunned." Shoot. Shoot, shoot. "I was hoping you'd call, but I must admit I didn't expect to be offered the job. I hate to ask, but is there any chance I can have a few days to decide?"

"Of course. How's Monday?"

"Yes. Monday's just fine." She hung up and then

covered her face with her hands. Darn it.

"Honey? What's wrong?"

She looked up at the sound of Paul's voice. His appearance at that moment was like a sign. She wasn't supposed to take the job.

"Is it something with your mom?"

She shook her head. She wanted to believe she and Paul had a future, but she wanted the job, as well.

"Then, what's wrong?"

"I was just offered the job in Milwaukee."

"Well, then, congratulations are in order. We'll have to go out tonight to celebrate."

Celebrate? Her leaving was cause for him to rejoice?

"When do you start?"

"I didn't say yes."

His eyebrows shot up. "Really? I thought you wanted the job."

"I didn't say no, either. I don't know what to do, Paul. I want the job. Really, really want it. But..."

"But..." The single word was full of expectation.

Looking up at him, she saw a glimmer of what she'd hoped to find in him. Marriage. Kids.

A family.

And then, the vision vanished. "I'm just not sure how Mom would adjust to a new place."

"Your mom. Of course." The sleeves of his crisp, white jacket bunched up at the elbows of his crossed arms.

"And I wasn't sure if I wanted to leave you."

His stance relaxed and the tight line of his mouth disappeared. "Really?"

She felt the urge to get up and run. Planting her feet, she nodded.

He pulled her up, wrapped her in his embrace, and nuzzled her neck.

She pressed herself up against him and concentrated on the feel of him against her. He'd said he loved her. She squeezed her eyes closed. Too bad professions of love didn't come with guarantees.

§

The question of who had paid his loans burned inside Matt while the next one hundred sixty minutes stretched into eternity. By the time Crystal stepped into the room, Matt had worked up fifteen different ways to broach the question. Before he could ask where his dad was, Crystal had crossed the room, leaned over the bed, and pressed her mouth to his. Whoa! Her tongue searched for his as though she'd spent the whole day anticipating this moment. The question of his loans became unimportant.

"Good lord."

"Oh, my."

Crystal pulled away at the sound of his parents' voices. His wait for questioning his father was over, but now he wanted his parents gone. Just for a while.

Crystal sat on the edge of the bed and gathered his hand in hers. Better than if she were sitting on a chair four feet away. But it felt as far away after that kiss.

"Any good news today?" Crystal asked.

For a sliver of a second, he wanted Crystal gone, as well. It was bad enough facing another day of paralysis without having to announce that it'd been another day without any improvement. He put on a smile. "Sure thing, babe. The lottery is over two hundred and fifty mil."

"Well, doesn't that make my day?"

"How about this?" He ran his hand over the mattress between himself and the guardrail. "I've been saving this place for you. All day."

Brad used to joke that Matt and Crystal only needed one chair because she used to sit so close to him. Those days had ended somewhere along the line, however, with one of the "down" times in their relationship. He expected Crystal to laugh off his invitation and move over to her folding chair, putting even more distance between them. Instead, she pushed the button that raised the head of the bed and then squeezed herself in next to him.

They could have used another couple inches to be totally comfortable, inches he could have easily given her if it weren't so damn hard for him to adjust his position.

Too tired after the day of therapy to even try, he slid his arm around her and called it good. She rested her head on his chest, and he decided it was better than good. This was how he'd envisioned their relationship. Deborah Stryker could keep her news bulletins to herself about Milwaukee Spine Care Center's openings. He wouldn't trade one evening of having Crystal in his arms for all the specialized therapists in the world.

He nuzzled his chin against the top of her head.

"Ow." She lifted her head and rubbed her scalp. "Aren't you tired of that beard, yet?"

"I'm certainly not tired of not shaving." But he was tired of her bitching about it. Looked like tomorrow he'd be adding shaving back to his list of things to do.

She finally settled against his chest again. He made sure, this time, to keep his chin away from her. With Crystal snuggled close, he addressed his father. "Remember that conversation we had a few nights ago? Where you said you'd help with my bills?"

His dad broke open a roll of antacids. "I may be old, but I'm not senile."

"What're the chances you paid my loans?"

His father frowned. "Was I supposed to? I thought you said you could handle it a few months."

"I can. So I'm confused why someone went and paid my loans for me."

Crystal wiggled next to him. The space was tight. He wished he could do the same.

"Well, it wasn't me," his dad said.

Grasping at straws, Matt looked at the top of his fiancée's head. "Crystal?"

"Yes?" she asked, her voice sounding innocent.

"Did you make my payments?"

She let out a laugh. "I'd love to say yes, but you know I don't have that kind of money."

"Not anymore. Not after paying my loans."

She lifted her head off his chest. Her gaze connected with his. "I didn't pay your loans."

Great. Two and a half hours of torture and he still

didn't know. "Well, someone did. If it's not you and it's not Dad, I guess I've got me a fairy godmother."

"Do you rent out your fairy godmother's services?" his father asked. "I could use her magic wand on Maguire's house. Seems a certain son of mine was off on his order for the bathroom tile. There's not enough."

"Uh, yeah. There is." Matt gave his head a little shake as he arched his eyebrows, tired of the same argument they had every time his dad asked him to calculate materials. He was equally annoyed that everyone seemed unconcerned that someone had paid a crap load of money on his loans.

"Uh, no. There isn't."

"You told me to get it as close as possible. There should be two tiles of each color left."

"I'd say it's closer to being about ten of each short."

"No. It's two each over." If he were back in Fuller Lake, he could oversee the project. As if his father would let him. Ridiculous thought. But, if his father would let him oversee the project, then he could prove in person that there were enough tiles. But, no, he was stuck here, seventy-eight miles away, with boat anchors for legs.

"Admit it. You miscalculated."

"No, I didn't. I'll show you." Matt reluctantly slid his arm from around Crystal's shoulder. He took the pad of paper and pencil from the over-bed table drawer and then pulled the table closer.

His father moved to the side of the bed while Matt drew out the room, pulling the measurements from memory. He wished he had a slide rule so he could get the scale right. Doing the best he could with the edge of tomorrow's breakfast menu, he drew in the tub surround. His father shifted his weight from one foot to the other. "It doesn't have to be perfect," his father said.

No, it didn't have to be perfect, but he wanted it right or his father would never believe him that the order was correct. He carefully laid out the tile pattern with shaded blocks. "See, if you lay it out just like this, there's plenty."

His father rubbed his chin while he examined the

diagram. "It could work."

Matt looked up at his father. "It will work."

His father continued to stare at the paper, working the figures in his head.

"It'll work, Dad. Trust me."

"We'll see." His father folded the paper and put it in his chest pocket.

"Have I ever been wrong before?"

His father grinned. "Not that we've noticed, but I think that's because you sneak in extra materials when we're not looking."

A devious idea. One he'd never thought of. Not like he'd ever needed to. But it surprised him that the thought had occurred to his father. Was it possible that devious thoughts came naturally to his father? Things he managed to hide with an expression of innocence? Things like paying his son's loans?

Matt laser-beamed his father. "You know anything about my loans?"

"Yeah, I do."

Finally, the mystery was almost over. In seconds, his father would say he'd made the payments. Instead of trusting that Matt could handle it on his own, dear ol' dad had felt the need to clean up the mess.

"Someone paid them," his father said. "But, like I said before, it wasn't me."

Matt sank into the pillow. The search was still on.

§

Friday came without much change in Matt's life. Like an obedient dog, he'd sat and he'd rolled over. Now that his "workday" was done, all he wanted to do was play dead. When the CNA brought him back to his room, he eyed the bed with longing. She pushed the wheelchair to the bed and positioned him for the transfer. Within ten minutes, he could be sound asleep.

But sleeping wouldn't get him back to his old life.

"I'd like to stay up for a while." Like he was a little kid asking permission.

"Sure thing. Just call when you want to get into bed."

Call. For help. Because, after five days of therapy, he still was little more than a helpless baby. So helpless that he apparently could no longer handle something as simple as paying his own loans. Even though his dad had said he hadn't paid the loans, Matt was betting his father was the culprit. Picking up after his irresponsible son.

"At least I can sit and roll over," he muttered to the empty room.

Barely.

Trying to stop himself from dwelling on his lack of improvement, he pushed his thoughts in another direction, one that didn't involve the damn loans. Unfortunately, the topic that came to mind was the group home, and it refused to be shoved away.

There was no way three men could complete the project by the deadline. They needed a fourth set of hands. If those hands didn't belong to Matt, then they'd belong to an outsider, something his father would never agree to. Which put them back at not being able to complete the project by the deadline. Matt's fault. Both for convincing his father to bid on the contract and for now being out of commission. Somehow, he had to figure out a way to stay a viable member of the crew, even if he remained stuck in the damn wheelchair.

He pictured himself on the ground nailing together the framing. A bit inconvenient, but doable. He'd be no help, though, when it came time to erect the walls. Installing the windows and doors would be impossible. He could help with the siding for the lower four feet, maybe even five—after that, he'd be useless. Forget helping with the roofing. Insulation? Possible...for the bottom half only. Drywall, no way.

The list of what he couldn't do far exceeded what he could. All in all, he'd be pretty close to useless. The only way to salvage the project was for him to not be stuck in the wheelchair.

Hoping for a miracle, he held his hand an inch away from his leg. *Please, God. Let me feel something.*

He dug his fingers into the muscles.

Nothing. He pulled his right leg onto his knee and tore off his too-white running shoe, tossing it onto the ground. He focused all of his attention on his big toe. *Move, damn it. Just a little. Move.*

His toe wasn't listening.

A heavy weight of responsibility pushed down on his shoulders as his thoughts shifted to Crystal. How fair was it to hold her to marrying him when the man she'd be getting wasn't the same man she'd said yes to? The right thing to do would be to cancel the wedding, at least until they knew if he'd recover or not.

Canceling the wedding might be the right thing, but if it meant losing Crystal, he didn't want to do right. How selfish was that?

He rubbed his forehead. *It'll be okay. It'll work out. Somehow, it's going to be just fine.*

"Is that some new fad?" came a familiar voice from the doorway. "Wearing only one shoe?"

Matt looked up to find two of his pool buddies standing there. Travis and Sam. "If you were hip, you'd already know that." He put out his fist and butted hands with both men in a modified handshake.

The visit helped distract him from his worries, and he found himself even more thankful he'd opted to stay at St. Luke's. In Milwaukee, there'd be no visits from the casual friend or distant relative. Or nightly visits from Crystal and his parents.

§

Abby sat in the quiet of the gym with an open directory of group homes and nursing homes. Thirty minutes gone and she had yet to find even one place that would give her mother better care than Eastlawn Manor. Looking at the list of homes she'd rejected, she wondered why she was bothering. Paul wanted her to stay. He'd said so last night.

Right after he'd said he loved her.

She grabbed the phone and dialed yet another number. The receptionist answered with a chipper, "Hot Springs Villa. How may I help you?"

Can you make my decision for me? That'd be a help. "I'm looking for a place for my mother."

"I'll connect you to our administrator. Hold, please."

Abby sighed. More wasted time for what was sure to be another dead end. She rocked her feet left and right, swiveling the chair. She'd give it two more calls. If she didn't find a place better than Eastlawn in two more calls, she'd take it as a sign.

"Charles Presthed." The clicking of computer keys accented his greeting. "What are your mother's needs?"

His abrupt question rendered her speechless.

"Her needs, please." The clicking of his keyboard never slowed down.

This was sure to be a bust. Tempted to simply hang up, she gripped the phone a little tighter and took a relaxing breath. "My mother had a head injury seventeen years ago."

"Her needs, Miss."

Could he be just a bit more brusque? "Supervision, I'd guess. She's like a child when it comes to the basics."

The clicking of the keyboard finally stopped. Unfortunately, it came with a sigh followed by a five-second stretch of quiet before he spoke. "All traumatic brain injured patients require supervision, and they're all like children when it comes to the basics. Is she on a respirator? Does she need assistance with feeding herself? Can she dress herself?"

If this was what the administrator was like, then she was afraid to find out about the staff. "I'm sorry. I don't think this is the right place for my mother."

"You obviously haven't heard our success ratio or you wouldn't be saying that. Seventy-five percent of our residents are released home within months of placement with us. Of the remaining twenty-five percent, three quarters are in less restrictive housing within three years. There is no other group home in all of Wisconsin that can make the same claim."

Her mother, in independent housing? No. That was impossible. "I'm sorry, but you must have missed the part where I said my mother's injury was seventeen years ago."

"Head injury, seventeen years ago, supervision, like a child. I heard it all. If you change your mind and wish to have your mother placed here, perhaps it'd be better for you to have her doctor call me." The clicking started up again. A moment later, he was gone.

"Of all the arrogant donkey's behinds." She dropped the receiver onto the cradle. "'Have her doctor call me.' I'll do just that you...you...uuurgh."

"Problems?"

Her stomach fluttered at the sound of Paul's voice. She looked up and met his blue eyes. It amazed her how one look at him had her wanting to melt into the safety of his arms. Just the way she'd felt with Jovan—before she'd found him in bed with another woman.

She scooted closer to the desk and further away from Paul. She hugged her arms across her chest. "Just a group home administrator with a stick up his behind. Whatever you do, if anyone ever asks you about Hot Springs Villa, tell them to run in the other direction, as quick as they can."

"Hot Springs? In Milwaukee? It's funny you should mention them because Cara said I should tell you about Hot Springs."

Cara, who batted her eyelashes at Paul. Little Miss Cara, who had to giggle and playfully slap Paul's arm every time she talked to him. Caaraa, who talked to Paul waaay too much, above and beyond the call of duty for a doctor's nurse. Gag.

Abby giggled and batted her eyelashes and playfully slapped Paul's arm. "What a coinkidink." If Hot Springs came with a recommendation from Cara, then it was all the more reason why she shouldn't place her mother there.

"She said she's heard great things about them. Did you know that ninety percent of their residents are back home within months?"

It's seventy-five percent. "Wow. Imagine that."

He pulled her up by her hand and wrapped her in his

arms, squeezing and suffocating. "You might want to give that place a chance." He nibbled her neck. "Just because you put your mom there doesn't mean you have to leave, too." His lips went lower, creating a new kind of tension. She arched her back, bringing her breasts closer, while wondering how she could ache to be with him while fearing it at the same time.

"After all," he said, his lips moving across her smock while his fingers probed her elsewhere, "your mom would be home in no time."

Her mother. Home. Not in a nursing home, but... Home.

It seemed like an impossible dream, but one that made her wonder if it could be a dream come true.

She cradled Paul's head and pressed him closer to her breast and sighed. Maybe her mother coming home wasn't the only dream that could come true.

§

Travis and Sam had barely left when Crystal appeared in Matt's doorway, dressed all in white. A white parka. White jeans. White fur boots. She looked like an angel. An angel who didn't deserve being stuck with a paralyzed man for a husband.

"Your parents will be up in a moment," Crystal said. "Your dad's parking the car."

She came closer and leaned in to him. Her lips felt like heaven next to his. So good, he didn't want to give her up, even if it were the right thing to do. He guided her onto his lap. Now that she was in his arms, he intended on keeping her there until her return to Fuller Lake forced them apart.

She made a move to stand. He held tight. "Stay."

"I don't want to hurt you."

"You're not going to hurt me."

"I might," she whispered. Her eyes shifted away.

He caressed her cheek. "No, babe. Trust me. This couldn't ever hurt."

She settled her head on his shoulder. Contentment filled him as he snuggled his arms around her. She rubbed his smooth cheek. "Thanks for getting rid of the beard."

As much as he hated to admit it, he felt more like himself with the beard gone. "Anything for you, babe."

Her hand dropped to her lap. Nothing concrete, but he sensed a shift in her. He closed his eyes and tightened his arms around her. Once he was home again, and walking, things would settle back into the way they belonged.

"We leave them alone for five minutes and look what happens." His father laughed. His laugh turned into a light cough.

Crystal squirmed her way off Matt's lap.

He loved his parents, but why couldn't they stay home, just once?

Except, he didn't really want that. He'd missed them as much as he missed Crystal. He just wished being with his parents didn't mean losing physical contact with Crystal.

His mother gave him a quick kiss and then dug into her bag. She held up a colorful drawing. "Kaylee made this for you."

A stick girl with yellow hair held hands with a black-haired stick man who was only one round head taller. Both people had smiles so large they spilled beyond the confines of their faces.

"Let me guess. That's Kaylee and me."

His mother nodded.

"She's grown a lot over the last week." A sad smile formed as he gazed at the standing figure that represented him. How long until her pictures had him in a grossly disproportionate wheelchair?

"I also brought your mail." She dug in her bag again and handed him a stack of envelopes.

Several cards. Bank statement. Too bad the statement wouldn't tell him who'd paid his loans. He moved to the next envelope. Credit card offer. He ripped it in half and then dropped it in the garbage. The last envelope was his cell phone bill. Thinking of the phone's glitch, he set the other envelopes on his lap and then ripped a tear in the cell phone bill envelope.

"Did you figure out who your fairy godmother is?" his father asked.

Matt looked up from the envelope. You? "Not a clue."

"Derrick said one of your pool buddies...Trevor?"

"Travis."

"Yeah, Travis, that's it. Travis told him the league set up some collection containers around town. Maybe they paid your loans."

Collection containers. Filled with cash. "Travis and Sam were just here. You'd think one of them would have mentioned it."

"Maybe they didn't want to spoil the surprise," Crystal said.

"Possible," Matt said as he set the stack of mail on the nightstand. Or, possibly, his father had found a good cover for what he'd done. He grabbed his cell phone and started dialing, earning a glare from his mother.

"Who are you calling?" Crystal asked.

"Travis. As pool league treasurer, he'd be the one to know."

"You can't do that," Crystal belted out as she grabbed the phone from Matt and pushed end call. "I mean, that'd ruin the surprise. Why don't you give it a few days?"

"Because it's bugging me now."

Both of his parents laughed.

"What?"

"Some things just never change," his father said.

Matt held up his hands and shook his head with a shrug. "What?"

"We'll tell you later, dear," his mother said.

"Tell me what? Why later? Why not now?"

Even Crystal laughed this time.

"What?"

"Crystal's right," his mother said. "If the pool league paid your loans, there's a reason why they've not told you yet. Don't go ruining their surprise."

"Errr," Matt growled. "I hate not knowing."

"That means you'll probably spend all night worrying about it," his father said and then grinned. "Sounds like a good time to challenge you to a game of Dummy Rummy. Maybe you'll be distracted enough to give the rest of us a fighting chance, for once."

"No," Crystal said. "Not cards again."

"We could play Scrabble," Matt said. Not that he liked Scrabble, but he had to do something or he *would* spend all night thinking about the damn loan payments, now that it was back on his mind. "I saw a game in the waiting room."

"No," Crystal said. "No games. None."

"What do you suggest we do for fun, then?"

"A movie. That sounds fun." She aimed the remote at the TV. "I'm sure there's something good to watch."

A movie. Great. Like that'd keep his mind occupied. "I'm sure Ma and Dad didn't drive all the way over here to watch a movie."

"Well, they didn't come here to play Scrabble, either."

"I'm good with a movie," his mother said.

His father hunkered down in the chair like he was settling in for the long haul. "Movie's fine with me."

Thanks for backing me up, guys.

Crystal operated the remote with the skill of a seasoned couch potato. She paused for a moment on each channel, just long enough to get Matt interested before moving on. The all-news channel stayed on the screen for less than a heartbeat, giving him only a brief view of a man who looked like someone he knew. "Wait. Go back."

"We're not watching news."

"Just for a second."

She sighed but flipped back.

The man stayed on the screen only a second before the view changed, but it had been long enough to convince Matt that the man wasn't anyone he knew.

The pretty newscaster smiled at the camera. "Mr. Smythe claims he still plans on going to work tomorrow, even after winning the two hundred and eighty-million dollar lottery." She looked at her co-host. "What do you say, Blake? Would you be coming to work tomorrow?"

The co-host smiled. "You bet'cha. Long enough to

clean out my locker."

"Lucky bastard," Matt said. "Two hundred and eighty mil. That's a shit load of money." With that kind of money, there'd be no need for handouts from collection containers. His father wouldn't have to pay his loans and pretend he hadn't. Better yet, he could say goodbye to St. Luke's and Milwaukee, as well. He could go home and bring in his own team of therapists. In no time flat, he'd be back to work.

"I'd settle for eighty million," Matt's father said while he peeled back the paper wrapping on a roll of antacids. "No need to be greedy."

"Since neither of you are going to win the lottery tonight," Crystal said, "can I change the channel now?"

"As you wish, babe." He leaned his elbow on the armrest and propped his head in his hand. He paid little attention to the pictures that flashed on the TV screen. Two hundred and eighty million. Crap load of money. Two hundred and eighty thousand would even be nice. Heck, he'd even be happy winning two hundred and eighty dollars, but he never won lotteries or raffles or drawings.

He might not be in line to win the lottery, but he felt lucky enough when he'd been transferred into bed and had Crystal nestled next to him. She hadn't even asked if anything new and exciting had happened. He leaned his head against hers and blinked, trying his best to stay awake. Couldn't even wiggle his leg to try to stay awake like he used to do in the old days. He looked at his father. Dear ol' Dad had fallen asleep five minutes into *You've Got Mail*.

Unlike his dad, Crystal and his mother were glued to the screen. How they could stand watching a movie they'd seen ten times already was beyond him. At least Crystal was snuggled up to him. Yep, he thought as he let his eyes close. If you had to watch a chick flick, may as well have a chick cuddled up next to you.

He woke up when Crystal pushed herself off the bed. Within seconds, she was standing by the window. "What?" he asked. "Where are you going?"

His father yawned and stretched his arms above his head. "Now that we men have had a nap, it's time to go home."

"You just got here."

"Shouldn't have slept through our visit," Crystal said, her smile teasing.

"Shouldn't have put on a movie we've already watched a thousand times."

"It's only been twice."

His dad stepped up to the bed and handed Matt a folded envelope.

Matt frowned at the paycheck-style envelope he'd seen hundreds of times over the years. "What's this?"

"Your pay."

"No," Matt said, pushing the envelope back at his father. "You already paid me through my last day of work."

"Consider it a consulting fee."

"For what? Showing you we had enough tile? I don't think so." Matt tore the envelope in half. "I'm not taking money I didn't earn."

His father nodded at Matt's mother. "You make out a new check tomorrow and deposit it in his account."

Matt stared hard at his father. Deposit money he hadn't earned in his bank account without his permission. Like his dad had done with his loans?

His father looked back at him. "I told you I had a plan. Stop messing with it."

Matt snorted out a laugh. "Your plan is to keep paying me for work I'm not doing? That's your grand plan? You go in debt trying to keep me afloat?"

"That's not exactly how I pictured it."

"Listen, Dad, I appreciate your help, but I'm okay."

"You're way too stubborn for your own good," his dad said, "you know that?"

"I learned from the best."

§

By eight o'clock on Sunday morning, Matt had already been awake two hours. Two long, boring hours. It wasn't likely the rest of his morning would be any different since he didn't have therapy on Sundays and it'd be hours before Crystal and his family arrived.

He wouldn't be so freakin' bored if he were home. But he wasn't home. All because he'd gone for a joy ride in an ice storm.

Why? If anyone knew, they weren't sharing. Whoever had paid his loans wasn't sharing, either. He should call Travis and ask if the pool league had paid them. He'd much rather find it'd been them than his father.

He grabbed his cell phone but didn't dial. Just because he'd been awake for hours didn't mean the whole world was up, as well. Especially when the free people of the world had probably been out until bar closing last night. Certainly wasn't because he wanted to be told the finger was still pointing at his father.

"Damn." He tossed the phone onto the bed. *What now? Count ceiling tiles?* He looked up at the plaster ceiling and sighed. It was going to be a damn long morning.

"Ho, ho, ho, bro. Merry Christmas."

Matt grinned at the sound of his friend's voice. Hallelujah. Salvation from boredom. "You missed Christmas by a few months."

"So I should take this back?" Derrick handed Matt a cashier's check.

"What's this?" Six hundred ninety-two dollars and eighty-three cents. Holy shit.

"It's the money the pool league collected so far. Pops told you about putting out the containers, didn't he?"

"Yeah." *He also said the pool league probably paid my loans.*

"Trav said to let you know he's sorry the check isn't bigger, but..."

Here it comes.

"...we just put the containers out a week ago. We're still collecting, though. Will be until people stop dropping money in the jugs."

Matt sighed and his shoulders deflated. If the containers had only been put out a week ago, there likely hadn't been enough money to cover his loan payments.

The finger was inching back toward his father.

"Do you need more?" Derrick reached for his back pocket. "I could probably spare a buck or two." He opened his wallet and pulled out two one-hundred-dollar bills, so crisp they looked ironed.

Matt waved away the offered money. "I'm fine."

Derrick set the money on the nightstand. "Consider it a loan. Cheap. Only thirty percent interest."

A loan. Matt looked at the money and then at Derrick. Paying his loans didn't seem like something Derrick would do, but he was grasping at straws now. "Is there any chance you…" Why would Derrick pay his loans and then give him an extra two hundred? Derrick, who darn near laminated every dollar he got to protect it until time's end. "Nah," he said, dismissing the idea.

"I what?"

"Nothing. It's just that someone paid my loans. I was wondering if it was you."

Derrick's dimple showed as he laughed. "Yeah, it was me."

It had been a long shot. And, really, he wouldn't have wanted it to be Derrick any more than he wanted it to be his dad. "Yeah, that's what I thought."

"Somebody paid your loans?" He looked away like he was embarrassed he hadn't been the one. "That's kind of strange, wouldn't you say?"

"Worse than strange. It's rude, sneaking behind my back like that. I don't understand why whoever it was didn't just tell me."

"Because they knew you'd want to pay them back? Because they're afraid you'd misunderstand their intentions? Who knows. It's not worth worrying over, is it?"

He wasn't *worrying* over it. It's just that the whole thing was bugging him.

"Rome wasn't built in a day, and you're not going to solve the mystery right now," Derrick said. "So what do you say we go for a little walk…uh, I mean, go for a change of scenery. I can buy you breakfast or something."

Sitting in the cafeteria over scrambled eggs, bacon, toast, and coffee added in for Derrick, Matt noticed how tired his friend looked. Derrick was sure to look even more haggard as the days went by, especially if Matt couldn't go back to work. Looking for the loophole he'd yet to find on his own, he asked, "How much help do you think I can be on the jobsite in this chair?"

Derrick looked up from his plate. His fork hung suspended in front of his mouth for a moment before he laid it down. "This is just hypothetical, right?"

"Of course." At least, he hoped it was.

"There's lots you can do. You can..." His eyebrows shifted and his mouth twitched as he apparently worked his way around the jobsite in a wheelchair. His face became more animated the longer he stayed silent. Finally, he said, "You can write up all the bids. Plan the projects. Order the materials."

Those jobs would be perfect. But his father would never trust him with that much responsibility. It didn't pay to even entertain the idea. "You mean I can be a secretary."

"Sounds more like a supervisor to me. But it doesn't matter because it's all hypothetical. You're going to be walking out of this place."

"And if I'm not?"

Derrick stayed silent.

"We need to find a way to get Dad to consider hiring someone to replace me, at least until I'm on my feet again."

"Yeah, like that'll happen."

"Dad'll listen to you if you tell him to hire someone."

Derrick held up his hands and violently shook his head. "Huh uh. I don't want your being replaced to be on my head." He put his hands down. "Don't you think you're jumping the gun, anyhow?"

"If we want anyone good, it's got to be now, before construction season starts."

A tapping sound came from beneath the table. "Yeah, you're right."

He was right, but this time he really didn't want to hear it.

"I'd go talk to Pops if I felt there was a need, but there's not." The tapping quit when Derrick leaned forward. His eyes narrowed. "You're going to walk again."

"And if I don't?"

"Then, I'll carry you around the jobsite, if I have to. I'll put in extra hours. I'll do whatever it takes to keep you on the crew." His eyes burned into Matt's. "Whatever it takes."

§

Abby curled up next to Paul, absorbing his body heat. She focused on the way his chest pressed against her with each breath. If only time could stop right now and she'd never have to make a decision about the job. If time stopped right now, she'd never have to worry about Paul leaving her. She could pretend, forever, that true love and happily-ever-after could really happen to her. She pulled away and made a pillow with her arm and stared at the triangle patch of hair in the middle of his chest. "Tomorrow's the day I have to tell Mr. Jones if I'm taking the job."

The triangle patch of hair stilled for a moment. "That soon already, huh?"

"Yes. That soon."

"What have you decided?"

"I've decided not to decide until I have to decide."

"That's my Abby."

My Abby. She 5loved the way that sounded. "Deciding to take the job at St. Luke's was so much easier after finding Jovan in bed with his ex-girlfriend. That pretty much told me where our relationship was headed."

"I suppose so."

"He said he loved me."

Paul rolled toward her, locking his gaze on hers. "I love you."

She wanted to believe him. "Great. Now, I'll find you in bed with some ex tomorrow."

"Not likely." He slid his hand across her bare skin. "Do you want to sleep here tonight?"

"I shouldn't."

"Then, I guess I shouldn't do this." He slid his hand between her legs.

Forty-five minutes later, he kissed her at his door. When he unlocked his lips from hers, he didn't release his arms. "I wish you didn't have to leave."

She gripped the lapels of his robe. She didn't have to leave. Not ever. All she had to do was trust him, that he really meant it when he said he loved her. She loosened her fingers. "I don't want the neighbors to talk."

"Believe me, they talk plenty already. They're all jealous of me, landing a hot chick like you." He planted another kiss. "If I said it again, that I love you, would you stay?"

Stay for how long? For tonight? Longer? Until he grew tired of her?

"I have to go home."

"I'll say it, anyhow. I love you, Abby."

His embrace felt too tight. Suffocating. She pulled away. "I'll see you tomorrow."

CHAPTER EIGHT

A beautiful pink filled the eastern horizon when Abby left her apartment the next morning. She paused to admire the sunrise, waved goodbye to her landlady, and then climbed into her Grand Am, like any ordinary day. In the wee hours of the morning, when she'd woken up alone, she'd made up her mind. Now, as she drove off to start another week at St. Luke's, she prayed it was a decision she wouldn't regret.

She used her employee pass key at the back entrance to the hospital and slipped through the quiet hallways of the obstetrics department, toward Paul's office. Since this decision involved him, as well, she figured he should know before she called Kyle Jones.

She cringed at the sound of her rubber soles squeaking on the highly polished tile—a fingernails-on-chalkboard sound in the otherwise quiet area. When she passed a darkened waiting room, another type of sound caused her footsteps to falter. A shushing noise? She stopped and listened. Her imagination. Then, she heard it again. Clearly, a person. Saying

"shhh." There was more. A sigh. A woman's sigh.

She backed up and peered into the darkened waiting room. On any given day there would be over a hundred men within the hospital complex who had thinning, light brown hair and doctor's coats, but only one she'd recognize with a brief glance. There was no denying that the man she now saw embracing a nurse was Paul.

With a feeling of déjà vu, the room pulled out of focus. The walls zoomed outward, while Paul and Cara seemed to grow to staggering proportions.

She wanted to run, but she couldn't make her feet move. As if Paul could sense her there, he slowly turned, and their eyes met. She saw on his face the same expression

Jovan had worn, the oh-shit-I'm-in-trouble look. He took a few steps away from Cara as though that'd clear him of any wrongdoing.

"Paul, just the person I was looking for," Abby said, forcing an upbeat tempo to her voice while willing her knees not to collapse on her. Paul's cheek was smudged with bright pink lipstick. Cara looked upset, like she hadn't wanted to get caught with her boss.

Abby focused her attention back on Paul and stared at the lipstick on his cheek. To think she'd actually believed, if only for a second, that he truly loved her. That she'd almost given up the job she really wanted, hoping this time love could be real. Thank heavens she'd come to her senses. Best to snatch up the job and leave Paul before he could leave her. But the joke was now on her.

"Abby, honey, this isn't what you think."

Honey? Not what she thought? He was so wrong. "Looks like my decision to take the job in Milwaukee was the right one."

With that, she turned and walked as calmly as she could for the door.

"Abby, let me explain. Cara was upset. I was just comforting her."

She kept walking. Her heart thumped and hot blood warmed her cheeks. The grapefruit she'd had for breakfast tried to work its way upward. She nodded at a young man pushing a cart filled with specimen tubes. Your average, everyday kind of morning.

Somehow, she managed to keep the tears at bay until she pushed open the door to the first restroom she came to. She pressed her hands against the counter and breathed deeply. What had she done wrong this time? Had she been too independent? Should she have spent the night with him? Maybe if she'd spent less time with her mother and more time with him. Whatever it was, she'd done something wrong, something to push him into Cara's arms.

She crouched into a ball with her hands clinging to the edge of the sink. Inside her head, more images mingled with the one of Paul and Cara. Jovan, naked, thrusting himself against an equally naked Belinda. And then, her father, handing her a cuddly brown teddy bear, just before he walked out of her life with a "see you later."

Her lips pressed together. Just one more lesson to prove there was no such thing as happily-ever-after. She should have known better than to fall for all that garbage she read in books.

She pushed herself upright. Never again. She was done with the books. Done with the fairytales. Done with men.

Her teeth bit into her lip and a tear crept down the well-traveled path. No chance for love. No hope for a family.

"Stop it," she said, as she straightened her spine. With angry swipes, she brushed her hands over her cheeks. She didn't need love. She was fine with it being just her and her mother.

She splashed cold water over her face. Her eyes were red and the skin around them puffy, but there was little she could do about it now. At least the tear tracks were gone. Still locked up inside the tiny bathroom, she pulled her cell phone from her purse. She settled herself into the corner by the paper towel dispenser and dialed.

At least something good came from this morning. She wouldn't spend her life wondering if she'd made a mistake in leaving Paul.

§

Matt listened to the silence while Abby worked his legs. It'd been at least five minutes since she'd said anything and then only to say, "Lay down."

What'd that bring her up to? Maybe forty words, total, between this afternoon's session and this morning's? He'd caught the stupid ball she'd thrown way left and he hadn't fallen over. She hadn't so much as smiled. No *Way to Go* when he rolled over every time on the first try. It didn't take a genius to figure out something was bothering her.

Not like it was his business. Her being quiet, for once,

was rather refreshing. Her sad eyes were another matter. He stared at the ceiling so he wouldn't have to look at her. Whoever had done the sheetrock had done a piss-poor job. The seam was as smooth as cottage cheese. Bad job. Real bad.

Bad. Whatever was bothering Abby had to be bad. Nothing like waking up in the hospital without being able to move your legs, but bad enough to shut her up. Bad enough to make him worry. He pushed himself up onto his elbows. Abby seemed to not notice. "Are you okay?" he asked.

"Fine."

One quick word. She didn't even look his way.

He lowered himself to the table again. And listened to the quiet.

His gaze shifted back to Abby. He felt a stab of pain at seeing those sad eyes again.

She wasn't fine.

He worked himself up again, all the way up, until he was sitting. He put his hand on hers, stopping her from moving his legs. "Talk to me."

Her lips disappeared between her teeth, and she blinked several times. He knew the signs of a woman on the verge of tears. He'd seen it enough with Crystal. With Crystal, he'd hold her and soothe her until the tears stopped. He planted his hands on the mat. "I'm a good listener."

She straightened her back and drew in a breath. "Everything's okay."

The hell it was. "If that's okay, I'd hate to see not okay."

"I'm fine. Really." She motioned him to lie down. "We should get back to work."

She looked about as fine as rough sandpaper, but he wasn't going to push. He started to ease himself back down onto the mat when he saw a man walking up behind her.

"You ready for me, Abby?" the man asked.

"We're just finishing up." She put on a smile that lasted only a second and hadn't looked anywhere close to natural. She motioned toward the newcomer. "This is Greg. He's from the medical supply store that has a contract with your insurance carrier. He's going to explain the differences in wheelchairs to help you select your permanent chair."

"Cool. My very own, permanent, forever wheelchair." Heat radiated throughout him. Abby's problems disappeared from his thoughts. "Thanks, but no thanks." He pulled his temporary wheelchair into position and then slid the transfer board under his thigh. He pulled himself across the board as though he'd done it a hundred times on his own instead of this being a first.

"Matt!"

Five seconds ago, he'd wanted the excited Abby back. Now, just when he'd gotten his wish, he wanted nothing more than to be far away from her. He grabbed his left leg and plunked his foot onto the foot rail. The lack of sensation mocked him. It seemed like cruel torture to have to move his other lifeless leg, as well. He glared up at Greg and realized he was taking out his anger on an innocent person, but he couldn't stop himself. "I—Don't—Need—A—Chair."

He wheeled his way around the man. Matt's arms stayed in steady motion as he pushed himself to his room. He parked in front of the window but paid little attention to the view. The wheelchair rolled backward a couple of inches as he slammed his hands against the windowsill. "Damn it. I've got to walk again."

An overwhelming sense of hopelessness pressed down on him. He wanted to give in to it. Just put his head down and cry. Instead, he slammed his hands against the windowsill again.

"Matt?" Abby's voice came from behind him.

He closed his eyes and willed his heart to slow to an unnoticed pace.

"You forgot your gloves," she said.

The gloves to prevent blisters as he grew used to wheeling the chair. The damn wheelchair he didn't want in his life. He opened his eyes. His chest rose and fell at such a rapid pace that he felt lightheaded.

She was behind him. He could feel her there. He didn't want a witness to his weakness. "Leave them and go." His voice came out husky. The words were choked.

"Are you okay?"

"Fine. Great. Peachy." He stared at the metal frame at the base of the window and struggled to slow his breathing.

"Good. I'd hate to think you were upset over anything."

Dirt had coagulated outside along the edge of the window.

"Especially when congratulations are in order. You did your first solo transfer."

He shifted his attention to an old cobweb outside. The silky threads quivered in the wind. He didn't remember getting into the chair. All he could remember was the intense feeling of fear. No, not fear. It definitely wasn't fear. There wasn't anything to be afraid of.

Still staring at the spiderweb that was now perfectly still, he said, "Big deal."

"It is a big deal. I didn't think you'd be ready to transfer on your own for another week. But you did it."

He finally turned and looked up at her. Although her expression was serious, there was a hint of a smile, like she was proud of him. She hadn't thought he'd be ready to transfer on his own, but he'd done it. Maybe she'd underestimated his ability to walk again, too.

With his gloves still gripped in one hand, she grabbed a chair and dragged it across from him, effectively blocking him in the corner. "I'm a good listener."

"Great. Glad to hear it. If I ever need a good listener, I'll holler." He wanted to back up, but he wasn't about to give her the satisfaction of knowing she'd trapped him.

"I caught my boyfriend with another woman."

The statement was like a gunshot in a quiet room. He couldn't figure out why she'd told him. Even more, he couldn't figure out why anyone would cheat on her. No wonder she'd been so quiet and on the verge of tears. The thought, alone, of Crystal with another man hurt. The reality would be ten times...no, a hundred times worse.

"I figure I can't expect you to discuss what's bothering you if I'm not willing to do the same."

"He must be an idiot." She picked at the Velcro closure on one of the gloves. "Thanks. I know you're right, but it still hurts. I keep seeing him with her, over and over, like it's stuck in my head and won't go away." Her fingers stopped moving. Creases formed across her forehead. Her eyes took on the same sad quality they'd had back in the gym.

"In time, it'll get better," he said.

"I should be happy, really. Being mad at him should make it easier to leave..."

Leave?

"...but instead of being excited about my new job, all I can think about is Paul."

She was leaving? The cheerleader was abandoning him?

She blinked twice and then rubbed her finger beneath her eye, leaving a moist track. "Enough about my problems. Your turn."

He still couldn't believe she was leaving. The news left him dumbfounded.

"Does this have to do with your hoping to walk again?" she asked.

Oh, yes. His hasty retreat from the gym. "Hoping? No, Abby, it goes beyond hope. I'm counting on it."

Her eyes locked on to his. "You know that might not happen, don't you?"

She didn't say it like it was an obscure possibility but rather like it was a given. His heart thumped uncomfortably, bringing back all the fear of moments ago. "Yeah. And the guy who just won the lottery might decide he doesn't want the money. The snow might not melt until late May. Crystal could decide to join the circus. Lots of possibilities out there, but I'm not banking on any of them."

"I'm serious, Matt." Her fingers cinched around the faux leather gloves, but her eyes never wavered from his.

"The sad fact is that less than two percent of all patients have any significant recovery. Every day you go without any sign of recovery makes it less likely there will be a recovery."

"It hasn't even been three weeks."

"Yes, I know. Almost three weeks."

The way she said it made it sound like three weeks was a lifetime. Maybe three weeks was a lifetime. Too long to hope to be one of the lucky two percent.

No. He refused to accept that. "I am going to walk again."

She leaned toward him, invading his space. "Matt, I hate to see you so focused on what might never happen that you're missing out on what has. Your first solo transfer." Her smile refused to be hidden. "Without any coaching. A week ahead of schedule."

He couldn't hear her praise. All he heard was her saying he'd probably never walk again. "Is it better for me to be so focused on what's happening now that I miss what could happen?"

"Does the phrase *one track mind* mean anything to you?"

"What?"

She held out the gloves. "I have some phone calls I need to make before it gets too late. If you change your mind and decide you actually do want to talk, I'll be in the gym. Page me. Come down. Whatever."

"Damn it," he muttered as he watched her leave. He lowered his head and stared at his lifeless legs. "Damn it."

§

Abby's mother chewed on air, pushing her tongue across dry lips, reminding Abby again of Paul with Cara and the kiss she'd caught them in. Paul claimed he'd only been comforting her. Said he'd have Cara reassigned to another department. If only Abby would stay.

He'd sounded so sincere that she'd almost bought into it, until she realized what she was doing. If she believed he'd been telling the truth, then, if only for a little while, she could believe she could be loved.

Realizing she was clenching her jaw, she forced her mouth to relax and then she forced her attention back to her mother and away from her thoughts. A pitcher of water sat inches away from her mother, but Helen's disconnected brain couldn't reason out that all she needed to do was pour herself a drink. Instead, she snapped her tongue against the roof of her mouth.

"Are you thirsty?" Abby asked even though the answer was obvious to at least one of them.

"Thirsty," Helen said.

The therapist inside Abby saw this as a perfect learning opportunity. "Your water pitcher is full. Pour yourself a glass."

Her mother looked at the pitcher as though she'd never seen it before.

"All you have to do is pour yourself a glass." Abby demonstrated with an invisible glass and pitcher.

Her mother reached for the pitcher. Abby nodded, pleased at how well her mother had picked up on the suggestion. She might not be worthy of love, but she'd make one hell of a damn fine therapist in Milwaukee.

Helen picked up the plastic cup. With her coordination compromised in the accident, she had a difficult time managing the two objects. She tipped both the cup and the pitcher.

"Maybe you should set the glass on the table." Abby guided her mother's arm, moving the glass toward the table.

Her mother's arm swayed as she held the pitcher above the glass. It pained Abby to watch her mother struggling. She kept her hands to her sides and instead encouraged with her voice. "Good job, Mom. Keep it steady."

Water drizzled down the outside of the glass as her mother's hand shifted before correcting her aim. "Good girl."

The water reached the top of the glass. The surface tension swelled above the rim and then broke, spilling over. Her mother frowned, but didn't stop pouring. "The glass is broken."

"No, the glass is fine." Abby grabbed the pitcher from her mother, interrupting the lesson as she let her impulses take over. "When the water gets to the top, you have to stop pouring."

Her mother lifted the over-filled glass, spilling water all over the table. Unaware of what she was doing, she tipped the glass before reaching her mouth. More water splashed over the rim, soaking Helen's dress, drizzling a line down her chest and over her stomach.

The flowing water was one straw too many. "Mother! You're making a mess!"

Without even a drop of water reaching her mouth, Helen threw the glass at the wall, spraying the remaining water on Abby in the process. "Sorry, I'm not perfect."

Abby breathed deeply. She'd lost her cool, which was unacceptable. As a therapist, she knew better. She was tired. So tired. All she wanted to do was go home. And cry.

The memory of Paul with Cara struck again and it struck hard. Tears burned her eyes. She tried to hold them back while wishing at the same time for her mother to comfort her the way a mother was supposed to comfort a daughter. Instead, her mother mumbled, "Nobody's perfect."

Abby pressed her trembling lips together. There was nobody she could turn to. Not her mother. Not Paul. Not her father. None of the foster parents she'd lived with. Nobody.

Milwaukee could be a fresh start. She'd be a better person this time.

She drew in one last deep, shaky breath. Her mother's mouth moved, chewing air once again, trying to work up spit to moisten her tongue since she'd never gotten any of her water. Abby wiped her eyes. "I'm sorry, Mom. I shouldn't have gotten upset with you."

"I try, but I can't do it. I can't do anything."

"We'll just have to work harder, Mom. Both of us."

"Is that why Danny doesn't come? Because of me?"

Abby settled on the bed next to her mother, offering

the comfort she needed herself. "No, Mom. Don't ever let yourself think that."

"Then, why?"

Because of me. "I don't know."

There was a knock on the doorjamb. One of the CNAs stood there. "Abby, Mrs. Addams would like to see you about your mother's transfer."

Helen stiffened in Abby's arm. "Transfer?"

"We're moving, Mom."

Helen stood. "No."

"You'll like Hot Springs Villa."

"I like it here."

She had no patience left. "We're moving, Mom. That's all there is to it. Like it or not, we're moving."

§

Matt stared at Abby's hand against his knee as she worked his legs the next morning. Soon, it'd be someone else. He wondered which of the other two therapists he'd be assigned to. There was ol' Gloom-and-Doom, the therapist he'd wished to work with on his first session. The one he'd since discovered never smiled. Or The Slug, who moved with all the energy and enthusiasm of a death-row prisoner running out of time.

Finding neither alternative pleasing, he pushed his thoughts to something more appealing. Like the bills sitting in his room that he'd been ignoring since Friday. Every time he thought about paying them, something distracted him. Things like Abby pushing him to order a wheelchair. Or wondering how he could get his father to confess that he'd paid Matt's loans. Or how they'd ever get the group home built with one guy short. Important stuff like that. No more putting it off. As soon as he got back to his room this afternoon, he'd write out the checks. Get it done.

"Matt?" Abby said as she rotated his hip.

"Umm?"

She straightened his leg and set it down against the mat. "I'm sorry about yesterday. I hope you're not mad about my forcing the truth on you."

Surprised by the apology, he worked himself up on to his elbows and stared at her. "I pushed you."

"Still, I had no right to say the things I said." Her shoulders slumped slightly and her head tipped forward. Like a little kid who'd just broken her mother's expensive vase.

He did a mental laugh. "That's right. You had no right to tell me the truth." He let a smile creep into his voice. "You evil bitch."

She grinned and motioned him to lie down again.

He watched as she bent his leg and then pushed his knee to his chest. She adjusted her grip. Her fingers brushed his calf, sending an electric tingle down his leg. So quick, it took him a moment to understand what had happened.

"Do that again," he said. He raised up on to his elbows.

She frowned. "This?" she asked as she rotated his ankle.

"No. My leg," he said too loudly. Fearing he'd been given a small window of time in which to feel the sense of touch again and that time was running out, he ordered, "Quick, touch my leg again."

Her frown deepened. She pressed her fingertip against his leg where she'd had her hand earlier. "Here?"

Nothing. She was doing it wrong. He pushed himself up all the way and leaned forward, feeling his leg in random locations. "I felt it. I know I did." His breaths increased with each deadened response. "It was real. I'm not making it up."

"Maybe you can't feel it now because you're trying too hard. Lie back."

He kept pressing against his leg, pushing harder, frantically. "No. I'm not giving up. I felt it, damn it. I felt it."

She gripped his hand with amazing force. "Matt, listen to me." Her grip softened, along with her voice. "I believe you." She gave him the lightest push against his shoulder. "Lie back, now. Relax."

The part of him who had to prove he'd felt something

wanted to resist. The tiny bit of him who remained rational knew she was right. He wouldn't feel it again if he was all worked up. Rational Matt took over. He laid back and closed his eyes. All of his attention zeroed in on the area where he'd felt the tingle. His heart pumped so hard, he wondered how he'd ever feel anything over the pounding in his chest.

For a long time, he felt nothing. Had he really felt anything earlier? Had it just been his wishful thinking?

And then, he felt it.

"Oh, God, Abby. There. Right there."

She touched the spot again. The tingle that spread from her fingertips made him sigh. He opened his eyes to find Abby smiling.

"Do it again."

She did.

"That feels so good."

Her eyes sparkled, giving him hope.

"I told you I was going to walk again."

She pulled her hand away, and the tingling sensation stopped.

"What?" he asked.

She shook her head.

Fiery heat flamed inside him. He wasn't sure if it was anger or fear, but it was there just the same. When the words came out, he noticed the desperation in his voice. "I'm going to walk again. Got it?"

"Sure, Matt."

At that moment, he wished she were already gone to her new job and that it was either Gloom-and-Doom standing there or The Slug. He touched his leg and felt the tremble of anticipation that came with the jolt of sensation. He was going to walk again. He'd prove it to Abby, even if he had to hunt her down wherever she was moving to.

§

At the end of his *work day*, Matt sat in his quiet hospital room with his left leg over his right knee and his fingers brushing over the quarter-sized patch of skin that tingled with his touch. Even though his parents and Crystal would be here soon, he wished they were here already. He couldn't wait to share the good news, news too good to tell over the phone. He sighed with pleasure as he felt the twinge again.

You're going to wear it out.

He laughed. It was impossible to wear it out. He could sit here until the end of time feeling the twinge in his leg and it'd never grow old. Still, sitting here feeling his leg wasn't getting those bills paid.

Reluctantly, he lowered his leg back into position and then wheeled over to the nightstand. He gathered up the envelopes, grabbed his checkbook, and wheeled over to the table. He flipped through the envelopes until he found the cell phone bill. The flap was already pulled loose on one edge from when he'd started to open it last Friday. He ripped it open the rest of the way.

Still amazed that he'd actually had a day with zero calls, he scanned the itemization of incoming calls. He paused when he saw an entry on the day of his accident—12:02 p.m. from Crystal's work number.

She often called on her lunch hour, but he didn't understand why the call hadn't registered in his phone's history. "Stupid piece of crap."

The next line in the itemization showed another call on January 28, this one from the local Ski-Doo dealer. Another call missing from his phone's history.

And another call, again from Crystal's work number, this one at 2:40.

He frowned as he looked at the next entry showing another call from Crystal, just before quitting time. Then, five more calls, all within an hour, all from Crystal's cell phone.

"No, this can't be right."

Still holding the bill, he grabbed his cell phone and thumbed his way through the menu. Scrolling through the history, the incoming calls still skipped over the day of his accident.

"Frigging piece of crap."

He looked back at the bill. The calls from Crystal seemed to jump from the page. Eight calls. Why hadn't she ever said anything? Like when he'd asked her about the accident.

"Hi, honey," Crystal said from the doorway.

Instead of eagerly wanting to share the good news about his recovery, all he could think of was that Crystal had called him eight times the day of the accident. "Where's Mom and Dad?"

"Your dad got a call just when we got here. Your mom's guarding him to make sure he doesn't kill anyone in the hospital with cell phone death rays."

He should have laughed. He couldn't.

She frowned. "Are you okay?"

"Yeah. Sure. Peachy."

"So, anything new today?"

Finally, he had a positive response to her question. Instead of sharing, he pushed the table out of the way. "Sit. We've got to talk."

After a moment's hesitation, she sat on the bed near him. Even though they were close enough that his feet nearly touched her leg, it felt like she was miles away. Or maybe it was him.

"What's up, honey?" she asked.

"Why'd you call me the day of the accident?"

"I don't know." Crystal wasn't looking at him. She fiddled with the zipper pull on her jacket. Up. Down. Up. "I can't remember that far back. I'm not sure I even called you."

He held up the bill. "You called. Eight times. Why?"

The zipper pull kept traveling up and down. He pulled her hand off the zipper. "Look at me."

Her head stayed tipped down, but her eyes raised and met his briefly.

"What'd you call me for?"

She reached for the zipper but changed paths and crossed her arms instead. "I don't know, okay? I don't remember. It was weeks ago." She looked toward the doorway. "I wonder what's keeping your parents. Maybe I should go check on them."

"Eight times, Crystal. It had to be important for you to call that many times."

"It was nothing." She stood and moved away. She picked up his water cup from the table, set it back down, and then moved a pencil away from the edge. "Probably something about the wedding. About the flowers, maybe. Or, what you thought of a song." She looked up. "I don't know, okay?"

"No, it's not okay. What aren't you telling me?"

From the corner of his eye, he saw his parents in the doorway. Crystal's shoulders relaxed. He could almost hear the relieved sigh she didn't actually utter. Without taking his eyes off her, he told his parents, "Crystal and I need a few minutes alone."

"They came to visit you, not to stand out in the hallway."

"I'm sure they can use some time alone, too." He shifted his attention to his dad. Even with how confused he was about Crystal, he noticed how tired his father looked. "Right, Dad?"

His father's gaze bounced from his son to Crystal and then back again. "Yeah, sure." He put his arm around Matt's mom. "Let's check out what's new in the vending machines."

Matt speared Crystal with his gaze again. "Talk."

She turned the pencil in circles on the table. "It was nothing, really. I wanted to know if you preferred roses or carnations or both."

"Flowers, huh? Sure it wasn't the music?"

She stopped moving the pencil.

She hadn't called eight times to ask about flowers. Or music. He'd bet his life on it. And he was damn sure she knew exactly why she'd called. It was just more of her refusing to talk to him, just like whenever she'd cry for no apparent reason. *What's wrong?* he'd ask. *Nothing,* she'd say.

"Do you want out?" he asked, wishing the second the words left his mouth that he could pull them back.

Where a moment ago she was a bundle of constant movement, she was now still. She seemed to not even breathe. She didn't say yes, but she hadn't said no, either.

He put his head down and rubbed his forehead. Every worry he'd had over the last two weeks disappeared for the moment—except for one. He was losing Crystal. He felt it. Deep in his heart. He felt her slipping away.

She crouched in front of him. She put her hands on his knees, and he realized it was the first time since the accident that she'd purposely touched his legs. "I don't want out," she whispered.

He tipped his head up, locking eyes with hers. She didn't look away. He wasn't sure he believed her, but he wanted to. Going with it, he pulled her into his arms and buried his face against her neck. A different answer to his stupid question and he wouldn't be holding her now. Or ever again. "I love you, Crystal."

She tightened her arms around him.

I don't want out. The answer should have satisfied him, but he couldn't shake free of the fact that he'd actually expected her to say she *did* want out. Or how about the fact that even though she'd said she didn't want out, he didn't fully believe her? What did that say about their relationship?

Stop it. Stop looking for problems.

Despite his little pep talk, he wished time would stop right now, with her in his arms having just declared she didn't want out. If time stopped now, he wouldn't ever lose her. But time wouldn't stop, and he couldn't hold her forever, so he kissed her neck and loosened his grip.

She leaned away from him but stayed crouched in front of him. "I don't want out."

Putting the subject to rest, he moved her hand to the tiny spot on his leg with sensation. "I can feel that."

She looked up at him with wide eyes. Her jaw hung slack. Questioning him if it were true. He nodded.

"Oh, Matt," she whispered. Her eyes glistened. She looked down where she touched. "Thank you, God."

She sounded more relieved than happy.

Relieved. Happy. The same emotion. Just different levels. But he wanted her to be happy. Not relieved.

By the doorway, his father peeked his head in. His father looked older than Matt remembered him ever looking before. His eyelids sagged, even as he raised one eyebrow at Crystal, all folded over in front of Matt, and then shifted to his son.

Matt put on an everything's-cool grin. "What can I say? She worships the ground I..." The smile fell away.

Crystal stood. Keeping her back to the doorway, she swiped a finger beneath her eye.

"May as well come in and relax," Matt said. He raised his voice. "Ma, you can come in, too."

His mother stepped into view while his father deflated into the closest chair. His father's head pressed back against the chair as though it had become too heavy to hold upright. He eyed Crystal for a moment before moving on to Matt. Apparently curious, but not asking.

Pulling forth that initial burst of joy from this morning, Matt managed a genuine smile. "I'm recovering."

CHAPTER NINE

Matt's father popped up from the chair, crossed the room in three strides, and clapped Matt on the back. "I knew you'd be okay."

His mother gave him a hug so tight it took Matt's breath away.

Matt peered between his parents at Crystal's profile. What was so damn interesting outside that she was staring out the window instead of crowding him like his parents?

"You'll be able to walk down the aisle at your wedding," his mother said.

Crystal's head dropped and her hands went to her mouth. He wheeled forward an inch, the closest he could get to Crystal with his parents in the way. He nudged himself forward a bit more, hoping his parents would move.

"Did the doc say how long until you'll be back to work?" his father asked. "To think, I was worried you wouldn't be back in time for the group home build."

Matt's hands froze on the push rims. His dad had him fully recovered and back to work. His mom had him walking down the aisle. All because of one quarter-sized tingly patch of skin that might not progress any further.

Now he was sounding like Abby. It *would* progress further. Far enough to get him walking again.

His father smiled at him with a grin so big it threatened to break his face. What would that grin do if Abby was right? What if one tiny, tingly patch of skin was all he got? "*Recovering* might have been a bit strong."

"Peshhh," his mother said, brushing away his statement. "This is just the start of things to come. You'll be walking out of here. I know it."

"You're too stubborn to let it stop here," his father

said.

Like how stubborn he was would make a difference in this case. "It's just one little spot of sensation, that's all. Not even as big as a quarter."

"Tomorrow it'll be—" His father coughed a phlegmy cough.

"Dad."

"It'll..." Carl Huntz coughed into a handkerchief from his shirt pocket. "It'll spread...huhhgh...Don't you... huhhgh...worry."

"You okay, Dad?"

"Of course, I'm okay." The rattling phlegm, when he cleared his throat again, made him sound anything but okay. He coughed deeply into the hanky, wadded up the cloth, and stuck it in his pocket. "Just like you're going to be okay. Like I knew all along."

Matt watched as his father settled into the chair again. This time, his father stayed upright, leaning slightly forward. Crystal looked equally relaxed standing by the window with her arms wrapped around herself. Two parents who had him speeding toward a recovery Abby didn't think would happen and a fiancée who looked seconds away from crying. Made him wish he'd kept his mouth shut.

Without thinking about what he was doing, he grabbed his ankle, brought his leg up onto his knee, and rubbed the patch of skin. Looking for affirmation that this was just the start. Three sets of eyes watched. All with expectation of things to come, a recovery he had no control over.

He put his leg back down, fitting his foot on the foot rail. The expectation was still there. Aiming for a distraction, he said, "Dad, you got those cards with you?"

"Of course." His father pulled the cards from his shirt pocket. The handkerchief came out with it and landed on the floor. He snatched up the hanky and shoved it back in his pocket.

Matt's mother set about clearing the over-bed table while Crystal remained perched by the window with her arms wrapped around herself, uttering not a single protest to the idea of playing cards. Neither of them saw what Matt had seen. He focused on the lump in the flannel pocket at his father's chest. Had it really been blood? Or, God willing, only a trick of poor lighting?

He gazed at his father's face. His dad stared back. The look was one Matt knew well. His father's just-leave-it-be look. Matt flashed a smile to cover up what he felt deep in his stomach. "Good thing you didn't need that lung anymore."

Instead of a witty comeback, his father gave him one of those smiles laced with another silent leave-it-be warning.

Leave it be.

His father dragged his chair closer to the over-bed table and opened the card box. "Crystal, you going to play?"

"I don't want to, but I will."

Matt looked at her, wondering what that comment meant. The entire day was wearing him down, bringing on a headache. For only a moment, he wished it were just him and his empty room. No expectations that the quarter-sized patch of sensation meant good things to come. No evidence that Matt's present condition was causing havoc with his father's health. No cryptic comments from Crystal that he just didn't have the energy to decipher. And then, he thought about how long the evening would stretch without his family to break it up. In roughly two hours they'd be back on the road. He could have his peace and quiet then.

Carl Huntz dealt the cards with much less enthusiasm than a week ago. This close, Matt could see all the fine lines in his father's face that had appeared over the last several weeks. Then, he saw something else that hadn't been there before. A speck of dried blood at the corner of his father's mouth. Sure bet it hadn't come from shaving.

His father's coming here night after night wasn't good. His father's trying to cover the work of a laid-up employee wasn't good, either. If he knew his dad, he was getting up before daybreak, working through his lunch, and then coming here directly from the jobsite. He wouldn't put it past his father to be putting in a few hours after getting back to Fuller Lake, either. No, this wasn't good. None of it. "You guys don't have to come here every night."

His father paused mid-deal. "Of course we don't *have* to."

"Maybe you should cut back to every other night." A drop in the bucket. "Or even every third night."

"Matthew, it's only for another month or so," his mother said. "We can survive just fine making the drive every night for that amount of time."

"And I can survive just fine being alone a couple nights a week."

"Of course you can," his father said. "But there's no need for that."

And there was no need for his father to work himself into an early grave, but as long as Matt was within driving distance, that's exactly what his father would do.

Driving distance, Matt thought as he eyed the blood at the corner of his father's mouth. Milwaukee wasn't within daily driving distance. He'd decided to have rehab at St. Luke's because it'd been what he'd thought was best for his family instead of being what he wanted for himself. Could he really do that again? Go against what he wanted for himself because of what was best for his family?

He looked at his mother. She thrived on taking care of her family. He shifted to Crystal. Their relationship might not survive time apart *and* a dose of paralysis. He looked at his father, who looked old and worn down. He could very well lose his father in trying to hang on to Crystal.

He stared at the wall, but he could still see all three of the people he loved. He grabbed Crystal's hand. Their fingers fit together so well. His father was an adult. He could take care of himself.

Except, he wouldn't.

Tightening his fingers around Crystal's, he said, "The social worker told me they have an opening in Milwaukee. I'm going to ask for a transfer."

§

With his eyes closed, Matt concentrated on the impression of Abby's hand on his leg when she worked his joints the next afternoon. She moved her hand, sending a tremor up his calf. He almost moaned from the sheer pleasure of the feeling. Something that felt that damn good had to be a good sign.

"I can't believe you're transferring to Milwaukee, of all places," Abby said.

He opened his eyes to find her grinning. Last time he'd seen a smile like that, he'd ended up as secretary for the pool league. Curious what this smile was going to get him into, he said, "It was either Milwaukee or a rehab center in Bermuda and Bermuda's already got enough problems with lost items."

She lifted one eyebrow.

"I have a reputation for losing things. Dad says I could lose an elephant in an empty room."

"David Copperfield gets paid big money for doing stunts like that."

He laughed. "I'll have to tell Dad that the next time I lose something."

She pushed his knee toward his chest. "Well, I, for one, am happy you picked Milwaukee over Bermuda. It'll be nice knowing at least one person when I move there."

He lifted himself to his elbows. "You're going to Milwaukee?"

"Milwaukee Spine Care Center. Just like you."

She'd be there. He'd be there. A therapist in need of patients and a patient in need of a therapist. "What do you think the chances are that they'll assign you to be my therapist?"

"Not likely, unless you get a brain injury within the next week. I'm going to be working with traumatic brain injury patients while I continue my schooling."

He flopped back onto the mat. So she wouldn't be his therapist. No biggie.

Abby's fingers brushed his ankle, sending a tremor up his leg. His toe jerked inside his too-white tennis shoe.

"Oh, God." He pushed himself upright.

"What?"

He grabbed his left leg and dragged it closer.

"Matt? What's wrong?"

Ignoring her, he ripped off his shoe and tossed it. "Move," he whispered to his sock-covered big toe. "Move, already. Move."

His toe barely moved a sixteenth of an inch, but it was enough for him. "Did you see?"

"You own a sock without a hole in the toe?" Her lips puckered just enough to show she was teasing.

"You are such a pain in the ass."

"So I've heard." She flashed him one of her buy-these-gloves smiles. "This is good, Matt."

Her. Saying it was good. The first words of encouragement he'd heard in weeks. "I'm going to walk."

She picked up his shoe from the floor where it had landed. The task obviously required every bit of concentration since she wasn't talking, for once.

"Abby. That's what it means, right?"

"It's a step in the right direction."

"I don't want just a step. I need a full recovery."

She busied herself with putting his shoe back on even though he was perfectly capable of doing it himself. Avoiding him is what she was doing. He could tell. "I need to walk again, Abby. You understand? I have to."

Still crouched down, she looked up at him. "*Want*, Matt. You *want* to walk again."

He snagged the fingerless faux-leather gloves off the wheelchair seat and pulled them on. "No, Abby. I *need* to walk again. I've got too many people depending on me."

Before she could lecture him on the definitions of want and need, he grabbed the chair and hurled his weight into the seat.

"Matt—"

"Save it for someone else. I'm done listening to your psychobabble about not getting my hopes up." It wasn't until he was out the door that he realized he'd gotten into the wheelchair without the use of the transfer board. His first impulse was to turn around, to go back to Abby, to bask in his milestone with her. A heaviness pressed on him. From here on out, he'd be basking in the milestones with someone else.

Didn't matter. All that mattered was getting well again.

He gave the wheels a hard push. Within minutes, he was back at his room. He turned the chair and gave a final push through the doorway.

Derrick stood at the bed with his back to the door. Even though he was happy to see his friend, he thought about putting the wheels in reverse. He didn't want company right now.

Derrick looked over his shoulder. "Hey, bro." The ceiling light glinted off the glass covering the framed picture of Crystal that Derrick held.

"Hey." Matt nodded at the picture. "Not thinking of stealing that, are you?"

"Wouldn't dream of it." Derrick put the frame back in place on the nightstand and then sat on the edge of the bed. He looked tired. More than tired. He looked…sad.

"You okay?" Matt asked.

His friend laughed. "You're the one in the hospital and you're asking me if I'm okay?"

"Yeah? So? You doing okay?"

"Just fine. Just a little tired, is all. Enough about me. I hear we've got something to celebrate."

Matt saw Abby with her this-doesn't-mean-anything look. "I wouldn't go polishing up my tools quite yet."

"Damn." Derrick grinned, his dimple deepening. "Wish you'd told me that before I spent all morning doing just that."

"Like you had time." The truth of the statement settled in. "I should be there with you guys, instead of here."

"You will be. Just give it time." Derrick raised his chin. "Pops said you're transferring to Milwaukee. I think that's a good move, especially now that you're recovering. We need you back, good as new."

He liked that picture—him, back, good as new. But it felt like a lie, even with as many times as he'd told Abby he was going to walk again. "And what if I don't come back good as new?"

"Don't think that way."

"I have to. Abby says there's less than a two percent chance of my having a full recovery. Two percent. That's nothing." Good lord. He was starting to sound like her.

"No. Zero percent is nothing. She didn't give you zero. She gave you two, and you can be one of those two percent as easily as the next guy."

Matt wiggled his one toe while he rubbed his leg in a spot where the sensation had spread from this morning. Derrick was right. He could be one of those lucky two percent. No, not *could*. He *would* be one of them. And now that Abby was going to be in Milwaukee as well, he could prove it to her without having to hunt her down.

§

By Monday morning, after a weekend in Milwaukee away from Crystal and his family and a full day with no further recovery, Matt was losing confidence that the two percent was within his grasp. His hands lay limp in his lap as the CNA wheeled him to his first therapy session. Without Abby.

He lifted his head. He was at the best spine care center in Wisconsin. He was going to have a therapist who only worked with spinal cord injuries. The best treatment at the best center. So what if he'd had a day without any recovery? He'd be walking out of this place, and he'd make sure Abby watched him do it.

The CNA parked him just inside the gym doors. He looked around the busy room filled with all the equipment he'd hoped for back at St. Luke's. Parallel bars. Weight equipment. Everything state-of-the-art. Everything he needed to get him walking again.

A plump older woman walked toward him. "Hi. I'm Esther Roper. I'll be your physical therapist."

The woman looked old enough to be his grandmother. If she'd ever touched a pair of ns, it'd been back when gas was a penny a gallon. Her lips curved into a warm smile, but he didn't feel any uncontrollable urge to buy into whatever she might be selling.

"I see from your records that your last therapist already had you working on wheelchair transfers. You even managed a transfer without a board. I'm impressed."

He didn't bother to point out that his progress in wheelchair transfers had been unplanned, anger-induced events.

"I think our best course of treatment would be to get you out on the wheelchair obstacle course. Get you working on wheeling up ramps, to start with."

Wheeling up ramps. Just like on St. Luke's flyer. Where were the braces and crutches? "I'm going to walk again."

"Of course you are." Mrs. Agreeable.

He waited for her to spout off some statistic to put everything in perspective. Instead, she said, "Until then, you need to be able to master whatever challenges stand in your way with the wheelchair. Speaking of which, I notice you haven't ordered a chair yet. I'll contact the medical supply store and have them send over someone to explain the differences in wheelchairs, so you can get that taken care of."

"I don't need to order a wheelchair."

She crossed her arms over a wide belly. He waited for her to protest. Instead, she said, "Well, then, how about we work on wheeling up some ramps?"

"Sure. Fine." Shouldn't she have told him how important it was that he have a wheelchair made just for him? "Sounds like loads of fun."

Loads of fun, it wasn't. Not in his morning session and even less so in the afternoon session. It was hard work, plain and simple. No harder than anything he'd done with Abby. It just felt harder without Abby's encouragement.

Back in his room, too tired and sore to move, he stared out the window at the parking lot. Four more days without Crystal or his parents. It felt like a lifetime.

He rubbed his right leg, just above the knee—a spot without sensation. He widened out the circle. When he felt the tingle of sensation where there hadn't been any before, he closed his eyes and breathed deeply. Thank God. He searched out more spots and found another new location. News this good he had to share, and he knew just who he wanted to share it with.

Ignoring the screaming pain in his shoulders and upper arms, he wheeled over to his cell phone and dialed Crystal's speed number. Listening to the ringing, he propped his elbow on the nightstand and leaned against the phone. Hearing her voice filled him with peace.

"I've missed you, babe."

"Me too. Anything good happen today?"

He touched the new area of sensation. One more patch didn't guarantee anything. He gave his head a quick shake. Positive thoughts only, he told himself. "The sensation's spreading again. I've got two new spots."

"Matt, how wonderful."

Wonderful indeed. All of it. The sensation spreading. The excitement in her voice. His mouth curved into a smile he couldn't hold back, even if he tried.

"What did your doctor have to say? This has to be a good sign, right? Oh, gosh, Matt. This is so great."

Her lips were flapping a mile a minute. So fast, he couldn't do anything but sit there with a sappy smile, soaking up her excitement.

"Soon, all of your sensation will be back. And you know what comes next, don't you? Walking. You'll be walking in no time."

His smile fell. She wasn't saying anything different from what he'd planned on himself. His believing this was proof he'd walk again seemed like a natural progression. Her believing it felt like a ton of responsibility dropped on his shoulders.

"Babe, it's just a couple patches of sensation. It could stop right there."

"No, honey. It won't. You're going to walk again. I know it."

His shoulders sagged with the excess pressure. He rested his head against his fingers pressed to his forehead. Like a recurring nightmare, the question pestered him.

What if he didn't walk again? Would she be content being saddled down with him and a wheelchair? He rubbed one of the new patches with sensation, trying to get the happy feeling back.

"Matt?" The excited tone was gone.

Rubbing his leg reminded him of how far he had to go. He pulled his hand away and cleared his throat. "So, what's new in Fuller Lake?"

"Oh, you know. Same old, same old. Nothing as good as what's happening down there."

He wanted to yell at her that it wasn't that great. Just two small, possibly insignificant, patches of sensation. Instead, he let his eyelids slide shut. His head pressed into his fingertips. "You have a good day at work?"

"It's work. What can I say?"

Silence filled the air. Silence that left him free to think. And worry. *What if I don't walk again? What's going to happen to us?*

"Got any plans for tonight?" he asked, hoping to quiet his mind.

"Nothing much. Just watching TV."

More silence.

"What are you going to watch?" he asked.

"Oh, I don't know. Whatever looks good."

Talking to her was becoming a chore. "What're you having for dinner?"

"Just a salad."

Like pulling weeds, one question at a time. Sad thing was, he couldn't think of anything else to ask. And she wasn't supplying any conversation on her own.

In the background came the sound of a doorbell. "Sorry, Matt. I have to go. Someone's here."

He was almost relieved to have an excuse to hang up. "Okay. I love you."

"Take care. See you Saturday." The phone went dead.

"I love you, Matt," he answered for her. Before he could bog himself down in self-pity, he dialed again. "Hi, Ma. Remember me? Your long-lost son."

His mother's laugh made him smile. "Which son would

that be?"

"Dad there?"

She hesitated. "No. Not yet."

He tipped his head back and closed his eyes. There was no winning. Without the nightly trips to Bakersfield to visit Matt, his father was filling his spare time working. "How is he?"

"Fine."

"No, Ma, don't lie to me. How is he? "

"You know your father. All he says is that he's got a little cold."

"Cold, my ass."

"Matthew, don't swear."

"I'm sorry, but I'm worried about him. He's so damn stubborn."

"He may be stubborn, but he's not stupid."

No, his father wasn't stupid. But he tended to think he was invincible. "Promise me, if he's not home in an hour, you'll go drag him home?"

"I promise. Now, tell me about your therapists."

Forty minutes later, he was still on the phone. He knew everything that had happened in his mother's day, right down to how many colors Kaylee used in the latest picture she'd drawn for him.

He didn't want to hang up, but he knew if he didn't, they'd stay on the phone all night. And his mom had something important to do. "Do me a favor. Go get Dad. Make him come home and relax."

CHAPTER TEN

At nine-thirty on Saturday morning, Abby exited Eastlawn Manor with her mother for what would be the last time. A fine dusting of snow covered every surface, turning the old, dirty snow to white. A fresh start.

Their feet slid on the slick pavement as they walked to her car. Abby shuddered at the thought of the trip ahead. One hundred eighty-three miles of snow-covered roads dragging a trailer. Would have been nice if the weatherman had warned her.

Her mother stopped moving the second the car and trailer came into view. She took a backward step. "Not moving."

Abby's shoulders tensed. "We have to. I have a new job."

"You go. I'll stay here." Her mother turned back toward the nursing home.

Abby grabbed her mother's sleeve. A layer of snow already clung to the wooly fabric. Why today, of all days, did the weatherman have to be wrong? "You can't stay." She pulled just a little to urge her mother toward the parking lot. "Please, Mom. We have to get on the road."

"Not going." Her mother stood firm.

Abby tugged on her mother's sleeve. Her feet slid. Just a little. The snow seemed to be coming down harder. Wet, heavy snow. Coating the roads. And her mother refused to cooperate.

She wanted to let go of her mother's sleeve, hold up her hands, and say "fine, stay if you want." She wanted to get in her car and drive away and leave her mother standing there. It was thoughts like these that made her a bad daughter—a bad enough daughter for a father to leave behind.

She let go of her mother's sleeve, but she didn't

leave. She put her hands on her hips. "We're moving to Milwaukee. You have five seconds to get in the car, or I'll go inside and get one of the orderlies. One." Her cheeks stung from the cold. "Two." *Please.* "Three." The snow covering her mother had thickened noticeably. "Four." Her eyes watered. She wasn't sure if it was from the cold or her frustration or both. Didn't matter because she refused to cry. "Time's up. I'm going for the orderly now."

Abby made it one step when she heard a very soft, "Okay."

"Thank you."

§

"Aw, hell," Matt grumbled as he looked outside before leaving for therapy. The snow was falling harder now. The flakes were no longer fat and fluffy. They'd become wet and heavy, the kind that accumulated more quickly. He hated to wait yet another week to see his family, but he'd hate it even more if they had an accident on the way.

He flipped open his cell phone and dialed his parents' house. The answering machine picked up.

"I'm thinking you guys shouldn't come down today. Not with the weather like this. I'll call you after I'm done with therapy. Love you. Bye."

He had to leave for therapy, but he wouldn't be able to concentrate until he knew for sure they weren't coming. He dialed his father's cell number. After two rings, the voicemail picked up. He got the same result with Crystal's cell phone.

"You all disappear into the Twilight Zone?" he muttered as he dialed his brother's cell phone only to get his voicemail, as well.

"Damn it." Calling off a visit shouldn't be this hard.

Giving it one last shot, he dialed Derrick's number and got an answer of a quick, "Yo."

Thank God. "What's the weather like up there?"

"On a scale of one to ten—shitty."

"I'm late for therapy. Can you get a message to my parents?"

"Sure."

"Tell them not to come this weekend."

"That would have been a good message to have about an hour ago. They've already left."

Damn.

Having already left, he could understand why his father, who was probably driving, wasn't answering his phone. But why wasn't anyone else answering? "Do me a favor. Keep calling Dad's cell. Make them turn back, okay?"

"Sure thing."

He hung up, linked his fingers together, and hung his hands on the back of his neck. Camouflaging his prayer. *Let them be okay. Please, let them be okay.*

§

Abby turned on the wipers to brush away the snow that had accumulated while she'd buckled in her mother. Helen sat beside her in a tight ball, her mouth pinched as tightly closed as her arms. She'd stay that way until Abby cajoled her out of her grumpy mood.

She hated seeing her mother like this, but there wasn't time to placate her. At least she was being quiet. Which was probably a good thing, she thought as she came to the first stop sign and heard her brakes chirp while her car barely skidded to a stop. This trip was going to require every bit of her concentration. She thought about postponing their move but dismissed the idea. Going back to Eastlawn would confuse her mother and create a bigger tantrum tomorrow. Besides, she'd turned in her key to her landlady and, as of ten minutes ago, her mother was no longer an Eastlawn resident. She'd driven in snow before, plenty of times. They'd be fine.

Coast clear, she stepped lightly on the gas. The tires spun and the car shifted slightly to the right before finding traction and bolting forward. With her cheerful mother pouting beside her and the beautiful road conditions, this was guaranteed to be a fabulous trip.

On the radio, *Rascal Flatts* sang about what hurt the most, about never knowing what could have been. A perfect theme song for her and Paul. Never knowing what could have been. Her eyes burned. She pinched her lips together. *You will not cry. You will not cry. You will not cry.*

Her chest ached. Her nose burned. She bit her lip, but the road blurred in front of her.

"Abby!" her mother screeched.

§

Pulled up close to the fake curb, Matt paid little attention as he tipped backward, bringing the casters off the ground. One second he was thinking about Crystal and his family, wondering if they were okay. The next, he was aware of the room shifting off kilter as he flipped over backward. His head bounced against the floor, and stars sparkled before his eyes.

"Matthew," Esther cried out as she crouched beside him. "Are you okay?"

His head hurt like a son-of-a-bitch, but there was no way he'd let on. "Dandy."

She peered into his eyes. "Are you sure?"

He put on a smile he had to work hard to keep in place. "Just fine."

She hesitated for a second before she stood and planted her hands on her hips. "Good, because now you can practice getting back into your chair after taking a tumble."

"My idea of fun." He'd prefer to just lie there. At least until his head stopped pounding. Instead, he worked himself out of the fallen wheelchair.

"With the right wheelchair, you wouldn't have tipped over so easily."

He propped himself up on his elbows. "And make this lesson meaningless?"

She crouched down. "You can't avoid ordering your chair forever."

"Sure, I can."

He waited for her to say something cheerful like what a bad sign it was that he'd gone three days now without a recovery. Or that even if he'd had some recovery every day of this last week, it still didn't guarantee he'd walk again.

Instead, she straightened and took a few steps off to

the side.

Using the wheelchair for leverage, he pulled himself into a sitting position. Her silence seemed wrong, like she didn't care what his outcome was, so long as he ordered the damn chair and learned how to use it.

"You know, I can move all my toes now," he said, enticing her to say something about his condition and not his therapy.

"Um hum." She nodded.

"All of my sensation's back." All was a rather broad usage of the word. It was only his sensation of touch that had returned, not the sensation of hot or cold, or the sensation of pain.

"I'm going to walk again," he added.

She waved at the chair, motioning for him to get back to "practicing."

He righted the chair and locked the brake. His "remarkable" recovery didn't mean diddlysquat. Not if it all stopped here. Ten wiggling toes and the ability to feel someone's hand against him wasn't going to get the group home built.

It was going to help even less if Derrick didn't reach his father in time and they had an accident on their way. It was bad enough that he was like this. To have his father or brother, or, God forbid, both of them, injured like this would mean an end to his father's business.

If only he knew where they were and that they were safe. "I need to make a call."

"We're almost done. You get yourself into the chair, we'll call it a day."

He brought all of his weight on to his arms. Pressure built behind his eyes. He pushed harder, lifting his weight higher. His arms shook from the effort. *Just a little further.*

Just when he thought there was no way he'd make it, he lifted himself higher. Throwing his head back, his weight shifted and pulled his body backward. With a little more effort, he got his body positioned. *Please, God, don't let my father or brother have to go through this, too.*

Without waiting for the okay from Esther, he left the

gym, mentally cursing himself for not having brought his cell phone with him.

The hallway between the gym and his room seemed to have tripled in distance. Fifty feet more. That's all. He pushed harder against the wheels.

Breathless and tired, he made a sharp turn into his room. His cell phone sat on the over-bed table like a beacon. No messages, he noticed as he snatched it up, unsure if that were a good sign or bad.

He pushed speed-dial-two. "Answer," he whispered. "Come on, answer."

The phone rang several times and then went to voicemail. He dialed Crystal's number and his brother's, as well, before switching to Derrick's number. He groaned when he got voicemail there, too. He should have called off the visit first thing this morning when he saw the first snowflake.

§

Through Abby's tears, she almost didn't see the SUV that had stopped in front of her with its turn signal flashing. Her reactions took over, and she stood on the brake pedal. Oh, God. She wasn't going to stop in time. Not with the weight of the U-Haul pushing her forward.

"Hold on," she screamed as she put out her hand to brace her mother. Even with her foot flattening the brake pedal, her car still skidded forward. There was nothing more that she could do but envision the impact and worry about how bad it was going to be. That, and wonder if this was how her mother had felt moments before hitting the tree. Now, she was putting her mother through that all over again.

The SUV pulled into the intersection at the exact moment Abby's car finally stopped. No collision. Ignoring the green light, she didn't move. Her heart thudded. Her muscles liquefied. What if the SUV had waited just one second longer? What if her mother hadn't screamed?

The realization that they could have been seriously injured brought on a whole new mass of tears. She had to pull herself together, but she couldn't.

The light turned red.

"It's okay," her mother said. "We're okay."

It wasn't okay. She'd put her mother in danger. Her shoulders shook.

A soft hand touched her arm. "It's okay, sweetheart," her mother said. "Look. We're okay. Really."

Her mother's impish smile looked so much like the one she'd always had before the accident, reminding Abby of the mother she'd lost. If only her mother could stay this way, like the mother Abby remembered. Even if only long enough for Abby to put her head against her mother's chest and cry over what she'd lost with Paul.

"The firefly turned grease," her mother said. Deep creases formed around Helen's eyes. In one swift motion, she pulled her hand from beneath Abby's, formed a fist, and then hit her head, over and over. "Damn words. Damn mixed up pea train."

The car behind them honked. Grabbing for her mother's hands, Abby realized the light had turned green again. The firefly turned grease.

Her mother struggled against Abby's grasp. "Get me where they can fix me. Please. Fix me." All of the fight left her. She slumped in a heap against the seat and whispered, "God, please, fix me."

§

At three-thirty, Matt dialed his father's cell phone for what felt like the hundredth time. The phone rang once. Twice. He didn't want to hear it ring a third time. What he wanted to hear was his father's voice.

The phone rang again. This time, the tone changed and he heard a tiny voice. "Unka Matyou, we here."

"Oh, God," he breathed.

"Unka Matyou?"

"Hey, munchkin." His voice shook. "Can I talk to Grandma or Grandpa?"

"Gampa say hold you horses. We parking now."

"You're here? Really here?"

"I told you aweady. We here."

Matt punched end call, tossed his phone onto the bed,

and then wheeled for the door. He made it all the way to the lobby before he saw the crowd coming to visit him. His mother broke free and wrapped him in a hug that had never felt better. He squeezed her a little more tightly than he'd intended. "Thank God you're here."

"Missed us, did you?"

"Where have you been?"

"Between towers," his father said, giving him a quick hug. "Changing a flat, taking bathroom breaks. You name it."

"You're okay. That's all that matters." His gaze landed on Crystal standing beyond Jenny and Brad, a squirming Kaylee in her arms. Crystal had never looked more beautiful.

She gave Kaylee a kiss and then set her down. She gave Kaylee a pat to the behind, sending the little one running. Not like the little bundle of energy needed any encouragement.

"Unka Matyou," his niece sang as she crawled onto his lap.

Just saving the best for last. He gave Crystal a final look before he turned his attention to Kaylee. Her bony knees dug into his thighs. It felt like heaven.

Matt's mother slid into his father's arm. His father grinned. He looked better, but not great. It *had* only been a week. Too quick for miracles.

Like their parents, Brad and Jenny also stood arm-in-arm. They looked more than happy to be temporarily relieved of their parental duties.

Crystal stayed in place, much too far away for his taste.

"Give Kaywe ride," his niece demanded, pulling his attention away from his fiancée once again.

"Your ol' Uncle Matt's not very skilled at driving this thing yet. But I bet, if you sit nice, we can convince Auntie Crystal to give us both a ride. Do you think?"

Kaylee nodded and then sat still. Crystal finally moved forward. She hugged him from behind with one arm while she brushed her finger across Kaylee's cheek. A tight band closed around his chest. This is what he wanted. Him and Crystal, with a child of their own. The start of a perfect family, just like his parents.

Crystal leaned forward, just far enough to give him a light kiss on his cheek. Not quite the kiss he'd been dreaming of all week. He moved his face closer to her, hoping she'd try that kiss again. "I missed you, babe."

She nodded and brought her lips toward him. Finally, the kiss he'd been waiting for. She settled in close to his ear and whispered, "Should we do that ride before someone starts bouncing again?"

The band around his chest tightened another notch. Where was the good kiss? At the very least, where was her *I missed you, too?* He forced some cheer into his voice. "Think we should move this party down to the family room where there are chairs for everyone?"

§

It was nearly four o'clock when Abby turned into the driveway at Hot Springs Villa. Her mother was quiet, her eyes half closed. Peaceful. Abby took her time parking the car, relishing what might be the last quiet moments until she was nestled in her new apartment. Alone.

Biting her lip, she focused on the building in front of her, a run-down version of the one she'd seen on their website. She squinted and tried to envision a wealth of colorful flowers surrounding the building like the pictures had shown. It didn't help. She still saw the shingles curling away from the roof, the flaking paint on the window trim, the faded and cracked vinyl siding.

Coming here was beginning to feel like a mistake.

Staying at St. Luke's, where she'd be running into Paul, would have been a bigger mistake.

With a deep breath, she pushed thoughts of Paul away before they could sink in good and deep. Plenty of time for that later. Right now, she needed to focus on her mother, getting her set in her new home. It wasn't the building that mattered. It was the quality of care her mother would receive. The success ratio Charles Presthed had quoted. That's what mattered.

This move was going to be a good one. For both of them.

Helen opened her eyes, looked toward the building, and then crossed her arms. "They can't fix me here."

"It's only a building, Mother. What counts is the quality of the staff."

"Take me somewhere else. I'm not staying here."

"Give it a chance." *Please.*

"You'll look for something else if I don't like it?"

"As long as you give it a chance."

Her mother sighed. "Let's get this over with."

Abby led her mother to the building. Two steps into the lobby, Abby stopped cold. Her lips parted. She felt like she'd stepped into the lobby of a five-star hotel. Soft instrumental music played from hidden speakers. Polished granite topped the reception counter. Gold tassels edged the heavy, burgundy drapes.

"They made a silk...potato out of a cowboy's ear."

"Purse," Abby said. "And I think it's a pig's ear."

"Whatever."

A woman stepped through a doorway. She smiled as though Abby were a close friend she hadn't seen in a while. "Hi. You must be Abby." The smile broadened. "And you're Helen." She held out her hand, not to Abby, but to her mother. "Welcome."

This woman obviously didn't take after the administrator.

"I'm Betty," the woman said as Helen took the offered hand. "Can I get you some coffee? Hot chocolate? Muffin? Freshly baked by one of our own."

Abby shook her head. "Thank you, though."

"I'll take a damn muffin," Helen said.

Abby's cheeks prickled with heat as though the words had slipped from her own mouth. She glared at her mother.

"What?" Helen's eyebrows dipped toward the center. "I figure I may as well get something good out of this place, even if it is only a damn muffin."

If Abby could have crawled under the carpet, she

would have. Betty's smile, however, never faltered.

"We'll drop off your daughter at Mr. Presthed's office on our way to the kitchen." Betty led Abby and her mother through the same doorway she'd appeared through just a short while ago. Like the lobby, the hallway was papered in elegant ivory wallpaper. Richly colored oil paintings hung on the wall. Her mother stopped in front of a painting of a girl enticing a sparrow to sit on her finger. Helen put out her own finger.

"Pretty, isn't it?" Betty said as though she had all the time in the world.

Such a difference from Eastlawn. Such a difference from the exterior.

When Helen let her hand drop to her side, Betty apparently took that as a sign to move on. A short while later, Betty stopped next to an open doorway and motioned for Abby to enter. "Mr. Presthed will bring you to your mother's room."

Abby stood in the doorway and watched as her mother wandered off with Betty without any snide comments. A good sign.

She finally turned and stepped into Mr. Presthed's office. He looked like he belonged in a *Godfather* movie instead of tucked behind a group-home administrator's desk. Dark hair speckled with silver at the temples. Expertly pressed black-on-black pinstriped suit worn over a black silk button-down shirt. The only thing missing were his henchmen standing guard.

Without giving her even the merest of glances, he continued jotting notes in a file. "Ms. Fischner, how nice to meet you in person."

His reception filled her with the warm and fuzzies. Made her want to sit down across from his desk and spend the evening basking in his company. Not. She remained by the door. "Nice to meet you, too."

He paused in his notes and finally peered up at her. He set down his pen and leaned back in his chair, his eyes steady on her. She felt like a specimen under a microscope. His eyebrows rose. "*You're* Abigail Fischner?"

"Yes."

He looked down at the file, frowned, and then looked back up at her. "The same Abigail Fischner who attended Rand University?"

How had he known that? She barely managed to keep from raising her eyebrows in surprise. Her answer came as a cautious, drawn out, "Yes."

"The same Abigail Fischner who graduated in the top one percent of her class?"

Instinct had her wanting to stand tall, proud of her achievement. Except her mind was whirling with suspicion. He'd dug into her past. *Her* past, which had nothing to do with her mother. Why would he do that? Better yet, what right did he have to do that?

She did stand tall, with her hands on her hips and her legs slightly spread. "I'm glad you spent valuable time checking out how well I did in school. We know how important that is when it comes to my mother's care. Speaking of which..." She moved forward, planted her hands on his desk, and stared him in the eye, refusing to look away. "What are your plans for her treatment?"

His eyes left hers. "I, ah, we have a top notch team." He leaned further back in his chair, bested in the staring contest. "That's why seventy-five percent of our residents are released home within months of placement. Three quarters of the remaining twenty-five percent are in less restrictive housing within three years."

She forced herself to remain steady. "Her treatment, Mr. Presthed. What are your plans for her treatment?"

His eyes met hers again. "Have a seat, Ms. Fischner."

She stared him down for two more seconds, which felt more like twenty minutes, and then took a seat.

"Our senior therapist has reviewed your mother's records. Although your mother has been at her mental capacity for much longer than anyone who's ever come to us, Jessica feels there's hope. It might take a bit longer, but I feel quite comfortable saying your mother will be able to move into less restrictive housing when she leaves here."

Her mother being anywhere other than a home with constant supervision was a concept difficult to wrap her mind around. Was it possible? Truly possible? She drew in a deep breath and sat tall. "So what do we do to make that happen?"

"We?"

"Yes, we. As I'm sure you already know, since you dug into my school records, my main focus has always been the mentally disabled. I want to be a part of my mother's treatment."

"The first thing we need to do is to start having her do everything for herself that she's capable of doing."

Abby nodded. She'd never dreamed of her mother living anywhere other than a care facility with strict supervision, but the longer Mr. Presthed talked, the more her hope grew. Yes, she thought, coming to Milwaukee was definitely a good move. A fresh start for them both.

§

In Milwaukee Spine Care's family room, Crystal sat beside the toy box with Kaylee. Brad knelt next to his daughter. He pushed a chunky plastic truck toward her while Crystal held out a floppy doll and made it dance. Kaylee looked at the truck, looked at the doll, and then picked up a plastic hammer. Like a true Huntz, she went to work "fixing" the toy box. If she were twelve years older, they might be able to put her to good use. Matt rubbed his thigh. The sensation was still glorious, but it wasn't enough.

"How are you doing?" Jenny asked as she claimed the chair next to Matt.

He watched Crystal for another second before he looked at his sister-in-law. "Great. Never better."

She tipped her head and arched her eyebrows, clearly not buying his bravado.

"Really," he said. "I'm doing fine."

"I know it's hard for you being so far away, but I want to say thank you for transferring to Milwaukee, for my own selfish reasons." Her mouth stayed straight, but her eyes gave away her excitement. "We don't get down here very much to see Faith. Seems wrong, somehow, to use you as a pawn, but I can't wait to see my sister again."

Matt knew exactly how she felt, and he'd only been without his family for a week. "Staying at Faith's five-star hotel tonight?"

Jenny nodded. "We brought the air mattress for Brad, me, and Kaylee. Figured we'd let your parents have the spare bedroom while Crystal gets the couch."

"Can't say I'm sorry to miss out on the slumber party," Matt said as he watched Brad push himself to his feet. His brother stretched to the left and then to the right. He hardly looked like someone who'd make it through the night sleeping on an air mattress. "Sounds like too many people in one apartment."

Truthfully, an apartment crammed with family sounded ideal. He'd gladly sleep in the bathtub with a shirt for a pillow if it meant he could spend the night with them. The only thing that'd make it better would be having Derrick there, as well. Then, the family would be complete.

"Sounds like too many people all fighting for the bathroom first thing tomorrow morning, if you ask me," Jenny said, "but I'll put up with it if it means having time with Faith."

Brad sat on the arm of Jenny's chair and slid his arm around her. He did a chin thrust at his brother. "Ma said you're coming right along with your recovery. Just like I told Derrick, you'll be back in time for the summer rush."

His brother was trying to be encouraging, but it had the opposite effect, reminding him that more people were relying on his recovery than just himself. He looked at his father. Even after the long drive, he looked relaxed. Tired and weathered, but relaxed. How relaxed would he look come summer, with Matt still in a wheelchair and only three men to build the group home?

His attention shifted to Crystal, who was still trying to interest Kaylee in the doll. How about her? How worn down would she look once she realized she was stuck with what he'd become, instead of the man he used to be?

He looked back at his brother and sighed. "I've still got a long way to go."

Brad became interested in a tiny hole in his T-shirt, a confirmation that Matt couldn't change the outcome of his recovery. Avoiding the possibility of his not recovering wouldn't change things, either. In roughly a month, he'd be home again. The chances were becoming better every day that a wheelchair would be coming home with him. Like it or not, it was probably time to order his own chair. And stop hiding from the other arrangements he had to make.

Matt clasped his hands behind his neck. Damn, how he hated the thought of putting in a ramp and making all the other modifications that'd make his house wheelchair friendly. Worse yet was acknowledging he'd need help when he went home. Twenty-six years old and he needed a frigging babysitter. Just didn't seem right.

"You look deep in thought," his father said as he joined the party.

Matt shrugged in answer while he inspected the fine lines that etched his father's face, especially those around his father's mouth. No traces of blood, but that didn't mean his father was out of the woods.

Maybe now wasn't the best time to bring up the remodeling he needed done on his house. Besides, what if he was jumping the gun? What if he had the work done and then his body finally decided to cooperate with him?

What if he wasn't jumping the gun?

Everyone was staring at him now. Everyone except Kaylee, who was still fixing the toy box, sawing on it with a chunky orange plastic saw. He wanted to be right there with her in the land of make-believe.

Murphy's law. Better to have the work done and not need it. "I was just thinking about having some work done at my house."

His father sighed, like he'd been waiting for this conversation and had been hoping this moment would never come.

Matt lowered his arms. "I'm going to need a ramp put

in. The bathroom needs remodeling. And I guess I'm going to need my bedroom moved downstairs."

"That sounds like you're giving up."

"Carl," his mother gasped.

Giving up. His father would see it that way. Matt, always the disappointment. "Forget it." His voice was louder than he'd intended. "I don't want a ramp. I don't want a wheelchair-friendly bathroom. I don't want a downstairs bedroom. I don't want any of it, and heaven knows, I don't want to be stuck in this wheelchair the rest of my life."

Crystal's mouth opened and she pulled back like he'd slapped her. And then her lip trembled and the tears started. He didn't have it in him, right then, to comfort her. And he didn't want to apologize for his outburst. All he wanted was to be alone. He pushed hard against his wheels and kept moving until he lost steam about two hundred yards down the hallway. He gave one final push and let his wheelchair coast to a stop.

He shouldn't have run out on his family. Not after he'd waited all week to see them. And not after they'd driven two hundred miles in a snowstorm to come see him. But he couldn't make himself go back.

He closed his eyes and pressed his fingertips to his face. His father was right to be disappointed in him.

Footsteps sounded behind him. Heavy footsteps. Left out Kaylee. Whoever it was, he didn't want a witness to him sitting here, wallowing in pity and shame. He especially didn't want his father to see him that way. But he couldn't make himself lower his hands.

"Kaylee's wondering where Uncle Matt went," his father said.

Damn. It would have to be him. Matt squeezed his eyes more tightly closed.

"It'll all work out, Son. Don't you worry. You want to come back now and discuss these changes you need?"

Want to? Hell no. He didn't *want* to ever discuss it. But, like it or not, it was beginning to look like he *had* to.

CHAPTER ELEVEN

On Monday morning, Matt wheeled to the physical therapy gym fifteen minutes early, just to escape the quiet of his room. The weekend had been way too short, and the next five days stretched out ahead of him like a year.

Parked just inside the door, he scanned the gym. Esther was with a patient across the room. Other therapists were working with patients, too. Everyone too busy to keep him company, but being here was still a damn sight better than being alone in his room.

A woman came into the gym, dropped a stack of files on the desk in the nurses' station, and then left. More people came and went until he lost track of the comings and goings. He barely noticed movement beside him.

"Well, look what the cat dragged in."

His heart raced a little when he recognized Abby's voice. With his gaze locked on Esther, he spoke with a gruff voice. "You people ever hear of shoes that make noise?"

"Sure have, but they're not as much fun."

He looked up at Abby in her purple smock top with her hair pulled up and her lips all shiny. A feeling of déjà vu hit him, remembering their first therapy session. Next, she'd say, *Speaking of fun, are you ready to start?*

Her lips parted. "So, who's your therapist?"

Feeling like she'd said the wrong line, he nodded in Esther's direction. "Esther Roper."

"She seems nice. I think you'll do well with her."

I was doing well with you.

"It's really great seeing you again, Matt, but I need to get back to work. Don't want to get fired on my first day."

He let her get several steps away before he called out. "Abby."

She stopped and turned toward him. Her smile made

him want to buy everything she had for sale.

He wanted to ask what it'd take to get her assigned as his therapist, besides a brain injury. "I'm glad you're here."

"I'm glad you're here, too." She gave him a little wave.

He laughed when he noticed the bounce in her step. Good ol' Cheerleader Abby.

"Well, well, well," Esther said as she blocked his view. "Look at this. Matthew Huntz, all full of smiles. Eager to get going with his therapy. You must have heard that we're jumping curbs again today."

"Oooh, curbs," he said, feeling the pleasant effects of being with Abby fading. "Should be loads of fun." Especially when he had to pick himself up off the ground when he fell again. Then he could have the enjoyment of listening to Esther tell him how much easier it'd be in his own chair. "Can't wait."

"I knew you'd feel that way."

His own chair. One he should probably be ordering. He tapped his fingers against the push rims as he glanced over at Abby. She was talking with a woman he had never seen before. A center employee, he guessed, based on the ID badge clipped to her suit jacket.

As if Abby knew she was being watched, she looked his way. He figured that buy-these-gloves smile would grow even broader if she knew he was thinking of ordering the damn chair. He looked back at Esther and wondered what her face would do if *she* knew what he was thinking. Him, ordering a chair. What was the world coming to?

Esther stared back. Her eyes burned into him.

Do it. Just open up your mouth and get it over with.

"The curbs are waiting," Esther said.

"Yeah, sure," he answered. Plenty of time to talk about ordering a wheelchair once they got settled into the therapy session.

At the wheelchair obstacle course, he stopped in front of the curb they'd been working with on Saturday. He knew what to do. No instruction necessary. Instead of popping the wheelie, he said, "Let's say I wake up tomorrow and

I'm able to move my ankles or bend my knees that means I'll be able to walk again, right?"

"It would certainly be a good sign."

Encouraging, but not the affirmative answer he'd been wanting.

"With your past patients, the ones like me who could only wiggle their toes at this point, have any of them walked again?"

"Every case is different, Matthew. You can't rely on what may or may not have happened with someone else."

Why couldn't she answer the damn question? "I just want to know what my chances are."

"I'm sorry, but there's no way to tell at this point."

Stepping around his question. Something Abby wouldn't have done.

"Shall we get down to business?" Esther asked.

He popped a wheelie. The trick was to hold the wheelie and roll forward at the same time. He edged forward. His weight shifted. He tried to hang on to the wheelie, but before he knew it, the room was tipping the wrong way. As his head raced toward the floor, his thoughts betrayed him. *This would be so much easier if you had a chair designed specifically for you.*

Esther crouched down next to him. "Matthew, are you okay?"

"No, I don't think so."

With a gesture that was becoming all too common, she held open his right eyelid and then checked his left eye. "Appears normal, but I'd better call the doctor."

"Don't bother. Call the wheelchair guy instead."

§

As Matt feared would happen, the week dragged by, with each day feeling longer than the last. But Friday finally arrived, and he found himself growing excited. He parked himself by the bed after his last therapy session and cradled Crystal's picture in his calloused hands. In just eighteen hours he'd be with her again, but tomorrow seemed a lifetime away. He closed his eyes and tried to imagine her laugh. Instead, it was Kaylee's giggle he heard, and that brought forth a whole new feeling of loss. He missed what Saturday afternoon would bring and Sunday evening would steal away. His family. Crystal.

"You're too morose." He put the picture back, adjusting it until it was just right, turned toward the bed where he could see it when he woke up.

Five more hours until bedtime. Five very long hours. Made him wish he hadn't already drawn out the plan for the ramp. He also wished he still needed to write up the materials list for the rest of the projects he needed done at home. Then, he'd have something to do.

He couldn't stand the thought of sitting in his room alone, not even for one second longer. There was sure to be activity in the common room, so he wandered out into the hallway. The common room was to his right, but he felt compelled to turn left. "What the hell." He turned left.

At the next intersection he paused as he considered his options. Right? Left? Straight ahead? His inner guide said straight. At the T-intersection he stopped again. There wasn't a whole lot to the left, but to the right was the center's lobby, another path to the common room, and the vending machines. Turning right made sense. He turned left, instead.

Within two minutes, he found himself in front of the closed therapy gym doors. There was no reason for him to be here, but this felt like where he was supposed to be.

A crack of light shone under the door. Behind that door was thousands and thousands of dollars worth of state-of-the-art weight-lifting equipment. Equipment he worked with in therapy but not to the extent he liked. If he were at home, all alone, he'd likely be up in the attic working out with his own weights. That was all he needed to justify opening the door.

Abby sat behind the desk that formed a hub in the center of the room. She looked up and smiled. A genuine smile that wasn't simply polite. Like she was happy her work was being interrupted.

"I was in the neighborhood and saw the light on," he said, a genuine smile of his own forming. "I was wondering if I could spend some time on the weights."

"Sure. I'll be here a while."

It appeared she was the lone therapist. "Did you get in trouble again and have to stay after class? Being forced to write over and over 'I will not be a pain in the ass.'"

"You know, I'm thinking I could get into trouble letting a patient use the weights after hours. I'd hate to get fired with only a week under my belt."

He wheeled a little closer. His gaze locked on to hers. "And I'm thinking that if you're here this late on a Friday instead of out enjoying yourself, that must mean you need to brush up on your social skills. What better person to practice on than me?"

She looked like she was struggling to hold back a smile. "Maybe someone who isn't so stubborn."

"Stubborn?" He pressed his fingers to his chest with mock indignation. "Me?"

"Yes, you."

Arguing with her was certainly more fun than sitting in his room. "Cool. I thought I was only disorganized and messy. It's nice to know I've risen above mediocrity."

She nodded at the exercise equipment. "Go knock yourself out."

He wheeled over to the pec machine. Within minutes, his movements became automatic, and his thoughts were free to roam. They went right where they'd gone a lot this last week. In roughly three weeks, he'd be going home. In less than two months, they'd be starting the group home build. It was getting harder and harder to hang on to the belief that he'd be of any help on the project.

In the back of his mind, he heard Abby spouting off percentages. He glanced her way. Her head was tipped forward. A lock of hair had pulled free of her ponytail and was hanging down by her cheek. Having even one hair out of place would have sent Crystal running for a mirror with a bottle of hairspray. Crystal wouldn't even step out of the house without her face fully spackled with makeup. And you sure as hell wouldn't ever hear Crystal reciting percentages.

Less than two percent of all patients have any significant recovery.

He looked away, but the thought was stuck there in his head. If he didn't recover, what did that mean for the group home build? Or, on a larger scope, what would it mean for his future as a construction worker?

Even though he'd already mentally navigated the jobsite in a wheelchair and determined it wouldn't work, he found himself doing it again, looking for the loophole he'd missed before. After twenty minutes, he came to the same conclusion he'd come to before—working in construction was probably one of the worst professions for a paralyzed man.

At the same time he noticed Abby walking toward him, he realized he'd quit working the weights somewhere along the line.

"Coming to kick me out?"

She sat on a weight bench next to him. "Nope. Just coming to remind you that I'm a good listener. It looks like you need one."

His impulse was to claim he didn't need her good-listener skills, that he was fine. But he wasn't all that fine. The stillness of the weights he was "working" with proved it. Abby's statistics might not be as encouraging as he wanted, but at least she didn't give him pat responses that didn't answer anything. "I can move all my toes now and the sensation has returned everywhere. That's good, right?"

"Definitely. Every move forward is a step in the right direction."

"Let's say I wake up tomorrow and I'm able to move my ankles or bend my knees, that means I'm going to walk again, right?"

Her eyes were locked with his. "I know you want me to say yes, but I can't."

Not what he'd hoped for, but it was exactly what he'd expected her to say.

"I can't say no, either. I can tell you all the statistics, but there's just no way of knowing what's going to happen."

Not a no, but not a yes, either. "I hate this not knowing."

"I would, too." She leaned closer. "Matt, I know it's not what you want to hear, but it really would be best for you to decide that this may be as good as it's going to get. You can't be disappointed that way."

"Okay, let's say this is all I get. How do I stay in construction if I don't walk again?"

"I'm not a construction expert, but I'm certain there are plenty of things you can do. There's got to be paperwork—"

"I'm a construction worker, not a secretary." As his father would be the first to agree. "I've been over it all in my head. There's close to nothing I can do in this wheelchair. That's why I've got to walk again, Abby."

She sighed. "I don't envy you the predicament you're in. It's got to be one heck of a balancing act to try to hold on to hope while facing facts at the same time. I wish I could be more encouraging, but the sad truth is that—"

"The odds are against me."

She nodded.

There it was. His stomach seized up like a pinched saw blade. He wished he were alone and that there wasn't some unwritten rule that men can't cry because he wanted to do just that.

Abby put her hand on his knee. "I'm sorry, Matt."

Through the pain came an awareness that wasn't unpleasant at all. He could feel her touch. Even if he never walked again, at least his body wasn't dead. He wasn't dead. When you got right down to it, that's what mattered.

He focused on the weight of her hand on his knee. "Life will go on."

"That it will." She pulled her hand away. "I usually do my paperwork after the gym closes down for the day. If you want to come back Monday night, I'll be here."

§

Matt took Abby up on her offer every night that next week. Wheeling into the dimly-lit gym the next Friday, Matt's gaze immediately went to what he now thought of as "Abby's desk." Seeing her smile made his heart feel lighter. Somehow, she'd gone from a pain-in-the-ass cheerleader therapist to a friend he looked forward to spending time with.

Halfway to the desk, he noticed she wasn't surrounded by patient files. She held a red plastic tumbler. He pointed at the Yahtzee score pad. "That what they pay you the big bucks for?"

"Actually, I've got all my paperwork done. I'm on my own time now."

A nice person would let her go home. Being nice meant giving up his time on the weights. It also meant giving up his time with Abby, afterward. "No paperwork left at all?"

"None. Zip. Nada."

Damn. "I'll skip the weights so you can go home."

"What? And take away all my fun? I like Yahtzee." She waved toward the weights. "Go knock yourself out."

She looked sincere. But it wasn't her responsibility to keep him from feeling lonely. "I like playing solitaire, but I wouldn't stay behind at a jobsite playing cards when I could be at home doing something else." He pushed himself backward. "See ya tomorrow."

"You really don't need to leave. I know how important this is to you. Besides, I really do like Yahtzee."

He should introduce her to Crystal, see if the Yahtzee-loving cheerleader could rub off on his game-hating fiancée. "You sure?"

She nodded.

Even though she'd insisted she didn't mind, he cut his time short to only fifteen minutes. He wheeled over to her desk and nodded at her score pad. "You win or lose?"

"I won, of course. I always do."

He gave her a half smile. "Sounds like a challenge."

"Take it any way you want."

He pulled off his gloves and slapped them down on the desk. "I take it as you wanting to see what it's like to lose."

She handed him a score sheet and a pencil. "Since I'm going to cream you, you can go first."

"I'll go first, but there's no way you're going to cream me." He picked up the cup and gave it a shake. Four of the dice displayed a single dot. Just one die away from a Yahtzee.

"Maybe I don't want to play with you after all," Abby said.

"I told you I wasn't going to lose." Despite his confident tone, the next two rolls failed to produce a Yahtzee.

Abby picked up the cup and watched as he entered his score in the ones box. "What? You're not going to put that in your four of a kind?"

"The idea is to get a high score."

"I know." She finally shook and let the dice fall to the desk. "I was hoping you didn't."

"That how you win? By cheating?"

"That's not cheating." She pushed aside two dice, scooped up the remaining three, and dropped them into the cup. On the next roll, she kept one die.

He liked this—sitting here with her in the quiet gym, playing games, just hanging out. "What made you decide to become a therapist?"

She hesitated, her bottom lip disappearing between her teeth like he'd seen her do whenever she seemed uncomfortable. "My mother was injured in an accident when I was ten. She hit a tree. There wasn't a lot I could do to help her, so I decided I'd help others. This is what I came up with." She gave a final shake and then pushed the cup toward him.

"Sorry about your mom," he said as he took his turn. "Is she...uh...paralyzed?"

"No." Her face crumpled as though fighting an internal war. "I often think paralysis would be so much easier to deal with."

Paralysis, easier? "Than?"

Her gaze hit him straight on. "Brain injury. She was thrown from the car and hit her head. Hard. Let's say she's got a lot of problems and leave it at that."

"Abby, I'm sorry."

She gave him a weak smile. "Me, too."

"What about your dad?"

She looked away. "He's...gone."

Gone. As in dead?

"I love my mother, but I was a daddy's girl. Losing him was hard."

As in dead. On impulse, he put his hand over hers. Her eyes went to his hand and then rose to meet his gaze. The gym suddenly seemed too quiet and they seemed too alone. He withdrew his hand. "Think we should get back to the game?" *Or, maybe I should just get the hell out of here.*

She gave the dice a shake. "Tell me about Crystal. How did you meet?"

"Crystal? I met her at a pool tournament. I saw her sitting at the bar. I couldn't seem to keep my eyes off her, she was so beautiful. Still is." He took the tumbler and shook. "She's smart. And she's fun to be with. She's really good with Kaylee. She's going to be a great mom." *If she gets the chance.*

He'd experimented late at night. Getting a hard-on was no problem now, but orgasms still eluded him. Even if he could climax, that still didn't guarantee anything. He knew from reading the brochures he'd been given that semen often backed up into the bladder instead of going out where it belonged. The joys of paralysis.

He shook the cup and let the dice fall onto the desk calendar. He set aside a four and dropped two threes, a two, and a five back into the cup.

"Don't you still need your small straight?"

"Why?"

"Because you had one."

He shrugged.

"Talk to me," she said.

What the hell. "Crystal and I wanted kids." He sighed. "I have no idea if that's possible now."

"Technology has come a long way."

"Damn it, I don't want technology. I want to be able to make babies the way God intended. Me and my wife, making love." He clasped his hands behind his head. *Be happy with what you've got. Be happy you're alive. Some people aren't so lucky.*

He thought of Abby's dad and how much she missed him. Which made him think of Abby's hand next to his. A touch between two friends. That's all. And he never would have thought otherwise if things didn't feel so off with Crystal. "I just want everything to go back to the way it's supposed to be."

"I wish I had some magic cure, but I don't. The best I can say is that things will get better."

He tightened his fingers and forced deep, even breaths until the blood stopped pounding inside his ears. When he lowered his arms, he found Abby staring at him, her head propped up on her hands.

"What?" he asked.

"I was just picturing you with a baby in your arms." Her face softened with her smile. "It's a beautiful picture, one I know will happen for you. You'll make a wonderful father."

He wasn't aiming for "wonderful." If he was half the father his dad was, he'd be satisfied. "I'm hoping I get the chance to try."

"You will," she stated with conviction.

He tried to picture him and Crystal with their child. Crystal refused to stay in the image. "I wish I felt as confident. About everything."

"Everything?"

Over a month had passed, yet he could still see Crystal's hand ricocheting off his leg. When he'd first gotten the sensation back she'd touched him, but now she was back to avoiding his legs. What if she couldn't handle his paralysis? What if they never had children, not because he couldn't provide the necessary ingredient but because Crystal wasn't around long enough to make it happen?

"Nothing." He picked up the dice and dropped them into the tumbler. "Think we should finish up this game?"

"Everything? Nothing? That's a sudden jump to the extreme, don't you think?"

He pushed the tumbler across the desk. "Shake."

"I see," she said. "You're going to hide from your feelings, huh? That it?"

"I'm not hiding," he snapped. Damn it. How had she gone from the annoying pain-in-the-ass cheerleader to someone who knew him so well?

"Then, talk it out. What's worrying you?"

He closed his mouth tight. His breaths blew across his upper lip.

"That bad, huh?" Abby asked.

She already knew something was on his mind. "What if Crystal and I get married only to find she can't handle everything that goes with my being paralyzed? What if I lose her?"

As soon as the words were out, he realized that Derrick was the only person he'd ever been this open with before.

"There's a very real possibility that might happen," she said.

"Thanks for the encouragement. I feel so much better."

"Do you want me to say it will never happen?"

He tightened his jaw and crossed his arms.

"Your injuries call for a lot of adjustments, not just for you but for everyone who loves you. *You* have to make these adjustments. Crystal doesn't."

"Yeah, I'm feeling better by the second. Just keep raising my spirits, okay?"

"If you're really worried about how she's going to accept the changes in your life, maybe you should do a trial run. Live together for a while before you get married."

"No." He answered without hesitation.

"Too bad you're so undecided on that issue."

"I'm human, Abby. Far from perfect, but I do my best, and I agree with what my parents taught me about marriage. What kind of a test would it really be, anyhow? If she could walk out whenever she wanted?"

"Would you rather she walks out after you're married?"

That scenario would kill him. Getting married. Thinking life's great, and then...wham! He could have the honor of being the first person in his family to get a divorce. Wouldn't that be a fine moment, facing his father with the news. He didn't even want to contemplate it. "I'd rather we finish this game."

"Fine. Have it your way." She picked up the tumbler. "Is talking about your childhood taboo, as well?"

"Why?"

"Because I have a feeling you're full of stories of you and Brad growing up."

"You don't know the half of it."

She crossed her arms and leaned forward. "So, tell me."

An hour later, he was still sitting at her desk with two squares filled in on their third game and his mouth flapping with yet another childhood memory.

"...and then I couldn't figure out how to put it back together," he said, "so I just screwed the cover on and put the toaster on the counter."

"Oh, no." Abby held the plastic cup above the desk like she'd forgotten she was about to roll the dice.

"Wouldn't you know, the very next morning, Ma decides to make toast."

She set the cup down without letting the dice fall, her eyes riveted on him. He loved the way she hung on to his every word. Like his stupid childhood memory was important. Like *he* was important.

"There I am, sitting at the table, trying my best to look innocent. Ma keeps frowning at the toaster, wondering why the bread hasn't popped up yet, I guess. She walks over to it, looks inside, and sees the heating elements are gone. Of course, she immediately looks at me."

Abby's eyes grew large as she pressed a hand to her mouth. So expressive. Alive.

"Don't know why she never looked at Brad. Anyhow, my dad made me work off the price of a new toaster at a quarter a chore. Took four months to pay it off."

"I'll bet you never did anything like that again."

He raised his eyebrows and smiled. "Actually, I was back at it within a week. I just made sure I paid attention to what piece fit where."

"You weren't kidding when you said you were inquisitive."

Even though they'd been laughing and having fun, their prior conversation hung in the air between them, unsettled. He shouldn't have cared, but he did. "Your idea about Crystal and me living together. It might be a good one, but it's just not me, okay?"

"Very okay. You have to do what's best for you." She rolled the dice and then looked up with a smile. "Look at that. Instant four of a kind."

"You're going to beat me again, aren't—"

Abby's smile had vanished and she was now looking over his shoulder.

He twisted around to follow Abby's gaze. His stomach dropped when he saw Crystal. He smiled and tried to ignore how hot the room suddenly felt. "Hey, babe. It's not Saturday already, is it?"

Crystal's gaze bounced between him and Abby. Had her eyes narrowed? Even just the littlest bit? He wasn't sure.

"Jenny wanted to spend some extra time with her sister, so I rode down with her." Crystal leaned up close to him and put her arm around his shoulder. Marking her territory. "What are you doing?"

"Just came to lift weights."

Crystal eyed his scorecard. "How nice."

He looked up at her, trying to gauge her expression. She sounded pissed, but she didn't look pissed. She looked like her normal, beautiful self. Still, he felt the need to explain. "I figured since Abby was nice enough to stay late, I should play a couple games with her."

Abby stood and extended her hand. "Hi. I'm Abby, one of the physical therapists here. You must be Crystal. He talks about you all the time."

"Why does that name sound familiar?" Crystal asked as she shook Abby's hand.

"Because I was Matt's therapist at St. Luke's."

"Small world."

Matt scrutinized Crystal's expression again, but her

face showed him nothing. How was it that his parents could hold entire conversations without saying a word, and he couldn't figure out for the life of him if Crystal was angry or if she was just making a statement.

"So honey, don't you think we should let Abby go home now?" Crystal caressed his neck. He noticed she avoided touching his surgery scar. "We need to go and make use of our alone time."

Her idea of making use of their time alone was to watch a movie on Lifetime. He looked over at her. She sat with her eyes on the TV screen, fiddling with her engagement ring. He took her hand in his. She looked at him, smiled, and then turned her attention back to the movie.

Just like an old married couple. Was that so bad? At least they were together

CHAPTER TWELVE

Matt whistled as he wheeled into his room following his Saturday morning sessions a week later. Crystal had been chatty every night this week when he'd called. Things with Abby had settled back into a friendship. Best of all, he'd been given a weekend pass. If things went well, in another week, he'd be on his way home.

The next twenty minutes dragged on. Finally, he heard their voices drifting down the hallway. When Crystal kissed him, he uttered a contented sigh as their lips met. The loneliness of the past week without her melted away. This weekend was going to be good. No. Scratch that. This weekend was going to be great.

"You ready to go?" his father asked. "Or do you still need to pack?"

Go. His heart did a little dance. He loved the sound of the word, even if go only meant leaving the center for one night. A trial run before they let him loose, for real. He nodded to the duffel bag by the door. "Everything I'll need for the night."

"Ready, then?" his mother asked.

More than ready. He grabbed his coat off the bed while Crystal claimed the canvas tote.

His father looked down at him. The corners of his mouth lifted. "This weekend will be nice." He nodded as though that cemented the thought.

"Next weekend will be better."

"Yes, next weekend will be better. It'll be good to have you back."

Back. The movement of Matt's arms faltered on the word. He'd be back home but not back at the jobsite.

Crystal fell in beside Matt. "I think Jenny will miss coming down here to see Faith."

"Well, I'm not going to stay here just to make her

happy. I'm eager to go home. Get back to real life."

Real life. What was "real life?" He'd expected "real life" to be what he'd left. Him, walking. One fourth of Huntz & Sons Construction. Future husband and father. Unless a miracle happened over the next week, he was going to have to alter his vision.

His father had parked Jenny's mini-van in one of the spots reserved for patient pickups, the space wide enough to aid in wheelchair-to-vehicle transfers. Matt had spent hours practicing with Esther, but he was far from "skilled," and he needed every inch of room allowed. He pushed the wheelchair arm away and inched himself toward the edge of the seat. *Piece of cake.* Brave words. He felt uncoordinated. Three pairs of eyes staring at him didn't help, either.

"Here." Crystal straddled his feet. She put her hands on his arms as though that'd help, somehow.

"I can do it," he said as he nudged her.

"I was only trying to help."

"You can help me more by getting out of the way." He'd tried to say it gently, but the words had come out harsh with his own irritation.

She stepped aside. Her bottom lip stood out.

"I've got to do it on my own, okay?"

The lip went back in, but she still looked miffed. Tuning her out, he focused on the sessions with Esther. Drawing forth her instructions, he hurled himself into the mini-van's front seat. A less than perfect transfer, but he felt good about it, anyhow.

Crystal got into the backseat beside Matt's mom and slid the door closed with more force than necessary. He'd never noticed before how childish she could be. He took a calming breath and then looked over his shoulder. "Babe, I know you want to help, but some things I just have to do on my own. Transfers are one of them."

"I know." She stared ahead.

"I appreciate that you want to help. The wanting to help, that's what matters."

The hard line of her lips disappeared. She looked his

way.

He gave her half a grin. "Believe me, babe, there's plenty you can help with."

Her gaze dropped, and she seemed to fold into herself. His heart fluttered. He looked forward, but he could still see her lowered eyes. He leaned his head back and stared through the front window. Was it possible for them to make it through this together, as a couple, intact to the end?

Fifteen minutes later, his father pulled into the parking lot for the apartment complex owned by Jenny and Faith's parents. This time, as he readied himself for the transfer, Crystal stood well off to the side. Out of the interference zone but still in the viewing section. He could feel her staring at him with that sad expression as he hauled his body into the chair. Steadying himself with one hand, he positioned his legs while she watched. His legs might not move on their own, but at least his toes did. That was sure to impress her down the road. Look honey, I can't stand, but look at those toes. Aren't you glad you married such a talented man?

His eyes met hers, and his stomach somersaulted when she quickly looked away. Yeah, she was impressed.

They barely made it inside the building when Kaylee came running down the hallway. Matt pulled her onto his lap and laughed as she covered his face with slobbery kisses. At least some things never changed.

"Go ride," she said as she bounced on him.

It wasn't easy to wheel the chair with a load on his lap, but he'd been practicing for an occasion such as this.

"Well, look at you," Faith said as he wheeled into the apartment. She looked like a shorter, wider, younger version of his sister-in-law. She waved him forward. "It's so good to have you here."

Without moving an inch, she gave him the grand tour. "Kitchen," she said pointing behind her. A point to the right. "Living room." She held out her left arm. "Down there's the bathroom and the spare bedroom, where your parents will room. Across the hall is my bedroom, where you can sleep."

He lowered Kaylee to the ground. "I'm not going to kick you out of your bed. I can sleep on the couch or something." The couch looked comfortable enough. In fact, he wouldn't mind trying it out right away. Just a quick nap. Take the edge off after this morning's therapy session.

"What? And take away my claim to fame?" Faith pressed her hands to her chest and laughed. "You did know that the goal of practically every girl at Fuller Lake High back in the day was to be your girlfriend, didn't you? Having you sleeping in my bed is good enough to make them all jealous."

He figured she was greatly exaggerating his role in the high school girls' dreams, but he felt heat rise to his cheeks, anyhow. He laughed like it was an inside joke. "I doubt your husband is as thrilled."

At the mention of her husband, her eyes sparkled the way Crystal's used to, once upon a very long time ago. "Russ knows my heart is with him." She nodded at the bedroom. "Come on. I'll show you to your digs."

"This is a nice place," Matt said as he followed her down the hallway. "Very efficient use of space."

"I'm willing to give it all up. First person I find to manage the building that Mom and Dad approve of, the job and this lovely apartment is all theirs." She led him into the room on the left and plopped onto the bed. "It's not like it's a hard job or anything, but I'm just tired of the hassle of trying to keep up with everything. It was fun when Russ was here." She shrugged. "Not so much fun with him gone."

"How long's he gonna be in Afghanistan?"

"Five more months. Then, when he comes back stateside, he's going to Fort McCoy for a year, but at least I can be with him. Mom and Dad'll just have to come back and watch their own damn apartments then because nothing's going to keep me from being with Russ." She sat there for a moment wearing a lonely expression. She sighed and pushed herself off the bed. "Well, anyhow, this is where you'll sleep tonight."

Jenny winked at Matt when they reemerged in the living room. "What were you doing with my baby sister for so long in there? Fulfilling all her high school dreams?"

Matt glanced at Crystal. A comment like that normally would have earned him a stare with narrowed eyes even though she knew it was only a joke. Now, she kept her eyes on the magazine on her lap. His heart gave an uncomfortable thump.

He pushed his head higher. Crystal was secure in their love, that's all. She knew she had no reason to be jealous.

His mother pushed herself off her kitchen chair. "Esther told us to put you into as many real-life situations as possible. What would you like to do, Matt?"

Sleep. Except, he didn't think that was what his mom had in mind.

"Real life?" Brad said. "That'd mean we men stay here and repair crap while you girls go out and spend our hard-earned money."

"Don't you mean you sit in front of the TV watching sports while we buy you snack foods?" Jenny's crossed arms didn't seem very threatening with the smile she was wearing.

"No, I think Brad's right," Matt said, liking the idea. Park himself in front of the TV. Close his eyes. Just for a little while. "I'm sure there are lots of odds and ends that need repair. If I know Dad, he's got tools with him."

"I think we *should* go to the mall," Crystal said.

Matt grinned. Sometimes Brad came up with the best ideas.

"All of us," Crystal said. "You men, included."

"What?"

"The mall is packed with real-life. You've got curbs and crowds and...I don't know. But I'm sure it'd be a good place to go."

"Need a new pair of shoes, do you?" Matt teased.

"No." So much indignation was packed into the miniscule word.

"I think Crystal's on the right track," his father said.

"Real life is annoying and there's nothing worse than a mall, so that means it's got to be the right choice."

Great. Not only was he not getting a nap, but he'd been sentenced to an afternoon in hell.

§

Ice cold grit soaked through Matt's knit gloves as he wheeled through the brown slush in the mall parking lot. The only good thing he foresaw about shopping was that at least the floors would be dry and it would be warm inside.

His father, just a few steps ahead of Matt, held open the door leading into the mall's food court. A herd of giggling teenagers pushed past Matt in a steady stream, taking advantage of the open door without so much as a "thank you" or "excuse me." He scrunched up his forehead and stared at the girls. What was he? Invisible?

A frigid wind lifted his hair and stung his cheeks and ears while he waited on the wrong side of the doors. Back in the old days, he could have squeezed his way in between the anorexic girls and joined his waiting family. Not now.

Seeing a break, Matt wheeled forward, only to be cut off by a mother pulling a screaming child behind her. He thought about saying "screw this" and heading back to the van, except that meant trudging through the slush again. Finally making it into the warmth of the building, Matt peeled off one wet glove and then the other. They'd never dry out in his coat pocket, but he didn't know what else to do with them.

"Ma...aatt," Crystal cried. "Those things are filthy."

"You want me to throw 'em away, or what?"

She shook her head and rolled her eyes.

A young woman swerved around Crystal and then paused for a heartbeat, her gaze trailing over Matt. Her mouth twisted and she looked away but not before radiating her unspoken thought. *What a waste.*

He closed his eyes and breathed deeply and slowly. That lady was wrong. He wasn't a waste. Still, he couldn't wait for his body to finally recover. He was tired of being tied to a wheelchair. Tired of wet gloves and dirty hands. Tired of people staring at him...or through him. Tired of it all.

He opened his eyes. "Let's just get this over with, okay?"

"Where would you like to go, dear?" his mother asked.

Home. "I don't care. Somewhere. Anywhere, other than here."

"Penney's," Jenny said.

"Build bear," Kaylee suggested.

"I'd like to go to Marshalls," Crystal said.

"Sounds like fun," Brad said, his tone indicating he'd rather not go to any of those places. "How about you girls go ahead and us guys'll check out that hat place we saw last week."

Hats? Yeah. Looking at hats was exactly what had first come to mind as a fun way to spend his time when he'd been told he was getting a weekend pass.

"I think we should stick together," his mother said. "This is Matt's outing. He should decide."

He couldn't imagine any place within the mall where he'd actually want to go, but the sooner they got going, the sooner they could go back to the apartment. "Marshalls."

Crystal beamed like she'd won a prize as she set off leading the way. Matt took up the rear, believing that his family would cut a path for him if they were in front. But just when he had a good speed going, his mother stopped, and he narrowly managed to swerve out of her way.

"Give me a signal before you stop like that." The words spilled out before he realized his lips had moved.

"I'm sorry. Something just caught my eye. Jenny, look." She pointed at a child's dress hanging in the store window. "Wouldn't Kaylee look adorable in that?"

And just like that, he ended up inside Kidz Korner, about the last place he wanted to be. For fifteen minutes, he followed the girls through narrow aisles with Hello Kitty dresses and Sponge Bob T-shirts swinging and swaying against his chair.

After two more detours, they finally reached Marshalls

where Crystal headed directly to the shoe department. Jenny held up a pair of shoes. "These are so cute. Crystal, don't you think so?"

He must have really done something horrible to deserve this kind of torture.

Crystal hung her purse on Matt's push handle. "You don't mind, do you, honey?" Without waiting for his answer, she turned her attention to her future sister-in-law. "Those would look nice with my pink jeans. And look at these." She pulled a pair of boots off the display table.

Before he knew it, Jenny had hung her purse and bags on his push handles, as well. He planted his elbow on the arm rest and propped up his head. At least he was useful.

He glanced over at Kaylee parked next to him in her stroller. She was all strapped in, unable to move. Shit. He'd struggled through growing up to end up just like a two-year-old. Stuck in a rolling chair. Unable to move.

Brad crouched down next to him and whispered, "Don't worry. I figure one more store and they'll forget we exist. Then we can go do something fun."

Two hours, one smoothie, and a soda later, the men were still stuck following the girls from store to store. His chair was decorated with enough shopping bags to start up his own mall. He'd been stared at and bumped into more times than he cared to count. He wanted nothing more than to go back to the apartment, spread himself out on the couch, and forget malls had ever been invented.

"Are we about done?" he asked.

"I'd like to check out the tool section at Sears," his father said, peeling back the wrapper on a roll of Tums.

"And we still need to stop by the hat place," Brad answered.

Traitors.

He sighed. Loudly. "In that case, I need to use the can. Where's the closest men's room?"

"There's one right down there," Crystal pointed.

"Then, that's where I'm headed."

He edged his way through the shoppers, going against the flow of traffic. Difficult enough of a task for the average, able-bodied person, it was compounded by the bulk of his chair and his inability to adjust directions quickly. Matt, seated below eye level, seemed to be invisible to the masses who were absorbed by their own little lives and agendas. He'd more than had his fill of crowds by the time he got to the restroom. Entering the quiet room was like stepping into heaven.

He wheeled to the handicapped stall. Just as he put out his hand to push open the door, he noticed the "Out of Order" sign.

"Damn."

He turned his chair, checking out the other stalls, none of which were designed for wheelchair entrance. What the hell good was having a handicapped stall if it wasn't available when someone needed it?

"Shit."

He left the sanctuary of the restroom and wheeled over to his father.

"Done already?" his dad asked.

Matt shook his head. "Where is everyone?"

"Well, the girls decided to go to the bathroom, too, and your brother's looking at T-shirts over there." He thrust his chin at the next store.

"Do you know where the next closest restroom is?"

His father's eyebrows raised, clearly wondering why Matt was asking. "About where we came in."

"Shit." There was no way he was going to wheel up to a urinal where everyone and his brother could watch him shove a catheter into his pecker. But he couldn't get inside a regular stall, and he didn't want to wade through half a mall's worth of people just to take a piss. The smoothie and the Coke no longer seemed like such a good idea.

With help, he could probably get inside a stall. His dad's help. The man he'd spent his life trying to impress. Now, he was supposed to ask his dad to get him on a shitter so he could take a piss.

He rubbed the back of his neck. "Where'd you say Brad was?"

"Right over there."

"I'll be back."

He found his brother looking at a shirt that said, *Carpenters Do it Level*. "I need your help," Matt said. "In the bathroom."

Brad raised an eyebrow. "I don't have a magnifying glass."

Asking for help was hard enough without his brother's wisecracks. "Just come help me, okay?"

"Yeah, sure."

Matt wheeled into the men's room and went to an open stall. "I need to get in there."

Brad looked at Matt, looked at the stall, and then looked back at his brother. "Can't you hold it?"

He wished he could. Damn, how he wished he could. "Just get in there and lift me up. I figure once you've got me up, you can swing me around."

Brad stood in the stall doorway. After putting his arms around Brad's neck, Brad lifted him up. Halfway to his feet, Matt realized the fatal flaw in his plan. Before he could say a word, Brad had him standing. The weight of all of the shopping bags sent the wheelchair crashing over backward.

Brad looked over Matt's shoulder. "Damn, I hope there wasn't anything breakable."

He almost hoped there was. "Maybe that'll teach 'em that my chair's for me, not for them, that it's not a hanger." Mentally planning out his next steps, Matt again wished he had skipped the drinks so he wouldn't be crowded into a toilet stall, relying on his brother's help. "Hang on to me tight."

Feeling his brother's arms tighten around him, Matt let go of his own grip and undid his button. At the sound of his zipper, Brad's wary voice said, "What are you doing?"

"What do you think? That I'm going to piss through my jeans?"

"God. I hope nobody comes in here."

You and me both. He lowered his jeans. "Turn me around and help me sit down."

They wouldn't have won points for style, but Brad

managed to get Matt centered on the toilet. And then, Matt remembered. "Somewhere buried under all that crap out there is my pack. I need it."

"Now's not the time to be fixing your makeup."

What they'd just done was bad enough, but to tell his brother what he needed totally pegged the embarrassment needle. "Just give me the damn pack, would you?"

"No need to snap." Brad dug out the pack, thrust it at his brother, and then slammed the stall door closed.

For a moment, all Matt could do was breathe. In. Out. Forcing out the anger and the embarrassment. Drawing in hope that this wasn't going to be his life forever. The stall door opened a couple inches as Brad let go. He caught flashes of movement and determined that Brad must be gathering up the spilled bags, mumbling under his breath the whole time about being owed, big time.

He didn't like the door not being closed all the way, but at least there wasn't anyone in the bathroom besides him and Brad. With one last deep breath, Matt opened the pack and took out a catheter. There wasn't any place to set the pack, so he tucked it under his arm and tried to work with his arm squeezed tightly to his side. On the other side of the door, Brad continued to grumble.

Just as Matt finished, Brad said, "I'll be right back."

Back? "Where are you going?"

The only answer he got was the sound of his chair being wheeled away. His chair. His freedom. "Wait," he shouted. "I'm done. Get your ass back here."

Like any good big brother, Brad ignored him.

"Damn it." Matt slammed his fist against the metal divider.

He was stuck in a damn toilet stall, of all places. He could imagine Brad standing outside in the hallway, laughing at how he'd pulled a good one.

"Damn it." He slammed the divider again, but he was just as trapped as before.

With a deep breath, he coiled the catheter back into its wrapper and jammed it in the pack. He stared at the backside of the toilet-stall door and waited. Thanks to the efficient mall maintenance employee who took his job way too seriously, there wasn't even any graffiti to read as he passed the time.

"He took my frigging chair," he mumbled while his shoulder muscles knotted. A lot of good the chair was if he was still dependent on others. He squeezed his eyes closed and breathed deeply and slowly, trying to force a sense of calm.

It was okay. Brad would come back. He wouldn't be stuck here forever.

As if to prove him correct, the outside door opened. Brad. Finally. But where were the sounds of his wheels rolling across the floor and the creak of the chair?

The door banged open, hitting Matt in the legs. It opened just enough to expose a gray-haired man, his eyes and mouth opened wide. And just enough to expose Matt to the man.

Perfect. Just perfect. Matt looked down, taking his eyes off the man who continued to stand there.

A lifetime later, the man said, "Oh, excuse me," and hurried from the restroom.

"I hate this," Matt muttered beneath his breath. "What did I do to deserve this?"

He sat there, mortified, his pants around his thighs and the pack nestled on his lap, with the toilet seat pressing a red ring into his ass that'd probably last for eternity. He wiggled his toes, willing the movement to migrate up his legs. If only he could walk. Just enough to get out of this damn stall.

I'll do anything, God. Just let me walk again. You name it.

God was silent.

Matt squeezed his eyes closed against the sudden urge to cry. *Just get me out of this. Please.*

The restroom door opened. This time, Matt heard the creak of his wheelchair.

"Where the fuck did you go? You took my chair and left me, damn it!"

"Sorry. I went to drop off the bags so your chair

wouldn't tip over again."

He tightened his jaw and glared at his brother's back as Brad took the pack and hung it on his chair, which was no longer decorated with shopping bags. He stayed quiet as his brother stood him upright, silently brooding about how much he hated every stinking moment of being paralyzed. He couldn't make it through a lifetime of this. He just couldn't.

Back in his chair, he wheeled out of the bathroom and over to his family. "I've had enough real-life situations for one day. I'm leaving, with or without you guys."

Without waiting for a response, he plowed through the sea of people toward the food court. He held his head high, but he had to bite down on his lips. Even then his vision still blurred, just a little. He blinked away the tears. He would not cry. Not here. Not now. Not ever.

CHAPTER THIRTEEN

Back at Faith's apartment, with the family gathered around the dining room table playing cards, Brad retold the men's room ordeal yet again. "Second I get him up, there goes the chair, crashing to the floor, with packages flying. Swear to God, we got some distance on Crystal's new shoes. You all should have been there. It was hilarious."

"A riot, for sure," Matt said while envisioning Brad choking on the potato chips he was shoving into his mouth by the handful. He glanced at the clock. Only eight o'clock. Felt a hell of a lot later. His gaze shot over to Kaylee playing on the floor with her new plastic horse. She looked like she had another four hours in her while Matt felt like he could close his eyes and fall asleep right there.

Across the table, his parents sat side by side, so close their arms touched even though there was plenty of room. Jenny sat next to Brad, with her head resting on his shoulder. Then, there was Crystal, beside him, yet far enough away that Kaylee could have stood between them. When had the distance formed between them? Had it always been there and he'd never noticed?

Brad snatched up another handful of chips from the bowl in the center of the table and set them on his plate. Jenny simply shifted her eyes, but it must have been enough for Brad to sense what she wanted. "My little health food nut," he said as he fed her a chip.

Like a baby bird, her mouth opened. She nestled closer to her husband as she chewed.

Matt put his hand on Crystal's thigh. He smiled when she covered his hand with her own. So what if she was sitting a little further away than he wanted?

More quickly than he'd have liked, it was Crystal's

turn to play and she took her hand off his, leaving his skin feeling like a cold wasteland. When he took his hand off her thigh to make his own play, he wondered if she felt the same sense of loss.

Her hand touched his leg and a rush of joy filled him. How lucky was he? But his smile had barely formed before she pulled it away. She reached for a chip and dropped it onto her plate without eating it. Only yesterday, it seemed, her hand had ricocheted off his leg when he'd been at St. Luke's, just like now. Nothing had changed.

And apparently, it wouldn't. Not unless he did something about it.

He took her hand firmly in his own. He put it on his thigh and held it in place. Her fingers squirmed beneath his hand like worms dropped on a hot frying pan. He focused his gaze on a spot on the wall while he worked hard to keep his face impassive. Inside, he was dying. What kind of marriage would they have if she couldn't stand to touch him?

As if she knew what he was thinking, her struggles stopped.

Then, it was her turn again. He let go of her hand. She held her fingers in place for a moment longer instead of making a quick escape. His eyes locked with hers. She smiled, gave his leg a squeeze, and pulled her hand away. After her turn, she scooted her chair closer and laid her head on his shoulder.

One second she was distant, the next, cuddled up to him. He had no idea which was real.

She kept her head on his shoulder until the next play. Slowly, with each subsequent play, she gravitated further away. He rubbed the tight tendons at the back of his neck. He was tired. That was all. He was reading in things that weren't there, something he wouldn't do wide awake.

He dropped his cards on the table. "Sorry guys, but I'm beat. I'm calling it a night."

His mother stood and gave him a hug and a kiss on the cheek. "Sleep tight, honey."

Jenny leaned over and gave him a little hug. "Thanks

for being such a trooper today at the mall. It was fun."

Fun. Yeah, right.

"Goodnight," Faith, Brad, and his father said as one.

Matt looked at Crystal. She was still for less than a second. Barely a blip in time. Still, as she leaned toward him and hugged him, he couldn't keep from thinking that it was all an act— Crystal doing what was expected and not what was real.

His mouth found hers. He searched out her true feelings as his tongue caressed hers. She met him, move for move, but it felt empty.

He felt empty.

And lost.

He pulled away. Tomorrow would be better. When he wasn't so damn tired. "Good night," he whispered.

§

Matt woke up early while the world was still dark. No Crystal cuddled in his arms. Not like he'd expected her to crawl into bed with him over night. Still, it would have been nice.

With much effort, he rolled over and closed his eyes, trying to fall back to sleep, but the apartment was too quiet. Realizing that trying to sleep would be futile, he decided to take advantage of the empty bathroom before everyone woke up.

Last night, he'd laid out the items he needed for bowel maintenance. He now put them to use and then waited until he could feel the little prickles at the back of his neck telling him it was time. Naked, he transferred into his wheelchair and covered himself with a bath towel, just in case he wasn't as alone as it seemed.

His bowels gurgled, telling him to hurry. That was one thing about trying to control what should have been a natural event. He'd discovered how little control he really had.

Since he couldn't feel pain, he couldn't feel the cramps building. His body alerted him in other ways, though. The prickles he'd felt earlier spread over his upper body. He grew hot. Things were moving more quickly than normal.

He was glad he'd given the toilet a test drive yesterday to get a feel for what he could grab on to in making his transfer.

He opened the door to the hallway. The apartment was dark except for a glow coming from a nightlight in the bathroom. The only noise was Brad's snoring from the living room. Trying to be quiet, yet hurrying at the same time, Matt wheeled into the hallway. A flash of heat struck. There wasn't much time. Damn good thing the bathroom was close.

Giving another push on the wheels, his chair stopped suddenly and his head jerked forward.

"What the—" He managed to cut off his words. Hopefully, before waking everyone up. He backed up the chair and groaned when he saw the luggage and bags stacked up against the wall, right in his way. He backed up further and edged closer to the other side of the hall, but the path was too narrow for his chair.

Another wave of heat struck. Sweat broke out under his arms, on the inside of his elbows, and at the back of his neck. He had to get in the bathroom.

He grabbed the closest bag and threw it. A duffel bag followed. He no longer cared about being quiet. All he cared about was getting to the toilet. His breath sucked out of him with another flash of heat, yet he reached for another bag.

"What's going on?" Crystal asked from behind him.

"Some idiot blocked my path to the bathroom."

"We needed room in the living room for sleeping. I thought putting it here was best, out of the way."

She'd done this to him? Crystal? The one person out of everyone who should have been looking out for him? "Have you never noticed how fucking wide my chair is?"

She crossed her arms. "There's no need to swear."

"The hell there isn't. I'm about to shit all over the place. I need to get in the bathroom. Now!" A cold sweat bathed him. "Oh, God." He squeezed his eyes closed as the prickles crawled beneath his skin while chills competed with another blast of sudden heat.

He sat upright, trying to push his ass as tightly to the chair as possible, hoping to delay things. "Just move the stuff, and make it quick."

She picked up a bag and carefully set it off to the side.

"Now!" he growled.

Another wave of chills hit him at the same time she moved the last suitcase. He raced past her, barely taking time to swing the door closed. He no more than got his ass on the toilet when his body let loose.

"Damn it," he growled, realizing what a close call that'd been. The sweats vanished as his temperature returned to normal, taking the prickles with it. He hung his head and pictured the mess there would have been had it taken him one second longer.

He shouldn't blame Crystal, but damn it. Any idiot could look at his chair, look at the hallway, and quickly determine he needed every inch. He shouldn't have to explain that to her.

§

The apartment was still quiet and dark by the time he emerged from the bathroom. Feeling heavy with exhaustion, Matt transferred to the bed and pulled the covers up. He closed his eyes, but a hopeless sensation he couldn't shake kept him from falling back to sleep.

A couple of months ago, his life had been so great. Now it was... He puffed out a disgusted laugh as the word came to him. Shit. That's what it was. Shit.

How had he drifted so far off track from where he was supposed to be?

A better question was, how was he supposed to get back to that point? If he didn't recover, he'd never get there.

Like he'd done so many times in the past, he focused on his toes, moving each one of them. Then, he concentrated on his ankles, willing them to move. Just the littlest bit would have made him happy. But it wasn't happening.

Someone moved in the hallway. A moment later, the bathroom door closed. It didn't take long before the toilet flushed. A second later, there was a light knock on his door.

He pictured Crystal. Except, she never would have left the bathroom without washing her hands. "Yeah," he answered.

The door swung open slowly to reveal Brad, his blond hair mussed. "Mind if I come in?"

"Yeah, sure. I wasn't doing anything important." Just fighting a heaping dose of depression.

Brad paused, like he was thinking of leaving.

"Just get in here, would ya?" Matt worked hard to sit up, conscious of his brother staring at him like he was a circus freak. Too bad he'd missed the early show. Matt dragged himself backward to lean against the headboard.

Brad finally came in, closing the door behind him. He sat in the wheelchair and fiddled with the wheels, moving himself forward and back. Which meant whatever he wanted to say was big.

"I doubt you came in here to play."

Brad pulled his hands onto his lap. "I was thinking about this group home contract. I know Dad told you to cut it close. Is the bid doable?"

"Would I write up a bid that wasn't?"

"No, I mean..." Brad looked away. He ran a hand through his hair, messing it up even more.

A rock dropped in the pit of Matt's stomach. "You mean is the bid doable with me stuck in a wheelchair, don't you?"

"Well, now that you mention it." Like Matt had been the one to start the conversation.

"Even though we all knew it was a possibility you wouldn't recover, none of us wanted to believe it. The build's only about five weeks away." He became interested in the wheelchair's brake.

"And..." Matt prompted.

"I, uh, I think we have to stop ignoring the fact that you're not coming back to work."

Not coming back to work.

The words worked their way through him. Like an insect beneath his skin. Gnawing. He crossed his arms.

"Who says I'm not coming back."

Brad looked up and arched his eyebrows. A who-are-you-kidding look. "Do you really think you can do the job in this thing? Hell, you can't even..."

The truth prickled beneath his skin. He didn't like the truth. A fight was much easier to deal with. "Can't what? Take a piss without help?"

Brad's only answer was a rise of his eyebrows.

"What do you want from me?" Matt spit out.

"I want you to tell Dad to hire someone in your place."

There it was. All laid out in the open like a deer that'd been gutted.

"I love you," Brad said. "I don't want you out of the business, but I've got a wife and kid who expect to see me longer than one hour a day."

The bathroom door closed. Out in the living room came the sound of Kaylee giggling. From across the hall came the sound of their father's coughing. Sounds of life.

"You know as well as I do that if you're on the payroll, that means we can't hire help. If we can't hire help, then that means we all have to work fifteen or sixteen-hour days, and we'll still be lucky to get the project done in time. I can't be away from my family that long."

"Sure, fine. How, exactly, do you think my quitting is going to help? You know Dad won't hire anyone but a Huntz."

"This job is important enough that he'll bend his rule. He won't admit it, but he wants the contract on the new build."

"And I want it, too. If you remember, I'm the one who wanted Dad to bid on this job. I'm the one who said it'd be good for our image if we did a job that was good for the community. I want to be a part of the build."

Brad went back to playing with the wheelchair, rolling it back and forth. More news he wanted to share but couldn't spit out without working up to it. Matt waited him out. What he really wanted to do was yell at his brother that the wheelchair wasn't a toy and to stop messing with it. As if Brad had read Matt's thoughts, he

stopped rocking the chair.
Here it comes.
"You remember what a hard time Jenny had when she was pregnant with Kaylee? How she had to spend those last two months in bed?"
"Yeah." They'd all been worried because she'd already lost a baby. Worried or not, he couldn't figure out what Jenny's bed rest had to do with anything.
Brad's eyes shifted, like he was making sure they were alone. He leaned forward. "She's pregnant."
Matt laughed. "Another little Kaylee?"
"Shhh. We haven't told anyone yet. We'll have to soon, though. She's five months along. She won't be able to hide her beach-ball belly much longer."
"Late July?" Matt asked, making the instant calculation.
"If she goes that long. You see, now, why I can't be putting in fifteen hour days? She's going to need me at home."
Faced with the real possibility of quitting, he wanted to dig in his heels and be as stubborn as his father. "Construction's all I've ever done."
A quiet knock sounded on the door followed by Faith's voice. "You two going to spend all day in there gossiping while we girls try to corral Kaylee?"
"We're coming," Brad said.
"I'll be out in a bit," Matt said as his brother stood. Brad gave him a quick, pleading look and then turned to leave. As soon as the door clicked closed, Matt focused his attention yet again on his ankles, willing them to move, just a fraction of an inch. The air turned too thick to breathe.
So, he couldn't move his foot yet. A month ago, he couldn't move even one toe. It'd come.
But would it come in time for him to be of any help?
The door opened. He forced a smile, praying he looked calm and collected instead of like the mass of gelatin he felt like inside.
"Unka Matyou, come play."

The smile became real. He patted his lap. "Come here, munchkin. Give your ol' Uncle Matt a good morning hug."

She crawled up on the bed and hugged him. He rubbed his bristly cheek against her soft one, smiling inside as she giggled. What a hole there'd be in his life without her. His smile faded. What kind of hole would there be if Jenny lost the new baby?

He gave her a quick squeeze. "How about you go find Grandpa? Let me get dressed. Then I'll come play."

She wiggled her way off the bed and then went running. "Gampa, gampa."

When he wheeled out to the kitchen a while later, his eyes immediately went to Jenny, who smiled back. His gaze lowered to her stomach. Sure enough, she had a roundness he was surprised he hadn't noticed and even more surprised nobody else had.

His gaze shifted to Crystal, who held Kaylee on her hip. She smiled the perfect smile. The one that said she was happy he was up, happy to see him, happy they were together. For just one brief moment, her eyes said something else before the expression shifted to match the smile.

"Hi, honey," she said. "Sleep well?"

"Yeah," he said as he stared into her eyes. In that brief moment, he thought he'd seen a glimmer of despair. Surely he was imaging things that weren't there. But he wondered, would there be a real glimmer in three months when they stood at the altar and she realized what she was getting herself into? How about a few months later? After she'd put up with him and his wheelchair long enough to know that wasn't what she wanted?

"What is all the noise?" his father said, stepping up beside Crystal. He tweaked Kaylee's nose. "This little girl is way too loud."

Kaylee giggled. It hadn't been noisy before his father stepped into the room, but it was now, and it stayed that way until breakfast was served and eaten. Brad and Kaylee moved into the living room and stretched out on the floor in front of the TV. Matt looked on with envy. He wouldn't mind getting down there as well, except it was too hard to get back into his chair. So he turned his attention back to the Sunday paper spread out in front of him, now open to the want ads. Bar None was looking for a bartender. The exact job he'd always wanted if construction hadn't panned out. Not.

Hansen, Nelson, and Jones wanted to expand their accounting firm by adding a new accountant on an apprenticeship program. Blue Moon Casino was looking for a blackjack dealer. Beaver Manufacturing needed a computer programmer who could read blueprints. Sally's diner was looking for a short-order cook.

His gaze went back to the Blue Moon Casino job. Too bad it was in Milwaukee and not Fuller Lake. He could almost see himself as a blackjack dealer.

He shook his head. What the hell was he thinking? He was a builder, not a card jockey. He'd be better off with the Beaver Manufacturing job. Other than the fact he wasn't looking for a new job, and he knew nothing about computer programming.

"I'll bet you're excited about going home next week," Faith said. "It's great your parents can move in for a while to help you out."

Matt looked up from the paper, his eyes landing on his fiancée. In that second, he realized Abby was right. He really needed to know Crystal could handle being married to him. "I was thinking Crystal should move in, instead."

The room turned silent. Faith's eyes darted from person to person, the crinkle of her forehead clearly showing her curiosity as to what she was missing.

Crystal was the first to speak. "I seem to recall you saying, and I quote, 'People live together because they don't believe in forever.'"

"I have no choice in whether I want to deal with all the crap..." He paused for just a heartbeat on the word that seemed rather poetic, given this morning's events. "...that comes with being paralyzed. You do. I want you to be sure you can put up with it now, before we're married, instead of finding out when it's too late."

Her fingers went to her engagement ring. She wiggled the ring back and forth over her knuckle. "I know what I'm getting myself into, Matt. It doesn't change my mind. I still want to marry you."

"Good." He punctuated the word with a nod. "And I'll feel that much more confident on our wedding day if I know you've had every opportunity to really see what you're getting into." He reached across the table and grabbed her hands, stopping her from playing with the ring. "I love you Crystal, and I would hate like hell if you decided to leave me, but I'd hate it even more if you did it after we got married."

"I think it's a good idea," Matt's mother said.

Everyone's eyes shifted from Matt to his mother. She shrugged. "Well, I do. Marriages have broken up over stupid little details like she can't stand his snoring or he can't stand the way she folds his underwear. This isn't a little thing."

"But it's not going to change how I feel," Crystal said as she pulled her hands free.

"Then what's the problem?" Jenny asked. "You're getting married in three months, anyhow."

Now, the eyes shifted to Crystal. She looked down as though to avoid the glare of ten spotlights. She rubbed her diamond with the pad of her index finger. "Fine." She looked up. "I'll move in. No big deal."

"Good. It's settled, then." Matt let his gaze shift to his dad and another realization settled in. "I need your help in the bedroom for a second."

He eyed the rumpled bed as he wheeled into the room. He tried to picture Crystal there. Next week. He'd be waking up with her. At his side. Together.

Forever?

All he saw was an empty bed.

He heard his father behind him. He turned the chair around. Damn, his father looked old. Not old in years, but old as in tired and worn down. "Close the door."

The door closed with a soft thud.

His breakfast gurgled inside his stomach. The room

became too stuffy. He looked forward to going home next week, but at the same time, he wished there was another month, or even longer—however much time he needed for his body to wake up and let him walk again.

His father stared at him with both eyebrows arched, patiently waiting, yet curious.

There wasn't another month, and time was running out. He drew in a breath. "I'm giving you my notice. Go hire someone in my place."

The curious expression and the look of exhaustion disappeared with a flash of narrowed eyes. "No. The name of the business is Huntz & *Sons*. You hear that *s*? Sons."

"Yeah. And one of your sons is useless— "

"Bullshit." His father rarely got angry, but there was no denying it now. Not with the veins straining his neck. "You are far from useless and don't you let anyone tell you that you are. Who's telling you this crap?"

"I am, Dad. I'm saying it."

"I did not raise you to quit before you even try." His father poked his finger in the air as he spoke, spittle flying from his lips. "You are not dropping out of the family business that I know you love, just because you're afraid of falling on your face."

"I'm not afraid." It was a true statement...for the most part. He was afraid he couldn't do the job. He was afraid of failing. But he wasn't letting fear keep him from trying.

"Good. Then this discussion is over." He held Matt's gaze. "Over. For once and for all."

"No, it isn't. You guys are working your asses off, trying to cover for me. Your health is going down the shitter."

"There's nothing wrong with my health."

Matt stared hard at his father. "Tell that to someone who didn't see you coughing up blood."

"That was nothing but a touch of bronchitis. I'm fine, now."

"Sure. And that's why you're single-handedly keeping the Tums factory going."

His father leaned close, his eyes burning into Matt's retinas. "There's nothing wrong with my health. And you are not quitting. This discussion is over. And that's final."

"That went well," Matt said to the empty room after his father stormed away.

A short while later, Brad came in. He leaned on the doorjamb. "What'd you say to make him so cheerful?"

"I told him I was quitting."

Brad's eyes widened. He looked down the hallway and then back at Matt.

"Yeah," Matt said. "As you can guess, he didn't accept my resignation."

"Shit, Matt, you've got to make him understand that he's got to hire someone else."

He understood where Brad was coming from, but he bristled at his brother's plea. "You want someone in my place, then *you* convince him."

"I can't do that." His eyes rounded with desperation. "You know I can't go to Dad and tell him to replace you."

"You could if you wanted it bad enough."

"Great. I'll get right on it." He leaned his head back, letting it thump against the doorjamb.

§

The sun broke over the horizon on Monday morning with a dazzling display of pinks and blues in a promise of a wonderful day. Matt knew better. This past weekend proved there would be no more wonderful days for him. Not as long as he was stuck in a wheelchair.

He sighed. So he'd had one bad weekend. That didn't mean his life was over. Put your chin up and move on, his mother would say.

Easier said than done, he thought as he backed away from the window.

"Knock, knock," Abby said from his doorway. Her voice sparkled just like her eyes. So alive and full of promise, lifting his spirits.

"How'd it go?" she asked. "Tell me everything."

"Everything?" Memories of the weekend pulled him back down into the pit once again. He didn't figure she really wanted to hear all the dirty details, but they spilled out, anyhow. "You mean like how my brother left me stranded in a public toilet?"

Abby's lips disappeared between her teeth and her eyebrows arched. He instantly knew she was working hard to hold in a laugh.

"It's not funny," he shot at her.

"I'm sorry. I just wasn't expecting that. You have to admit, of all the places to be stuck, a toilet's right up there. I hope he at least left you with a good magazine."

Against his will, he laughed. He had to admit, laughing felt a whole lot better than being angry. "A guy walked in on me. You should have seen his face. I never heard anyone scurry from a room so fast in my life. Once he got moving, that is."

"The sight of you on a toilet is that frightening?"

"Must be." He sighed. "The weekend was nothing like I'd expected. You name anything that could have gone wrong, it probably happened."

She sat on the edge of his bed. "I'm sorry things didn't go well."

He snorted out a sad little laugh. "Didn't go well? That's an understatement." She was five feet away, plenty close enough for any conversation, yet he wheeled closer until their knees nearly touched. "If that's a taste of what real life's like, I don't want it."

"It won't always be that hard."

"What if it is? I can't live like that." He'd used up two months of his eighteen-month window for recovery. There were times when he wished the eighteen months were over, so they wouldn't be hanging over his head as a constant reminder.

She put her hand on his knee. Her eyes locked on to his. "You're stronger than you think, Matt."

The way she said it made it sound like she believed it were true, instead of just spouting off words of encouragement. He flattened his palm against his thigh, bringing their hands closer together. "What if I'm not?"

"You are."

He loved that about her. The way she believed in him, even when he didn't.

The sun stretched past the trees, shedding light into his room and bathing Abby's hair in golden highlights, like a newly anointed angel.

"I can do this, can't I?"

"You can." She pressed her fingertips lightly into his knee, as though pressing the truth into him.

His lips parted and his heart gave an erratic beat as he became fully conscious of her touch. Her, touching him. Like he was just average ol' Matt instead of a paralyzed man. He concentrated on the feel of her hand against his leg. "I love the way you do that."

Her nose twitched just a little as she frowned. "Do what?"

"The way you touch me."

Pink highlights colored her cheeks. Like a cut rubber band, her hand sprang away. She stood and crossed her arms, her hands tucked against her sides. "I really should be getting to the gym."

"Damn it." The words slipped out. Now, not only was she not touching him, she was leaving, too. He should have kept his mouth shut.

Her eyebrows arched with understanding. "Crystal doesn't touch you anymore, does she?"

He tried to smile like it didn't matter, but he could tell by how tight his facial muscles pulled that he was failing.

Abby crouched and put both of her hands on his legs. "You have to give her time. I'm sure she's having as hard a time adjusting as you are."

He slid his hands closer to hers until their fingers touched. "And what if she never adjusts?"

"She will." She said it with confidence, like she was an authority on the subject. The important part was, he let himself believe it was true.

"Thanks, Abby."

"You're welcome." She stood. "And now, I really must go." She took three steps before she turned back, her mouth bent in a smile. "Your brother really left you in the bathroom?"

He laughed. "Really."

"That story I need to hear, Mr. Huntz."

"Tonight."

She gave him a little wave and, all too soon, he was alone. He brushed his thumb over his leg where her hand had been. Remembering her touch, he closed his eyes and said a little prayer while thinking of Crystal. *I want a wife who's not afraid to touch me. Please, God. If you're going to leave me stuck in this chair forever, just let that happen. Let me have a wife who'll touch me.*

CHAPTER FOURTEEN

The sound of weights clanging serenaded Abby as she filled in the last of her patient charts the following Thursday. She glanced at her watch. Seven, already? Matt was usually done and out of here by now. Of course, she was usually long done with her charts by now, as well. She'd moved more slowly tonight, stretching out their last night together.

The noise from across the room stopped. She watched Matt from the corner of her eye, like she always did, while he pulled on the fingerless leather gloves. He was one well-put-together man. She gave a little laugh as she remembered their first meeting, his fear that he wouldn't be able to please Crystal. He had no idea that there was absolutely nothing lacking in him. Not in looks and most certainly not in personality.

He wheeled across the room and stopped by the desk. "Once again, thank you for letting me tie up your evening."

She put down her pen. "My pleasure." She wondered if he knew how much truth were in those words. The time she'd spent with him were cherished moments. Moments she would miss once he left.

"What are you going to do with all your spare time now that you're not going to have to stay late for me?"

"Oh, I'll still have my paperwork."

His fingers were wrapped around the push rims, but he didn't look eager to leave anytime soon. "Really, I do appreciate your letting me come here every night. The talks afterward, too."

"The talks were nice." More like the highlight of her day.

He scratched his fingernail in a groove on the desktop. He wanted to ask something. She could tell. Just working up the courage. She gave him the space he needed.

Finally, he pulled his hand away. "You said something once about how every day that goes by without some recovery makes it that much less likely to have more of a recovery." His gaze rose to meet hers. "It's been a month since there's been any change. Does that mean this is all I get?"

She wanted to lie and tell him he'd walk again, but that wouldn't do him any good. "The truth? Or something soft and gentle?"

He shrugged.

"Statistically, you've probably reached your plateau."

He put on a brave smile that wavered before it held. He nodded. "Thanks for the truth."

She couldn't leave it at that, because she wanted a happy ending for him as much as he did. If there were any way to make it so he'd walk again, she'd do it. "Should you give up? No. The Internet is full of miracle stories of people beating the odds, having a recovery they were told would never happen. We don't know, Matt. That's the problem. We simply don't know." She reached across the desk, wanting so badly to grab his hands and fill him with her own energy, to somehow heal him. Instead, she pressed her palms to the scarred laminate top. "If anyone's a rule breaker, it's you."

His eyes turned cloudy. He nodded. The muscles of his jaw tightened, relaxed, and then tightened. Matt, working his way from what he wanted over to reality. It wasn't even a guess on her part. She already knew him that well, which made her thankful he was leaving. If he stayed any longer, she might start thinking of him more as a man and less as a patient. Nothing good could come from that.

"Just stay on this side of hope, the real side," she said. "Don't let hope rule you, and you'll be fine."

He crossed his arms and stared hard at her, his head tipped. He reminded her so much of the man she'd met that first day, but, at the same time, he'd come a long way. His eyes bored into her once again. "What?" she asked.

"Just thinking back to that first day. What a pain in the ass you were. You're still a pain in the ass, but I've gotten used to you." He laughed. "Damn, I can't believe I'm about to say this. I'm going to miss you."

"I'll miss you, too, Matt."

"If I gave you my number, think we could keep in touch?"

A light and airy sensation filled her. For just a second, she pretended there was no Crystal. She pretended love wasn't a four-letter word. She pretended fairytales were real. And then, the second was over. She forced herself back into the real world. Like it or not, Crystal did exist. Love was the ultimate four-letter word. Both Paul and Jovan had proven that fairytales were nothing but fictional stories. She was thankful Matt had allowed her their friendship, but that was all it was and all it ever could be. Now it was time to let go. "I'd like that, but I really don't think Crystal would."

"Yeah, you're probably right."

"Probably?"

He laughed again, the tone deep and rich, a sound she wished she could bottle and keep forever. "Not much question about it." He rapped his knuckles on the desk. "I should go."

"In case I forget to say it tomorrow, I hope things go well with you and Crystal, and that you get that big family you want."

Again, his jaw twitched like he was working his way from what he wanted over to reality. "Thanks."

§

Matt's arms stayed in steady motion as he wheeled down the hallway the next morning after his last therapy session. His goal was to be packed by the time Crystal and his parents arrived. Get the car loaded up before the engine had time to cool off. And be on their way. Home.

He had the wheelchair humming so fast he had to grip the push rims to slow down when he reached his room. His parents were already here, fowling up his "be packed before they showed up" plan, but he couldn't think of a better plan to get messed up.

His mother dropped the shirt she'd been refolding and

rushed toward him. Her hug threatened to squeeze the air from his lungs. He looked around the room the best he could while being pinned to his chair. His father stood by the window, grinning. He looked better, much better than when Matt had transferred from St. Luke's. But he still looked older than he had before Matt's accident. Maybe now that he was going home, that'd change.

His father left his perch and patted his wife's shoulder. "Honey, let go. He's turning blue."

The greeting cards and Kaylee's drawings that had papered the walls were gone. Boxes and bags lined a pushcart by the bed. Everything seemed to be in order for his release, except for one thing. Crystal was missing.

Crystal said she'd come. She'd asked for time off work as soon as they'd known his release date.

"I'm sorry." His mother's words came out choked. "It's just this day's been a long time coming."

This day. His homecoming. After eight and a half long weeks, he was going home.

Reality struck hard. He was really going home. Today was no longer some abstract date in the future. It was today. Now.

His father stared at him with that shit-eating grin. The man who'd mentally had him back to work with that first quarter-sized patch of sensation.

His mother still hovered close by. The woman who'd had him walking down the aisle.

And his fiancée, the woman he was supposed to escort down that aisle, was nowhere to be seen.

The wheelchair suddenly felt too hard, pressing against every part of his body. He took small, quick breaths. None of his plans were panning out. The damn chair wasn't supposed to be a part of this moment. He was supposed to be walking out of here.

"Honey?" his mother said.

His father stood straighter. "Matt?"

Matt forced a smile. "Just surprised by how much you got done already." Where the hell was Crystal?

The toilet in the little bathroom flushed. His gaze shot

to the bathroom door. Water ran in the sink. He held his breath. After what felt like a lifetime, the door finally opened and Crystal filled its void.

"You're here."

She laughed. "Of course I am." She gave him a hug, one that felt one hundred percent genuine. "Are you ready to go home?"

Home. With her. He nodded and placed his hand in hers. "More than ready."

The doctor knocked on the doorjamb and then entered the room. "I see you're ready to go. However, I have some last-minute instructions."

Matt nodded while the doctor reminded him to redistribute his weight often to avoid sores. He waited for the doctor to say something along the lines of *Enjoy the wheelchair because you're going to be in it forever.* There'd actually be a level of relief in hearing those words. Something that would allow him to move forward without the pressure of maintaining the hope that he'd walk again. Something that would allow him to look his father in the eye and say, "Sorry, Dad, I screwed up. This is the best you get."

The doctor was saying something about outpatient therapy. Before he knew it, the doctor was shaking his hand. No grim news that he may have reached his healing plateau. No release of responsibility.

"Good luck, Matthew. If you have questions, feel free to call."

The doctor barely disappeared from sight when Esther came into the room, along with one of the CNAs. She held three glittery gift bags tied closed with curled ribbon streamers. "These are just some homemade cookies. Going home presents." She put the bags on the cart. "Are you ready?"

Matt looked at his mother. The clothes were all packed, the suitcase now on the cart. She nodded. He tightened his fingers around Crystal's. "Yep. I'm ready."

Esther stepped behind him and gave the wheelchair a push. "I never did quite figure out this policy. We spend hours in therapy teaching you how to operate the chair in every possible situation, but we don't let you wheel yourself out of the center."

The cart rattled behind them, manned by the CNA. Esther pushed him down the hallway. She stopped at the intersection to let a woman pushing a food cart pass. He looked toward the doorway to the gym. Behind those doors, Abby was busy being a pain in the ass with someone other than him.

He tightened his fists. Abby wasn't his future. Crystal was. He looked back at his fiancée, grounding himself to his dreams. Home. He was going home.

The food cart moved down the hall and Esther turned to the left. Within minutes, they were in the lobby. Through the window, he could see Jenny's mini-van parked in the first patient pickup spot. Esther pushed the button mounted on the wall and the doors parted. The wheelchair moved forward. He looked over his shoulder. "Let me."

With a nod, she released the wheelchair. He placed his palms against the rims but didn't move. The doors closed.

His palms grew sweaty. He let his gaze rove around the lobby and then looked through the glass at the outside world. Once he passed through those doors, this was going to be one hundred percent real.

His father cleared his throat.

His mother squeezed his shoulder. "You'll do fine."

His heart fluttered.

Crystal stood in front of him. She smiled and nodded at the doors. He moved his head up and then down, just a tiny fraction. Esther pushed the button and the doors slid open. A light breeze touched his cheeks. He took a deep breath and then pushed forward.

He was going home.

CHAPTER FIFTEEN

The passing landscape of fields and woods, broken by the occasional town, had a mesmerizing effect on Matt. Through half-closed eyes, he stared at the back of his mother's headrest while the speakers cranked out an old Pink Floyd tune. Something about dogs. A song he could easily live without, just like the rest of the CD. Unfortunately, the tune blipped through his head, anyhow.

Crystal had curled up against him somewhere around Fond du Lac, and she'd been asleep pretty much ever since. He wished he could have fallen asleep, as well. Then he wouldn't have to listen to his father's crap music. But now, they were almost home.

He blinked and tried to force his eyes open, but his eyelids went back to half-mast. Through tiny slits he saw the sign welcoming them to Fuller Lake. Population eight thousand three hundred and twelve. As if she had some built-in GPS, Crystal lifted her head. "We're home, already?"

"Umm," was his answer, but her words had a revitalizing effect on him. Home. He was back home. He looked from window to window at his hometown, soaking up all the sights, like he'd been away two years instead of two months.

The tires thumped over the cracks in the road. A rhythmic sound. *Hurry. Hurry. Hurry.*

"How does it feel to be back?" Crystal moved her hand. Sunlight bounced off her engagement ring.

He stared at the ring much the way he'd stared at his mother's headrest earlier, wishing he could remember what had happened the night of the accident.

Forget it. Don't wreck today with things you're never going to figure out.

Today was a good day. He was on his way home. With Crystal. She'd already moved her necessary possessions to his house, mingling her belongings with his. Just like a married couple.

Hurry. Hurry. Hurry.

But they weren't a married couple. Not yet. And if this trial run failed, it'd be never.

The scenery flashed by too quickly now, as if life were zooming toward the unhappy conclusion of this test run. Certain his father was stuck on highway speed, he looked at the speedometer. Thirty. Five over the limit. Technically speeding, but allowable speeding.

Hurry. Hurry. Hurry. Hurry. Hurry. Hurry.

He put his hand against his ear, pressing it flat enough to feel the suction, but he could still hear the road's mantra. *Hurry. Hurry. Hurry.* His mind countered with—*Stop. Stop. Stop.*

"Matt?"

He tightened his arm around Crystal and told himself to chill out. She wasn't going to leave. "It's going to be good, babe."

With determination, he told himself it would be good. Tomorrow, he'd wake up with Crystal at his side. Later, when they finally got out of bed, they'd make breakfast together, shower together, go shopping together. From now on, their lives would be spent...together.

Crystal settled her head against him again, trapping him between her and the seat. They passed the lake the town's name was based on. It was actually a wide spot in a narrow river that cut through the city. To the west was the two-block stretch that made up the entire downtown. Most of the townsfolk complained about Fuller Lake's small size, but that's what Matt liked best. In a small town, everyone knew each other and there was a sense of family. In a big city, you simply were lost among the masses.

They proceeded north. Eight blocks later, his father slowed and turned on to Park Street. Matt watched as they passed familiar houses until they reached his block.

He sat up straighter and scanned the left side of the block. Balloons and streamers hung from the gingerbread trim around his porch roof. A banner was spread across the white spindle posts. "Welcome home." A mound of snow separated the driveway from a browned lawn. After a few more warm days, that snow would be gone, as well, and the lawn would go from brown to green.

His father slowed and pulled into the driveway. He came to a stop in front of the garage that was filled with Matt's toys—motorcycle, snowmobile, riding lawnmower. Crystal's CRX was parked on the lawn between the garage and the house.

The scene looked so normal. The only thing missing was his two-year-old Chevy Silverado, too mangled in the accident to salvage.

His gaze shifted toward the back of his house. A few feet of the newly constructed ramp showed. So much for "normal." His father slid out from behind the steering wheel. A moment later, he reappeared, the empty wheelchair in front of him. Yup, so much for "normal."

Matt looked over at his neighbor's house. Mrs. Mezmitz peered out through the crack between the curtains. She waved and then let the curtains close. He knew she was still there. Watching him from behind the sheets of lace. He pulled the wheelchair into position. He could feel Mrs. Mezmitz watching as he awkwardly hauled his body into the chair. As long as there was a show, she'd watch. Putting an end to the entertainment portion of her day, he wheeled up the ramp that ran the length of his deck. His mother held open the door. The scent of fresh varnish filled the air. The kitchen looked the same, other than the addition of a coffee machine and new trim around the doorway leading to the hall.

"We had to widen the door," his father said.

Matt gave the countertop another inspection. Other than the coffee maker, nothing had changed. Which was wrong. There should be more than just the coffee maker. The countertop should be filled with Crystal's cat cookie jar and her canisters and all of the rest of her kitchen counter crap.

"Come see the bathroom," his mother said, motioning him forward.

He wheeled his way around the refrigerator, through the doorway, and into the hall. He stopped in front of the open bathroom door. Like the kitchen, there was a lack of that feminine touch he'd been expecting. However, there were changes from the bathroom he used to know. The pedestal sink that had been in hibernation in the garage since December was now in place, the mirror lowered to his eye level. Gone was the claw-foot tub. In its place was a modular shower stall. A manual showerhead was visible through the opaque glass, the showerhead placed three and a half feet from the floor. A plastic shower bench was visible, as well. A built-in wood cabinet filled the space between the wall and the shower unit.

Everything perfect for a paralyzed man.

"What'd you do with my tub?"

"It's in the storage shed for now."

Matt nodded, but he wanted everything put back where it belonged. The claw tub back in the bathroom. The pedestal sink back in the garage. The "paralyzed-man" shower stall back at the home improvement center.

He started to back out of the room but stopped when he noticed something shiny on the wall next to the toilet. He rubbed his hand over his mouth as he stared at the handrail. The lowered showerhead was bad enough, but a friggin' handrail. In his house. For his use.

He wiggled his toes.

If anyone's a rule breaker, it's you.

Hang on to the hope, he reminded himself as he backed out of the bathroom. He was more than happy to escape the room so full of evidence that he was no longer the same man he'd been the last time he'd been in his house.

The varnish scent almost gagged him as he followed his father into the room that used to be a den. The carpet had been removed, the hardwood floors resurfaced. A closet had been built in the corner of the room.

He'd expected to find Crystal's frilly comforter and bed ruffle. Instead, his old blanket covered the bed that was centered on the wall with access from either side.

Her comforter, his blanket—didn't matter. What mattered was that the bed wasn't just his anymore. Tonight, Crystal would be there with him. Maybe sooner, if he could convince her to take a nap with him. The second wind he'd gotten was winding down.

A lot of time and care had gone into the remodeling project. Other than the missing tub and the addition of the handrails, he liked the changes. He looked up at his dad. "I appreciate you having done all this for me."

"Actually, you should thank Derrick," his mother said. "He did most of the work."

He'd have to thank Derrick when he came over later. There weren't plans in the works for a visit, but he couldn't imagine his friend staying away.

Matt wandered over to the closet and ran his fingers against the glossy doors. Like usual, Derrick had done an outstanding job. With a head full of brains, Derrick could have done anything with his life. Instead, he'd forgone college to work for Matt's dad, something Matt never could understand, but it'd been to his father's benefit.

He opened the closet door. The clothes rod was lower than normal, putting the hangers in Matt's easy reach. More proof of how much his world had changed.

His shirts were evenly spaced across the rod. His mother's touch. Matt gave the clothes another look, a frown forming. "Crystal? Where are your clothes?"

"I put them upstairs."

"Why?"

"So my clothes would be where I am."

Why'd she have to make this so difficult? Especially now, when he was too tired to deal with it. What the heck did she think she'd be sleeping on, anyhow, since his bed was now down here?

He turned the chair toward her. "Babe, you forget the idea of you moving in was so you'd know what you're getting yourself into as my wife? Won't work if you're not here—" he waved his hand through the air "—with me."

Someone knocked on the outside door. A second later, he heard his niece call out. "Unka Matyou. Where Unka Matyou?"

He felt pulled in two directions, eager to get a hug from his niece but also needing to know Crystal understood. He held his ground.

Crystal looked down. "Fine. I'll sleep here."

He didn't like being a concession. Before he could say anything further, his niece came bounding through the door like a puppy. "Unka Matyou."

§

His brother, Jenny, and Kaylee had been just the start of the visitors who flooded his house, taking away any chance of a nap. Within an hour, it looked like he was hosting a party, complete with food and beer that had appeared like magic, along with all the people.

Across the room, Crystal sat with her back toward, him chatting with Jenny. Earlier, she'd been talking to his mother. Before that, with Travis. Every time he'd looked at her since Brad and Jenny had arrived, she'd been wrapped up in one conversation or another. Always with someone else. Which was okay. He'd have her all to himself when everyone left. And there was tomorrow. When he'd wake up with her beside him. They'd have all the alone time they needed then.

The only person Crystal hadn't struck up a conversation with was Derrick. Because Derrick was probably the only person in all of Fuller Lake who hadn't made an appearance yet. He'd be here, though. No doubt about it. No way his best friend would miss his coming home.

"Quite the party." Sam pulled a chair closer.

"Yeah." Quite the party. Noise and smoke and Crystal a hundred miles away on the other side of the room. And him, without a nap. "It's great you all popped in like this."

"Man, it's so good having you back again. I tell you, pool just hasn't been the same with you gone. Think you can shoot in that thing?" He waved toward the wheelchair.

"We'll see." The way he felt right now, it wouldn't be

anytime soon. Not with him being so tired.

"Maybe we can convince the league to give you extra shots, on account of the chair." Sam winked. "If you don't need the extra shots we can just keep it a secret, give our team a little edge."

Win by cheating. Sam always had been lax on sportsmanship. "Sure. Great idea."

"If you get nothing but air, you get a do-over. And you'd get one free scratch per game."

Twenty minutes later, Sam was still brainstorming ways to use Matt's wheelchair to their advantage. In the meantime, visitors came and went. Matt propped his head up with his hand and nodded like he was taking in all of Sam's suggestions.

He liked Sam, but he wanted him to shut up and go home and take everyone with him. He wanted to crawl into bed and call today done—and it wasn't even eight yet. How sad was that?

His eyelids drooped. He shook his head, trying to hang on. He couldn't go to sleep. Not when Derrick hadn't come yet. His eyelids slid closed. He left them closed. Just for a minute, he told himself. Just to rest up so he'd be raring to go when Derrick finally showed up. Where was he, anyhow?

Sam's voice blended in with the steady hum of background voices. Someone laughed. Matt wondered what was so funny, but he wasn't curious enough to check it out. Sleep. He just wanted sleep.

Just when he was about to surrender, he felt a miniature mountain climber scaling his legs. "What have I got here?" he asked as he tickled his niece.

She stood on his thighs and wrapped her arms around his neck. "Nite, nite, Unka Matyou."

Brad had his arm wrapped around Jenny's shoulders. Her baby-bump had blossomed over the last week, preventing them from keeping her pregnancy a secret any longer. "We're going to take off. Jen's getting tired."

"Sure, blame it on the pregnant lady." Jenny swatted Brad's chest, but it was really just a tap. She looked back at her brother-in-law. "Looks like you should be going to bed yourself."

"Soon," he said.

Brad lifted his daughter off Matt's lap. "You really do look tired. I can kick everyone out if you want."

"Nah, that's okay. I'm sure they'll all leave soon."

"You look tired," Crystal said, plopping down on the couch close to his wheelchair for the first time since the party started. "Why don't you go to bed?"

He let his gaze roam around the room. Sam had wandered off and was now talking with Travis. Neither looked like they had immediate plans to go anywhere. His mother was busy alphabetizing his CD collection while his father dozed in the recliner. Derrick still hadn't shown up.

"I'll discretely shoosh everyone out the door." She gave his chair a little push. "Go ahead. Go to bed."

He gave her a sly smile, playing with her. "Only if you promise to join me as soon as everyone's gone."

"I'll be there as soon as I can."

He arched his eyebrows. He'd expected her to protest, somehow. He gave his guests another visual once over. Nobody would miss him. And he was tired. "I'll warm the bed up for you."

After a visit to the bathroom, Matt wheeled to the bedroom. Exhaustion took over, and he was glad he'd let Crystal strong arm him into going to bed. The back-to-back visitors had been exhausting, but it was nice to know so many people cared about him. His last thought before he slipped over the edge from awake to asleep was about Derrick, wishing he could have stayed awake until his friend had come.

§

The house was silent when Matt woke up. The sun was just starting to rise, casting his room in a soft glow. He was still on his right side, just like when he'd fallen asleep. Not a good thing since staying in one position too long could mean bedsores, the very thing the doctor had warned him about just yesterday. He should roll over now. If he wasn't so damn tired.

He closed his eyes again. There was too much quiet. No nurses chatting in the hallway. No pages on the intercom. No TVs playing in neighboring rooms.

No Crystal breathing softly beside him.

No sounds of Crystal in the kitchen or bathroom, either. Not even the scent of the fresh-brewed coffee Crystal needed in order to feel human.

He strained his ears, listening for evidence of her moving around, but all was quiet. He pushed himself upright and then transferred into the wheelchair. He paused at the foot of the stairs, but he still didn't hear her moving around upstairs.

He found her in the living room, curled up on the couch with the afghan his grandmother had made pulled over her. One corner of his mouth went up as he watched her sleep. Obviously, playing hostess had tired her out, as well. So tired she'd fallen asleep watching TV.

The curve to his mouth disappeared as he looked at the TV, the screen as black as midnight on a cloudy evening. He turned his attention to the lamp on the end table. The lamp was turned off. The muscles at his jaw twitched as he stared at his fiancée, who'd obviously opted to sleep on the couch instead of with him.

She opened her eyes. She pulled the afghan closer around her. "Good morning."

"If you say so." He wheeled from the room and headed for the kitchen. He wanted to give her the benefit of the doubt, but he couldn't come up with any reason why she'd slept on the couch instead of in bed with him.

He looked at his mostly-bare countertop and sighed. Crystal loved "stuff." Her house was filled with knickknacks. Her own kitchen counter was end-to-end decorative clutter. With an uneasy feeling, he backtracked. He wheeled into the hallway to find her coming out of the bedroom, the afghan flowing around her shoulders.

Before he could slip into the bathroom, she zeroed in on him. "There you are."

"Didn't know I was that hard to find." He stared beyond

her. "Especially last night, when I was in bed."

She leaned against the wall, the afghan wrapped tightly around her. "I was afraid if I came to bed I'd wake you."

His focus shifted to her. "And that would be bad, why?"

For a quick moment, her mouth became pinched. "Because you needed your sleep." She sighed and then stepped closer. Her voice was much softer as she said, "Honey, you were exhausted. I slept on the couch for you."

"For me, huh?"

She crouched in front of him. The afghan slipped, revealing a bare shoulder, save for the thin satin strap of her nightgown. Her fingers rested on his leg for only a second before she put her hand on his arm. "Yes. For you."

The heat of her palm burned his arm. He locked his eyes on hers. "You can touch my legs, you know."

She looked away. "I know."

He moved his face in line with hers. "Do you have a problem with touching me?"

She didn't move her head, but her eyes shifted. "No."

"Good, 'cause I'd hate to think that my future wife couldn't stand the thought of touching me."

"Not a problem." Her eyes connected with his. She put her hand on his leg. It felt like a mannequin's hand. If that was what her touch was going to be like, he'd rather she kept her hands to herself.

He pushed her hand away. "I have to take a piss."

He went into the bathroom. A second later, the sound of a cupboard being opened and closed drifted from the kitchen. He heard water running and then being poured into what he figured was the coffee maker. He listened to her moving around. Nice sounds. He wished he could block out the prior ten minutes and just keep the memory of right now.

Inside the cabinet he found a small basket with Crystal's curling iron, blow dryer, and makeup essentials. Far from the bathroom clutter she had at home, but at least it proved she'd intended on spending the night. He grabbed a sealed catheter and wheeled over to the toilet. He was sliding the catheter home when he realized he wasn't alone. Crystal's gaze rose from his hands and met his eyes only briefly before she turned and walked away. He found her in the living room. She was curled up on the far end of the couch, her feet tucked beneath her and her arms wrapped around her waist. She continued to stare out the window even though he knew she'd heard him come into the room.

"I knew you had to do that," she said, "but I just never expected...you know, for it to be like...that."

The bitter scent of coffee drifted in from the kitchen.

"It doesn't hurt, if that's what you're worried about."

Her eyes came to him for the briefest of seconds before lowering to his lap and then zipping back to the window. She seemed to shrink into herself, and she blinked rapidly several times. "I'm sorry, Matt, so sorry this happened to you."

Sorry this happened to me? Or sorry this happened to you?

He pinched his lips tight. Thoughts like that weren't going to solve anything. "Like it or not it has happened, and we've got to face it, babe, or it's going to tear us apart." He wheeled closer. "Yeah, I've got to shove a tube in me just so I can piss, but my dick still works. I might not be able to move more than my toes, but I can feel. And I might need my rest, but that doesn't mean you have to sleep on the couch." *Look at me, Crystal. Let me know we're going to be okay.*

Her eyes closed and her mouth convulsed. The thin fabric of her nightgown jerked with each breath. And then the tears came.

As he watched her cry, he hated her just a little. Not a lot. Just enough that he couldn't make himself wheel closer to comfort her. Not when he felt like crying too.

This was so not what their first morning together was supposed to be like.

CHAPTER SIXTEEN

Matt wheeled through the house, full of restless energy he didn't know how to release. He'd been home three weeks, and he still hadn't figured out how to make good use of his time.

He stopped at the base of the stairs and listened. From the kitchen came the off-key sound of his mother's singing as she prepared lunch. From the living room came the Winnie the Pooh theme song, along with Kaylee's singing, only marginally worse than his mother's. Two flights up was an attic full of weight-lifting equipment. Nobody was singing off key up there.

It'd be slow going, but he figured he could get upstairs, somehow. Maybe sit on the bottom step and then lift his ass from step to step using his arms. That'd take care of his excess energy and kill time, as well. It'd get him upstairs, but it still wouldn't get him into the attic, which meant going up a ladder that pulled down from the ceiling.

Maybe he could get Brad and Derrick to move some of the equipment into his old bedroom. If he could get Derrick to grace his home with his presence for more than lunch. Every day, people Matt barely knew came to gawk, using the pretence of being a "good friend," while his true friend made himself scarce. Didn't make sense. He pushed the wheelchair away from the stairs, giving up on the weights. Wouldn't be the same without Abby across the room, anyhow.

Too bad today wasn't a therapy day. Going to therapy at least got him out of the house while burning a couple hours of his day. Unfortunately, it also wore him out in a way a full day of work never had.

"Work," he mumbled. That's what he really wanted to be doing right now.

His father no longer coughed hard enough to hack up

a lung. And in the three weeks Matt had been home, he hadn't seen his father take even one antacid. Apparently, it had just been bronchitis, like his father had said.

He no longer felt responsible for his father's health. But he wanted to be on the job with them again. He wanted to be at one of the houses they were remodeling. What he wouldn't give to be figuring out the best way to lay out the drywall boards to save on waste. Something challenging while being useful.

Useful. That was the key word. He wanted to be useful again.

Heavy truck doors slammed shut in the driveway, one a fraction of a second after the other. A few seconds later, the back porch steps groaned. Matt made his way into the kitchen to where his father, Brad, and Derrick stood, pink cheeked, their jackets zipped up to their chins. Matt wanted pink cheeks and a jacket zipped to his chin too.

"Close the door," Matt's mother said as she pushed behind the men to do the very thing she'd just said to do. "You're letting in all the cold."

Derrick pulled off his coat and hung it on the back of a chair. "I swear, it was warmer in the dead of January than it is today."

"Come on, boys, wash your hands," his mother said. She pulled the cover off a stock pot. The scent of spicy chili bit at his nose.

"Daddy, daddy," Kaylee sang as she came running into the already-crowded kitchen. Brad lifted her into his arms and blew raspberries into her cheek.

Derrick washed his hands and then took a place at the table. Matt wheeled into the open spot where the chair had been removed. He grabbed a cornbread muffin, handed it to his friend, and then took one for himself. "You know, you can come here at nighttime, too, not just for lunch."

Across the table, Matt's father's eyes lifted from his bowl.

"Just giving you and Crystal space," Derrick said. "Letting you settle into this marriage thing you're trying out."

"Nice plan. Unfortunately, the rest of Fuller Lake doesn't agree. It's been like Grand Central Station since I got home."

"All the more reason for me to stay away. You've got enough to handle without my hanging around."

Like a man watching a ping pong game, his father's eyes tracked from Matt to Derrick and back.

Matt peeled the paper liner from his muffin. "No. All the more reason for you to be here. Act as a reinforcement. Us against them."

"Did you wash your hands?" his mother asked.

"'Course I did." Over two hours ago. When he'd gone to the bathroom.

"Matthew." His mother pointed at the sink.

Matt shook his head and rolled his eyes while Derrick hid his smile behind a big bite of muffin. Matt wheeled to the sink just long enough to wet his hands. He grabbed the towel from the oven bar, did a quick job at drying his hands, and then dropped the towel onto the counter. His mother came behind him and hung the towel on the bar.

His father returned to his lunch. The kitchen filled with the sounds of the four men slurping up chili between bits of conversation. Matt had missed this, the male bonding moments with his mother hovering around them like they couldn't manage on their own. Even more, he'd missed being with the guys at the worksite. The physical exertion of hard work. The process of seeing their ideas shift from blueprints into reality. He wanted to be back with them instead of spending his days napping and watching cartoons. What he wanted and what he was capable of were two different things.

His father dipped his cornbread into the chili. "You have therapy today?"

Matt shook his head.

"If you feel like it, you could come to the jobsite for a while."

He felt a tingle of anticipation at the thought of joining them at the jobsite. An outlet for his restless energy. He wanted to say yes. Damn, how he wanted to say yes. But he knew he'd be in the way. And while he was wide awake now, that'd change within an hour or so. Just what his father needed. A sleeping crew member that everyone had to step around. He felt enough like a failure without having to prove it. "Maybe tomorrow."

His father's fist seemed to tighten around his spoon, his knuckles whitening. His jaw looked as tight as his grip on the spoon. Tomorrow, obviously, wasn't what his father had wanted to hear.

Matt stared at the kidney beans and ground beef that littered the red juice in his bowl. Just once, he wished he could make his father happy instead of always falling short.

"I know you're still feeling your way around, but what about project management?" his father asked. "Think if I brought the book over you could handle that?"

Bottom of the barrel work. His father scrambling to make use of his least-helpful employee. "Sure. I'll borrow one of Crystal's dresses and paint my nails while I'm at it."

"If you don't feel ready, just say so."

"No, Dad, it's fine. Bring the book over."

He'd agreed to do what his father wanted, but his father still had a scowl. He should have agreed right away without the remark about Crystal's dress. When was he going to learn not to be such a smart ass?

Brad's cell phone rang. "Hey, honey." His smile quickly deteriorated. "Maybe you should go to the doctor."

Everyone except Kaylee stopped eating.

"You're the boss, but you call me if things change." Brad flipped his phone closed and then sat there staring at the phone, his finger tapping against its cover.

"Is it the baby?" their mother asked.

"She said it's just an upset stomach, but she's going home to rest." Brad's eyes met with Matt's, a reminder of how precarious her pregnancy was.

Matt's chili and cornbread no longer seemed appetizing. Not that he knew much about pregnancies, but he did know that the baby wouldn't survive if Jenny delivered now. She'd have to take it easy, which meant she'd need to rely on Brad more. Which meant Brad couldn't spend his evenings working.

"We better get back on the road." Matt's father pushed back his chair. "See if we can get you home at a decent hour tonight."

Brad and Derrick both shuffled to their feet.

Matt dropped his spoon into his bowl. "Dad, there's something I need you to look at in the bedroom for a second."

Matt led his father to the bedroom and then turned his chair around.

"We've got to quit meeting this way," his father said.

"I've been thinking about work. I doubt I'll be back in time for the build. You should hire someone."

"I'm not replacing you." His jaw took on a chiseled look.

He wondered what his father's reaction would be if the therapist determined he'd definitely reached his healing plateau. Would he still be determined to keep his useless son employed? Or would he finally get his head out of his rear and hire a damn outsider? Truthfully, Matt didn't like either outcome. Regardless, his wonderings were just that...mindless pondering. The therapist hadn't offered any opinion. Good or bad. And he wouldn't lie to his father, even if doing so would benefit the business. "Just temporarily, Dad."

"No. That's final." His father stormed out of the room, his heavy boots thudding against the hardwood floor in the hallway.

"That went well," Matt mumbled. He'd barely made it to the kitchen when he heard the truck roar to life outside.

His mother wiped Kaylee's hands with a wet washcloth and then moved to Kaylee's face. "What put a hornets' nest in your father?"

"I asked him to hire someone to replace me."

She nodded. "Ah."

"Can't you talk some sense into him?"

She lifted Kaylee from the highchair. With a little pat on Kaylee's back, she said, "You better check on your babies, see if they're hungry."

Kaylee went running from the room with the thunderous roar of a herd of elephants. His mother turned her attention back to him. "I'm with your father on this one."

"If we don't come in on budget and on time, Rex Johnson's going to smear Dad's name all over town. We'll be lucky to even get a job building a damn doghouse."

"You're exaggerating, dear." She gathered up the dirty dishes from the table. "And if you listened to what you just said, you'd know exactly why your father won't hire a replacement."

"What? That we'd be lucky to get a job building a doghouse?"

She smiled a you-got-it smile.

He curled his lip and eyed her through tiny slits. "Doghouse? I don't get it."

"We, honey. You said we. You're no more ready to cut yourself out of the business than your father is."

She was right. He wasn't ready to cut himself out of the business. But that didn't mean he wanted it to go down in flames, either. "The group home is an important contract. It really is going to have an impact on future contracts."

She sat down and regarded him. "Your father didn't start the company to get rich. He did it with the hope it'd be something he could share with you and your brother. If you end up building doghouses, that's okay with him, as long as you're all building doghouses together."

They both were insane. It was obviously up to him to make the build a success. Which meant he needed a frigging miracle.

A hint of a memory tickled his brain. Miracle. It was something to do with a miracle. And Abby. She'd said something. What? It'd been just before he'd been released. They'd been in the gym. Their last night together. He nodded as it came to him. He'd asked her if there was any chance he'd recover, and she'd said the Internet was full of miracle recovery stories. That was it. The Internet.

He went to the computer, logged on, and then typed in "paralysis cures." The screen filled with lines of text. One hundred twenty-nine thousand hits. A lot of it guaranteed to be crap, but the key to his recovery might be hidden somewhere in all those websites.

He scrolled through the lines, looking for anything promising. He saw a hit that said, *Woman cured after two years of paralysis.* Two years. That was well beyond the eighteen-month mark he'd been told would mean the end of hope. With his heart pounding, he clicked on the website, only to find it dealt with a woman who'd had a stroke. He clicked on the printer icon anyhow, just in case there was something helpful he'd missed.

He clicked on entry after entry, printing anything that looked hopeful. After two hours, his eyelids started to droop. He propped his head up with a hand and scrolled to the next entry. The words in front of him started to blend together. He closed his eyes. Just for a second.

§

He was aware of movement beside him. It took him a moment to realize his head was tipped forward and his eyes were closed. He'd drifted off to sleep. Something heavy dropped onto the desk. He looked up just in time to see Crystal walking away. The thick stack of printouts were no longer haphazardly stacked in front of him but were off to the corner, right about where he'd heard the thump. *Damn.*

"Crystal," he called out. She didn't stop. He backed away from the desk and went after her.

She stood in the kitchen, facing the counter, her back to him. Her purse sat on the table next to a plain plastic shopping bag.

"Don't you think it's time to move on?" she asked.

"Move on?" She, the queen of I-won't-touch-you, couldn't possibly be saying such a thing. "You mean like you have?"

She turned to him. "What's that supposed to mean?"

He went to the fridge, pulled out a beer, and popped the tab. The liquid was cold, and he felt it all the way down to his stomach.

"Matt." Not a question, but a demand.

"Why do *I* need to move on when you refuse to accept my paralysis?"

She squished up her face and gave a little shake of her head. A movement he used to find cute. *Used* to.

"I have accepted your paralysis."

He took another drink and then stared her down. "That's why you still refuse to touch me? Because you're so accepting?"

Her eyes shifted away.

"I can feel, Crystal." He ran his hand down his thigh. "Here." He touched his stomach. "Here." He laid his hand flat against his heart. "But most of all, here."

She opened her mouth. No words came out.

He put his beer can on the counter. "I'm looking for a cure so I can be the man I used to be. The man you once loved."

He wanted her to correct his claim, to say she still loved him.

She stepped closer. With her eyes on his, she knelt and placed her hands on his legs. "My feelings for you haven't changed, Matt. Not one bit."

"That's what scares me, Crystal. Things haven't been all that great between us in a long time. I've tried to do whatever I can to make you happy, but it's impossible when I don't know what's wrong."

"Nothing's wrong." Her eyes didn't meet his.

"Well, I feel so much better now." He tried to wheel away from her, but he was trapped between her and the refrigerator.

"I know I've been rather distant lately, but it's only because your accident shook me up. You could have died. I guess, in my own little way, I've been protecting myself from further hurt." She moved her hand higher up his thigh. "I'm sorry, honey."

At that moment, he no longer wanted an apology nor

did he want to quibble with explanations. What he wanted was for her hand to move two inches higher. It had been way too long.

He brushed her cheek. "Babe, don't you know it'd take a lot more than a scrawny tree to take me down?"

She covered his hand with hers, pressing his fingers to her skin. Tears gathered in the corner of her eye. "I'm sorry."

The floodgates were about to open unless he found a way to stop them. "You're sorry?" He motioned toward his lap. "What about him?" He stared deep into her eyes. "He's missed you."

"I've missed him too." She covered his crotch with her hand and gave a light squeeze before pulling her hand away.

"That's all he gets?"

"I have to get dinner going." She stood and picked up the shopping bag.

He pictured a fighter jet spiraling from the sky and then crashing into the ground in a burst of flames. That was their relationship. "That's right. Dinner trumps sex any day."

"I just don't want to be eating at nine, okay?"

"Sure. Fine. Dinner it is." He took a deep breath and willed his anger away. Not worth the effort. He nodded at the package clutched tight to her chest. "What'd ya get?"

"If you must know, it's a treat I was going to save for this weekend."

He made a grab for the bag. "What kind 'a treat?"

She twisted away from him. "You just never mind."

"That's not fair. You know I hate surprises."

Her mouth twisted. He couldn't for the life of him figure out what she was thinking. Her mouth snapped back into place. "Fine. You want to know so bad, go get undressed and lay down on the bed."

He felt hope reviving. Any surprise that started with those words was just fine with him. "You getting undressed too?"

Keeping her body between him and the bag, she

wiggled past him. "Just go, like I asked. Lay face down." The stairs creaked a moment later.

Still backed up to the refrigerator, he looked up at the ceiling, picturing where she was based on the sound of her footsteps. His old bedroom. Other than when she'd moved her clothes back downstairs, he couldn't remember her going upstairs for anything.

"Are you naked yet?" Her voice drifted down the stairwell into the kitchen.

At the word naked, he decided he really didn't care what she was doing up there, as long as she didn't plan on leaving him stranded in bed alone.

She came into the bedroom just seconds after he'd settled himself chest down on top of the covers. The satiny slip that she wore shimmered as she moved. One hand was hidden behind her back. He thought he'd died and gone to heaven when she straddled him, her weight resting lightly on his upper thighs.

There was a snap, like the sound of a flip-top bottle opening. "This might be a little cold," she said.

"What might be cold?"

"Shhh." A rose scent filled the air. Something dripped on his back. She slid her hands up his back toward his shoulders.

Body oil and a soft touch. He'd never felt anything so heavenly in his life. "Where did you have that stuff hiding?"

Her fingers stopped moving for just a second. "Nowhere. I just bought it, from Judy at work. She had one of those naughty parties."

Her fingers kneaded little circles high on his shoulders. It felt truly wonderful, but naughty thoughts were now running through his head. Her, lying back, legs bent and spread while he worked her to a frenzy with a vibrating toy. "What else did you buy?"

"Nothing."

"Too bad."

Her hands, warm from the oil, moved away from his shoulders, going lower. The sensation changed when she crossed the injury line. The warmth of her hands changed to just a sensation of touch. Her fingers slid over his hips and then cupped his ass.

"I always liked your naked behind," she said.

"Ditto." He sighed as she squeezed his right cheek and then moved upward again, this time at a faster pace until she reached his shoulders.

"I can turn over, if you want," he volunteered.

"Later." Her hands remained at his shoulders and neck, her thumbs making paths around the edges of the surgery scar, never crossing directly over.

"I can give you a massage," he offered.

"Later."

He gave up on trying for more and concentrated on the feel of her touch. It did feel nice. The sexual thoughts lessened as he became more relaxed. His breathing slowed. His cheek and ear sank into the pillow. His body melted into the comforter. Even if he'd had the , his legs he wouldn't have been able to at that moment. As it was, it'd take more strength than he possessed if he needed to get into the wheelchair.

Her hands stopped moving. A moment later she whispered, "Matt."

He took one more breath and then drifted off to sleep.

When he awoke, the bedroom was cast in shadows. He cocked his head, thinking he heard noises upstairs. When nothing further came, he lifted himself up to his elbows and looked at the clock. Seven forty. Damn, he'd almost missed the whole evening. He turned himself over and then dragged his naked ass into his wheelchair. At that same moment, he heard a sound so quick he couldn't quite place it. Footsteps on the stairs? He sat still and listened. Water ran in the bathroom sink. Obviously, he'd been wrong about the origin of the noises.

He wheeled out of the bedroom at the same time Crystal came out of the bathroom. She looked like a vision, still dressed in the satiny slip. Her hair was mussed, only slightly neater than after a great round of sex. Color brightened her cheeks.

She took one small step back. Her head dipped. "I didn't know you were awake."

"Just woke up." He grabbed her hand and pulled her onto his lap. He snuggled his face against her chest. She smelled good. Flowery. Like the scented oil. "But I can easily go back to bed, if you want. Use some of that oil on you now."

"I think we should probably have dinner."

He slid his hand beneath her slip. "My thoughts exactly. I'm very hungry." He wanted her so much he ached. He worked his fingers between her thighs and wiggled his way around her underwear. She was warm and wet, just the way he liked her.

"Matt, dinner, remember." Despite her protest, she spread her legs slightly. His finger went in easily. Damn, she felt better than he remembered. So wet, like she'd spent the past hour dreaming of this moment.

She tipped her head back and spread her legs even further while she purred like a kitten. He slid in another finger. About the only time he could remember her feeling this loose was right after he'd made love to her. He pictured the plastic bag she'd had earlier. It'd had a lot more in it than just a bottle of oil. She'd bought toys, and she'd been keeping herself busy while he'd been sleeping. Busy taking care of herself when he'd have been more than willing to please her.

Shaking off the bad feelings before they could find a permanent home, he decided he'd just have to show her how much better he was than a vibrator. He pressed his fingers deeper inside her. She might have started her party solo, but he was going to finish it. Oh, he had plans for her. Bring her to the brink of a killer orgasm and then pull his fingers free. She'd have no choice other than to finish herself off in front of him or straddle his love machine. He didn't care which, as long as she wasn't hiding from him.

She thrust against him and moaned softly. So close. So close he could almost feel it. One more second and he'd be giving her his ultimatum.

The phone rang and she went still. He tried to get her back in the mood.

She pushed against his hand. "The phone."

"They can call back."

She freed herself from him. "It might be something important."

"Nothing's more important than this." He tried to pull her back to him. He'd love to strangle whoever it was on the other end of the phone line.

She stepped into the kitchen. The phone quit mid-ring followed by her breathless, "Hello." A second later she shoved the cordless phone at him.

"Your timing is impeccable," he said as a greeting.

"I figured you'd be happy to hear from me," Derrick said. "I was thinking we should go out, get a couple brewskies."

Leave it to Derrick to finally decide to get together. Matt eyed Crystal flitting around the kitchen in the slip that clung to every curve she owned. No way was he leaving now. "Great idea. I'm free next week on Tuesday."

"I meant tonight."

Crystal had hamburger in a frying pan, sizzling. Dinner in the making. Make-out time was obviously over. But that didn't mean it couldn't be resurrected later. "Tonight's not good. How about you come over...tomorrow."

"Tomorrow's no good. I've got plans. Maybe next week, then."

"Yeah. Next week."

"What'd he want?" Crystal asked after Matt hung up. Her back was to him. The slip shifted over her hips as she chopped an onion.

"Just to see if we wanted to go out tonight, but neither of us are exactly dressed for the occasion, so I said no."

She brought her arm up, like she was wiping her eyes. She sniffed.

"You okay?" he asked.

"Darn onions."

She set down the knife and turned to face him. Her eyes glistened. "You know what we should do tonight?

Let's watch a movie. I can make some popcorn. Maybe you'll sit next to me on the couch?"

"Sounds like a date, babe." In his book, a date was a hell of a lot better than being an old married couple. On a date, he had a chance and a half of getting laid.

§

A soft glow filled the bedroom when Matt awoke the next morning. Even though he'd never gotten to finish what Derrick had interrupted, the evening hadn't been totally ruined. Crystal had cuddled up next to him on the couch while they'd watched *You've Got Mail*, and then, not even a minute after he settled into bed, she came in and slid herself into his arms. He'd take a night with her snuggled up to him anytime.

They'd drifted apart over night but she was still next to him now, a tantalizing vision with her lips slightly puckered in sleep. He worked his way closer to her. She rolled away and pulled the covers over her head. So, they'd just cuddle he decided as he lifted himself to his elbow.

"Could you stop jiggling the bed?" She rolled further away.

He flopped onto his back.

"All I want is another hour of sleep, okay?"

"Sure, babe. Another hour." *Another hour with me lying here, wide awake, wishing you weren't so far away.* He dragged his body to the edge of the bed and reached out to grab hold of the wheelchair, but he got nothing but air. "Where the hell is my chair?"

"I moved it," she mumbled from beneath the covers. "It was in my way."

She'd moved his chair. Because it was in her way. What if he'd gotten sick over night and had to get up? Or maybe just to take a piss? Or what if there'd been a fire? The house could have been filled with smoke by the time they woke up. Valuable time would have been wasted searching by touch for his chair. Time that could mean the difference between life and death.

"Damn it, Crystal. You can't move my chair like that. That chair is my legs."

Still burrowed within her cocoon, she said, "I'm sorry. I won't do it again."

He glared at the bump beneath the covers. The bump that hadn't made any effort to get the chair that was out of reach. The chair that was out of reach because the bump under the covers had moved it. "Are you going to get my chair, or do I have to fall off the bed and crawl over to it? Where the fuck is it, anyhow?"

She threw back the covers and stomped to the closet, which put her at the furthest point of the room. She yanked the chair away from the wall, her feet slapping the hardwood floor as she stomped her way back. She shoved the chair at him and then rounded the end of the bed. For someone so tiny, the bed shook an awful lot as she crawled back in on her side and pulled the covers over her head again.

He made a face at the lump under the covers and then made his transfer. He got to the hallway before he remembered he was naked. Every stitch of clothing he owned was behind that closed door. With Crystal. The last person he wanted to be near at that moment.

Too keyed up to relax, he wheeled into the bathroom and glared at the shower stall. He wanted his claw-foot tub back. Not that he ever chose baths over showers, but he wanted to be able to take a bath if the mood so happened to strike him. He closed his eyes and breathed deeply. What he really wanted was to be walking again. To be the man he used to be, the one who didn't have to rely on a frigging wheelchair to get around.

But wishing didn't change anything. The fact was, he was stuck in the damn chair whether he liked it or not. And the shower wasn't going to magically change back into his tub. Taking one final deep breath, he wheeled closer to the shower and transferred onto the plastic bench—another piece of his life that he despised. On a roll, he thought about Crystal in the next room, buried under the covers. He'd envisioned Saturday mornings with Crystal starting out with them making love and then moving their lovemaking into the shower where they'd caress each other's soapy bodies.

The only good thing about the shower was that the water was hot. The bathroom filled with steam that hung in the air like a London fog. After a while, his resentment loosened its hold. By the end of his shower, he felt much better. Refreshed. Rejuvenated.

He transferred back into his chair and towel dried his chest and arms. The bedroom door opened. A floorboard outside the bathroom creaked as Crystal walked by. Feeling much more optimistic about life, he realized Crystal would need to shower. He was still mostly wet. Maybe the morning wasn't a complete loss, after all.

"Hey, babe," he called out. "Shower's all warmed up for you. I can wash your back."

"I'm busy." The coffee machine was already gurgling as it brewed a fresh pot. A cupboard door opened and closed, followed by another door opening and closing.

So much for salvaging his honeymoon dreams he thought as he loaded his toothbrush with toothpaste. Another cupboard door closed loudly in the kitchen. He shoved the toothbrush in his mouth and then wheeled to the kitchen in time to see Crystal slam another cupboard door.

"What gives?" he asked as he laid his toothbrush on the counter.

"Where are the mixing bowls?"

"Top shelf, far left cupboard, over by the clock."

She opened the door and stretched to reach. Her fingers barely brushed the shelf. "Stupid place for mixing bowls."

"I never used 'em, so it seemed the best place for 'em."

"Sure. You're tall. What would you care?" She dragged a chair over and then pulled down two mixing bowls.

Water dripped from his hair onto his shoulder and then ran down his back.

Still standing on the chair, she looked at him. "Are the measuring cups something you don't use often?"

"Next cupboard over, top shelf."

Another drop of water drizzled down his neck. He

grabbed the kitchen towel from the oven bar and rubbed it over his head. Crystal crawled down from the chair in time to see him pull the towel from his head and drop it onto the counter. She glared at the towel and then shifted her gaze to him.

"What?" He had the urge to back away, but he held his ground.

"Why do you do that? Why do you drop the towel on the cupboard like that?"

He picked up the towel and started to hang it on the oven bar. Her horrified look stopped him. "What?"

"You just used that on your hair."

"So? My hair's clean."

She rolled her eyes and gave him a you-can't-be-that-stupid look.

"I'll put it in the hamper, okay?"

"It won't dry out in the hamper. Hang it on the towel bar in the bathroom." She turned around, pulled out a drawer, and then pushed it back in with a thud.

"Now what'cha looking for?"

"Measuring spoons."

"Why don't we make breakfast together? You tell me what you want and I'll get it for you." The idea was perfect. A way to give them that *together* time he wanted.

She shoved her fists on her hips. "Why? You think I can't make pancakes on my own?"

He held up his hands. "I just thought we could do something together. You don't want my help. Fine. I'm out of here."

"Ma...att."

He shook his head and wheeled from the room. In the bathroom, he stared at the faint reflection of himself in the steamy mirror while he tried to shake off his anger before it could take root. This wasn't how *marriage* was supposed to be. She was driving him crazy. Up one minute. Down the next.

"I'm sorry, Matt," Crystal said from the bathroom door. "I wanted to surprise you, but I couldn't find anything I needed. I guess it'll take time getting used to your kitchen."

He turned his wheelchair toward her. "It's not *my* kitchen. It's yours. You move the stuff so it's where you want it, okay?"

She nodded.

He opened his arms, hoping she'd curl up on his lap. She took a step back. "I need to get back to breakfast or it'll be lunchtime before we eat."

An empty hole opened inside him as he watched her walk away. *Give it time. All new marriages have to go through an adjustment phase. Even those without a wheelchair.*

She'd barely left when she came back.

Decided you want to cuddle after all, huh? He spread his arms and grinned.

She plopped his toothbrush down on the edge of the sink and then stalked off. From the hallway he heard, "And he wonders why he can't ever find anything."

He dropped his arms to his side. His fingers curled into fists as he stared at the empty doorway. *If I die when I'm seventy-six, then I only have to make it through eighteen thousand two hundred and forty-three more mornings with her.*

§

"We should do something," Crystal said a few hours later after the breakfast dishes had been washed and put away. She shifted her position on the couch, pulling her legs from beneath her. "Go out. Have some fun."

Matt thought about the massage oil and wiggled his eyebrows. "We can stay here and have some fun. Finish what you started last night."

"Ma...att." She made a face like he'd asked her to do a strip tease on Main Street. "It's not even noon yet."

"Yeah? So?"

"Think of something else."

"We could play a board game."

"Sure. Or we could pluck all the hair on my legs. Then I won't have to shave tomorrow."

"Well, what do *you* want to do, Ms. Smartypants?"

"We could go shopping." She smiled. "That sounds

like fun."

"I'd rather you pluck all the hair on *my* legs."

A vehicle pulled into the driveway. Crystal's eyes narrowed slightly below arched eyebrows. "Company?"

Matt shrugged. The visitor traffic had decreased to a trickle over the last two weeks. He wheeled to the kitchen just as footsteps sounded on the deck. His father. Through the window, Matt saw Brad and Derrick sitting in his father's truck. Exhaust curled out of the tailpipe. A stop in between jobsites.

"Forget where Mr. Jones lives?" Matt asked as he held open the door.

"Came to bring you this." His father set a stuffed three ring binder on the table. The project book. Pages stuck out of it at haphazard angles.

Matt leafed through the book. Only about a fifth of the pages had actually been fastened into the binder. The rest had been shoved inside in what appeared to be a random order. "Gee. Thanks. Crystal and I were trying to figure out how to entertain ourselves. You just solved that problem. For about the next month."

"You're lucky the pages are with the book. It's been a hectic couple of months."

Matt easily read between the lines. Hectic couple of months as three men did the work of four. The disorganized binder was Matt's penance for taking an unplanned, extended vacation.

"And if I don't want it to get worse," his father said, "I've got to go."

"Thanks for stopping by." Matt swung the door closed. He leafed through the first couple of disorganized pages and sighed. "Thanks a lot."

Crystal came and stood in the doorway. "What'd your father want?"

"To ruin my life."

She looked at the binder, raised an eyebrow, and sighed. "Can you handle being on your own for an hour?"

"Do I look like a baby?"

She closed her eyes. Her mouth turned tight. Counting

to ten, he guessed. Apparently, it took a lot of patience to deal with him. As he watched her for those ten seconds, he wondered why he was with her. Because there were times when he really didn't like her. Then, when the ten seconds were up and she opened her eyes and the tightness disappeared, she looked like the woman he'd fallen in love with, so beautiful with her hair done up just right and her makeup so expertly applied. Right at that moment, he couldn't imagine ever being without her.

"I don't have to work on the project book right now."

"From the looks of it, you're going to need every spare second of the next century to get that thing back in order." She leaned over and kissed his cheek. "I'm going shopping. Call my cell if you need me."

She slid her leather jacket on over her fuchsia silk blouse and grabbed the expensive purse that'd cost more than he made in a week. With a wave, she left him all alone with his father's mess to clean up.

"I'd rather go shopping," he mumbled as he listened to her car start up.

For the next hour, he worked on the first step—organizing the pages, grouping them by project. They had a contract on a garage build, cabinet installation, window replacement, installing a new roof, and a re-siding project. And those were just the big jobs. There was a one-room painting job, a replacement of a sidewalk, adding a railing to a porch, and putting in wood flooring in a den. None of this included whatever projects they were working on today that might take them through the coming week.

Eliminating the unknown jobs the guys were currently working, he quickly calculated how many man hours it'd take for three men to complete the projects. Unless they worked sun up to sun down, there was no way they'd get it all done before the group home build started.

They *had* to go into the group home project with a clean slate.

Even if Matt had the energy to go back to work, he couldn't physically do enough of the work to make a dent in it.

He closed his eyes and buried his fingers in his hair. Somehow, he had to figure out a way to get his father to hire someone.

CHAPTER SEVENTEEN

Matt wheeled over to the weights that had been brought down to the bedroom. *Eighteen thousand two hundred and thirty-two*, he thought as he listened to Crystal moving around in the bathroom, although that number didn't seem as frightening as it had a week and a half ago. All he had to do was keep in mind that she wasn't a morning person, that's all. Keep that in mind and they'd be just fine.

The blow dryer started up. He pictured her standing in front of the sink wearing close to nothing, just two scraps of light pink satin. Catching her in just her bra and panties made the morning mood swings almost bearable. Catching her in just her bra and panties at night though, that was even better.

"Yeah, right," he muttered as he pulled on the weights. The body oil had come out only once since she'd bought it.

He knew there was more to marriage than sex, but it'd been over a month. Five long, sexually stagnant weeks.

May as well concentrate on something more encouraging. Like Huntz & Sons Construction's backlog of work. They were supposed to start the group home today, but the little jobs were still not finished. If only he could be of more help than keeping the project book in order, doling out the jobs, ordering the materials, and placating the homeowners who were getting restless.

If only his legs would cooperate and start working again. He was on page eighty of the Internet listings, and he still had yet to find anything useful.

The blow dryer went silent. A moment later, Crystal came into the bedroom looking like a Victoria's Secret model. Her gaze fell on him for the briefest of moments as she walked toward the closet. There was something cruel about living with a woman who looked that hot but didn't care about sex.

He tightened his jaw and tugged on the weights. It wasn't sex she had a problem with, at least she never used to. What he couldn't figure out was if it was his useless legs that freaked her out? Or was it him?

"I don't know how you can work out so early in the morning," she said. "It's all I can do to get up enough energy to take a shower."

"I'm used to being at a jobsite already." Thinking of their unfinished jobs, he wondered how impossible it'd be to put in a porch railing while being confined to a wheelchair.

She turned around and pulled a floral dress over her head. "The point is, you're *not* at a jobsite. You could be sleeping."

"Other than my internal alarm going off at five and my not being able to fall back to sleep." He could mix the cement for the sidewalk, but there was no way he could dig up and remove the old cement.

She leaned against the wall, her gaze burning into him as he worked the weights. A hint of a smile formed, apparently liking what she saw, which gave him an idea. Tonight, when she got home from work, this was where she'd find him. With any luck, his sexual dry spell would come to an end. If he couldn't be a success in the workforce then be a success in bed, right?

"Speaking of jobsites," she said, "if you have enough energy to lift weights at seven-thirty in the morning, don't you think you're strong enough to go back to work?"

He yanked harder on the weights. "You sound like my father."

"You won't know what you're capable of doing if you don't try."

He let go of the ropes and the weights fell with a clang. "Yeah, I do. I would love nothing more than to be back at work, but I know there's nothing I can do." Nothing useful, anyhow.

She shook her head and sighed deeply. "You're so

damn bullheaded."

"Thank you."

"I wish you'd just try, honey. If it doesn't work, it doesn't work. Anything you can do at the jobsite is going to help your father more than you sitting on the damn computer all day looking for miracles that belong to other people."

He tightened his jaw and stared through her. *Eighteen thousand two hundred and thirty-two.*

She sighed again. "I'm sorry, Matt. I told myself I wasn't going to nag you about the computer, but I just can't help myself." She came closer and knelt before him. "It hurts to see you like this, that's all."

He focused in on her again. "If I never walk again, so be it. But what if there's some crazy treatment that can fix this? What if the answer is out there on the Internet and all it'd take is one more day's search to find it? I can't give up, not if it means I could be a real, honest-to-God help to my father again."

She stood and gave him a quick kiss on the cheek. "I'm going to be late for work."

He listened to her make her way through the house, pausing in the kitchen long enough to gather up her purse and lunch and to slip into her shoes. The imprint of her kiss clung to his cheek. Was this really what married life was supposed to be like? A kiss on the cheek without so much as a goodbye or a have-a-nice-day or an I love you from either of them?

She hadn't left yet. It wasn't too late. He navigated the wheelchair through the bedroom as quickly as he could and then raced down the short expanse of hallway to the kitchen. She stood by the counter with her left arm wrapped around her waist and her right hand pressed to her mouth. Her cheeks glistened. Seeing her like that made his chest ache.

"I'll stop searching, babe. If it means that much to you I'll stop."

Without looking his way, she brushed her fingers across her cheeks. "I have to go." She grabbed her purse strap and the bag with her lunch and then turned for the door.

"I love you," he said just as she reached the door.

She paused. *Turn around, babe. Turn around and say you love me, too.*

She nodded and then pulled open the door. His chest ached with each breath as he listened to her footsteps on the deck. *Why are we even pretending?* he wondered as her car door opened and then closed. A second later the engine fired to life. He heard her little Honda CRX back down the driveway. And then she was gone. For just a second, he wished she'd never come back.

§

It had been easy to avoid the computer. After Matt finished up his half hour on the weights, he showered. Then, his mother and Kaylee arrived, and they all had breakfast. He took Kaylee for a walk while his mother did the dishes. After his outpatient therapy session, he worked on the project book, looking for any smidgen of work he could do to help on any of the projects. He'd come up empty.

Now, he sat with Kaylee in front of the TV where a cucumber dressed as a superhero cried out, "I am that hero." The first time he saw Larry Boy and the Bad Apple, he thought it was cute. Somewhere over the last month of daily viewings, however, it'd lost it's charm.

"Wouldn't you rather watch *Little Mermaid?*" he asked, fully aware that right now his father, Brad, and Derrick were doing important work. He envisioned them sawing the two by fours, laying out the walls, hammering together the framework. He should be there, too, wielding his hammer.

"Lawwy Boy," Kaylee insisted, turning up her nose at his suggestion of changing movies.

Matt crossed his arms, something Larry Boy couldn't do since he had no arms, which made it really amazing that he was a super hero. He wondered if good ol' Larry Boy had Googled *Armless Super Hero Stunts*. Maybe that's what he needed to do. Google *Legless Super Construction Stunts.*

Kaylee laid her head on the arm of the couch and popped her thumb in her mouth. She blinked. He gave her five minutes before she fell asleep. Then, he could have the TV to himself. As if soap operas were any better than the twentieth viewing of Larry Boy.

Kaylee's little eyes were soon shut tight. Didn't even take the five minutes Matt had given her. He wished he could crawl onto the couch and take a nap with her, but he wasn't the least bit tired. Which only gave him more time to be bored. More time to be aware of how *helpful* he was to his father. More time to wonder if just one more day's Internet search would lead him to the cure he sought.

He felt the pull of the computer. Didn't mean he had to look for miracles. He could play Spider Solitaire. Or maybe he could look for a cheap used car. He couldn't expect his mom to keep on running him everywhere he had to go.

The guys would arrive soon for lunch, but he still had time to run a few searches.

Leaving Larry Boy to his super hero stunts, Matt wheeled over to the computer and logged on. He typed in *used cars, central Wisconsin* and then wondered why he was looking for a car. He was never alone long enough to need to go anywhere by himself. He backspaced and stared at the blinking cursor, acknowledging the true reason he'd logged on to the computer. He'd promised.

Two...no, five...five more websites and he'd call the search done. Five or six searches wasn't bad, was it? She couldn't really complain if he looked at just seven or eight more sites.

As he backed out of his tenth site, he wished his eighteen months were over. He could tell his father: "Sorry, I'm never going to walk again, don't count on me for the group home." His father would have to hire someone then. He could stop worrying about impressing his father.

Except he didn't want to be stuck in this chair forever. So he clicked on another site.

He was scanning his fifteenth website when he heard the truck doors slamming in the driveway. He hadn't found any nuggets today, but he was certain there'd be at least some little glimmer of hope this afternoon. He stashed his printouts in the lower drawer and then wheeled out to the kitchen. His father, brother, and friend were dusted with bits of sawdust. Their smiles were broad. Invigorated. Just like whenever they started a major project. Matt crossed his arms and glared at each of the guys like it was their fault he'd spent the morning watching cartoons instead of slinging a hammer. It wasn't their fault. It was his own.

"Got the group home all built?" he asked as he forced his arms to unwind.

His mother held a finger to her lips. "Kaylee's sleeping."

Derrick nodded and then whispered, "Got one side framed in already."

Matt had wanted to be there for that first cut, the first nail, the first everything. Working on the group home had been his idea, and now it was barreling along without him.

He dried his hands and then dropped the towel on the countertop. Lunch didn't even appeal to him today.

His mother picked up the towel and hung it over the oven handle while Matt took his place at the table. The place where the chair had been removed. His father and Brad were working on their food like there was a race. Derrick dished up a heaping serving as though it were his last meal. Matt filled his plate with twice the amount he'd eaten on any day since coming home. If he couldn't be like the guys at the jobsite, then he'd try to fit in at the table.

When the plates were nearly cleaned for the second time, Matt felt an overwhelming sense of suffocation. They'd be leaving soon. Back to the jobsite. Back to life. Matt's big plans for the afternoon were to clean his bellybutton and trim his nose hair, maybe alphabetize the useless printouts detailing other people's miracles.

"We could use a fourth set of hands out at the site," his father said, looking at Matt.

He felt a stronger tingle of anticipation than he'd felt the other times his father had tempted him with going back to work. He wished going back was as simple as saying yes, but he'd mentally worked the jobsite numerous times. The little he could do wasn't enough. He put on a smile to soften his words, as much for himself as for his father. "Then I guess you'd better be hiring someone."

His father's jaw tightened. "You need more time, then tell me you need more time. But don't you dare give up before you even try."

Jenny's stomachache last week had been just that—a stomachache—but she wasn't home free. Matt flashed a look at his brother. *Back me up here.* Brad pushed a tomato-soaked macaroni noodle around his plate. *Thanks for the help, Mr. I-Need-To-Be-Home-With-My-Family.* "I don't need to try it, Dad. I know I can't handle the job."

"Your arms still move, don't they? You can swing a hammer the same as any of us can."

Matt stared back at his father and thought about how happy Crystal was going to be. Give her her frigging wish. "Fine, Dad. I'll come swing the damn hammer, but only if you promise to hire someone when you discover I'm no help."

"The day you prove there's not one single thing you can do, that's the day I'll hire someone. But not one second before."

"Anybody ever tell you how stubborn you are?"

His father smiled, knowing he'd won. "And I'm damn proud of it."

Despite resisting going back to work, Matt felt a tremor of excitement when they filed out of the house toward his father's truck. In one of the rare moments where he wanted to be wrong, he hoped his mental wanderings around the jobsite were nowhere close to reality.

His excitement faltered when he realized how high up his father's truck was. "Maybe I should have Mom bring me over in the car."

"Can't," Brad said. "Kaylee's sleeping. Unless you want to wait until she wakes up."

No, he didn't want to wait. Not now that his going back to work was set into motion.

"We can get you in the truck if that's what you're worried about," Derrick said.

"Worried? Me? Hell, no." Him. The rock climber who used to be able to lift more weight than any of them. Unable to get into the truck on his own.

His father put his hand on Matt's shoulder. "There's no shame in asking for help."

Matt stared at a pebble embedded in the floorboard because he couldn't stand to look at any of them. If he couldn't get into the damn truck, how was he supposed to be any help at the jobsite?

Not wanting to go down that road, he forced himself to sit up straighter. So, he couldn't get into the truck on his own. That didn't make him useless. "Fine. I need help."

Derrick took one side and Brad took the other. Together, they boosted Matt upward until he could grab the handle built into the frame.

"Now what?" Brad asked as he gripped the waistband of Matt's jeans.

"I don't know," Derrick said. "All I know is I wish we had my truck instead of Pop's." Derrick's truck was a souped-up low-rider, one of the few purchases he'd consented to spending some hard-earned cash on.

"How 'bout I just hang here," Matt said. "If you get up enough speed, I can fly like a kite."

"Nah, we'll figure this out," Brad said, as though Matt had been serious.

Three-ring circus, Matt thought as he hung there. He couldn't see Mrs. Mezmitz hiding behind her curtains, but he knew she was there. He hoped she was getting her money's worth. "Why don't one of you get inside the truck and pull me in, already?"

His father ran around the truck, got in the driver's side, grabbed a handful of Matt's jeans, and then reeled him in. Matt rotated his shoulders. "One more minute and I'd have been buying my shirts at "Apes R Us"."

"You already do, don't you?" Brad asked.

Matt curled his lip at his brother and then smiled. Damn, he'd missed this. Excitement vibrated within him. He was going to work. Finally.

In less than fifteen minutes, they arrived at the jobsite. The south wall was framed in and braced into place. Two by fours were laid in position on the ground to form the frame for the east wall. They'd been busy, but there was plenty of work to be done, and Matt was raring to go. He pushed open the door and remembered the fiasco of trying to get him into the truck. Getting him out should be a laugh and a half.

Derrick came around and scooped Matt into his arms, like Matt was a Russian mail-order-bride and it was their wedding day. It had been bad enough having Brad and Derrick give him a boost, but being in Derrick's arms was just plain wrong. Trying to cover his unease, he batted his eyelashes. "My hero."

Derrick plopped him into the wheelchair and then stretched his back like a hundred and ninety pounds was about a hundred pounds more than he could manage. "Yeah, well, sorry to say, you're not exactly my idea of a damsel in distress."

"I need more makeup, huh?"

Derrick laughed. "Try about a case full."

Matt looked at the beginnings of a building. Adrenaline pulsed through him. This was what construction was all about.

Brad opened the tool trailer and strapped on his tool belt. Matt worked hard to push his chair over the upturned soil. Derrick and his father had their tool belts on by the time Matt reached the trailer. He grabbed his belt and buckled it on. The sounds of hammering echoed all around him. He worked his way over the bumpy terrain, eager to get to work. Brad and Derrick were busy fitting the studs into the frame and hammering them into place.

Matt looked down at another stud ready to be secured. He mentally tried out different positions. Without pounding in one nail, he determined he'd have to leave the framing to the others. But there was still plenty to do. Lots of opportunities for him to prove his worth. Like cutting the studs.

He put all his strength into bouncing his way over to the pile of two by fours. His head and shoulders jerked forward when his chair got hung up, one front caster hanging free in the air. "You can work yourself out of this," he mumbled.

"Need help?" Derrick hollered loud enough for the entire neighborhood to hear.

"I'm fine. Thanks."

With a lot of wiggling and leaning and jerking and four minutes gone forever, he managed to free himself. He made it though. That's what mattered. Then, he was by the stack of two by fours. Holding on to the edge of the wheelchair, he leaned over, grabbed a plank, and then hung there. Rock hard biceps and triceps apparently didn't matter when it came to lifting the stud off the ground. Not even ten minutes on the site and he was at two-to-zero on the scale of what he couldn't do versus what he could.

"Need a little help?" his father asked.

He wanted to say no. Damn it, he should be able to say no. He looked away and stared at a rut he was going to have to pass over in order to get to the saw. He'd probably get hung up on that one too. His father was still staring at him. Damn, how he hated admitting he couldn't pick up a frigging two-by-four, especially to his father. "Just a little."

"Tell you what. I'll carry the studs to the saw. You measure and cut."

"Wonderful plan."

His father had the stud on the saw and the measurement marked by the time Matt worked his way over the rough ground.

"Both cuts are marked for you," his father said as he went to get another two-by-four.

Matt pulled the blade across the wood. Mixed in

with the scent of fresh-cut pine was an acrid scent, like burning plastic. He leaned closer and sniffed, but all he smelled was pine. Such a wonderful smell.

He grabbed hold of the stud to turn it around and then puffed in frustration. Stuck in the chair, it'd take him forever to reposition the stud to cut the other end. Not impossible but impractical, considering he needed to keep ahead of Brad and Derrick or they'd be twiddling their thumbs. He should just wave the white flag now and go home.

His father came up behind him with another two-by-four. He looked at his son and then at the uncut end of the stud. Looking back at Matt he sighed. "Do you think if I put the stud across your lap you can take it over to Brad and Derrick?"

Forty feet of bumpy ground stood between him and where Brad and Derrick were working. Forty feet of bumpy ground he had to cover while balancing a stud. *Hell no*, was what came to mind, but he knew his father wouldn't let him give up that easily. If he could master rock climbing, then he could do this. "Sure."

It took his father only a minute to turn the stud, make the cut, and then lay it across Matt's legs. Matt pushed against the wheels, but his arms immediately hit the stud. Put him on smooth, even blacktop, he could probably get there without a decent forward push. Stuck in the ruts from the backhoe, there was no way in hell he'd get across the lawn.

Brad patted his tool belt. "Shit."

Derrick looked up and grinned. "Didn't load yourself with nails again, huh?"

"Shut up."

Finally. Something he could do. "I'll get you some," Matt said. He threw the stud as far as he could toward its final destination. He worked his way to the trailer, filled his own belt with nails, and then bounced his way back to his brother.

Derrick swiped his wrist over his forehead. "Damn. A cold Coke would be good right now."

"I'll get it," Matt said. He made it halfway back to the tool trailer before he realized his worth in the crew. A gofer. That's all he was good for. Nothing but a damned gofer. Not even a good one, considering Brad or Derrick could have been to the tool trailer and back before Matt even shaved off a quarter of his trip.

He eyed the framed-in wall spread out across the ground and pictured them lifting it into position. There was no way he'd be any help. Then there'd be the rafters, another job he couldn't do. Forget roofing. He'd pretty much be useless with the siding. He couldn't put in drywall.

Other than running for nails or sodas, he was useless. His being here would do nothing more than slow down the project. He pulled his cell phone from his pocket, ready to call his mom to come get him. To hell with what his father expected of him. He'd disappointed his father his whole life. Why stop now?

He dialed in the first few numbers. His father came up beside him and put his hand on Matt's shoulder.

"We'll figure it out," his father said.

"Dad—"

"Just give it some more time."

He could almost hear the unspoken *please* hanging in the air. "Fine. But if I can't do anything more than run for soda and nails, you're hiring someone—got it?"

His father answered with a smile that had no power behind it.

Matt went back to the framework. Nailing might be difficult, but not impossible. He eased himself from the chair onto the ground and then reached for his hammer, only to find it was missing. He looked at his brother who waited a heartbeat before he offered his own.

While Matt set his first stud, Derrick pounded out three. Brad managed two, and that was with him running for a new hammer. Matt wanted to throw the hammer across the lawn, but he held tight. So, he'd only nailed in one stud. The point was he *had* nailed in a stud. He wasn't totally useless.

As he continued working, he perfected his awkward method. After a few studs, it no longer took his full concentration to balance his weight while swinging the hammer. He set another nail into place. His arms ached. Somewhere along the line, he'd slowed down. One stud to four of Derrick's and Brad's. The hammer felt like it weighed three hundred pounds. He lugged it back up and swung, hitting his thumb instead of the nail. "Shit mother almighty," he swore as he threw down the hammer. "Shit, damn, fuck."

His father came over and crouched. "You've put in a good day's work. Maybe it's time we have your mother come get you."

His thumb throbbed. "I haven't even been here two hours."

"You haven't been out of the hospital all that long, either. I don't expect miracles."

They stared at each other until Matt looked away.

"We'll bring you back tomorrow after lunch. We'll make you work for two full hours and then some, no matter how much you beg us to let you stop earlier."

Matt laughed, but he wished he had the confidence his father had.

"That's better." His father had nothing but love in his eyes. "Little by little, it'll come."

He wanted to buy into what his father was selling, but he couldn't. He could come back tomorrow and the next day and the day after that and he didn't think it'd make any difference. What he couldn't do would still outweigh what he could.

"You look beat." His father stood up, pulled out his cell phone, and punched a few buttons. "Why don't you rest while waiting for your mother."

Brad and Derrick kept pounding in studs, but he knew they'd heard. *That's right boys. Little Mattie's going to take a nappy while waiting for his mommy.*

He stared at the hammer laying where he'd tossed it. There were still nails in his belt. It'd take at least twenty minutes for his mother to load Kaylee and her favorite doll into the car and make the trip across town. Plenty of time to hammer out a few more studs and pretend he was one of the boys. But what was the use? Two or three studs more didn't prove anything.

The throbbing of his thumb reached up through his arm all the way to his temple. The thought of having to work himself back into the chair seemed like an overwhelming proposition. Then, he still had to navigate the hills and valleys left by the heavy machinery. He'd be lucky to make it to the driveway by the time his mother showed up.

With his version of waving the white flag, he popped the clasp on his tool belt and abandoned it on the ground not far from the hammer. At this point, he didn't care if it laid there through eternity. Brad and Derrick kept working, but he felt them watching as he hefted his ass onto the chair's leg strap. His muscles quivered and almost gave out as he worked himself higher. What he wouldn't give to be able to stand, for even a second. He threw his weight backward, throwing his ass onto the seat.

Using his final reserve of energy, he pushed his way out of the construction zone, going over ruts that seemed as deep as the Grand Canyon. Him, without his rock-climbing gear. When he reached level ground, he dropped his hands onto his lap, closed his eyes, and waited. Behind him, he heard the whack, whack, whack of hammer to wood. The table saw whined as it chewed off excess lumber. Work in progress.

They'd be better off if he'd died in the accident.

Deep down, he knew that wasn't true, but right now that fact seemed fuzzy. He hung his head and wished for a freak accident to take him out of his misery. Then he thought about never holding or kissing Crystal again. His thoughts expanded to not making it to his wedding day only two months away. To never seeing Kaylee grow up and get married. Never seeing the new baby. Never having the chance to have children of his own. Plenty of reasons to want to stay alive.

Like his father had said, little by little, it'd come.

Somehow, he'd prove his worth.

He lifted his head and opened his eyes. The sun was bright and the sky was filled with cotton candy clouds. Much too beautiful a day to waste with bad thoughts.

"It'll come," he whispered.

His father walked toward him. There was nothing out of the ordinary in his father's stance, yet Matt knew he was about to deliver bad news. Matt looked down the road, wishing to see his mother's car. The road was traveler-free.

"Your mother just called. Mrs. Mezmitz needed a ride to her doctor's appointment, something about her daughter being sick and couldn't take her. It's going to be about an hour before she can get here."

That kind of bad news he could live with.

Since he had time on his hands, maybe he could try putting in a few more studs. His thumb still hurt but it'd quit throbbing, and it wasn't like it was the first time he'd ever had to work after whacking his thumb a good one.

He turned his chair and looked across the minefield to where Brad was crouched over the framework. It looked to be a mile away. *If you can scale a rocky cliff, you can make it over that again.*

The saw started up. Almost immediately, there was a high-pitched squeal. Matt looked that way in time to see the puff of smoke and Derrick jumping back like he'd seen a rattlesnake.

"What now?" his father grumbled as he ran toward the saw.

By the time Matt made it over the mountains and valleys, Derrick had the motor cover off and was poking at the melted wires. "Who wants to perform its last rites?"

"A better question is, who's got time to run to the hardware store?" Carl asked.

"I'll go," Derrick said. He looked at Matt. "Want to do a road trip?"

"I think I could take time out of my busy schedule."

"Make it quick," Carl said as he unplugged the deceased saw.

Each rut in the lawn seemed more difficult to cross than the one before. Matt tried to ignore the burn in his arms as he lagged behind Derrick. He grunted like a wuss when he hurled himself into Derrick's passenger seat, sighing as he eyed the empty wheelchair. Pulling off the wheels and storing the parts seemed like more effort than it was worth.

"I can put it in the back," Derrick said.

"Nah. Leave it. I'll just stay in the truck. You can move faster without me, anyhow."

"You sure?"

Matt nodded. Now that he was sitting stationary, his arms felt rubberized and he wished he hadn't given up afternoon naps.

Backing onto the road, Derrick said, "It's great having you back. Feels like old times."

They were still a sight short of old times, but it was getting there. Twice now, Derrick had picked Matt up and they'd gone to the Hideout, just the two of them. They'd stayed out too late, and he'd gotten too drunk, but it'd been fun. The only thing that would have made it better would have been having Crystal along and whatever girl Derrick was dating this week. *That* would be *old times*.

"How's married life treating you?" Derrick asked.

Matt's thoughts went back to this morning. "Great. Wonderful."

"That good, huh?"

"I love her, but I really didn't think living with her would be so hard. I know a lot of it is getting used to all the crap that comes along with the wheelchair, but it's been over a month and it's not what I'd hoped for."

"I'm sorry."

Matt shrugged. "It'll work out, right?"

"I'm counting on it. I already called a bunch of guys about the bachelor party. Sure would hate to cancel all those nude dancers."

Matt laughed. "Sounds like a good enough reason to get married right there."

Derrick pulled into the parking lot of the building

supply center. "I'll make it quick."

Ten minutes later, Matt still waited. The air turned hot in the truck, but Derrick had the keys and Matt had no way to lower the electric windows. With a car parked to his right, he could only open the door a crack, which didn't help much.

He waited two more minutes, fanning himself with his hand while sweat trickled from his brow. He needed something more than his hand. A map would work, and Derrick was just the type to own a map *and* keep it someplace handier than back home on a shelf.

He opened the glove box. Three maps to choose from. A Wisconsin state map, a Milwaukee street map, and a Minneapolis/St. Paul map, all folded so neatly it appeared they'd never been used. He chose the Wisconsin map because it was bigger and had more oomph. With the first swish through the air, a slip of paper fell onto Matt's lap—a bank receipt.

Seeing his bank's logo at the top, he realized he hadn't gotten any further calls about his loan payments. His benefactor must have given up.

"Thank God." He started to toss the receipt back into the glove box. He hesitated. Derrick didn't bank at Fuller Lake Community Bank.

Didn't matter. Wasn't his business.

Still, he scanned the receipt, feeling guilty for invading Derrick's privacy but curious enough to override the guilt. His stomach plummeted when he recognized his own account number. His loan payments. Blood pulsed at every pressure point as he stared at the receipt. He couldn't have felt more betrayed had he just learned Crystal was cheating on him.

The truck shifted when the tailgate was opened and the miter-box carton loaded onto the bed. The tailgate closed with a solid bang. Then the driver's door opened and Derrick hopped in. "Sorry it took so long. I ran into..."

Matt shifted his gaze from the receipt to his friend. Derrick's grin faded. He looked down at Matt's hand. "Oh, shit."

CHAPTER EIGHTEEN

"Why?" Matt held up the receipt. "Why did you do this?"

"Because you don't deserve what happened to you."

"Of course I don't deserve this." He slammed his fists against his legs. "But that's not your responsibility." He waved the crumpled receipt in the air. "My bills aren't either. Damn it, paying my loans behind my back and not telling me was wrong. Just plain wrong."

"I just wanted to help. I never meant to hurt you."

The thing was, it did hurt. Not that Derrick had paid the loans but that he'd kept it a secret. "Why didn't you say something, especially when I brought it up?"

"Because I know how you hate taking help from anyone. Admit it. If I'd offered you the money, you wouldn't have taken it, would you?"

"Of course I..." He sighed. "No."

"I knew your parents couldn't afford it any more than you could, but I also knew they'd do whatever it took to get you the money. I did this as much for them as for you."

It was hard to stay angry when faced with such an explanation. Matt knew his family meant as much to Derrick as they did to him. Still, it hurt that Derrick would do such a thing. "Thank you." His voice was harder than he'd intended. "Don't do it again, though. Okay?"

Derrick held up his hand, index and middle finger spread apart and the other fingers curled down. "Scout's honor."

Matt slugged Derrick but laughed while doing it. That's what being friends is all about, the way you can be angry and still find something to laugh about. "You weren't ever a scout and that's the peace sign, you idiot."

"Hey, I want peace."

"Then don't go paying any more of my bills. I mean it."

Derrick nodded but his eyes didn't meet Matt's.

"What else did you do?" Matt asked.

"I sort of bought you a car."

"Der...rick." His loan payments. Now a car. What next? His friend held up his hands. "If you don't want it, you don't have to keep it. I can sell it, easy. But it's already being set up with hand controls."

To say he didn't want it would make him look like an ungrateful jerk. "What you paid, all of it, including the car, that's a loan. I'm paying it back. Just as soon as I can."

"Wouldn't have it any other way."

"Good." He shoved the bank receipt back in the glove box with the map. He grinned. "What kind of car?"

"A '67 Camaro SS. Mint. Candy apple red."

"Der...rick!"

"I'm just kidding. It's a '98 Grand Prix, but it runs and it's got low miles."

"Good, 'cause that's all I need."

"Admit it though, the Camaro would have been cool."

"That it would, indeed." He leaned back and shook his head. Thanks to Derrick, he'd have wheels again. He was sitting pretty well financially. He was back to work.

Life was looking up.

§

Crystal's CRX was already in the driveway by the time his mother brought him home. He dragged his chair into the front seat and then grabbed one of his wheels. He had the wheel on and was reaching for the other when he remembered. He'd been on the computer.

Where were the printouts?

What about the computer? Had he turned it off?

He couldn't remember.

"Since Crystal's already home," his mother said, "would you mind if I don't stay?"

"No, that's fine." Better than fine. He had a feeling it was going to be safer for her and Kaylee that way.

Wheeling into the kitchen a moment later, he put

a smile in his voice. "Hey, babe," he called out. "Home already?"

He noticed her standing in the kitchen doorway, her pretty floral dress replaced with a designer running suit, her idea of dressing down. Then he noticed the stack of printouts in her hands. He had only enough time to notice how closely matched the color of her outfit was to her red cheeks before she slammed the ream of paper down on the counter. "Damn it, Matt. You promised."

"I was looking for a car." Weak excuse, and he knew it.

She picked up the top page. "Michigan dog walks after four months of paralysis." She crossed her arms, smashing the paper to her stomach. "How the hell is a Michigan dog going to help you find a car, Matthew? No, scratch that. How the hell is a Michigan dog being able to walk going to help you walk? Because that's what this is all about, isn't it? You walking." She wadded up the page, threw it at him, and then turned and stormed away.

He sat there with the wadded-up paper ball in his lap and his eyes riveted on the stack of paper on the counter. She didn't understand. The dog hadn't shown any improvement in four months, and then one day it just started walking. That could be him. Maybe one day he'd wake up and, like magic, he'd finally be able to walk again.

She just didn't understand any of it, and she didn't want to even try. He picked up the wadded paper and brought his arm back, ready to hurl it across the room while mentally he saw himself wheeling away from the house. Where he'd go didn't matter. Just away from here. Away from her.

He let his arm drop to his lap with the paper still in his hand. He didn't want to be away from her. Not really. He loved her. Deep down, he did, even if right then it was a little hard to remember how they had once been.

A loud bang came from the front of the house. Just what he needed, after the day he'd had. He thought about leaving her to stew in her anger. He thought again about leaving. Just wheeling away and never coming back. And then he pushed those thoughts from his mind and went after her. The curtains on the front door still swayed when he got to the living room, and Crystal was nowhere to be seen.

He wheeled onto the front porch and found her curled up on the swing, her knees pulled tight to her chest and her arms wrapped around her legs. She quickly turned her face away from him but not before he saw the tears glistening on her cheeks.

Today had been chock full of stress. All he wanted to do was go back into the house and leave her to act like a baby, if that's what she wanted. He couldn't do that. Not with her crying. But he couldn't go to her, either. Not when he was scared shitless that she was crying because she felt trapped.

"All day long that's all you do, isn't it?" she asked. "You sit at that damn computer and look for cures."

"No, that's not all I do. I went to work today, just like you've been begging me."

She looked his way. "You went back to work?"

"Yeah. They started the group home today. Dad asked me to, said he needed my help."

She shot out a laugh while she rolled her eyes and gave a quick shake of her head. "Your father. I should have known."

"What is your problem?"

"I shouldn't have to explain." She pushed herself off the swing and stomped past him, back into the house.

"What the hell does that mean?" The woman was driving him crazy. He tipped his head back and stared at the porch ceiling. "You love her. You really, really do."

§

Four days later, Matt still had no idea what Crystal had meant, but at least he no longer had to remind himself how much he loved her. And as an added bonus, today was Sunday, which meant he didn't have to pretend to be a help on the jobsite.

He looked at his brother nestled on their parents' couch next to Jenny, who was rubbing her very round belly. Hard to believe just six weeks ago nobody knew she was pregnant. He let his eyes shift to Crystal. He tried to imagine her stomach round, but he couldn't make the vision stick. Probably because it was impossible to get pregnant without having sex.

"Have you gotten the invitations yet?" his mother asked Crystal. "I can help address them if you'd like."

Crystal shifted on the hard wooden chair. "I meant to order them last week, but time got away from me."

Matt studied his fiancée while wondering who that woman was because it sure as heck couldn't be Crystal. The real Crystal had recited the wedding checklist over and over until he knew it better than he knew his shoe size. The invitations needed to be mailed six weeks before the wedding. That gave them only two weeks to get the invitations in the mail. Invitations that hadn't even been ordered yet.

Invitations she was hoping to not need?

Choosing to believe there had to be another reason, he forced a smile. "Planning on staying up all night addressing them, babe?"

Crystal glared at him. "No, I was planning on you helping and our staying up only half the night."

"Sure. 'Cause we know how neat my handwriting is." He said it in a teasing tone, but Crystal's expression didn't change.

"I know," Jenny said, her voice full of excitement. "We'll make a party out of it. We girls can address the invitations while the guys entertain Kaylee. Maybe I could convince Faith to come up. Surely she can leave the apartments for a few days."

"You miss your sister, don't you?" his mother said.

Jenny nodded. She caressed her stomach. "She was in Germany for Kaylee's birth. I hope she can be here for little junior's birth."

Brad's hand joined Jenny's, their fingers meshing while they both caressed their unborn child. "It could be another girl, you know."

"No. This one's a boy. I can tell. Brad Junior." She

snuggled her head onto Brad's shoulder. "Faith said she interviewed someone to take over the apartments, but the guy has a criminal record. Some disorderly conduct charge from ten years ago. Mom and Dad would never go for that."

"Your parents ever hear about this little thing called giving a guy a second chance?" Matt asked.

Jenny shrugged. "They want someone they feel a hundred percent comfortable with."

"That leaves me out." The job would be perfect for him. If the apartment complex wasn't in Milwaukee, that is.

"No, they like you. Mom always wanted you to hook up with Faith." Jenny quickly looked at Crystal. "Not that he was ever interested in her, mind you. The crush only went one way." Jenny's eyes grew large. "It's over, the crush. Faith's not interested in Matt any longer." Her gaze shot to Matt. "Not that she wouldn't be. She still thinks you're cute. It's because of Russ. She's married, you know."

"Honey," Brad said. "Maybe it's time to be quiet now."

Jenny nodded. She pressed her lips together like she was afraid of saying anything else.

§

When they got home later, Matt said to Crystal, "I can order the invitations. Save you from having to do it."

"It's fine. I can do it."

"When, babe? On your lunch hour? When you should be eating? I can do it when I go for therapy."

She turned away from him. "They need a deposit."

"So? I think I can hand them a check as easily as you can."

"Matt, we don't have the money right now."

Money. The simple explanation he'd been looking for earlier. If he could have stood and danced, he'd have done it. He wheeled to her and pulled her onto his lap. "Is that why you haven't ordered them? Because of money?"

She looked down.

"Have you been worrying about our money situation?"

Her head rose and fell once.

"Aw, babe." He snugged her up tight to his chest. "You

don't need to keep your worries to yourself. We need to discuss things like this, okay?"

She nodded again.

He brought his mouth to hers and kissed her once. "I love you." He kissed her again. "We have enough money in savings. You go tomorrow and order the invites, okay?"

After she nodded, he kissed her again, deeply and with need. He thought of Jenny with her round stomach and pictured Crystal cradling Kaylee. They'd planned on starting their family as soon as possible after getting married. He didn't want to wait. He wanted her pregnant now. He slid his hand beneath her shirt and cupped a satin-covered breast. He pulled his mouth from hers. "Let's go to bed."

"I need to write up the information for the invitations."

"It's waited this long. I don't think another hour or so will hurt."

She nudged his hand. "Did you see the expression on your mother's face? I wouldn't be surprised if she showed up here with address labels so we'd be ready when the order comes in. Speaking of which, do you have a list of people you want to invite?"

He pulled his hand out from beneath her shirt. A hopeless feeling that was becoming way too common struck another blow. What was the point in having a wedding when it seemed like all they'd be is roommates? "Sure thing. Got it all written out."

CHAPTER NINETEEN

After a week and a half of running for nails, sodas, and forgotten tools, Matt was starting to get used to being nothing more than a gofer. He sat in the shade of the tool trailer and watched his brother and Derrick line up a piece of siding. His father stood off to the side with Rex Johnson. Based on the waving of hands, he could tell Mr. Johnson wasn't happy about the progress of the project. It didn't help that every day at least one of the guys had to leave for a while to chip away at their backlog projects.

His father patted Rex Johnson's shoulder, reassuring. Matt could imagine his father loading on a pile of bullshit. *We're right on target, Rex. Don't you worry. We'll have this puppy tied down in plenty of time.*

Bullshit. That's what it was. A big, steaming pile of shit. And it was all Matt's fault.

They needed a miracle if they were going to get the group home done in time. He concentrated all of his thoughts on his right ankle, willing it to move. Nothing happened. Not even a quiver.

Mr. Johnson got in his truck. He didn't look happy as he drove away. Obviously, he knew a pile of shit when he stepped in it.

His father stood there, staring into space. Probably doing mental yoga trying to bring calm into his life. Matt gave up on his ankle. Looking at his father was just as depressing, so he watched Brad and Derrick install a piece of siding. He frowned as he estimated the board's length. They'd cut off sixteen inches to vary the length so the joints didn't land in the same location each run. Sixteen inches wasted. Lopped off too short to be used anywhere else and not look like a job done by a bunch of amateurs.

"No, no, no." He wheeled over to his brother. "I had it

all planned out so we'd be down to the exact amount of siding we needed. Didn't you look at the diagram?"

Brad held the siding in place with his hammer and looked down the ladder at his brother. "Sure I did, but who can read your writing? This made sense, so we went with it."

"No. It doesn't make sense. You cut off thirty-two inches, we can use it somewhere. We can't use sixteen."

"Who the hell made you boss?"

Their father joined the party, a roll of antacids in his hand. He popped a couple tablets in his mouth and then said, "I did. When it comes to materials, you listen to your brother."

"But—"

"But nothing, Bradley. You know your brother has a knack for making materials stretch. You also know, since he made the bid, that if anyone knows how close we are on materials, it'd be him. If he says not to make a sixteen-inch cut, then you listen to him."

Matt's heart thumped as he watched his father chomping the antacids that he thought were no longer a part of his life. This wasn't good.

"Yes, Dad." Brad glared at Matt.

Matt scanned the building, checking what had already been done. It looked like they'd be okay. He nodded at his father. "We'll be fine." He sighed, wishing he'd been talking about more than just the siding.

"Glad you were here. That could have cost us." His father looked up at the sky. "Weather looks like it's going to hold. We should probably make use of it and stain the trim even though we're not going to need it for a while. If I lay out some boards, you want to get going on that?"

Did he *want* to get going on the staining? Hell, no. Of everything his job entailed, staining and varnishing were his least favorite. But he read between the lines. His father was scrambling to find something for his least helpful employee to do. "Sure. I love staining."

His dad set up some boards in the cavernous living room/dining room area, right where weather conditions didn't matter. He tried to tell himself it was okay. At least he was doing something productive.

The sawhorses were the perfect height for someone standing. Not so perfect for someone sitting. Fifteen minutes later, he worked a kink out of his shoulder. A headache throbbed behind his watering eyes. Nothing like shoving your face right in the fumes. He eyed the boards lined up along the wall, all waiting for the grand treatment, and then looked at the few boards he'd done so far. It would take him until Christmas to finish.

"Great idea, Dad," he muttered as he moved to the next board. The room swam before him. He paused a moment until the sensation passed.

He had to get out of here. Get out in the fresh air. Hell, he needed to go a lot further away than just outdoors. He couldn't do this anymore, come to work every day and pretend he was useful. He put down the stain can and wheeled from the building where he sucked in fresh air. His father came running.

"Son, are you okay?"

Acid rolled around in his stomach, but the stain fumes had little to do with it. From the first time his father had brought him to a construction site, this was what he'd wanted. To be like his father. And now it was over. "I think I'm going to be sick. I have to go home."

By the time he pulled into his driveway, the nausea had passed. The headache still throbbed, but his eyes had stopped watering. He almost wished for the blurriness to return as he eyed the kitchen counter that in recent past had housed only the bare essentials. At least fifty various items were now crammed along the back wall of the counter. A cat cookie jar. Metal wildlife canisters. A giant mug that held pens and pencils. Decorative clutter. He'd told her to make the kitchen hers and she'd done just that. In his wildest dreams though, he couldn't have envisioned how much space her crap was going to take up.

Just like he hadn't envisioned turning into an old married couple so quickly when he'd suggested they live together. Not that he'd wanted sex every night, but once in the last six and a half weeks would have been nice. She obviously didn't feel the same.

He wondered how much of it had to do with his lifeless legs.

She claimed it didn't bother her. Easy to say, harder to live by. Still, he'd like to believe her because if he didn't, that made for a pretty bleak future. So he looked for another reason. Could simply be because she was a woman. Women and men had different ideas when it came to sex. Men wanted instant pleasure and then they were done. Women wanted all the crap that led up to the sexual act, the romance.

Romance. He just about whacked his forehead with the *ah-ha* awakening. That's what Crystal needed. Wasn't that what she'd been trying to tell him with the body oil rub? That she needed some tenderness.

Well, if romance was what she wanted, then romance was what she was going to get. He'd cook her dinner. Turn the lights low. Watch one of those chick flick movies with her that'd turn her teary-eyed. He'd sit on the couch with her even though it was easier to stay in the wheelchair. Romance wasn't about easy. It was about showing the other person how much you care.

Excited about his plans, he wrote up a grocery list and headed to his car. Within an hour, he was back home. Fresh cut flowers filled a vase that he'd put in the center of the table. Just call him Mr. Romance, he thought with a smile.

Instead of spaghetti sauce from a jar, he dug out a recipe he'd gotten in home-ec. Making sauce from scratch had to prove how much he loved her. Within minutes, the sauce bubbled, speckling the stovetop with red droplets. He boiled water in a pan and then dumped in a box of spaghetti noodles. He tossed the empty box onto the counter next to dripping, empty tomato sauce cans.

His grin spread. This was going to be so great.

§

Crystal pulled into the driveway while Matt was cutting

lettuce for a salad. *Here we go,* he thought with a grin as he grabbed the towel and wiped his hands. She was going to be so surprised. And happy. Nothing better than a surprised and happy woman. He dropped the towel onto the counter next to the tomato sauce cans and then turned toward the door.

"Home already?" She made it two steps into the kitchen and then stopped dead. Her gaze went to the counter where the empty tomato sauce cans sat. She sighed and her shoulders sagged. "Been home a while, I see."

Not quite the reaction he'd hoped for. Thank heavens he'd gotten the flowers. He motioned toward the vase. "Tonight's your lucky night."

She dumped her purse on the table so close to the vase that one of the straps fell against a tightly-closed rosebud. She turned away from the table and sighed as she stared at the counter where most of the clutter had accumulated. "Oh, I'm lucky all right."

Crystal's nose scrunched as she picked up a dripping tomato sauce can. The hairs on the back of his neck prickled as the can landed in the sink with a tinging whack. Why could she see the cans, but the vase filled with thirty-dollar roses was apparently invisible?

He took a deep breath as she picked up another can and threw it in the sink. "I can clean later," he said. "Dinner's done. Why don't you sit down?"

As if he'd spoken in a tone only animals could hear, she picked up another can and tossed it in the sink. With two fingers, she picked up the towel from the counter. "Damn it, this towel is ruined." She slammed it back onto the counter. "Why aren't you at work instead of home... cooking?"

He gave up on the illusion that romance was what she needed. "Because I'm useless there, just like I'm useless here."

She rinsed a can and then dumped it in the recycle bin under the sink. "You're not useless."

"Well, I obviously can't do anything right."

Another can landed in the recycle bin. He felt about

as important as the vase of flowers. Not even worthy of a *Don't be stupid, Matthew*. This was so not what he wanted in a relationship. None of it. He didn't think he could stand being with her another hour let alone another eighteen thousand two hundred and seventeen days.

"This isn't going to work, is it?"

"This what, Matthew?" She closed the cabinet door a little harder than necessary.

"Us. Our relationship."

"Sure, it is." She took the dirty towel and wiped it across the counter.

It all became so clear. He loved her. But he didn't want to be in this relationship alone. Not even to keep from telling his father he'd screwed up, once again. "No. It isn't."

He waited for her to protest.

She rubbed at the counter with a clean corner of the towel.

"Look at me, Crystal."

She turned, but her gaze seemed to settle somewhere above his head. Eighteen thousand two hundred and seventeen days wouldn't make any difference. It'd just be the both of them putting in their time, which wasn't what he wanted.

He knew what he had to do but he didn't think he could. If he called off the wedding, there'd be no going back. Their relationship would be over.

He stared at her as she stared at something else that wasn't him. Something shifted inside him, a reckoning. Their relationship was already over. It had been for quite some time. The hole in his chest deepened. "I'll call Pastor Ron and tell him to cancel the wedding ceremony."

Apparently forgetting the dirty towel in her hand, she hugged herself. Her gaze stayed focused above him. "That isn't what you want."

"Hell no, it isn't what I want." His voice boomed so loudly his half-deaf elderly neighbor could probably hear him. "I want us to be married until we die together at a ripe old age. I want us to fill this house with kids. I want us to spoil our grandchildren and great-grandchildren rotten." *I want what my parents have.*

His chest hurt. Every breath was a knife to his heart because he knew that every breath from here on would be without her. "What I don't want is a divorce in five years, and that's exactly where we're headed, if we even make it that long." He wheeled closer, wanting so desperately to hold her. He stopped when she was still just out of reach. "If that happened, if we got divorced, it'd kill me."

Her eyes lowered.

"Look at me, Crystal. Look at me and tell me I'm wrong. Tell me you haven't thought that it'd be okay to marry me because you could always get a divorce when it got too hard?"

The single tear that trailed down her cheek told him everything he needed to know. His own tears blurred his eyes but he refused to cry. He looked away from her. He stared at a pull knob on the cupboard. "If you get me all the numbers, reception hall, florist, caterer, I'll call everyone and cancel." He pushed his wheelchair backward, away from her, away from the future he'd wanted. "You can take as long as you want to move out. You can sleep in my old room upstairs."

He turned his chair around, toward the door. "I need to be alone. I'll be back later."

"That's it, Matt?"

He stopped but he didn't turn around. He couldn't. If he looked at her, he'd never be able to leave.

"You're just going to walk away again?"

Again? What the hell did she mean *again*? Hell, he couldn't even walk, let alone walk away *again*.

"Is there a reason not to?" He closed his eyes and listened hard, willing her to give him any excuse to stay. Even a hiccup and he'd be turned around and across the room, pulling her into his arms.

Silence. Nothing but silence behind him.

With , motions he wheeled forward, giving her time to stop him. How the hell was he supposed to tell his father he wasn't getting married? He kept his head high and rolled down the ramp, doing his best to act like this was any ordinary day—and that he wasn't dying inside. He made it to his car without her coming to the door to stop him.

It was really over.

He got in his car and drove aimlessly. The further he got from home the bigger the hole in his heart grew. How'd his life get so screwed up? Just three and a half months ago he'd been an active construction worker with a wedding so close he could smell the wedding cake. Now, he was nothing. A pile of waste.

He came to the area where he'd had his accident. He looked at the tree he'd crashed into and thought about crashing into it again. Just ending it all. What point was there in living? Every last plan he'd had for his future was gone. Kaput.

If he killed himself, he'd never have to face his father as a total failure.

It'd be so easy. Just turn the wheel. Apply more gas.

His tire crossed the center line. He envisioned the jarring crash. And then, darkness. Nothing. Over. Done.

He squeezed the gas lever a little harder. Then, he thought of Abby's mother. Brain damaged. She'd crashed into a tree and hadn't died. He hadn't died the last time he'd hit the tree. There was no guarantee he'd die this time, either. He could end up like Abby's mother. And then he'd definitely be of no use to his father.

He corrected his path, swerving back into his own lane. But now his thoughts were on Abby, wondering what kind of chipper advice she'd have for him right now. Too bad she wasn't here. She had a way of lifting him from whatever deep pit he'd fallen into. She'd been a good substitute for Derrick.

With that thought, he knew exactly where to go.

Back in the hospital, Abby had been a perfect substitute for Derrick. Now the tables had turned. It was Derrick he was going to use as a substitute for Abby.

He drove to Derrick's and stopped at the end of the driveway. He stared at Crystal's CRX parked next to the garage, seeming to glow in the flood-light on the side of the house. As Matt's friend, Derrick was also Crystal's friend. But it still surprised him that Crystal would turn to Derrick instead of one of her girlfriends.

He thought about backing up and going home, but he didn't want to go to an empty house. Maybe Crystal being at Derrick's was a sign. Maybe she'd realized she didn't want to call off the wedding. She'd come here thinking this was where he'd go.

Praying that was the case, he pulled in behind her car. He rushed through the process of putting the wheels back on his chair. With eager hands, he wheeled up the ramp Derrick had built for Matt's visits. He raised his hand to knock on the screen door and then hesitated when he saw Derrick through the open door with Crystal in his arms. For just a second, he felt a stab of jealousy, and then he talked himself out of it. Crystal was upset. Obviously, Derrick would comfort her.

She tipped her head back, and Derrick's mouth covered hers.

Feeling sick to his stomach, Matt grabbed the chair's push rims. He turned to leave and hit the door casing with his foot, the sound much louder than the creaking deck board. Derrick and Crystal stood frozen.

"Oh, God." He pushed backward on the wheels. Kept pushing. Had to get away. "Oh, God."

His wheel caught in the groove between two deck boards. He pushed hard. The next thing he knew, he was bouncing backward down the steps. He grabbed the wheels, trying to stop his backward motion. The chair flipped and went in one direction while he went in another, landing hard on the pavement. Stars sparkled all around him.

The back door opened and closed with a slam. "Oh, no. Matt." Crystal's voice mingled with the sound of footsteps. Derrick and Crystal crowded around him.

Matt grabbed his wheelchair and pulled it upright.

"Are you okay?" Derrick reached out, ready to help Matt.

Matt pushed away Derrick's hand. His head throbbed. "You're bleeding." Crystal poked lightly at Matt's head. *Gotta get away.* Derrick reached out again to help. Matt glared at him. "Don't fucking touch me."

Derrick and Crystal stood like stone statues while Matt worked himself into his chair, his head throbbing with every movement. Blood dripped down the back of his head, seeping through his hair. He could do this. He had to.

His eyes went to Derrick as he struggled to lift himself. The man who'd been his best friend for the last eighteen years had been kissing Crystal. The truth lodged hard in his stomach. This kiss hadn't been their first. Acid tickled the back of his throat. He took quick, deep breaths. The acid rose, bringing with it the urge to vomit.

Needing to get away, he gathered all his strength and pushed himself up that last little bit that brought him into his chair. His breaths came faster, in quick pants. He had to get away.

He wheeled forward, aiming as best he could for his car. It felt like the world was tipped at a crazy angle, pulling his chair toward the grass instead of down the driveway.

Derrick stopped the chair's forward movement. "I can't let you drive like that."

Matt's attention shifted to the man who'd just been kissing his fiancée. Something inside him snapped. He turned and pushed against Derrick's stomach, forcing him to take a backward step in order to stay upright. "How long have you been fucking my fiancée?"

"Shhh," Crystal said.

"What?" Matt screamed. "You afraid of what the neighbors will think? Afraid they'll find out you were fucking him while you were living with me? Pretending you wanted to be my wife?"

"It wasn't like that," Crystal said.

"How could you?" Matt demanded, hitting Derrick in the gut at the end of each sentence. "She was my girl. You were my best friend. How could you do this?"

Derrick's eyes slid closed. He shook his head. "I never meant to fall in love with her. It just happened."

Fall in love?

The world tilted again. Matt struggled to stay in balance. "Oh. I feel so much better now." He turned on Crystal. "And you. You were making plans to marry me." He tossed up his arms. "You know what? You two deserve each other. You're both sick, twisted people."

Unable to stand being near them anymore Matt pushed his way around them. With each movement of his arms, a puzzle piece fell into place. Derrick paying his loans and not being straight about it. Buying him a car. All the work he put in at Matt's house. All of it to cover his guilt.

What about Crystal's insistence that she hadn't talked to him the day of the accident, despite her calling his cell phone over and over? What about the calls having been deleted from his phone's history? Derrick advising him to forget about the accident.

They knew why he'd had the accident.

He turned his chair around. He eyed Derrick and then Crystal before his gaze went back to Derrick. "You know why I had the accident, don't you? You both know why I was out there."

Crystal and Derrick looked at each other. In that split second, they held an entire conversation without words, just like Matt's parents. The way he and Crystal never could. Derrick said, "Not out here. Come into the house."

Going into the viper pit was the last place Matt wanted to go, but a perverse need to know had him following them up the ramp and into the house.

Derrick sat on the edge of the couch while Crystal stood in the doorway with fifteen feet of air separating them. Even that far apart, they seemed connected.

"I want to make it clear," Derrick said. "We never meant to..."

"...hurt you," Crystal finished

Matt laughed.

"It's true," Derrick said.

Matt looked at Crystal. She shrugged. "I really did love you, Matt. When you asked me to marry you, I was so happy. But I have to admit I had feelings for Derrick, even then. Feelings I kept pushing away. Until..." Her gaze dropped. Color rose to her cheeks.

Sick, morbid curiosity filled him. Unable to keep his mouth shut Matt said, "Until...?"

"Until we kissed."

The reality hurt more than he'd expected. His stomach churned. He no longer wanted to know.

"Last Labor day," Derrick said, grinding in the truth. "When we were camping. You'd gone on a bike ride. Crystal wanted to go for a hike. I knew you wouldn't want her to go alone."

Matt wanted to put his hands over his ears. Wanted to sing a nonsense song to drown out Derrick's words. La-la-la-la-la.

"She almost fell and I grabbed her, to stop her fall. That's when it happened. When we kissed."

"We tried to hide our feelings," Crystal said. "We agreed it'd be best to stay apart, but you kept pushing, kept saying how we should do things with Derrick. I couldn't say no. Not without making you wonder why."

Matt laughed. "So it's my fault? You two go off and have an affair because I thought I should be able to do things with my fiancée *and* my best friend at the same time?"

"We're not blaming you," Derrick said.

Well, he felt a hell of a lot better knowing that.

"That day, the day of your accident," Crystal said, "I decided I had to finally break it off with you. I wanted to meet you at The Hideout."

"Somewhere public where I wouldn't make a scene."

Crystal looked away. "It seemed like a good idea at the time."

"All the calls on my cell phone. You were calling to arrange a meeting."

Crystal nodded.

He fought the truth. "But we never talked. I lost my cell

phone. I made it home. I crawled through the window."

"And then I called you at home."

A headache throbbed behind Matt's eye.

"I told you we had to talk. That it was important. I told you to meet me at The Hideout, and then I hung up."

Matt rubbed his forehead. "And I ran right out to see you, just like you knew I would." What an idiot he was. Crystal calls. Matt jumps.

Crystal slid down the wall and crouched on her heels. She closed her eyes. Her arms went around herself in a protective hug. "When you came in, I almost chickened out. Before I could say a word, you asked if I was finally going to tell you what was wrong. So I told you. Everything. Right down to Derrick.

"You just sat there. Staring at the ring on the table. When I stopped talking, you gave me a kiss, wished me luck, and then you left. An hour later, your parents called to say you'd had an accident. A bad one. I have no idea what happened after you left. I don't know why you had the accident. I only know why you were out."

All of the air in the room sucked outward through every crack, leaving nothing inside for him to breathe. He dropped his head forward and pressed his hands to his face. For all he knew, she could be lying. But he didn't think so. The woman he loved so much, he'd walked away from without a fight. And now he'd done it twice.

What had he done then? After he'd left her that first time? Had his anger erupted after he'd left the bar? Had he rammed his truck into a tree? Like he'd almost done less than an hour ago? Or had it been as the word implied? An accident? Nothing more?

A strong hand appeared on his shoulder. The fingers were heavy. "I'm sorry."

Matt looked up at the man who'd been his friend. More than a friend. A brother. The hurt that cut through him was worse than Crystal's betrayal. He pushed away the hand that had once given comfort.

He wheeled outside with a sense of loss, knowing this would be the last time he'd leave this house.

Back home he saw evidence of Crystal and Derrick everywhere he looked. The very car he sat in was thanks to Derrick. The roof Derrick had helped shingle. The flowers Crystal planted. The evidence was inside, as well. The new trim around the door Derrick had widened. The light green paint Crystal picked out. The hardwood floor in his bedroom Derrick had refinished. The lamp Crystal had helped him pick out.

He picked up Crystal's picture from beside the bed. The photo from that fateful camping trip. How could she claim she'd fallen in love with Derrick that weekend? This picture proved otherwise. She stared out from the frame with so much love it could have brought him to his knees. Every bit of love, directed at him, straight through the camera's lens.

Every bit of love, directed straight through the camera's lens—to the person holding the camera.

His stomach turned as he remembered. Derrick had taken the picture. Not him.

The picture slipped from his fingers and landed on his lap. It seemed to grow, Crystal's smile mocking him.

The love that had helped Matt through his lowest days in the hospital whenever he'd looked at this picture had been a sham.

He hurled the picture across the room. It hit the doorjamb and crashed to the glossy hardwood floor Derrick had so expertly refinished. The glass shattered, its shards glittering in the lamplight like the diamonds in Crystal's engagement ring.

His whole life was a lie.

He could find thousands of miracles on the Internet, but that didn't mean he would ever walk again.

He could go to work every day, but that didn't make him a contributing member of Huntz & Sons Construction.

He could pretend he was okay with letting his best friend have a relationship with his ex-fiancée, but he wasn't okay with it. Not okay at all.

His tires crunched as he wheeled through the broken glass and headed for the fridge. As the cold beer made its way down his throat, he planned how to right what had gone wrong. First thing in the morning, he'd go to his father. With just a few words, he could get Derrick fired, and he wouldn't feel even one bit guilty. His ex-friend didn't deserve to be a member of the Huntz crew.

§

Bright sunshine streamed into Matt's bedroom the next morning. Crystal's side of the bed stretched out in front of him. He knew she was gone but he listened for sounds of her anyway. Hearing none, he closed his eyes, but he couldn't sleep. A gut-wrenching pain filled him.

His alarm clock went off. He silenced it with a slap of his hand, but he made no effort to get out of bed. Why should he? Nobody would miss him at the jobsite. In fact, they'd probably be thankful he wasn't there slowing them down.

The phone rang shortly after nine o'clock. He didn't answer. He couldn't answer. He couldn't make himself move. A mechanical version of his voice filled the air, telling the caller he was out having fun and to leave a message after the beep.

Fun? Is that what this was? Felt a long way away from fun.

"Matt, are you okay?" his mother asked the recorder. "Your father said you didn't show up for work. Matthew?" Her voice took on a worried tone. "I'm coming over."

He didn't want that. Her here, fussing over him. He grabbed the phone by the bed. "Ma, I'm fine. Just tired. I had a big night."

"Matthew?" The single word held all the worry in the world. No matter what he said, she'd still come to prove to herself he really was okay unless he proved it to her first.

"Tell Dad I'll be at the jobsite in an hour, okay?"

"Are you sure you're okay?"

"Just fine, Ma." He squeezed his eyes closed. Could a person live with a heart that had been torn to shreds? A tear slipped free. "Just fine."

True to his word, he was at the jobsite in exactly one hour. His father was deep in a conversation with Rex

Johnson, but Matt barely noticed. Instead, his gaze went directly to Derrick standing by a stack of siding. Derrick pulled a pair of tin snips from his belt and clipped the wire band wrapped around a bundle of siding. Matt tightened his grip on the steering wheel. The movement of Derrick's legs were so automatic. Hate filled him. Hate for Derrick being able to stand. Hate for Derrick being a productive member of Huntz & Sons Construction. Hate for Derrick being what Matt used to be.

Unable to stomach Derrick any longer, he looked over at his brother standing on a ladder propped up against the building. Brad seemed to be paying more attention to their father than to the siding.

"What's up?" Matt asked as he wheeled up to Brad.

"Rex ain't a happy camper. We should be much further along than we are. He's threatening to pull the project."

"He can't do that. We've got a contract."

"It's his money. He can do whatever he wants."

Derrick came back and climbed the ladder. Unlike Brad, he was like a mad-man on speed. Constant motion. If Matt's father had any chance of getting this project done in time, he needed Brad *and* Derrick. It was Matt who was expendable. Even though Derrick deserved to get fired, Matt couldn't make it happen. Not now.

Keeping Derrick on wasn't enough. They needed another crew member, someone who wasn't useless and in the way. As long as Matt was around, his father would refuse to hire another worker.

An idea took seed.

"Is Faith still looking for someone to manage the apartments?" he asked his brother.

"This contract is falling down around us, and you're worried about the damn apartment building?"

"Is Faith still looking for someone?" He enunciated each word.

"Yeah, she is."

Her parents liked him. He figured all he'd have to do was say he wanted the job and it'd be as good as his. But that would put him two hundred miles away from the people he loved, people he'd need in the coming days as he faced life without Crystal.

A truck door slammed behind him. The motor caught and revved. Tires spun on the gravel. Matt looked over his shoulder. His father stood in place, his head tracking Rex Johnson's retreat. He ran a hand through his hair.

For a long moment, there was no sound. Matt realized both Brad and Derrick were watching his father, as well. His father lowered his hand. He looked toward his crew.

"What are you staring at? Get those hammers moving."

With long strides, his father crossed the jobsite. He disappeared into the tool trailer.

"Think Rex will really pull the contract?" Matt asked.

"No doubt about it," Brad answered.

Moving to Milwaukee was the perfect answer, but Matt didn't think he could do it. How could he leave his family now? When he had nobody in his life but them? He had to convince his father to replace him, but there had to be a way that didn't involve moving away. He wheeled over to the tool trailer. His father was kneeling, his head bowed and hands clasped. Praying for a miracle.

"Dad?"

His father lowered his hands and grabbed a square from a hook in the pegboard in front of him. "Just looking for the square."

"Dad, I'm quitting."

"Damn it, Matthew. Not now."

Matt held up his hands, non-threatening. "Yes, Dad. Now. I'm slowing things down. You can't hire someone who can actually help as long as I'm on the payroll. Don't you see? The only way to save this project is for me to quit."

He'd already spent over a month in Milwaukee, and he'd lived through it.

But this time it wouldn't be for just a month. He couldn't expect his family to drop everything to come visit him every weekend. And he probably couldn't abandon the apartments to come to Fuller Lake weekly either.

His father pushed his way out of the tool trailer. "I

won't hear of it."

He'd be in Milwaukee longer than a month, but it wouldn't be for a lifetime. As soon as he was walking again—and he *would* walk again—he'd be back. As soon as he could take back the life Derrick had stolen from him. "Doesn't matter," he told his father, "'cause it's not your decision. I quit."

His father ran his fingers through his hair again. "Matthew."

"Just shut up, okay? If I find a replacement, will you hire him?"

"No." The word shot out without hesitation.

"Well, you're going to have to. I took a job down in Milwaukee," he said, sealing his fate. "It starts right away. I'm going to call the other builders. See if they have someone they can spare or if they know of anyone looking for a job. When that person shows up reporting for duty, you're going to hire him. You got it?"

"I said no. I need you here."

"I can't stay. Crystal and I broke up." The words he hadn't meant to say. Not yet. Not until he was used to the idea and it no longer hurt. But the words were out and he couldn't pull them back. So he told the truth. "Don't you see, Dad? I can't stay here, not when I'll keep running into her. I need to leave."

His father leaned against the tool trailer like all the air had been sucked from him. "I'm sorry. What happened?"

He thought about Derrick, about his plans to get him fired. But his father really did need Derrick's help. "It just wasn't working. That's all."

"You sure you need to leave?"

Matt nodded.

His father's jaw turned hard, but he didn't protest.

Matt nodded in Derrick's direction. "I just need to talk to him a sec and then I'll be on my way."

He wheeled over to Derrick. Without looking at the man who'd been his friend, he said, "Meet me by my...the car. Now."

Without waiting to see if Derrick had heard or whether

he was obeying, Matt wheeled over the hard, bumpy terrain one last time. He got in the car that was only three percent his and ninety-seven percent Derrick's and worked on removing his chair's wheels. The passenger door opened. The car shifted slightly as Derrick sat down and then pulled the door closed, reviving Matt's anger. Derrick might have bought him a car, but Matt hadn't asked him to. And he certainly hadn't given Derrick permission to steal his fiancée. He had half a mind to tell Derrick he could have the damn thing back, but he really needed a car now that he'd come up with this great plan to move.

Matt put the wheels in the back and then hauled his chair into the car. When everything was in place, he put his hands on the steering wheel and stared ahead. It hurt to be cooped up in the car with the man he'd always thought would be his friend. "I came here today ready to get you fired. I could do that, you know. All I'd have to do is tell Dad what you did, and you'd be out of here before you could blink. Even now, with this project coming down around us."

"What changed your mind?"

"I love my father more than I hate you. Like it or not, my dad needs you. You're a good worker."

"Thank you."

"Don't thank me. Like I said, I'm not doing this for you. I'm doing it for Dad." He finally looked at Derrick and was surprised by the dark circles under Derrick's eyes. He looked away. "I'd like you out of my car now."

Derrick looked a little bit lost as he got out of the car. Matt didn't care. Derrick wasn't his concern. Not anymore.

Matt went home and pulled out the phonebook. Within an hour he had a new employee lined up for his dad. And just like that, Huntz & Sons was now Huntz, Son, & Two Unrelated Dudes. Now it was time to make the call that'd take him away from Fuller Lake.

But first he wheeled from room to room in the house he loved, the house so much like the one he'd grown up in, the house he'd bought with a family in mind. A family with Crystal.

He stopped in the kitchen and stared at the canisters and knickknacks that still filled the counter. Clutter. Had it really been only yesterday that he'd complained about all her crap? Now he couldn't stand the thought of the cupboards being bare again.

This house was just that—a house—no longer a home. He flipped open his cell phone and dialed Faith's number. She was speechless as he told her his idea. They'd swap houses. He'd manage the apartments. She could stay in his house until Russ came home from Afghanistan. The only thing was, he wanted the move to happen as soon as possible. Tomorrow.

That done, he pulled out his checkbook and wrote out a three-thousand dollar check to Derrick he that couldn't really afford. If he had to, he'd eat stale bread and water until he'd paid Derrick back every cent he owed. Being in debt to the traitor was one monkey he didn't want choking him any longer than necessary.

CHAPTER TWENTY

Matt wheeled a triangle in Faith's compact apartment. He'd never think of it as *his* apartment. Dining room. Kitchen. Living room. Then back to the dining room. A caged lion. That's what he was. A caged lion separated from his pride. Three weeks without his family. Three weeks cooped up in this tiny apartment. Three weeks with a social life that amounted to listening to his neighbors' arguments through the wall followed by the sounds of them making up.

On a trip back to the living room, he caught sight of the phone. Back in the old days, he'd have called Derrick to go shoot some baskets with him or go fishing. Those days were gone. Forever.

He faced the TV, turning his back on the phone. His reflection stared back at him from the forty-two inch screen. A lonely man in need of a haircut and a shave and a purpose in life.

He took a long draw from the bottle of Miller that had been tucked between his legs. Barely past noon, and he was drinking already. Alcohol. The perfect substitute for friends.

The telephone rang. He snatched it up before the second ring. It could be a salesman and he wouldn't care, although it was Derrick who came to mind. Like he'd really want to talk to the back-stabbing son-of-a-bitch. "Hello."

"Good, I got you."

It wasn't Derrick. Not like he really thought it would be. Nor did he want it to be. "Hi, Dad."

The whine of a saw competed with the echo of hammers in action. Matt could almost smell the scent of fresh-cut pine. He should be there, adding to the hammer symphony.

"I'm looking at your diagram for the lobby's tile. I can't tell from your notes if we're using the six inch tiles or the four inch. Do you remember?"

"Six inch. Bigger room, bigger tiles." Which his father already knew. It was, after all, his rule. "The fours are for the bathrooms."

"That's what I thought, but I wanted to be sure."

"How's the build going?" What he really wanted to ask was how Derrick was doing. Was the jerk as lonely as he was? Or was he too busy with Crystal to be lonely? "Back on schedule?"

"Close enough to make Rex happy."

Based on the relaxed tone of his father's voice, Matt read that to mean they were back on target. Spending time on needless chit chat wouldn't keep them that way, but he didn't want to hang up. "And the new guy?"

"Doesn't know shit about making materials stretch, and he's got a total lack of vision."

"So he's working well, huh?"

His father grunted. A "yes" without admitting it. "How's the manager job?"

"Keeps me busy." In three weeks, he'd fixed one electrical problem. That's all. It'd taken him all of fifteen seconds to diagnose the problem and flip the wall switch the tenant didn't realize controlled the outlet.

"Too busy to write up a bid for me? Gotta line up some fall work."

"I think I can squeeze it in."

"Good. I'll email the details later when I get home."

"Sounds like a plan." *Don't hang up. Not yet.*

"While I've got you, do you have any idea what's eating Derrick?"

Guilt, he hoped. "No idea."

"I thought maybe he would have said something to you."

"No. We haven't talked much." Did *not at all* count as *not much*?

"Something going on between you two?"

Not anymore. "Of course not."

"Well then, maybe you could feel him out the next time you talk."

"Sure. I'll do just that." When hell freezes over.

"Your mother wants to come down for a visit. Probably not this coming weekend, but we'll make it soon. As soon as we have a comfortable lead on the group home."

We'll come visit. But not right now. Like a carrot jerked away from a hungry horse. "I'll get out the good china then."

His father laughed. "Chinet instead of Dixie, huh?"

"And Cool Whip bowls instead of the cheap brand." Anything to keep his father talking.

"Well, Son, I've got to go. Take care. I love you." And then he was gone.

"I love you too, Dad," he said to the dial tone, already missing his contact to home. He held his thumb on the reset button and pinched the bridge of his nose with his other hand. A tear managed to escape, anyhow. Just like he was some kind of girl.

"Pathetic," he mumbled as he swiped the back of his hand across his cheek. Not like it mattered. There wasn't anyone to see him crying. Nobody to care. He was in a city of six hundred thousand people and he'd never felt more alone. Him, Matthew Huntz, the guy who'd always had a pack of friends—all alone. No family. No friends. No Derrick.

"Who needs him?" Matt slammed the phone onto the cradle harder than he'd intended. "Who the fuck needs him?"

He wheeled to the kitchen, to the dining room, to the living room, and back to the kitchen.

Why Derrick? If Crystal had to cheat, why couldn't it have been with someone else? And why, of all the women in the world, why'd Derrick have to pick Crystal to finally fall in love with?

"They deserve each other," he mumbled as he grabbed a fresh Miller from the fridge. "I don't need him, and I don't need her. I'm fine on my own." He wheeled to the living room and parked in front of the blank TV again, facing the lonely reflection in need of a haircut, a shave, and a purpose in life. "Just fucking fine."

He watched his reflection as he took a drink of his beer. Getting drunk wasn't going to get him back to work. He should be figuring out a way to get his legs moving again. At the very least, he should be at a health club lifting weights, keeping in shape, doing whatever he could to prove that Derrick hadn't won.

Tomorrow. He'd find a health club tomorrow.

He finished off his beer and wheeled to the fridge for another. He twisted off the cap and took a deep swig. He could feel the cold liquid all the way down his throat. He just wished he could feel it clouding his brain, wished desperately for the numbness he sought. Instead, everything was too vibrant. The emptiness inside him too deep a cavern. The loneliness too present. His family, too absent. And him, too fresh out of friends.

An image of Abby flashed in his mind.

He set the bottle on his knee. Abby lived in Milwaukee. The rehab center was only a few miles away. Next to Derrick she'd been the only person he knew who he could bare his soul to, and heaven knows he had a lot of baring to do these days.

He wheeled to the phone. As he dialed Milwaukee Spine Care Center's phone number, he realized he must be well on his way to being drunk or he never would have called her.

"Milwaukee Spine Care Center. How may I direct your call?"

"Abigail Fischner, please."

This is stupid, he thought as he listened to canned Muzak while waiting to be connected. He and Abby weren't really friends. Talking with her had been nothing more than a way to pass the time. And she certainly had better things to do than keep him company.

He was about to hang up when the music died off and he heard Abby's voice. "Abigail Fischner."

What the hell. "Hi. It's Matt Huntz, in need of a good

listener. Can you meet me at Bar None after work?" He chose the bar based on location. "It's not that far from the center. About a fifteen-minute drive." Just around the corner from the apartment. Close enough he could wheel home drunk, if need be.

For six long seconds he heard not a sound. Abby trying to figure out a polite way to say no. But just as he was ready to write her off, she said, "I have to visit my mother right after work, but I can meet you at six thirty, if that's okay."

Six hours. He took a swig of his beer. He'd be so drunk by then he wouldn't remember what he wanted to talk to her about. He liked the not remembering part. "Sounds perfect."

Waiting at Bar None sounded like a much better alternative to staying cooped up in the tiny apartment for the next six hours.

Outside, he squinted at the bright sunlight. Had the sun always been this bright?

Bar None was the complete opposite of the outdoors. He sat just inside the doorway for a moment while his eyes adjusted to the hazy darkness. A man with a *ZZ Top* beard wiped down glasses behind the bar. A woman wearing shorts that were so short her ass hung out and a tank top that looked two sizes too small carried a tray loaded with dirty glasses and beer bottles.

Laughter came from a booth at the far end of the bar. People who knew how to have a good time.

A man and a woman sat at the bar. The man rubbed her leg while he spoke.

Two men at the pool table took turns pretending they knew what they were doing. In the few seconds Matt watched them from across the room, he decided he could probably teach them a thing or two, even stuck in a wheelchair.

People, Matt thought as a smile formed. All around him, people. Too bad he hadn't come here *before* calling Abby. Then he could have saved her from wasting her time.

He wheeled to the back of the bar and took a place at one of the tables close to the pool table. He'd watch for a while, study the men's techniques, and then offer a challenge. Good way to kill an afternoon. Too bad he hadn't thought of coming here earlier, like three weeks ago.

The waitress laid a napkin in front of him. Her breasts spilled over the top of the too-tight knit shirt. Breasts like that could help him forget Crystal. Breasts like that could help him forget he'd lost his best friend. Putting on his best smile, he reached into his shirt pocket for some money, but his keys were in the way. He dropped the keys onto the table and then pulled a crumpled ten from his pocket. "Miller Draft. And a drink for yourself."

She eyed his wheelchair. "Thanks, but Charlie don't like me getting too chummy with the customers."

Pretending she was staring at him and not his chair, he said, "But he doesn't mind you becoming dehydrated?"

Her eyes came back to him. "De...hide...what?"

Silicone poisoning, he decided as he pushed the crumpled ten closer to her. "Just bring me a Miller, okay?"

One of the men at the pool table looked his way and nodded a polite greeting. The perfect opportunity to strike up a conversation. Matt nodded back, but looked away.

Why are you still sitting here, you dip-shit? You wanted to shoot pool, so get your ass over there.

A billiard ball smacked against another one, followed by the sound of the ball rolling over the felt before ricocheting off the bumper. The game was underway again. It'd be rude to interrupt. As soon as he heard a lull, he'd go over.

He shifted his attention to the couple at the bar. The man smiled and nodded at the exit. The woman crawled off the barstool. The man slid his arm around her waist and led her to the door.

Even though it had been a long time since Matt had walked with Crystal, he could feel the memory of her nestled against him. He crossed his arms, but they still felt empty. Sure bet Derrick's arms didn't feel as empty.

A tightness formed in Matt's throat.

Needing a distraction, he turned his attention back to his pool-shooting pals. What he saw was himself and Derrick shooting pool, laughing, having a good time. His chest constricted and his eyes burned. *God, please, don't let me start crying. Not here.*

The blonde with the breasts brought him his beer. Concentrating on the exploding display of skin helped take the edge off his loneliness. She had a little mole deep in her cleavage that looked a little bit like a heart. Staring at the mole, he asked, "You sure I can't buy you a drink?"

"I'm up here, sugar."

He lifted his eyes.

"I told you, Charlie don't like me drinking with the customers."

"Charlie would get over it."

"No, he wouldn't. He's my boyfriend."

Great. He hadn't come here to get himself killed by a *ZZ Top* wannabe. He lifted the beer. "Then, I'll drink this one for you."

As soon as she left, he set the bottle down and wrapped both hands around it. He stared at the mouth as though it were a crystal ball that held the answers that'd fix his life. All he saw in the crystal ball was the opening to a pit of nothingness.

He drained the last of his beer from the defective crystal ball and held up the empty, indicating he needed a refill. The waitress brought him a fresh beer.

§

Abby stood outside Bar None and finger-combed her hair. Her stomach fluttered at the thought of how close Matt was. In less than a minute, she'd be seated across a table from him. Would it be like their after-hours chats? Her stomach fluttered again. If she were smart, she'd turn on her heel and run as fast as she could to her car.

She wasn't smart though, because she saw her hand reaching for the door handle. *Lord, don't let me regret this.*

Just inside the door, she scanned the faces through the dim lighting. There were several men at the bar clumped in groups of two or more. Two men were taking turns hitting balls around the pool table while two more men waited for their turn. No Matt. Maybe he'd changed his mind. Which would be a good thing.

Someone by the pool table moved, revealing the lone man sitting at a table tucked in the corner. Forty feet separated them but she recognized Matt as though she'd seen him yesterday, instead of months ago. His hair was longer. Much longer. And he needed a shave. But it was him. She could tell by the way her heart was pounding.

She moved toward him. Ten feet still separated them when she noticed the empty beer bottles and the loose change on the table. Either he'd been there a while, more than a couple of hours based on the number of empties, or he'd chosen the dirtiest table in the joint.

He downed the rest of his beer and waved the bottle in the air before he added it to his collection, making her reasonably sure he hadn't picked the dirtiest table. She thought again about making a dash for her car. Chances were good, with that many empties littering the table, he'd never notice she hadn't shown up. She took a step backward. Then he looked her way. A wave of heat flushed through her as his dark eyes locked onto hers. She pressed her hand to her chest and acknowledged that she was about to dive into the deep end without a life vest.

CHAPTER TWENTY-ONE

Although Abby had finally reached her goal of working exclusively with brain-injured patients, the victory had barely carried her through each day these last two months. Her world had seemed flat without the after-hours visits with Matt. Even her mother's progress had seemed less astounding than it should have. Now, as she slid into a chair across from Matt, her world felt complete. She smiled, even though she knew the happy place she'd reached was a bad thing. It would be that much further to fall. "Long way to come for a drink, isn't it?"

"Not when *home* is just around the corner."

She arched her eyebrows. "You live here? In Milwaukee?"

"That's what my mailing address says."

"But I thought you loved Fuller Lake and your house there."

He croaked out a laugh. "The house got a little too big and Fuller Lake got a little too small."

She wasn't sure what to make of his answer. "How does Crystal like living in Milwaukee?"

"She doesn't. Live in Milwaukee, that is."

The meaning of what he'd said sank in. She put her hand on his arm. "Oh, Matt. I'm so sorry."

He pulled away from her touch. "Don't be. It's over and done with."

His words sounded tough, but he didn't look tough. He looked broken. There was a sad edge to those dark eyes. He didn't look like a guy overjoyed to be free of the *old ball and chain*. Like so many times during their past discussions, she felt the urge to wrap him in a hug. He wasn't her patient. He was no longer engaged. Two good reasons to get up and leave.

"She was messing around with my best friend," Matt

said.

"Derrick?"

A pained expression pinched his mouth and eyes as he nodded.

"Oh, Matt." She leaned into him before she realized what she was doing. "I'm sorry." She wrapped her arms around him. He felt solid against her. For a moment, he stayed stone still. Then he relaxed all of that solid weight against her. His arms went around her. His breath warmed her shoulder. She gave a silent sigh.

Matt turned his head, just a little. He kissed her neck. Just a little. Just enough to get her heart pumping. And to make her want more. If she turned her head, just a little, his kiss would move to her lips. She tensed her muscles, refusing to give in. As quickly as they'd come together he pulled away, the moment gone.

"I'm drunk," he said. "More drunk than I'd thought, 'cause for a second there—just a second mind you—I forgot what a pain in the ass you can be."

Her world felt off kilter. She wrapped her arms around herself. "And I forgot how darned stubborn you are."

The waitress chose that moment to walk past the table. He downed the rest of his beer and waved the bottle. "Bring me another, darlin'."

The waitress stopped and eyed his mounting collection. "I think you've had enough."

With his attention centered on the skin spilling out of the top of the waitress's shirt he said, "Trust me, I'm not drunk enough yet. Bring me another."

This wasn't the Matt she knew.

"One more," the waitress said. "And then I'm cutting you off."

He watched the waitress move away, the short shorts creeping up, showing off twin pale crescents of soft flesh. When she moved out of view, he turned his attention to the most-recently emptied beer bottle, picking at the label with a fingernail that needed cutting.

"Damn, that waitress might be right. I must be damn drunk 'cause I can't believe I told you about Crystal and

Derrick." His eyes raised to her. "I haven't told anyone, not even my parents. They think I left town because I needed a change of scenery. They had no idea part of it was because I couldn't stand seeing Derrick, knowing he'd been messing around with her."

She touched Matt's arm again. "I'm sorry."

"He's back there, in Fuller Lake, still working for my dad, while I'm stuck in this hell hole of a city in a life I hate with a body that doesn't work." He lifted the beer bottle and peered into its depths.

She fought the urge to comfort him more. "Maybe you just need to find something you like to do and start doing it."

"I already have." He tipped the bottle toward her. "I enjoy drinking."

With a nod at his collection of empties, she said, "Then you need to find something more challenging because you've mastered the fine art of drinking."

He peered into her eyes with the same intensity he'd given the beer bottle. "What I need is to stop being such a fuckup. When I asked Crystal to marry me, I thought I was finally getting my life together."

"You're not a...you know. It's understandable you're feeling down, but you and Crystal breaking up isn't a reflection on you."

"You don't understand. Dad married Mom the day after her high school graduation. He'd just turned nineteen. Brad was born nine months later, me a year after Brad."

"My parents married young, too. That's what people did back then."

"It's still how it's done in my family." He tipped back an empty, shaking it against his tongue before setting it back down. "Where's that damn waitress with my beer?"

She placed her hand on his, hoping to distract him from the alcohol he didn't need. "You're far from being an old spinster, or whatever they call it for guys."

"Tell that to my dad. My twenty-fifth birthday he takes me aside and tells me I'm not getting any younger and that it's time I think about settling down. I met Crystal two months later and six months after that we were engaged."

"You asked Crystal to marry you just to make your dad happy?"

"Yes." He shook his head. "No. I mean, I would have asked her to marry me anyhow, but I would have waited if it'd been up to me."

"You wouldn't get back together with her just to make your father happy, would you?"

"No. I'd do it to make *me* happy." His voice cracked. His Adam's apple stroked his throat as he swallowed hard. He turned his face away. Keeping his head down, he pulled a crumpled wad of bills from his shirt pocket. "Tell the waitress she was right. I'm plenty drunk." He dropped a ten on the table and then wheeled out of her life.

§

"Talk about baring your soul," Matt grumbled as he wheeled to his apartment door. He should have known better than to turn to Abby. She had a way of digging all of his deepest, darkest secrets out of hiding.

He reached into his shirt pocket for his keys and got nothing but air and lint. He patted his front jeans pockets. Nothing. "Happy welcome home." He wiggled the doorknob. Locked. "Just frigging great."

Couldn't even break in like he used to do back in Fuller Lake, not from the wheelchair. Sure bet Derrick wasn't going to happen along with his key ring either.

Where'd you find them?

In the tool trailer behind the miter box under the sandpaper.

He closed his eyes against the memory, but he could still see Derrick in his hospital room holding up the key ring.

"I don't need you," he snarled as he leaned forward to check his back pocket even though he knew he'd never have put the keys there. Being paralyzed, his balance was already compromised. Being drunk only made it worse. Gravity sucked at him and, before he knew it, he was tumbling forward. His forehead smacked against the doorjamb on his way down.

"Perfect. Just frigging perfect."

The center of his forehead throbbed.

Just kill me he thought as he lay there. He had no desire to try to get back into the chair. *Just let me die, right here, right now.*

He touched his forehead and then looked at his fingers. No blood. Another wish unfulfilled.

The outside door clicked as someone opened it. One short walk down the breezeway and they'd be at the main hallway. Just what he needed, one of the tenants finding him lying here smelling like a brewery. He could say goodbye to the apartment manager job. Make dear ol' dad real proud.

Even though it was too late to cover the fact that he'd fallen, he grabbed hold of the wheelchair, hoping the tenant would ignore him if he looked like he had things under control.

Trying to hurry, he fumbled with the wheelchair's brake. A simple device that he seemed to have forgotten how to operate. Part of him wanted to say the hell with it, let him be discovered in his drunken heap. Let him get fired. It wasn't like he was all that fond of the job, anyhow. Heaven knows, he'd had his fill of Milwaukee. Then, he remembered his father, how disappointed he'd be learning that Matt couldn't even handle a job that required no skill. That was enough to get him moving again.

From the sound of the footsteps, the person would be entering the main hallway any second now. No way would he make it, but he wasn't ready to give up. With his head throbbing, he worked himself upward.

"Ma...att."

Abby?

He lost his grip on the chair. He didn't fight as he lost his balance and flopped onto his side. *Please, God, just kill me now.*

Abby crouched next to him. She brushed his tangled hair away from his face. "Matt, are you okay?"

Her fingers against his skin felt nice. He soaked up her touch. "Never better."

"Do you often take naps in the hallway?"

"As often as I can." A horrible thought came to him. She'd expect to be invited in. He'd have to tell her he'd lost his keys, like it wasn't bad enough she'd caught him in a drunken heap. "Thanks for asking. You can leave now."

Abby flopped down and crossed her legs. Settling in for the long haul. Leave it to Abby to do the opposite of what he asked.

"Very nice," she said. "I can see why you like sleeping here. Saves on changing the sheets, too." She ran her hand over the industrial carpet, and he imagined her caressing him that way.

Shit, man. She gives you a hug and now you want the whole package—a package you don't need. "What do you want, Abby?"

"Mainly, to give you these." She held out his keychain.

Where'd you find them?

In the tool trailer behind the miter box under the sandpaper.

The thought of Derrick brought an ache deep in his chest. His eyes watered. Crying was bad enough, but doing it with an audience was unacceptable. He closed his eyes and felt his lip quiver. *Stop it. Pick yourself up.*

He didn't think he could. The ache had already buried itself too deeply.

Maybe if he started crying she'd leave.

Or...she'd comfort him.

Hugs. Holding hands. Sitting with Crystal snuggled in his arms. He missed it all so much. The tears pooled behind his closed eyelids. He turned his face toward the floor as a tear broke free. How frigging pathetic.

He heard movement. Abby leaving? He'd be alone. Free to cry. He didn't want to be free to cry. He didn't want to be alone. He opened his eyes to find Abby turning toward his door. The keys jingled against each other as she looked for the proper key.

Would she open his door, help him inside, and then

be on her merry way? That'd be best but it wasn't what he wanted.

"And...?" he asked as he tried to sit up. The combination of his throbbing head and Miller-induced coordination complicated the task.

The jingling noise stopped and she turned to him. Creases formed between her eyebrows as she gave him a confused look.

He'd managed to sit upright. "You said you came mainly to give me my keys. That means there's another reason."

"I was worried about you. I wanted to be sure you were okay."

He puffed out a sad laugh. "And what did you decide?"

She crouched down with her arms resting on her knees. "Messed up beyond belief."

"Thanks."

She smiled a nice, warm, comforting smile. "But it's temporary."

Damn, he hoped so.

"What do you say we move the party inside?" she asked. "The carpet is comfortable, but I'm sure your couch is even better."

§

Abby followed Matt into his apartment, wondering why she hadn't just given him his keys and been on her way like she'd planned. Of course, she hadn't expected to find him lying on the floor looking so lost and helpless.

The apartment was compact but pleasant, and much cleaner than she'd expected, given Matt's ragged appearance. The end tables and TV appeared to have been recently dusted and the carpet still bore evidence of vacuum tracks. In contrast, a hairbrush lay on the dining room table and a towel was bunched up on the arm of the couch.

"Interesting decorating technique." She nodded toward the toothbrush shoved into an empty vase.

"I've been looking for that." He grabbed the toothbrush. "Can I get you something? Water? Coke? Beer?"

"Water would be fine, but I can get it myself."

"So can I."

She pulled out a dining room chair and sat. "Fine. Water. Thank you."

He reached into the fridge. She smiled when she noticed he no longer held the toothbrush after closing the door. He'd be surprised when he found it in the refrigerator tomorrow.

The path that brought him back to her was a little wobbly, and his aim wasn't the best as he handed her the bottle of water.

"I probably don't need this," he said as he popped the tab on a can of Miller.

Darn tootin'.

"No matter how much I drink, I just can't seem to drown out the memories. I don't know what's worse, remembering the feel of her next to me or seeing them kissing over and over again, like it's stuck on some endless loop in my head."

Having been there herself, she could relate. At least she hadn't been engaged to Paul or Jovan. And they hadn't cheated on her with her best friend. That had to hurt. "You've told me about Crystal. Now tell me about Derrick." On the surface, the question seemed cruel, but she sensed he needed to talk about Derrick.

For a long moment Matt was silent, and she wondered if she'd been wrong. And then, he started talking. "When I asked him to sit at my table at lunch that first time, I never expected we'd turn out to be friends. He was so damn serious, but it was nice being with someone interested in more than seeing how far he could blow milk out his nose.

"Even after I started dating Crystal, Derrick and I stayed tight. I suppose that was part of the problem. Crystal and I did as much with Derrick and whatever girl he was dating as we did alone. Maybe if I'd dumped our friendship when I got serious with her we'd still be together."

"You can't undo what's already done." A wish she'd

made more than once in her life.

"With a sad laugh, he said, "I wish we could. Maybe then I wouldn't have gone out that night and I'd still be walking."

And we never would have met.

"But then..." His gaze kissed her face before landing on her lips. "...I wouldn't have..." He leaned forward. Like a magnet, she felt herself being pulled toward him. "...met..." He blinked and shook his head. He looked away and set his beer on the table. "Damn, I think I've had more than enough to drink."

She sat back. Her heart thumped all the way to her stomach. Had they really been about to kiss? No. Of course not. And she didn't want to, either. Definitely not.

"I think I need some food." He wheeled backward, away from her. "Soak up some of this alcohol. You hungry?"

Food. Something innocuous. Safe. Non-intimate. "Yes. Food. Sounds great."

"There's hamburger and buns in the fridge, or we could order a pizza."

Pizza. With pepperoni. Onions. Lots of cheese. And thirty minutes to wait. Thirty minutes for her to think of ways to fill their time. Her attention shifted to his lips. She popped up out of the chair. "I'm fine with hamburgers. I'll help you cook."

Matt opened the refrigerator. "What the..."

Remembering his toothbrush, she bit her lip, desperately trying to hold back her smile. Surprised indeed. And she'd been lucky enough to witness it.

He set the toothbrush on top of the microwave. "Never know where that damn thing's going to turn up next."

"I have a pretty good idea where it won't turn up."

He looked at her with one eyebrow raised.

Two friends. Having fun. Nothing more. And that was more than enough for her. She grinned. "The toothbrush holder in the bathroom."

"Since you're so smart, you can make the burgers." He handed her a cellophane-wrapped package of hamburger.

"Only if you make the potatoes."

"Deal." He washed his hands and then reached toward the drawer next to the sink. He paused. With his fingers dripping, he looked toward the stove. Looking for a towel, she assumed. Which was probably the one on the couch.

He opened a drawer, pulled out a fresh towel, and then dropped it on the counter as soon as his hands were dry. She snatched it up, dried her own hands, and then hung the towel on a pull handle on the closest drawer.

While she patted the hamburger into patties, Matt washed potatoes. When he grabbed the towel she'd just hung up, she knew without a doubt where that towel was going to end up. *Bingo*, she thought as he dropped the towel onto the counter.

With a quarter pound of hamburger sandwiched between her hands, she watched as he placed two potatoes on the glass tray in the microwave. "Did you poke those potatoes with a fork?"

"I was planning on doing that after they're cooked. You know, when I'm eating."

"Were you going to clean the potato chunks off the inside of the microwave before or after you ate what was left? You have to poke the potatoes or they'll blow up. Get a fork and I'll show you." She plopped the patty onto the frying pan and then washed her hands.

He came to her with the fork. One inch closer and his wheelchair would be pressed against her leg. She could smell spiced cologne beneath the scent of beer. He was so close she could easily thread her fingers through his without moving anything but her arm. She shuffled a bit further away, grabbed the towel from the counter, and dried her hands.

She started to thread the towel back into the handle and then stopped. With a smirk, she held the towel over the counter. "This is where you keep it? Right?" She let the towel drop.

"You are such a pain in the ass."

"I know. Now, give me a potato." She jabbed the potato randomly with a fork. He stared at her as though she were doing something complicated.

"I don't think I've ever seen you with your hair down like that. It makes you look older."

She shoved the fork into the potato deeper than she'd planned. "Older? Thanks. A woman always wants to hear that she looks older."

"No. I mean it looks nice. You look older in a good way. Not so...cheerleaderish."

"Cheerleaderish?" She yanked the fork free of the potato.

"I was trying to say you're..." He shook his head. "Never mind me. It's the alcohol. I'm toasted, remember?" He wheeled away from her, turned, and then held his hand up. "Toss me a tater."

Figuring she'd be picking the potato up off the floor and washing it, she gave it a toss. Like a pro, he tipped his head away from where he was reaching, countering his weight, and snatched the potato from the air. Toasted or not, he was an athlete.

"And the crowd goes wild." He made some cheering noises as he pretended to slam dunk the potato into the microwave.

"Interesting the way you mixed baseball and basketball together there." She thought back to the first time she'd met him and of their discussion on wheelchair basketball, which gave her an idea. Matt needed a new hobby, something other than drinking, and she hoped she'd just found it. She knew someone who knew a guy who coached a wheelchair basketball team that was always looking for new members. Tomorrow morning she'd give him a call.

"Did 'em both," he said as he caught the second potato. "Bowling, darts, pool too. Did it all..." His smile fell. "...with Derrick."

Her mental planning came to a halt. Maybe basketball would be too much of a reminder.

He opened the fridge. She heard the *pop, shhhh* before she even saw the beer in his hand. Watching him tip back the beer, she figured that doing nothing would hurt him more than any basketball-induced reminders of Derrick would.

With a little prayer, she hoped she wouldn't be proven wrong.

CHAPTER TWENTY-TWO

Matt stared at his reflection in the TV. He'd taken care of the shaving part, but he still needed a haircut. He could probably find a barber open on Sunday, but he didn't care enough to hunt one down. Just like he figured he could find a health club easily enough in the phonebook, but he couldn't summon the energy to look.

You need to do something more than just sit here and stare at yourself.

He closed his eyes, no longer staring at himself. A cop out but he didn't care.

He should be looking at the bid information his father had sent, but he had no desire to do so. If only he could turn back time. All the way back to when he started dating Crystal. He'd do it right this time. He'd keep Derrick and Crystal apart. Then he'd have Crystal back. He'd still have his friend. He'd still be working for his dad. And not writing up a stupid bid, either.

There'd be no Abby.

"So what?" he asked as he opened his eyes. With Crystal and Derrick back, he wouldn't need Abby.

But Crystal and Derrick weren't here.

Last night had been fun. Even if he'd been too drunk to really enjoy it. He wasn't drunk now. He planned to keep it that way. The new and improved Matt.

New and improved Matt could call Abby.

Or the new and improved Matt could go back to bed.

That plan had definite possibilities.

He put his palms to the push rims, ready to go back to bed. The telephone rang. His mother, he figured. Or his father. He didn't even want to talk to them. His father would ask if he had the bid ready. His mother would ask him a hundred times how he was doing.

He reached for the phone. "Hello."

"Matt, it's Abby."

He sat up straighter.

"I was wondering if you had plans for this afternoon."

"I had a hot date lined up with Jessica Alba, but it can wait. Why?"

"I have a little surprise for you, that's all."

"What kind of surprise?"

"A surprise kind of surprise. I'll be there in about twenty minutes."

"But..."

She'd already hung up.

He wheeled to the bathroom and checked his shave job to be sure he hadn't missed anything. Should he change his shirt? he wondered as he reached toward the toothbrush holder. His shirt was clean, but it had a tear on the sleeve.

Where the hell was his damn toothbrush? He opened the cabinet above the sink. No toothbrush, but he did find the bottle of glue he'd lost earlier in the week.

Spreading toothpaste on his finger, he thought about the meager supply of shirts he'd brought to Milwaukee. Why hadn't he brought anything nicer than a T-shirt? Like it really mattered. The shirt he had on was good enough for anything Abby had planned, which was probably nothing more than her giving him a printout of some paralyzed superman who'd conquered Kilimanjaro. *You can do this too,* she'd say, and then leave, and he'd have changed his clothes for nothing.

He spit into the sink and then wheeled out to the living room where he parked himself by the front window.

A man walked by with a dog on a leash. He'd often thought about getting a dog until the reality of his hectic lifestyle woke him up. That and Crystal, who wasn't a pet person. An over-active lifestyle no longer stood in his way. Neither did Crystal.

He leaned closer to the window, his eyes tracking the mutt's bouncy movement. He wondered if Abby liked pets. Maybe she'd want to go to the pound with him. Pick out a dog. Some floppy thing with big feet that little Fido would trip over. He and Abby could take Fido to the park, throw him a Frisbee. Take him camping too. He and Abby could borrow Brad's boat and take Fido fishing.

"Good lord," he muttered although he realized he was smiling. Maybe getting a dog was exactly what he should do.

The doorbell rang. His heart beat a strange tattoo. "It's just Abby." *Just Abby.* He drew in a shaky breath and then let it out slowly before he reached for the door.

Abby greeted him with, "You shaved. You look good."

She did too. Her hair was down and brushed to a brilliant shine. Her plain-Jane jeans were just tight enough to display curves he'd never noticed before. Soft curves. Cuddly curves.

"So, are you ready?" she asked.

"For what, exactly?"

"You'll see." She nodded toward the hallway. "Come on."

Before he could close the door, she yelled out, "Wait."

"What?"

"Do you have your keys?"

"Yes, I have them right..." He patted his shirt pocket.

"Try the kitchen counter. That's where you put them last night."

Sure enough. That's exactly where his keys were. Right next to the beer he'd started earlier. He looked over his shoulder. Abby was busy fluffing one of Faith's floral arrangements, not paying a bit of attention to him. He could take a quick draw. Two even.

No, he warned himself as he grabbed his keys and pocketed them. He didn't need alcohol. He turned his chair around with more force than necessary. "Where are we going?"

"You'll see." She led him down the hallway.

"I've never been one for surprises. Just ask my mom."

"Is there a childhood story involved?"

He laughed. She always seemed to love hearing his stories. As soon as they got into the car, he said, "Just before my ninth birthday, I found my presents in my parents' closet. I opened every present and then wrapped it all up again." But not before he'd dragged Derrick into the closet to show off his stash.

"Did you get into trouble?"

"Ma never said anything, but she had to have known because I wasn't exactly the neatest kid on the block. Also, she became more creative with her hiding places after that."

She looked his way. One corner of her mouth lifted. "Creative?"

"One year I found my presents hidden behind the pots and pans. Another year they were in the laundry hamper. The best one, though, was when she hid them in the freezer."

"You've grown out of this, right?"

He raised his eyebrows and smirked. "Of course."

"Why don't I believe you?"

"Actually, it is the truth. I quit looking right around the same time I moved into my own house." The house back in Fuller Lake that he didn't live in anymore.

He looked out the passenger window. Buildings flashed before him like a sideways slide show. He breathed deeply, trying to ward off the depression that seemed to be an all too constant companion.

The flashing building slideshow came to a crawl as Abby turned into a parking lot.

He eyed the stretched out brick building with the sign reading *Hoover Elementary*. "Why are we at a grade school?" he asked as she parked between a van and a Toyota truck.

She patted his arm. "Patience is a virtue. Haven't you ever heard that?"

He followed her into the school and down the hallway lined with empty coat hooks. Laughter and voices came from somewhere down the hall. The sound of a thumping basketball gave him a jolt of anticipation. The sounds grew louder as they made their way past the closed classroom doors. A basketball game in progress. Was that her big surprise?

"This must be the place," Abby said, stepping through the open doors where the noise was coming from.

With his attention focused on the sight before him, he almost rammed into Abby when she stopped. Ten people were in the midst of a basketball game. The teams were made up of both men and women, their ages from mid-teen to upper fifties. Every one of them in a wheelchair. Four additional wheelchair-bound people sat on the sidelines.

One of the four, a middle-aged man, looked their way. He made his way over to them and extended his hand. "Matt, right? Glad you could come. I'm Ryan. I guess you could say I'm the coach." He looked up at Abby, his smile growing with obvious appreciation. "And you must be Abby."

Ryan's hand was still meshed with Abby's, and she was making no attempt to free herself. Matt crossed his arms and stared out across the court, but he could still see Abby with her hand nestled in the coach's. On the court, a man in his mid-twenties wearing a green tank top crowded the teenage boy who had the ball. Green Shirt looked like he was out for blood as he blocked the pass, bringing back memories of Matt's own aggressive style. He pretended the coach wasn't gushing over Abby and put himself in Green Shirt's position on the court. The kid with the ball twisted and then aimed to another player. Matt mentally intercepted while Green Shirt did the real interception.

"We're always looking for new people," Ryan said. "Right now we play for fun, but we'd like to form a team for competition. Think you might be interested in joining us?"

Matt shrugged like he wasn't itching to get on the court. "Yeah, I guess. Until I go back to Fuller Lake, that is."

"Abby says you're athletic. I take it you know the rules of basketball?"

"Lettered three years in high school." Derrick had been captain.

"The rules are the same with a few modifications." He motioned to the court. "Watch Alex, the kid in the green shirt. See how he handles the ball."

Green Shirt bounced the ball and then dropped it into his lap. He pushed against his wheels twice, bounced the ball, and then put it on his lap. He wheeled forward. Green Shirt made it look easy, but Matt knew he could make it look better.

"We can't push our wheels more than twice without dribbling, passing, or shooting the ball. Got that?"

"Yeah." Piece of cake.

"Now watch Chuck, the amputee in the blue shirt." When Alex came close to Chuck's chair, the man stuck out his only leg, effectively snagging Alex's chair. One of the bystanders blew a whistle and pointed to Chuck, who raised his hands as though to imply he was innocent.

Ryan nodded. "I knew he'd do that. He's always cheating. That's an example of the physical advantage foul. All players must stay seated at all times. If you use a functional leg in any way, that's considered a foul."

What he wouldn't pay to be able to manage Chuck's maneuver. "Don't have to worry about that with me."

"That's right. Abby said you have no lower mobility."

Heat prickled the back of his neck and cheeks.

"That'll come in handy if we ever compete," Ryan continued. "Each player is rated for mobility. There can only be so many class points on the court at one time, so the teams can stay relatively even. You're a T1 complete I believe Abby said."

A T1, as though his injury defined him. But that slid into the background compared to hearing the shotgun blast word "complete." The equivalent of permanent. He narrowed his eyes at Abby who held her hands out while she shook her head.

"My mistake," Ryan said. "Abby said you had no lower function."

"No lower function, my ass. I can move my toes." The words sounded stupid as they spilled from his tongue.

He wiggled his toes as he looked back at the action

on the court. Trying to prove his injury wasn't complete. Praying that he hadn't reached the end of his recovery even though it'd been over three months since there'd been any change.

Someone blew a whistle and the players drifted to the sidelines. Green Shirt wheeled toward them. "New blood, huh? Glad to have you." He put out his hand. "Alex Easterbury."

Matt raised one eyebrow. "Easterbury?"

"Don't even go there. You can't possibly come up with something I haven't heard already." Alex looked up at Abby and squinted. "Don't I know you?"

"I'm a physical therapist at Milwaukee Spine Care Center."

"No." He shook his head. "That's not it."

"I used to work at St. Luke's in Bakersfield."

"That's it. I was there for a few days until I transferred out. I had…" He snapped his fingers. "Some Brady Bunch chick."

"Marsha."

"Yeah. Marsha was my therapist, but I saw you around the gym."

Chuck wheeled over and kicked Alex in the shin. "Nice shoot'n Tex." He looked at Matt. "You gonna join us?"

Matt couldn't wait to get out there. Show off his stuff. He shrugged and tried to look indifferent. "I guess, as long as I'm here."

Chuck turned around and pointed to the teenage boy. "That's Noah. He's pretty good for being a young pup. Sandy, the chick with the purple streak in her hair, she ain't so good but she sure is pretty to look at, so we let her hang around. Rolland, the big muscular dude, him you got to look out for. He'd just as soon tear out your throat as to let you score. Cheats too. Man does he cheat."

The names started to blur as Chuck gave a commentary on each person. Matt was relieved when the break was done and Chuck went back onto the court. Except they'd all gone back to the game, and Matt was left on the sidelines. Green Shirt, his name already forgotten, intercepted the ball right away. Matt mentally aimed the ball and shot. Behind him, Abby and Ryan were carrying on a quiet conversation.

"How is Alex doing?" Abby asked.

"He had a rough go of it, but he's really changed since coming here, more confident, not so moody. Hell, I know it's helped me feel more normal, if you can believe hanging around with a bunch of guys in wheelchairs could make you feel normal."

Never, Matt smirked as he watched the girl with the purple stripe reach up to grab the ball. Never, ever would being with this gang make him feel normal. At the last second, the girl brought her hands close to her face. Matt winced in anticipation while wishing he could stop the inevitable. The ball smacked her hard in the face.

"Oh, shit. That's going to leave a mark." Ryan moved onto the court and made it halfway to the girl when he turned around. "Hey, Huntz. You want to go in?"

"You bet."

As soon as Matt hit the court, the big dude Chuck had warned him about tossed him the ball. Matt put it on his lap and then gave his wheels a shove. The ball rolled down his lap and fell to the ground. Chuck stopped it with his foot and then tossed it back to Matt with a bit of advice. "Gotta wedge it in there tight."

The ball stayed in place through three pushes on the wheels.

"Hey, he didn't bounce the ball," the teenage boy yelled.

"Cut him some slack," another person yelled. "He's new."

New. The hair on his neck prickled. New. Like he didn't know how to play basketball. He'd show them new. He bounced the ball to the right of his chair. It hit the frame and rolled away. Green Shirt grabbed it and headed for the basket, making it look easy as he dribbled every couple pushes.

This wasn't what Tuesday nights had been like. A hard pit formed in his stomach at the thought of his old life.

Back when life was fun and Derrick wasn't the enemy. Forcing his attention back on the game, he tried to block the pass. Green Shirt spun his chair and then zipped around Matt and scored.

When they got to the other end of the court, Chuck passed the ball to Matt. The teenage boy got in his face. Instinctively, Matt wanted to zig to the left, but the limitations of the chair stopped him. He wheeled backward and crashed into another chair.

"Foul."

Five minutes into the play, Matt had gained possession for the fourth time without scoring, but he was seconds away from rectifying that record. He aimed the ball and shot. It fell two feet short of the hoop.

"Glad you're playing for us," one of the guys on the other team yelled as he scooped up the ball.

Matt held his ground while the rest of the guys turned and moved toward the other end of the court. He didn't need to put up with this crap. Except, he couldn't prove himself as a player if he left. Having lost ten feet of ground, he raced to catch up. As soon as he got the ball back, the teenage boy snagged it away. Matt grabbed the kid's chair and got another foul called on him. And then he got a foul for violating the four-second rule.

Basketball wasn't supposed to be this hard he thought when he finally got the ball back and tried to manage dribbling and wheeling. When Green Shirt snagged the ball during a dribble, Matt turned his chair away from the action. "Screw this." He pushed hard on the wheels, eager to be out of the gym and away from these people.

Abby caught up with him halfway down the hall. "Matt, what's wrong?"

Blood pounded behind his ears. He whipped past the closed classroom doors. "That game is a joke, is what's wrong."

She hurried beside him. "I don't get it. I thought you were having fun."

"I'd rather have my nuts squeezed in a vise." He yanked on the door that led to the parking lot and then wheeled for the playground. The woodchips scattered around the equipment tugged at his wheels. Where was a fucking beer when you needed one?

He hurled one of the swings toward the frame, the chain clanking as it wrapped around the metal tube. He grabbed swing after swing and launched them until every seat was in motion. The anger was still there.

"What was the point in that?" he screamed, turning to Abby while the swings on either side of him careened back and forth in a drunken path. If he couldn't even do something as simple as playing basketball, how could he ever hope to be any help to his dad? "Trying to show me what I can't do?"

She crouched in front of him. "No, Matt. It's to show you what you *can* do. Didn't you look at those people? They're all disabled in some way."

She didn't say it, but he heard the words she'd held back. *Just like you.* His cheeks prickled with heat. He stared past her at the wire fence surrounding the playground. His breath squeezed in and out of a chest that had gone tight. This, being stuck in a wheelchair, was not the real him, and he was getting tired of waiting to be the man he used to be. The need for a beer pulsed through him as readily as the blood flowing through his veins. "Do you know what it means to letter in a sport? It means you're one of the best."

"That bothers you to not be the best?"

"Hell, no." His eyes connected with hers for a fraction of a second before he looked away.

She tilted his face toward hers. Her fingers were soft against his cheek. He wanted to cover her hand with his own. Instead, he pushed her arm away.

The soft edge to her face stayed in place. Without a hint of anger, she asked, "Who do you admire most?"

"What kind of stupid question is that? What the hell does it matter?"

"Just play with me here, Matt, okay? Pick someone famous."

Dealing with her was so frigging frustrating at times,

this being one of those times. He knew she wouldn't give up so he said, "Fine. Lance Armstrong."

"Do you think he could have won the Tour de France the first time he rode a bike?"

"You think I don't know that I can get better with practice? Twenty years of practice isn't going to change the fact that I'm not the man I used to be." That's what hurt the most. No matter what he did he'd never be the man he used to be, not stuck in this wheelchair. If he couldn't be that man, there was no way he'd ever make his father proud of him. He turned around and pushed toward the car. He made it half way when he heard a male voice behind him.

"Hey, wait up."

Matt stopped and looked over his shoulder. Green Shirt wheeled toward him. "You aren't leaving, are you?"

"I'm sure the hell not staying."

"Damn." Green Shirt coasted the final feet. "I was finally having fun out there. You're good. Best competition I've had since joining the team."

Competition his ass. Matt turned away and made another push toward the car.

Green Shirt laughed. "No way. I couldn't have been that bullheaded. Was I really that stubborn?"

"Stubborn?" Abby asked, sounding puzzled.

"Yeah, Ryan said I was just like Matt here when I first joined the team. But I can't believe I was such a baby."

Matt abruptly changed course and wheeled back to Green Shirt. "Who you calling a baby?"

The guy held his ground, his smile never wavering. "You went through therapy insisting you were going to walk again, didn't you? Probably tried to go back to your old job."

Matt took another push closer. "You have a point or are you just naturally a prick?"

"I've been there. Broke up with my girlfriend because it was easier to claim I was doing her a favor than to adjust to my disability. Then I spent the next four months drunk on my ass until I found out cocaine was more effective at deadening the pain. You're not there yet, are you?"

Not waiting for an answer, Green Shirt shook his head. "No, and if you listen really close to what I have to say, maybe you can save yourself from the mistakes I made. Cocaine doesn't take away the problems and neither does the alcohol. It just makes a whole new set of problems. I OD'd. Ended up in a treatment center after I got out of the hospital. My counselor got me hooked up with these guys. It's weird. Playing wheelchair basketball is so far removed from my old life, but when I'm out there, I feel like my old self again."

"Yeah? Well, I felt like a loser."

Green Shirt grinned. "Maybe that's what you were in your old life."

He wanted to slap the grin off Green Shirt's face. No. What he really wanted to do was cream him on the basketball court.

"So, are you going to come back in? Give it another try?"

Abby touched his shoulder. She kept her hand there, feeding him courage through her palm. She leaned close and whispered in his ear. "Tour de France, Matt."

Pent up frustration burned through him. He needed a release. "The slave driver said my options are to play another game or go a couple months without sex. I guess I'll try the game again."

Abby swatted his head. "A couple months? Try a lifetime."

Matt fell in beside Green Shirt. "Does it really get better? Or are you feeding me a line of shit?"

"It gets better. Day by day." Green Shirt looked over his shoulder and grinned. "I'd say your life can't be too bad considering your girl stuck with you." He shook his head. "What are the chances of you dating a physical therapist and then finding out you need one?"

"About a zillion to none."

His second attempt at wheelchair basketball wasn't much better than his first, but it didn't bother him quite so much this time around. Especially not when Green Shirt,

Alex, became his personal trainer, giving advice. At the end of the game, when everyone was going their separate ways, he realized he was actually looking forward to next Sunday, getting together for another game.

Back in Abby's car, he felt good. Hopeful, even. As if life might not be quite so bad. He even saw himself back in Fuller Lake one day, back at the jobsite with his father.

He leaned back against the car seat and let his head roll toward Abby. So pretty in her cheerleader fresh way. He liked that Alex believed a guy like him had a chance with a girl like her. "So, I did like you wanted. I played basketball. I get sex now, right? I mean, that was the deal."

Her eyes remained on the road. "I don't remember making any such deal." She glanced his way. "I will agree to you taking me out for dinner, though."

He shrugged. Not like he'd honestly thought she'd say yes. "It was worth a shot."

She put her hand on his, and he decided he liked it there. "Honey," she said. "You aren't ready for me."

"That sounds a lot like a challenge. You know how much I like a good challenge."

"Yeah. And I'll remind you, last time you took me on, I beat you. I am the Yahtzee champ."

"Yeah, but you haven't seen me in bed yet."

§

"I shouldn't have made that sex crack." Matt squeezed and released the beer can and then squeezed it again just so there'd be noise in the apartment. "Stupid, stupid."

Abby had played along, acted like it was all a joke, just like he'd meant it to be, but she'd been quiet after that. Then she'd declined his invitation to come up for a drink when she'd dropped him off at the apartment. A polite, "I'm sorry. I have plans. But I'll call you."

And he'd believed her that she'd call.

He squeezed the can but didn't let go this time.

Five days.

He downed the rest of the beer and then smashed the can against the countertop.

Five days and no word from her.

He twisted his mouth. He hadn't called her either. Last he'd heard, the phone lines worked both ways.

Instead of going to the phone, he went to the fridge. *You forget you weren't going to do this anymore? There's a health club less than five miles away. Or you could earn the two hundred Dad sent for doing another bid.*

Or you could call Abby like you really want to.

He went to the phone and dialed Abby's number before he could talk himself out of it.

One.

She probably wasn't home, anyhow.

Two.

Unlike him, she had a life.

Three.

At the same time he pulled the phone from his ear, he heard her breathless, "Hello."

He thought about hanging up, anyhow. But then he remembered how empty his apartment was. And how lonely he'd been this past week.

"I've got a movie here that I don't want to watch alone," he said, "and a pizza I don't want to eat alone. What do you say you come over and cure that *alone* problem?" World's best pick up line.

"I have to go somewhere, but I can be there in a couple hours."

Instead of being happy she'd agreed to come over, all he could hear was her saying she had to go somewhere. Plans with some guy, he figured. Which probably explained why he hadn't heard from Abby all week. He tucked the phone between his shoulder and chin and wheeled closer to the fridge. "That's okay. Tonight's probably not a good night, anyhow." He laughed to make it sound like it really was okay.

"I'm sorry."

"No big deal." Just as well, he decided as he chugged the beer after disconnecting the call. Who needed a cheerleader when he had his good friend Miller to keep him company?

§

Abby flipped on the right blinker as she approached the turn that would take her to Hot Springs. A left turn would take her to Matt's. Where she could be headed if she would have visited her mother right after work. Mom was expecting her. Matt wasn't. She turned right.

At the next intersection, she again had the urge to turn left, to go around the block and head straight to Matt's. She punched the accelerator and sped through the intersection, but her thoughts stayed with Matt.

He'd sounded like he was in good spirits, but there'd been an edge to his voice. Something beneath the words that said he didn't want to be alone. "Beneath the words?" she muttered. He'd outright said it. *Come over and cure that alone problem.*

Another intersection brought forth another chance to question herself. Straight for Hot Springs. Left for Matt's. Intuition told her, despite his teasing words, the edge really had been there. At the last second, she turned the wheel. Just to check to be sure he was okay. Then she'd be on her merry way.

Matt greeted her at the door with a beer can tucked between his legs. Even though she had no interest in drinking a beer, nor did she have the time, she nodded at the can. "Do you have another one of those for me?"

"In the fridge. Help yourself. Grab me another while you're at it."

She took two cans from the nearly full twelve pack. She popped open her own and broke off the tab. She felt only slightly guilty when she took stock of his garbage as she threw the tab away. He was eating well, but he was drinking better. Would he one day add cocaine to his daily diet like Alex had?

Time was ticking by and she had to visit her mother. Leaving Matt with an almost-full carton of beer didn't seem like a good idea, though. She could take the beer hostage. Claim she was *really* thirsty. 5Except that'd slow him down only until he made his way to the corner bar.

She could take Matt away from the beer. Which meant

taking him to visit her mother. An insane idea. He was a big boy. If he wanted to spend his night drunk, who was she to try to interfere?

Matt tipped his head back as far as he could and tapped the beer can pressed to his lips, trying to get the last drop. A poster child of someone who shouldn't be left unsupervised with an almost full twelve pack of ice-cold beer. She put the beer she'd gotten him back in the fridge.

"Hey, the deal was you get a beer and I get a beer."

She turned her can upside down over the sink. "Now we're even. Go brush your teeth and splash on some aftershave. We're going out."

"Where are we going?" The relief that showed in his eyes said they could be on their way to the toothpick factory to hand count inventory and he wouldn't care.

"Out." She shooed him with her hands. "Get moving."

She watched him wheel off to the bathroom. Had it really been only a week since he'd found his way into her life again? It felt like he'd been there so much longer.

But it *had* been only a week. And now she was taking him to meet her mother. What in the world was she thinking?

Her eyes went to the closed bathroom door. She wasn't thinking. That was the point. Instinct was guiding her and nothing else.

He emerged from the bathroom a short while later. His hair was still a touch too long, but it was clean and now freshly combed, as well. With the hint of a smile, he looked quite handsome. When he got closer, she decided he smelled good, too.

"Where are we going?" he asked as she led him to her car.

"To visit my mother." *Then, we're going to find an all night psychiatrist and have my head examined.*

As soon as she walked into the room, her mother sprang from the bed where she'd been sitting cross legged. She held a blue blob of clay in her hands. "Abby, look."

Such a difference from how her mother had been at Eastlawn, Abby thought. Coming here really had been a good move.

"Helen noticed Matt. She took a step back, hugged herself, and looked away.

"Mom, this is my friend, Matt. He won't hurt you."

Helen turned further away.

Great. This was sure to be an exciting evening.

"Can I see what you have, Mrs. Fischner?" Matt asked.

Still turned away, her mother looked at him. He flashed a smile that could have melted a snowman. Her mother looked away again. Her arms tightened around herself.

"It looks pretty cool," Matt said. "Can I see it?"

Her mother snuck another glance at him. Her eyes tracked him from head to toe. "Why are you in a... chairwheel?" She grimaced as the wrong word came out.

"I had an automobile accident. I hit a tree."

"I hit a tree."

"I know. Abby told me."

Helen held out her hand, displaying what could have been a bird. Or it could have been a turnip.

"What a nice blue jay," Matt said.

Her mother beamed. "Yes. A blue jay."

Abby raised one eyebrow as she stared at him. How had he gotten a blue jay out of the blob of blue clay?

Her mother handed it to him. "You like it, you take it."

He ran his finger over it like he was petting a real bird. "Thank you. I'll put it on my windowsill at home."

"Are you Abby's boyfriend?"

"Just a friend," he said but his eyes raked across Abby, and she felt her stomach flip.

Her mother frowned. "Too bad. Abby needs a boyfriend."

What Abby figured she needed was to duct tape her mother's mouth. She put her arm around her mother's shoulder and steered her back to the bed. "I think we need to find an activity."

"You do need a boyfriend," her mother insisted while Matt attempted to hide a laugh behind a fake cough.

"Are those coloring books?" Matt asked as he nodded at the bookshelf next to her mother's bed. "I haven't colored since I moved to Milwaukee."

"You color?" her mother asked.

"Heck, yeah. One of my favorite things."

Next thing Abby knew, Matt and her mother were sharing space on the bed table and he looked like he was enjoying himself. Abby watched Matt through new eyes. This man was truly amazing.

They stayed an hour longer than she'd planned, but Matt hadn't seemed to mind. He'd cheerfully done every activity suggested. When it came time to leave, her mother asked, "You'll come back?"

"As long as Abby says it's okay."

Her mother speared her with pleading blue eyes.

Abby held up her hands. "It's not up to me."

Matt grinned. "I'd say that's a yes. I'll come as often as I can convince Abby to bring me."

Her mother leaned close to him, cupped her hand around his ear, and whispered something. His eyes connected with Abby's while he listened, a natural smile forming. He nodded and told her mother, "I might take you up on that."

"You come back," her mother reminded Matt as they headed for the door.

"You can count on it." He held up the blob of blue clay. "Thanks again for the blue jay."

What did she tell you? Abby silently asked as she and Matt headed down the hallway. The question burning inside her, she said, "You were very good with her. Thank you."

He shrugged. "No thanks are necessary. Your mom's pretty cool. I had fun."

"Still, you were amazing. So patient."

"I appreciate you bringing me. It was nice being with a family again."

Her footsteps faltered. "Family?"

Matt stopped pushing against the wheels and looked up at her. "Yes, family. A small one, but you're a family just the same."

She started walking again. Family, huh? She'd never thought of her mother and her as anything other than mother and daughter, but he was right. They were a family.

She waited until they got into the car before she asked. "Okay, so what did she whisper to you?"

"Can't tell you. She swore me to secrecy."

"Ma...att."

"Do you realize how cute you are when you say my name that way? The way your nose crinkles up?"

"My nose doesn't crinkle."

"Sure. Whatever you say."

They drove a block further before he spoke. "I still have that pizza and movie at home. Interested?"

"Certainly." She looked his way and saw him grinning. A wave of heat pressed through her. She looked back at the road and tucked her lip between her teeth while her heart fluttered beneath her breastbone. *Interested* indeed.

§

Fifteen minutes after Abby left, Matt transferred into bed and slid his arms beneath his head. He felt good. Real good. Good enough he didn't feel the need to drink his bedtime beer sitting on the nightstand. Tonight had been the best night he could remember in a long time. He smiled at the thought of Helen's whispered message. *Abby likes you. Ask her out on a date.*

Did feeding Abby a frozen pizza and watching a rented movie count? he wondered as he closed his eyes. To be on the safe side, he figured he should call Abby tomorrow and ask her out on a real date. Maybe they could take her mother somewhere. Start out with the park, maybe. Then ice cream.

His eyes popped open. What in the hell was he thinking? He couldn't ask Abby out. Him and the cheerleader? No way.

He and Abby were friends. That's all. He closed his eyes and tried to remember the feel of Crystal in his arms. Instead, he saw her in Derrick's arms, Derrick's mouth attacking hers. His best friend and his fiancée. Refusing to leave his thoughts now that they'd invaded.

"Damn it," he whispered as he reached for the beer.

CHAPTER TWENTY-THREE

June turned hot over the next two weeks. Even with her hair pulled up, perspiration formed on Abby's neck. She smoothed her hand over the top edge of a sheet of wallpaper that seemed as wet as she was. As soon as she pulled her fingers away, the paper curled away from the wall. She stood back and surveyed her work.

Twenty minutes of her life gone, and all she had to show for it was one crooked strip of peeling wallpaper with an air bubble bloating a patch of flowers. What had seemed like a great idea when she'd been watching the home-improvement channel now seemed foolhardy. At the very least, she should have saved this project for when the weather turned cooler instead of sweltering in an airless kitchen on a Saturday afternoon. She could have called Matt and asked him to go to the lake. But no, she'd come up with this stupid idea instead.

She wiped her hands on the old kitchen towel and then unrolled another length of paper. She grabbed her ruler. Forty-six and a half inches? Or was it fifty-six and a half? She turned to re-measure the strip on the wall. The top edge had rolled back even further.

"No," she cried out and pressed her hands to her face. The telephone rang. Her fingers stuck momentarily to her face as she pulled her hands away, the skin pulling slightly before the glue released its hold. She watched as the paper on the wall peeled back further. Deciding she'd had her fill of papering, she reached for the phone.

"What'cha up to?" Matt asked.

His voice sounded upbeat but there was an edge to it. The same edge she'd heard the night she took him to meet her mother. "Pretending I'm a wallpaper pro."

"Pretending, huh?"

The single strip of paper crept closer to the floor. "You

wouldn't happen to know anything about wallpapering, would you?"

He laughed. A real laugh. One that eased her worry.

"Uh, Abby, that's part of what Huntz & Sons does. We mostly do remodels, which includes painting and wallpapering."

She stood straighter. "I'd pay you to come help. Pizza. Except the pizza's just a frozen one, but I'd really appreciate your help."

"Frozen pizza, huh? Best offer I've had all day. I'll be right over."

She hung up and leaned against the wall. By the time Matt got there, her only strip of paper would probably be puddled on the floor. She thought about trying to press it back into place. Recognizing the futility in such an attempt, she pushed herself away from the wall and left the scene of the crime.

Her spirits weren't bolstered much when she stepped in front of the mirror a moment later. She looked like a victim from a slasher movie. Wallpaper paste smudged her cheek. Several locks of hair hung loose from her limp ponytail. Matt would probably take one look at her and turn tail and run, screaming in horror. Either that, or he'd double over laughing. Neither prospect was favorable.

After washing her hands and face, she pulled her hair free of the elastic band and brushed her hair smooth. Her face looked pale in the bathroom light. She applied a dusting of blush and then ran some gloss across her lips. Just a touch of eye shadow. Maybe a little mascara.

"Why don't you just spend an hour curling your hair while you're at it?" she asked, disgusted with herself. He was coming to help her wallpaper. That was it. She gathered her hair back into its ponytail, secured it in place with the elastic band, and then left the bathroom.

When she opened the door for Matt five minutes later, he didn't double over laughing. He didn't turn tail and run, either. He simply said, "Lead me to the project." She wondered if he would have noticed if she'd shown up at the door in a string bikini?

She took him to the kitchen where it looked like a paper bomb had exploded. A roll of wallpaper was stretched out on the table next to a ruler and a pencil. Additional rolls of paper were propped up against the cabinet. The strip on the wall was still clinging on for dear life, but just barely.

His lips twitched before he covered his mouth with his hand. He nodded. His mouth still covered, he said, "Honey, I'm going to have to teach you the meaning of *pretend*."

She put her fists on her hips to keep from whacking him. "What?"

"*Pretend* implies you have a basic knowledge of what you're doing."

She held out her hands. "What'd I do that was so wrong?"

He looked at the lone piece of paper making a desperate attempt to cling to the wall. "Need I say more?"

"It's my first attempt."

Moving closer, he visually followed the pencil line she'd drawn halfway down the wall. He rubbed his hands over his face as though he was already exhausted. "Let me guess. You drew that horizontal line by measuring off the ceiling."

He said it like that was a bad thing, so she simply shrugged.

"Bad thing is the morons who built this place obviously never heard of a level." He pointed toward the cabinets. "Your ceiling slopes upward in that corner by two inches. Therefore, so does your line."

His eyes went to the rolls of paper waiting to be used. "That all the paper you have? Or is some of it hiding in fear of what you might do to it?"

"Might I point out that no rolls of paper came crawling out of hiding when you showed up."

"So you don't have any more. Is that what you're saying?"

She swatted him.

He wheeled over to the strip she'd applied to the wall.

He grabbed the loose corner. To press it to the wall again, she assumed. Instead, he pulled the sheet free. Her hard work. Gone. In one quick yank. "What'd you do that for?"

"You're going to run short if you stick with the match pattern you've established. We can make it stretch if we move your line down just one inch."

"But—"

He gave her a hard look.

"But—"

He widened his eyes.

"Fine. You're the expert."

"That, I am." He handed her the strip. "Fold this so the glued sides touch and put it somewhere safe. Bathtub would be a good spot."

When she returned to the kitchen, he was gone.

"Matt?" There was no answer. She threw her hands in the air. "Great. Rip off my wallpaper I spent twenty minutes on and then leave. Some help you are."

Her telephone rang. She grabbed it. Matt said, "Can you bring that cute little ass of yours out here to my car?"

She hung up and smiled. Maybe he *would* have noticed if she'd opened the door wearing nothing but a string bikini.

Don't get your hopes up. He's going back to Fuller Lake someday, remember?

Still, her step was light and bouncy as she made her way across the lawn to his car. His trunk lid was open and he was leaning into it, but he wasn't moving. From her vantage point, he appeared to have his hand covering his eyes. The edge in his voice she'd heard earlier came to mind.

"Matt?"

For as still as he'd been, he became the complete opposite as he dug in the trunk. A man with a sense of purpose. She tried to get a look at him, but he managed to keep his face pointed away as he started handing her tools, almost as though he knew she was trying to get a look and he had something to hide.

He handed her a metal *L* thingy and a plastic gadget with a crank on the side. A level and a tape measure. A mini paint roller without the fuzzy covering. A bucket of paste and a paint brush.

"I need all this?" she asked when her arms were full.

"Unless you want it to look like Kaylee was in charge of your wallpapering."

"Yeah. Thanks."

He looked and sounded like his normal self right down to the teasing, and she wondered if her concern was unwarranted.

Back in her apartment, he took the level and the tape measure from her. She dumped the rest of the tools on the counter while he started measuring and drawing lines. She watched in wonder as he moved down the wall. His T-shirt strained with every movement he made, defining the rock-hard muscles across his shoulders and upper arms. Watching him was better than any movie she could have picked out at the video store.

The line he'd made shifted dramatically from the one she'd drawn. When he got to the end, he looked at her. Embarrassed he'd caught her staring, she said, "I hope you're not afraid of spiders. You had one on your shoulder." She tapped her own shoulder. "I kept an eye on it to make sure it stayed on your shirt."

He twisted his neck farther, checking out his shoulder, and then turned those chocolate eyes back on her with his eyebrows arched. He clearly wasn't buying her story.

She shrugged. "Must have gotten away."

"Hand me that chalk line." When she hesitated, he said, "The green plastic thing with the crank and the pull ring."

Within minutes, they had a horizontal blue chalk line snapped on the wall and a vertical line snapped twenty inches from the corner.

"What made you decide to start with the bottom?" Matt asked as he picked up a roll of paper she'd chosen for the top half of the wall. He had a smudge of blue chalk at the corner of his lips.

"Because that's the pattern I like the best." She let her gaze stray away from the smudge of blue to roam across his lips. She'd never seen a set of lips that she'd wanted to kiss more. She forced her attention away from him.

He peeled off the plastic wrapping from the roll. "For future reference, that's not how you decide on which paper to start with. You always want to start at the top. Especially if you're going to use this pre-pasted crap."

"The lady at the store said the pre-pasted paper is easier."

"The lady at the store doesn't know shit. You do enough wallpapering, you learn that it's best to use paste and a brush. It's messy, but your paper sticks."

Having taken her eyes off him hadn't helped. She pictured his lips sucking lightly at her neck before they moved lower, kissing her along the lace edge of her bra.

He leaned back in his chair. His gaze ran the length of her countertop. "About the only thing you did right was clear off the countertop."

"I didn't clear off the countertop."

"You're kidding? You don't keep your counter cluttered with wall-to-wall decorative crap?"

"I like to live sparse. Less to pack if I have to move." She frowned, wondering why she'd said that.

"You move often?"

Was eight times in seventeen years *often*? "Only when I screw up the wallpaper so badly that it's easier to move than to try to fix it."

"Then, it's a good thing I'm here to save this project because I'd really hate for you to have to move."

He didn't want her to move? She became giddy with the thought that he cared. In a flash, she advanced through time—their first kiss, getting married, having children. Thoughts of Matt in her future came too easily. The air in the enclosed kitchen became stale and heavy. She took a step away from him and focused on the roll of paper on the table. "Time's wasting. Shall we?"

They had two strips on the top half of the wall when Matt's cell phone rang. She guessed it had to be his mother or father. One of them seemed to call whenever she was with Matt. She ran her finger lightly over the papered wall while he answered. Even though she'd applied the paper herself, she couldn't believe what a difference there was between the strips she'd put up with Matt's help and the poor thing she'd tortured earlier on her own.

"Hi, Dad."

Bingo, she thought. His father would also ask about materials.

"You're still out at the jobsite?...Three blues and then a black. That's the pattern we decided on."

Abby measured the next strip and then grabbed the L shaped metal thing. Square, she corrected herself. She lined the square up like she'd watched Matt do. She looked at him for his approval. When he nodded, she ran a straightedge blade along the square and smiled, pleased she'd done it on her own.

"I'm pretty sure I left you detailed instructions on this," Matt said. "Yeah, sure. I understand my writing's not the neatest...Sure, you can have Mr. McCofsky call me. I'd be happy to look over his bid...Two hundred's more than enough...No, I'm not at home. I'm out...No. Just out, okay?...No, you don't have to worry about me. I'm fine. Really...Yeah, I love you guys, too."

Abby dunked the brush in the paste and then slopped it on the paper, brushing it out like Matt had shown her. A few hours later, the top half of the longest wall was papered. Abby stood back. "That looks nice."

"I think you can be trusted now with that poor piece of wallpaper I rescued from you earlier. Can you get it?"

She got the piece and handed it to him.

"See this clump of flowers here?" He pointed to where she'd cut the paper at the top edge of a bouquet of flowers. "Now, look at the bottom. You've got one inch of this same section of flowers showing. That means to match the next row, you now have to cut off twenty inches from the top of your next sheet. By moving our line down on the wall, we've managed to eliminate all that waste."

"Wow. You're really good. No wonder your father's

always asking for your advice."

"Don't be fooled. My dad uses it as an excuse to call because he and Ma worry too much."

"That's not true. I mean, sure they worry. They're parents. But your dad values your opinion."

Matt patted her arm. "Honey, reality called. It said come back to earth."

So darned bullheaded. She wanted to cuff him upside the head. Like Deborah Stryker had said a zillion years ago when Abby had first become Matt's physical therapist, once he got an idea in his head he clung to it. Somehow, she had to get him to see that even in a wheelchair he still had worth.

He handed her back the strip of paper. "Slap some glue on here and put it in place. Then, we'll cut off the excess."

She was in the middle of hanging the strip when Matt's phone rang again.

"Yeah, Ma," Matt said. The edge was back in his voice. "I'm fine." After a pause he said, "That's 'cause I'm not at home...No, I'm just out, okay?"

Holding the paper in place, she looked over her shoulder. Matt shook his head while he shrugged. "Parents," he whispered. He nodded as he said into the phone, "Love you, too. Bye."

He hung up. "I think they have separation anxiety."

The separation anxiety went both ways. She'd heard the wistful tone whenever he was on the phone with his parents. As soon as the hurt over Crystal and Derrick wore off, he'd be on his way back to Fuller Lake, a fact she'd be wise to keep in mind.

Only one strip was left to be put into place on the large wall when they decided it was the perfect time to break for dinner. She'd be done with the wall and have time to clean up a bit before the pizza came out of the oven.

It felt perfectly natural when Matt put himself in charge of cooking while she prepared the last strip of wallpaper. He washed his hands and grabbed the towel from the bar on the stove. She smiled when he dropped the towel on the counter, just like she'd expected him to. He picked a frozen circle of pepperoni off the pizza and popped it in his mouth.

He'd just slid the pizza into the oven when his phone rang a third time. She paused as she brushed the paste onto the back of the paper. It was common for him to get a call from one of his parents when they were together. Once, he'd even gotten calls from both of his parents. Three calls was unheard of.

"I'm going to shut this damn thing off," he said as he flipped open the phone. "Hi Ma," he said without giving the caller a chance to speak. "Oh, hi." His eyes shot to Abby while he spoke into the phone. "Hold on a sec."

He set the open phone on his lap. "I'll be back in a moment."

The glue bucket and brush became unimportant as she watched Matt wheel from the room. He'd never left the room for one of his parents' calls.

She remained still as she listened to his movements. He went to the end of the hall and then on into the living room. She heard a muffled, "I'm back."

For a long time, there was silence. Matt listening to whatever the caller was saying. Abby turned her ear toward the doorway and listened hard, waiting for his reply.

"Yeah, I wish it would have turned out differently too. But it didn't, did it?" His voice was harsh. The conversation didn't sound like anything she'd expect him to have with his parents, and certainly not in that tone.

"I think I have a right to be pissed, Crystal."

The paintbrush fell from Abby's fingers.

"You cheated on me. With my best friend, of all people. Don't you get how much that hurts? I have to go."

Abby snatched up the paintbrush and hastily dipped it in the glue, trying to make it look like she'd been busily working the whole time he'd been gone. The paintbrush blurred. She shook her head and focused on spreading the glue, but she couldn't get the call off her mind. Crystal had called. There was only one reason she could come up with.

Her hand stopped moving.

She'd known all along that one day he'd return to Fuller Lake. Not once had she thought it would be because Crystal wanted to get back together.

His wheelchair creaked. She spread out the paste and positioned the wallpaper sheet on the wall. As she smoothed it out, she realized Matt was still down the hallway.

She wiped her hands on a towel and dropped it on the counter before tiptoeing down the hallway. Her feet barely touched the floor as she moved into the living room doorway. The sight of Matt took her breath away, his head bent and his fingertips pressed to his forehead. Even though she'd been mouse quiet, Matt looked up. Her heart beat hard four times as he stared at her, saying nothing. Then his lips bent into something she assumed was supposed to be a smile but came off more like a grimace.

"You got that piece up?"

Instead of answering, she walked into the room and crouched down in front of him. "Are you okay?"

"Yeah, sure, peachy." He looked away. "Never better."

"I'm a good listener, remember?"

"Why can't I move past what they did? Why can't I just forgive her?"

Abby took his hand. "Maybe because you're not the same person you were when you asked her to marry you."

He turned his hand over and threaded his fingers with hers. "Today was supposed to be my wedding day."

The world stopped. "I'm sorry. I didn't realize."

His fingers tightened on hers, like he was clinging to her for support. "I'm glad you needed help with your wallpaper. I didn't want to be alone today. Ma said they would have come down this weekend, but I knew Dad didn't feel comfortable leaving the guys to work alone on the group home."

"Me and my wallpaper are hardly a good substitute for family." Her thighs ached from crouching. She wanted to shift positions, but she was afraid it would distract him. "You should be with them."

"I could have gone home for the weekend, but I knew my mom would have smothered me. That's not what I needed today. I needed...a friend."

He'd chosen to be with her instead of his parents? The idea was both thrilling and frightening. "And you got stuck with me?"

"If this is being stuck, I like stuck." He rubbed his thumb against her hand. "You may be a pain in the ass, but I'm so thankful you met me at the bar that night. I don't know why you didn't blow me off right then and there."

"I couldn't. You needed help."

"Thanks for being my friend. Heaven knows, I needed one. Bad."

She felt drawn to him. She'd never felt this close to anyone other than her parents. Not even Paul, before she discovered he was like everyone else. "Maybe not as much as I did."

He laughed. "You? Need a friend? You must have more friends than you know what to do with."

"Nobody I'm close to." Her thighs screamed and her right calf felt like it was seconds away from cramping.

"Oh, come on. Don't give me that crap."

"Really. I mean, why get attached to someone who's just going to leave?" Matt was going to leave her too. He'd go home, pick up where he left off with Crystal. It was just a question of when.

"You say that like it's a foregone conclusion."

She shifted positions and knelt before him. "It is, isn't it? Tell me how many close friends you've had in the past who you're still close to now. Someone who really means something to you."

He opened his mouth but closed it right away. Not the reaction she'd wanted. She'd hoped he could prove her wrong. And convince her at the same time that he wasn't going to leave her someday, as well. "See. It's not worth it."

"What Derrick did hurts. I'll admit it. But I still wouldn't trade in all the years we were friends. And what he did won't stop me from making friends in the future."

"That's because your father didn't leave you." She winced the second the words were out. Even though she hadn't told Matt her father had died, that's what he believed, and she'd never felt the need to correct that misconception. After all, why point out that the most important person in her life hadn't found her worthy of sticking around?

His eyes turned to little slits while those kissable lips scrunched up. "You said your dad was—"

"Gone."

"He didn't die in the accident?"

She hadn't lied to Matt, but it sure felt like it now.

"Go sit down." He nodded toward the couch.

She did as he asked and arched an eyebrow when he transferred to the couch. He put his arm around her. She hesitated only a moment before she settled her head against his chest. He rubbed her shoulder. Staying here like this was wrong, but she couldn't make herself move. Not yet.

"What happened?" he asked softly.

She rubbed her finger in a circle on his arm. Even as she stayed silent, biding her time with her slow circles, the story formed in her head.

"You don't have to tell me," he said.

"It's simple, really. Not much to tell." She closed her eyes and concentrated on Matt's arm around her, the weight of his hand on her shoulder, the way his fingers glided back and forth. The scent of the cooking pizza filled the room. Someone should check on it. In a bit. "We were a very close family. Three peas in a pod. My father adored my mother and she loved him so much that she still asks about him even though she hasn't seen him in seventeen years. Shortly after my mother's accident he took me to California to visit with my mother's aunt while he went on a business trip. He never came back for me."

"Maybe he couldn't. Maybe he'd had an accident, as

well."

"Honey, reality called. It said to come back to earth." For a long time she'd let herself believe the same thing Matt had suggested. Right up until she'd found out her father was sending Aunt Norma money to take care of her. That's when she'd known he'd left because she'd done something wrong. "He didn't have an accident. He simply chose to turn his back on my mother and me. It took me a long time to feel comfortable with Aunt Norma and Uncle Joe, but in time I grew to love them. Then, Aunt Norma got pregnant. With twins. They already had four children and now two new babies on the way. They decided I'd be better off living with Aunt Norma's oldest sister, Gretta. "Aunt Gretta was sixty. She'd never had children. She had no idea what to do with an eleven-year-old who'd been dropped into her life, but she bumbled through. Just when I let myself get comfortable, she became ill and died. There I was, thirteen and being dumped off to live with a family I'd never met. There were two more families after that, but I swore right then and there that I'd never let myself love anyone again. And I didn't until I met Jovan in my last year of college.

"I fell for everything he said. We were going to get married. I passed up a really good job on the other side of the state so we could be together. Then, I found him in bed with his old girlfriend. That's when I moved to Bakersfield."

Matt cradled her head, pressing her forehead to his cheek. "I'm sorry, honey. That had to be hard."

"It was. Hard enough that I never dated anyone more than a couple dates. Until Paul."

"Paul?"

"He was a doctor at St. Luke's. The one I told you about. The one I caught with a nurse in his department."

"I remember."

"Like with Jovan, I lost my head when it came to him. I hoped it could lead to marriage." The scent of the pizza grew stronger. It was probably burning. She didn't care. She let her head rest heavily against him. "Silly me."

"Not everyone's like Jovan and Paul."

"No, but they are all like my father."

His phone rang again. She mentally groaned. She wasn't ready to separate herself from him.

He let the phone ring. "I can understand where you're coming from, but that doesn't mean everyone you meet is going to abandon you."

The ringing stopped only to start up again. "You better get that," she said.

"Why? It's probably my parents calling to make sure I'm *really* okay."

"All the more reason to answer it, then." She reluctantly freed herself from his arm.

He sighed. "I guess you're right." He pulled the phone from his pocket and flipped it open. "You said you wouldn't call anymore...No. It's too soon."

Abby's stomach tightened at the tinge of hysteria in his voice.

"I'm coming home. Now." He flipped his phone closed and looked at her. "Jenny's having the baby. I've got to go." He grabbed the wheelchair and pulled himself further away from her. She stood while he made the transfer. He pushed against the wheels once and then patted his pockets. "My keys. Where the fuck are my keys?"

She put her hands on Matt's shoulders. "Relax. We'll find your keys. Just relax."

"I can't. Jenny's having the baby and it's too soon. She's not due for another month."

She rubbed his arms. "Let me turn off the oven. Then I'll help you find your keys. And then I'll go with you to Fuller Lake."

"You don't need to do that."

"Unless I want to be your therapist again, yeah, I do. Because you're in no condition to drive."

CHAPTER TWENTY-FOUR

They arrived at the hospital around midnight. Matt wheeled to the waiting room like it was the finish line of a race. Abby picked up her pace to a jog to stay with him. Only four people were in the waiting room, but even if there'd been a crowd of fifty she could have easily picked out Matt's parents. The family resemblance was that strong.

His mother lifted her head from his father's chest. As soon as she saw Matt, she stood and rushed forward, enveloping her son as though she hadn't seen him in years. His father's arm stretched out across the back of the chair, waiting for Matt's mom to fill the void again. In the chair next to him sat a girl who looked a lot like what she remembered of Jenny, only younger and plumper—most likely, Faith. Kaylee was nestled on her lap, sound asleep.

"How's Jenny?" Matt asked. "Did she have the baby yet?"

"She's still in labor," his mother said.

"She's having a hard time," his father said, "but the baby's heartbeat is good."

Matt ran his fingers through his hair. "That's good, right? That the heartbeat is good?"

"It means the baby's hanging in there," his mother said as she returned to her seat. His father's arm immediately snugged around her.

"She can't lose the baby. That wouldn't be fair."

Abby put her hand on Matt's shoulder. He covered it with his own. The girl next to Matt's parents looked at Matt and Abby's clasped hands. A hint of a smile formed. "Aren't you going to let your girlfriend sit?"

"We're not dating," Abby said, quick to clear up any misconceptions. "I'm not his girlfriend."

"Oh?" Matt's mother asked, her eyebrows raising a bit.

"Oh." The girl's eyes sparkled.

"Faith," Matt said, but his eyes were on his parents. "This is my *friend*, Abby. Abby, this is Jenny's sister, Faith."

Matt's father hesitated before he said, "It's good to have friends."

Matt pulled his hand away from Abby's and nodded toward the row of chairs. She sat on the end chair and he parked his wheelchair next to her.

Even though she'd just said they weren't dating, it hurt to hear Matt confirm it, more than she'd thought possible.

Within seconds, Matt's hand latched on to hers again. His grip was tight. A little too tight, but she let him be. She understood. She leaned close. "You're fine, Matt. Everything's going to be okay."

An hour passed. Matt's mother's head had returned to his father's chest. Her eyes were closed, but Abby doubted she was asleep. Matt's hand tightened around Abby's. "You'd think they'd come and let us know how she's doing."

"I'm sure she's doing fine," his father said.

"Still, it's rude leaving us in the dark like this."

"They're busy taking care of Jenny and the baby."

Fifteen minutes went by before Matt broke the silence again. "All this waiting is driving me crazy."

"Now you know what it was like for us those first days you were in the hospital," his father said.

"And we spent five days in the waiting room," his mother said. "Not just a few hours."

"The doctor assured us you were holding your own, but it was still hard waiting for you to wake up."

"Five days of this? I don't know how you guys stood it." He tugged on Abby's hand. "I can't just sit here. I need to go for a walk."

They barely got three feet down the hall from the waiting room door when Matt stopped. He looked up at her with the saddest eyes she'd ever seen. "As one friend

to another, can I tell you I could use a hug?"
She smiled and crawled onto his lap. A sigh filled her as his arms closed in around her. She put her arms around him and rested her head on his shoulder. The big wheelchair tire pressed uncomfortably against the back of her leg, but she wasn't about to complain.

"Thanks for coming," he said.

"You owe me. Big time. A sundae with lots of caramel and hot fudge and peanuts."

"I'll buy you two."

"One's fine. I'll even share it with you." She rubbed the back of his neck, her finger brushing over the hard ridge of his surgery scar. His hair was soft against her hand. She wanted to bury her fingers in it, but she held back. His right thumb caressed her shoulder blade. The wheelchair tire pressing against her leg grew more uncomfortable. Sitting on his lap for too long wasn't good for his circulation. She should get up. But she couldn't. Not yet. Just for a while longer, she wanted to be in his arms.

"What if something happens to her?" His lips brushed against her head. "What's Brad going to do? Kaylee needs her mother."

"Women give birth every day."

"But not a month early. What if the baby dies?"

She hated to pull away from him, but she needed to look into his eyes. "If something horrible happens, we'll deal with it then. Not now."

"But—"

She pressed her finger to his lips. "Worrying about what ifs doesn't accomplish anything. Why spend all of your energy worrying about something that probably won't happen?"

He pulled his head back just enough to free his mouth from her finger. "Has anyone ever told you that you're—"

"A pain in the behind?"

"Well, that too, but I was going to say smart." His eyes stayed connected with hers like he couldn't bear to look away.

She loved the way he was looking at her. Too much. She didn't want to get up, but it was time to put some distance between him and what she was feeling. She pushed herself off his lap. "You wanted to go for a walk. We should probably do that."

"No. I don't want to leave. In case something happens." He took her hand. "Thanks."

He wheeled back into the waiting room. His eyes went straight to his father with a silent question. His father shook his head.

"I'll take that as good news," Matt said.

He parked himself next to the chair Abby had sat in earlier. Again, his fingers linked with hers, but this time his grip wasn't as tight.

A tall man stepped into the room. "Any news yet?" he asked.

Matt's fingers tightened on Abby's.

The man looked their way. His eyes met Matt's and his footsteps faltered. Tension filled the air between the two men. She knew without asking that the newcomer was Derrick.

The air crackled with tension. She glanced at Matt's parents, wondering if they felt it, as well. His father frowned as he looked between his son and Derrick. His mother lifted her head from Matt's father's chest. Confusion filled her eyes.

Derrick looked away. His feet started moving again. "How's it going?"

Carl Huntz stared at Matt a second before looking up at Derrick. "We still haven't heard anything."

Derrick shifted his weight to his other foot. "I can't stay. Tell Brad I stopped by and that I'm wishing all the best for them. Call me as soon as there's news, okay?" Without waiting for a response, he turned. He walked past Matt as though there was only empty space.

Matt's fingers remained tight around Abby's. He stared at the now-empty doorway.

"What's up with you two?" Matt's father asked.

"Nothing," Matt said, looking away from the door. She

could read both the anger and the sadness in his eyes.

"Don't give me *nothing*. What was that all about?"

"I guess he just doesn't like hospitals or something."

"My bet's on the *or something*," his father said. "So what is it?"

"How the hell am I supposed to know?" His grip threatened to cut off the circulation in Abby's fingers. "I'm not his keeper. You'd have to ask him."

"Precisely what I plan on doing."

Matt's head tipped back. His jaw muscles twitched. He had the look of someone who knew they'd been given only a short reprieve and that the next battle was going to be twice as deadly. She touched his arm, giving it a gentle squeeze. He looked her way. She offered an it's-going-to-be-okay smile. He didn't smile back but his jaw relaxed, and that was good enough for her.

A man stepped into the doorway. Blond hair escaped from the bottom of the cap he wore, but the face was Matt's. A mask hung around Brad's neck, and the paper booties that covered his feet matched the gown. His proud smile told the outcome of the last several hours. "I've got a son. A little guy. Five pounds, one ounce, but the doctor says he doesn't think there'll be any problems."

"How's Jenny?" Faith asked. Kaylee stirred on her lap and then settled back into sleep.

Matt's parents got up from the couch as one unit. His father's arm stayed around his wife's shoulder as they walked toward their oldest son.

"She's great. A bit uncomfortable. Happy it's over. But she's great."

As Matt's parents surrounded Brad in a joint hug, Abby could tell Matt wanted to be in there with them. She gave his hand a little squeeze and then let go. He wheeled over to his family and slugged his brother on the arm. "Had a little runt just like yourself, huh?"

Brad grinned as he looked down at his brother. "I'm not so sure you can call me runt anymore. Not when you have to look up to me now." He bent down and hugged his brother. "I'm glad you made it. It means a lot to have you here."

"Thank Abby. She's the one who got us here in one piece."

Brad nodded her way. "I've got to get back to Jenny."

Everyone settled into their original seats, but there were happy smiles now. Glad to be a part of it all, Abby looked over at Matt. Her smile faded as soon as she saw Matt's closed eyes. His breathing seemed labored. His parents had probably forgotten the scene with Derrick, but she was certain Matt hadn't. "Hey, you." She tapped his arm. "Now it's my turn to drag you on a walk. No excuses this time."

He followed her from the room. She stepped to the side so he could fall into place next to her. "Penny for your thoughts," she said.

"I'm happy everything turned out fine."

She looked over at him. Although the worry of earlier was gone, he looked far from ecstatic. "Did it?"

He let go of his wheels. "Yeah. Baby's fine. Jenny's fine. Everything's fine."

"Everything except with Derrick."

Matt looked away. He gave the wheels a push. She trotted beside him to keep up until he got to the end of the hall. He slammed his fists down on his thighs. "That should have hurt." He buried his fingers in his hair. "I need a drink. God, how I need a drink."

She knelt in front of him. "No. You don't. What you need is to accept that you're hurting inside. It's okay to be angry with him."

"I hate him. I hate what he did to me. I hate it even more that when I first saw him, I was happy he was there. I miss him, Abby. I miss the Tuesday night basketball games. I miss shooting pool with him. I miss working with him on the jobsites. How can I feel that way? How can I hate him so much and miss him at the same time?"

"Because you treasure the people who mean something to you. That's what makes you so special, Matt."

"I'm not special." He hooked his fingers around the push rims of his chair. "I'm not special at all."

She locked gazes with him. Was it possible he wouldn't disappear from her life like everyone else? "Yes, you are."

§

Sunday dawned early after the late night, but Matt felt exhilarated, anyhow, as he sat in Jenny's hospital room surrounded by his family. He looked down at the little baby—Lucas Matthew—snug in his arms. He smiled as he listened to the room buzzing with multiple conversations, all going at once. Such chaos. Amazing how it filled him with a sense of peace.

Abby crowded closer to him and lifted Lucas's hand. The baby's fingers, no fatter than roofing nails, closed around her thumb. When she smiled and looked at Matt, he felt a wave of emotion unlike any he'd ever felt before, like everything in his world had settled into place. Nothing mattered other than this moment, this place, and the people he was with. Abby included.

Matt's eyes stayed locked with hers for much longer than he could remember ever having looked at Crystal. He had no desire to ever look away. The baby stretched and let out a mewing wail like a newborn kitten, drawing Abby's attention away from Matt in the process.

As he looked away from Abby, he caught sight of his father across the room staring at him, his gaze as intense as hers had been. Even though he knew he'd done nothing wrong, Matt still looked away like a guilty child caught with a screwdriver in one hand and a brand new toaster in the other. He sensed his father still staring at him. Probably soaking up the view of Matt holding Lucas since it'd probably be the closest Matt would ever come to having a baby.

Little Lucas pulled Abby's thumb to his mouth. "I think the baby's hungry," she said.

"Would you like to feed him?" Jenny asked.

Abby's eyes widened. "May I? You wouldn't mind?"

"Knock yourself out."

Abby took Lucas from Matt. Like an expert, she cradled the baby in her arms and took the bottle Matt's mother offered.

Matt's father stood from his perch on the windowsill. "Too much sitting," he said. "I need to walk. Matt, you want to join me."

Not a question.

Matt glanced over at Abby. She looked beautiful holding Lucas. So happy. He hated missing even one second of this.

His father cleared his throat.

Abby's gaze connected with Matt's, silently asking what was brewing. Matt shrugged. She thrust her chin at the door, saying he'd better go before his father dragged him out. "I'll make sure little Lucas doesn't do anything cute while you're gone."

"Good luck with that."

Feeling very much like one of the many times he'd been called to the principal's office, he followed his father from the room. The walk ended halfway down the hall when his father led him to the waiting room where he immediately took a seat.

Matt's mind whirled while he tried to figure out what he'd done to deserve this special one-on-one.

"How serious are things with you and this Abby girl?"

He almost laughed. That was what his father had pulled him away for? "I don't know, Dad. We don't have our comedy routine ironed out yet. Does that make it serious?"

His father crossed his arms.

"We're just friends. That's all."

"Then there's no reason for you not to come back home and try to make a go at things with Crystal."

Not what Matt expected to hear. At all. "Nothing other than the reasons why we broke up in the first place." Like the fact that Derrick still existed.

"I think it's time you come home and work on those reasons. Faith will be moving out of your house in a couple months. You can stay with your mother and me until then."

Nope, not the conversation he expected at all. "I need more time."

"Then I'll buy you a couple of watches." There was no hint of teasing in his father's expression.

"I can't come home yet."

"This have something to do with Derrick?"

Matt's gaze shifted to the picture behind his father. Being called to the principal's office would have been much easier. "There's nothing with Derrick."

"He's not seeing Crystal, if that's what you're worried about."

His eyes shot back to his father, and his mouth started flapping as the words flowed from his heart. "That doesn't make it any easier to accept what they did." His brain caught up, and he frowned. His father knew about Crystal and Derrick?

"That son-of-a-bitch." His father sprang from the chair.

Matt sighed as he closed his eyes. His father had been trolling for information, and he'd latched onto the bait—hook, line, and sinker.

"Why didn't you tell us?"

"Because you need him on the job."

"Well, I certainly don't need him anymore."

Matt rubbed his forehead. Last night had been too long and too filled with worry. He was too tired for this conversation. "They made a mistake. You can't fire him over a mistake."

"You're defending them?"

Matt's eyelid pulled and stretched as he made circles on his forehead with his fingertips.

"Okay," his father said. "Fine. Forget Crystal. Forget Derrick. We've only got another couple months on the group home. This was your project. I want you to come home and help finish it."

Like Matt's being there would make a difference.

"You've already got all the help you need."

His father stood. "Just come home."

Matt closed his eyes and listened to his father's footsteps carrying him away. Yup. Would have been better to visit the principal. Three days of detention and it'd be over.

§

Abby's step was light and airy as she walked down the hallway to visit her mother the next day. The memory of Matt holding his nephew made her smile. It amazed her how gentle he could be with something so tiny. And he was a natural. He was going to make a wonderful father. She just wished she could get him to believe the things she kept trying to prove to him. That he was a value to Huntz & Sons Construction, in or out of a wheelchair. That he could still have the life he'd planned, even without a recovery. That he was such a special man.

She stepped into her mother's room, not one bit surprised to see one of the other residents sitting at the other end of the bed. "Hi, Mom. Sandra."

Her mother's eyes lit up. She held up a clay form that was recognizable as a bird. "Look what Matt made for me."

Abby's smile fell. "Matt?"

Her mother nodded. "Matt came. He made this."

Abby held back a groan. She never should have brought Matt along that one time. Her mother had asked when Matt was coming back every day since she'd brought him. Now, like the imaginary visits from her father, she'd have to put up with fake visits from Matt, as well.

Sandra hugged Abby's mother. "I go now that Abby here. See you 'morrow."

"'Morrow," Helen parroted as she waved to her friend.

Abby sat beside her mother and eyed the bird. The clay model was very detailed. Complete with feathers and shaped wings. She wondered where it'd come from. "Shall we color?" she asked, hoping her mother wouldn't bring up Matt again.

"Matt colored me a new picture." She pointed to a neatly colored picture taped to the wall.

So much for that plan. "Well, Matt's been very busy, hasn't he?"

Her mother nodded. "He was activity leader today. He'll come every day, but not on Wednesday. We cook on Wednesday. He said he doesn't cook. But he said he might come to eat." She rubbed her stomach. "He likes to eat."

Knowing it was best to humor her mother, she said, "Then you make sure you cook him something good, okay?"

She pulled two coloring books and a box of crayons from her mother's shelf and returned to the bed. Opening one book to a random page, she handed it to her mother, who promptly closed it and picked up a word search magazine.

Amazed pride spread through Abby as she watched from the corner of her eye while Helen ran the tip of her pencil above the paper, looking for the first word. Such a change from the woman who hadn't been able to figure out how to turn a page not that long ago. A change that Abby, the physical therapist Abby, should have been responsible for and not the staff at Hot Springs.

She gnawed on her bottom lip.

It didn't matter if she'd been responsible or not. Her mother was making strides. That's what mattered. If her mother kept up at this pace, Charles Presthed might very well have another success story to add to his résumé. As much as she disliked the man, she had a feeling she'd be tempted to hug him if her mother was released to independent living.

She pictured her mother in a group home like the one Matt's father was building. Hopefully, her mother would be able to move into such a home. Such a wonderful thought.

Turning her attention back to her coloring book, she flipped through the pages. An already colored-in picture caught her eye. It was the picture Matt had done the night she'd brought him with her. In the lower right corner, he'd printed M. L. H. She looked at the picture taped to the wall. A wave of emotion washed through her when she noticed a blur of writing in the same location.

She picked up the clay bird from the table where her mother was solving her word-search puzzle. Her heart skipped a beat. The initials M. L. H. were etched into the bottom.

What was he up to? she wondered as she picked a purple crayon out of the box and colored in a fish. Since the move to Milwaukee, she usually welcomed her time with her mother. Tonight, time dragged because she needed to call Matt. Finally, her mother yawned. Abby knew she shouldn't be happy, but she was. "Looks like someone's about ready for bed."

Her mother nodded. "Go to sleep so tomorrow comes. Bring Matt with it."

"You say hi to him." Abby gave her mother a hug. "I love you." As the words came out, she realized they were true. She did love her mother. Very much. She gave her mother an extra squeeze and a kiss and then waved goodbye.

As soon as she got outside the building, she pulled her cell phone from her purse and dialed Matt's number. "Did you have an interesting day?"

"You just visited your mom, didn't you?"

"What do you think you're doing?"

"Chill, okay?"

She clenched the cell phone. "Not until you tell me what you're up to."

"I'm not up to anything. I went to visit your mom, that's all."

"That's all, huh? That's not what I hear. I hear you're working there now."

"Your mom was in the activities room. I helped out. Next thing I know, this arrogant jerk is offering me a job."

"Charles Presthed?"

"Yeah, Prickhead. That'd be the guy."

"So you *are* going to be working there." What he did with his time was his business. So why did it bother her so darn much?

"It's not like I've got anything better to do. Where else am I going to get paid to play all day?"

She flashed forward through the future. She saw her mother becoming dependent on Matt. Then Matt disappearing from their lives with an *I'll see you soon.* Her mother would be crushed. That's what bothered her.

"Matt, you cannot take the job."

"Why not?"

"What if my mother becomes dependent on you?"

"So all the other employees there should quit, too? Just to keep your mom from becoming dependent on them?"

"You know what I mean," she snapped, angry because if what he'd said made sense, then what she'd said didn't.

"No, Abby. I don't. If I take the job, how am I different from any other employee there?"

"Do what you want, Matt. Just don't you break my mother's heart."

"Isn't it your heart you're worried about?"

She punched the end call button and stormed across the parking lot, her fingers clenched around the phone. How dare he suggest she was worried about herself and not her mother.

The phone vibrated, announcing an incoming call. Matt, she assumed. The vibration spurred her to walk faster. Five feet from her car, the phone went still, as did she while she waited for the quick buzz to indicate he'd left a message.

A car drove into the parking lot and then turned around. Too much time had passed. He hadn't bothered to leave a message.

She hunched her purse strap higher on her shoulder and took a step forward. So he hadn't left a message. Big deal. She hadn't wanted a message from him, anyhow.

The phone vibrated again. Another incoming call. She looked at the display. Matt's number. Her legs felt weak and her heart raced and her stomach floated inside her. How could she be happy he'd called when she was still mad at him? She punched the answer button. "What?"

"Abby," he said with a gentle voice. "If you don't want me to take the job, I won't. If you don't want me to visit your mom, I won't. If you want me to drop dead, well, sorry, you're on your own with that one."

She let out a little laugh and hated him and loved him all at the same time for his managing to work that reaction out of her.

"I like your mom. But I like you more. You tell me what you want, okay?"

She knew what she wanted, but she couldn't allow herself to go down that road. As soon as she let herself believe she had a future with him, everything would get all messed up and he'd be gone from her life. She couldn't stand that. "I worry about her."

"I know you do."

"I wish you'd told me before you went to visit her."

"I'm sorry. It was a spur of the moment thing. After being home this weekend, I guess I was a little homesick. I couldn't be with my family, so I spent time with yours."

She wanted to tell him no, he couldn't take the job, but she couldn't do it. "You decide, Matt. If you want the job, take it."

"Thanks, Abby. Any chance you haven't eaten dinner yet?"

She laughed again. "I rarely get to eat before I visit Mom."

"I'm just heating up some of that lasagna Ma sent home with me. It's more than I need to eat by myself. And I'd like your company."

"I'll be over." The words slipped out before she could stop them.

CHAPTER TWENTY-FIVE

July melted into August, and life with Matt settled into a comfortable friendship, free of romance. Which was just fine with Abby. She didn't need him to be anything more than a friend. What she did need, though, was to knock some sense into him. He was so stubborn, and he was totally stuck in his belief that he had to give up the life he'd planned. But she had an idea. A little dream he'd once mentioned that she was about to bring to reality.

She eased the borrowed SUV to a stop in front of Matt's apartment. Pulling a camper had been no different than pulling a U-Haul, although she'd be more than willing to pass over the driving responsibilities to Matt once she let him in on his surprise outing. Thankfully, the SUV belonged to Ryan and was all set up with hand controls.

She climbed out of the Ford Explorer and noticed Matt wheeling out of the apartment building. A sudden ache in her heart fought the usual weightless sensation upon seeing him. Two nights cooped up with him in a tiny camper. If she made it through this weekend pretending she was content being just friends, it would be a miracle.

His chocolate brown gaze went from her to the camper. When it came back to her, his eyes melted into her, bringing with it that floating sensation again.

"Surprise," she said, praying the surprise wouldn't be on her.

"You're taking me camping?"

"Door County."

"Biking," he said, reciting his dream vacation. "Taking in the view. All those orange and red leaves."

"Unfortunately it's too early for the leaves to change, but I think I can manage the rest of your dream vacation." As long as he'd forgotten the sex part. Because that *wasn't* going to happen. Not even so much as a kiss. Or a hug.

Nada. None. Not if she had any hope of keeping him in her life.

"We get to live the dream until Sunday evening," Abby said. "Then it's back to reality."

§

Abby had chosen the perfect weekend for their camping trip Matt thought the next afternoon as he pedaled behind her on his new hand-control bike. Not too hot. Not too cool. Everything perfect, even with the trees full of green leaves instead of orange, red, and yellow. Not like he would have paid attention to the leaves if they had been in full color. Not when the view in front of him was more appealing. Hair pulled away from a neck he wanted to nibble. Pedals being pumped by shapely calves he wanted to caress. The occasional glimpse of the outline of plump breasts he'd love to lick.

He kept his speed steady as she slowed down, bringing them side by side. The view only got better. "Thanks for renting a recumbent style bike for yourself," he said. "I'm getting used to the looks whenever I go somewhere, but it's kind of nice to blend in every now and then."

She laughed. Like he'd said something funny.

"What?" he asked.

"You? Blend in? Don't you know that you turn heads wherever you go and your chair's got nothing to do with it?"

He didn't get it. Whenever he looked in the mirror, he saw an average looking man. Nothing special. Yet, for some reason, women found him attractive. He was surprised, however, to discover that Abby did, as well.

She hadn't seemed the least bit fazed when she'd burst into the camper this morning. There he'd been, face down, buck naked, checking his skin with a mirror for breakdown, and she'd looked him straight on and asked where the matches were. Not even a hint of pink had colored her cheeks. If she hadn't been affected by his naked ass, then it was unlikely she had any opinion on his looks. "Must be the huge wart on my nose."

"Yeah, that'd be it." She flashed that damn buy-these-gloves smile and then appeared to be enthralled by the scenery and not the wildlife pedaling the bike next to her.

How different she was from Crystal, who stared at the ground in front of her tire as though the road were the only thing that existed.

"It really is beautiful here, just like you described," she said.

"And camping? What do you think of it, so far?"

"Well, other than that frightening view this morning, I'm enjoying it."

Frightening? His naked ass had been frightening? He'd almost rather go back to believing she hadn't noticed he'd been naked. "You could have knocked first."

"I'll keep that in mind for the next camping trip."

Next camping trip. He could easily be convinced to come camping with her again.

"Oh!" Abby stopped pedaling. Her eyes widened and her lips parted.

He stopped pedaling, as well. Off to the left, not a hundred yards away, a mother deer and her two little ones grazed in the field. A beautiful sight. One that would have left Crystal shrugging her shoulders with indifference, unlike Abby who seemed enthralled. She planted her feet on the pavement and looked as if she'd be content sitting there until the deer left or night fell or they got run off the road by a passing motorist. Enjoying the simple things in life.

He watched her instead of the deer. She glanced at him and smiled before her eyes went back to the critters. Such an amazing creature. How different might his life be now if it'd been Abby he'd fallen in love with first, instead of Crystal?

His hand slipped off the pedal. "Oh, God."

"I know," she whispered. "It's really amazing, isn't it?"

It wasn't possible. They hadn't even kissed yet. He couldn't possibly be in love. Could he?

The truth set in. He did love her. And he had for quite some time. He just hadn't realized it because he hadn't been looking for it. Not like with Crystal, where he'd been evaluating his feelings from their first date, searching for a relationship that would satisfy his father while hopefully satisfying himself, as well. After a couple dates, he'd convinced himself he'd hit two out of two with Crystal. If only he'd known what love really felt like.

He let his gaze drop to Abby's feet planted on the asphalt and then shifted to the single back tire on her bike. Her bike might look similar to his, but it was nothing like his, just like she was nothing like him.

Abby looked his way, her eyes alight with an excitement he couldn't remember ever having seen in Crystal. He rubbed his leg and sighed. Why in the hell couldn't he have met Abby before he'd met Crystal? Back when he'd been whole.

§

The warm afternoon had turned chilly as the sun began to set. Parked close to the crackling fire, Matt skimmed the *Milwaukee Journal Sentinel* while he waited for Abby to join him. Too bad he hadn't acted on his idea of getting a dog. It wouldn't be so lonely if Fido were curled up next to him. Dang, it felt like Abby had been in the camper for hours even though he knew it'd been less than five minutes. Funny how he could miss her when she was only fifteen feet away.

Funny how he could have fallen in love with her without even realizing it was happening.

He turned the page and noticed he'd reached the classifieds. With nothing better to do, he scanned the listings.

Bouncer. A job he could have done without working up a sweat before the accident. Now, he'd just get laughed at.

Computer programmer. He could surf the Internet, but that was about as far as his computer knowledge went.

General construction worker.

He rubbed the back of his neck as he stared at the black type on the newsprint paper. A reminder of the man he used to be. That man might have had a chance with Abby. He wasn't sure the man he was now had a chance.

The camper door opened. He looked over the top of his paper. Abby had changed clothes. Her department-store shorts and tank top had been exchanged for inexpensive sweat pants, a hooded Mickey Mouse sweatshirt, and well-worn tennis shoes. Real clothes, he thought with a smile. Not a pair of designer jeans, a frilly blouse, and three-hundred-dollar fashion boots like Crystal would have been wearing. Abby smiled...at him...like he was the most important person in her universe. He wanted to be worthy of that smile.

"You want a soda?" she asked as she reached into the cooler.

She had about twenty pounds on Crystal, but the extra weight only made her curvier, not heavier. He imagined how soft she'd be next to him, and sighed.

Still bent over she looked his way. "Soda?"

"Yeah. Thanks."

Settling into the lawn chair next to him she handed him the Coke. "Anything good in there?"

"A job at Blue Moon Casino. Blackjack dealer. Hourly wages, tips, bonus, benefits. Must have reasonable math skills." He laughed. "Leaves me out." His father would never approve of such a job.

"Over qualified, for sure." She took a sip from her can, her lips lightly suckling the rim. "Why are you looking at want ads?"

"Killing time."

"You could have set up the Yahtzee game."

"Professional Yahtzee setter-upper. There ya go. Too bad there's no such job."

"You can be my professional Yahtzee setter-upper. I'll pay you a quarter."

"Wow. What would I do with that much money?"

"Buy your favorite girl a present."

He liked that. His favorite girl. "My favorite girl deserves better." Better than a guy stuck in a wheelchair. He hastily folded the paper and tucked it beneath his thigh. "Make it a buck and I'll buy you a taco when we get back to Milwaukee."

"How about you set it up for free, and *I'll* buy *you* a taco when we get home."

Home made him think of Fuller Lake, not Milwaukee. His house was empty now. Russ had arrived at Fort McCoy a couple weeks ago, and Faith had moved out last week. Even if she'd still been living in his house, Fuller Lake would always be home.

"Matt? What do you say? You set up the game and I'll buy us tacos when we get home?"

"I don't want to be a kept man."

"Okay, then, what do you want?"

You. As my girlfriend. As someone I can have a future with. Both of us, living in my house. "I want to go back to work for my dad, but that's not going to happen."

"Says you."

Yeah, says me. And whoever's in charge of my recovery. "I need your expert opinion." And a whole lot of good luck. "Dr. Meyer said I had eighteen months before there wasn't any hope of a recovery. But it's been six months since I've had any change. Is my time up?"

"I may not be a math-whiz, but last I heard, six isn't even half of eighteen."

"Abby, you know what I mean."

"Do you still have a chance of walking?"

Locking onto her eyes, he nodded just the tiniest bit. His breath held. He needed to know he still had a chance—at walking again, at working for his father again...and at being worthy of having a serious relationship with Abby.

"You know there isn't any way to know for sure."

An answer he would have expected from Esther. Not from Abby. "Don't wimp out on me."

Her eyes clouded over but remained on his. "Do you really want to know, Matt? Really, truly, and honestly?"

Did he? Even if her answer took away all hope?

Say no and he could be stuck in limbo for eleven more months. Or he could have his answer now and get on with his life.

His heart beat so rigidly that he felt it in his shoulders. "I can't stand it anymore, Abby. I need to know."

Her lip disappeared. Not a good sign. For a smidgen of a second he thought about saying he'd been kidding. Instead, he said, "Please."

Still, she paused a second. Then she shifted her chair until she was directly in front of him. She took his hands in hers. He wanted to stop right there in that moment, her hands meshed with his, her eyes locked on his, nothing left in the world except for him and her.

"I believe you've reached your plateau."

An instant sadness washed through him, filling every nook and cranny, suffocating. Deep down he'd known that would be her answer, but he'd hoped, God he'd hoped, to hear he still had a chance. He closed his eyes. In the darkness, he clung to her hands. It was over. He wasn't ever going to return to work for his father. He'd never make his father proud. And he'd probably never have more than a friendship with Abby.

For as tightly as he held Abby's hands, she managed to wiggle free. The next thing he knew, he was in her arms, snug to her shoulder.

"I'm sorry, Matt."

He tried to focus on her touch, but instead all he could feel was the pain ripping through him. The wheelchair he sat in seemed to swallow him. The wheelchair that would always be a part of him.

Tears burned his eyes and throat. He tried desperately to hold them back but failed. And once that first tear slid free, he was lost. His shoulders shook as he clung to Abby.

All of the plans he'd had, gone. All because...

The night of his accident remained a blank, but he no longer needed to remember to know what had happened. He was pretty sure he'd crashed into the tree on purpose. His father would be disappointed. More than disappointed. Ashamed.

As long as he never said anything, his father would never know.

But Matt would.

From the time he'd been seven years old, he'd known he wanted to be just like his father. From that point on, he'd lived his father's life instead of his own. And now it was over.

All of it.

Gone.

Forever.

§

Abby lay beneath the covers on her side of the camper. Across the room came the gentle sound of Matt's snoring. He'd fallen asleep quickly. Crying as hard as he had would do that to a person. She knew from personal experience. At least he was at peace now.

Outside, the wind picked up.

Lightning flashed through the darkened plastic windows, reminding her of the day Daddy had left. She could use a little of Matt's peace right now. Or the teddy bear Daddy had given her to protect her from the storm. She hugged her wadded up Mickey Mouse sweatshirt to her chest. It was a poor substitute for the bear she'd clung to the night Daddy had left. Matt could protect her, except he was on the other side of the camper, dead to the world, and she was over here, all alone. She closed her eyes and hugged the sweatshirt more tightly. Thunder crackled in the distance.

One, one thousand. Two, one thousand. Three. Lightning flashes lit up the camper.

She wiggled her leg. *Make it stop. Make it stop. Make it stop.*

Heavy raindrops pounded the canvas. She buried her head under the covers. Still, she could see the flashes of lightning. Daddy had left her in a storm. Matt would leave her, as well.

Make it stop. Make it stop.

Lightning cracked and thunder roared in deafening booms overhead. She let out a scream.

"Abby? You okay?"

Her heart pounded. *Save me.*

Another rumble of thunder filled the air. She whimpered, hoping Matt wouldn't hear her while hoping, at the same time, that he'd come rescue her.

"Abby? I know you're awake. Come here."

She wanted to run to him, but she stayed where she was. She pressed the sweatshirt to her mouth, but she rocked hard, just like she'd done when she was little and scared.

"Would you just get your ass over here?"

"I'm fine," she mumbled through the sweatshirt.

"Then I'll come over there. The storm will probably be over by the time I make my way across the camper, though." He pushed back his covers. Thunder cracked. She jumped from her bed and ran across the camper. No hesitation as she climbed into bed with him and buried her face against his chest.

He pulled the covers back into place and wrapped his strong arms around her. Just like she'd always thought, she felt safe with him. His fingers stroked her hair. "It's okay, honey. It's just a storm. It can't hurt you."

Being in his arms for the second time that night was as much a curse as it was a blessing because it reminded her of what she'd be missing. "Yes. It will hurt. I know it will."

"No. Trust me. Nothing bad's going to happen. I'm here. I'll take care of you."

She wanted to believe him. He continued to run his fingers through her hair. In time, she relaxed against him. Her breaths evened out in a rhythmic pattern. The storm was still raging outside, but inside she was calm.

§

Abby awoke in Matt's arms. For a second, she thought she was dreaming until she remembered the storm. With her back snug against his stomach, she realized they were a perfect fit. Like two adjoining pieces of a puzzle.

His stomach pressed against her back with each intake of air. With each exhale, she felt his breath on her shoulder. His hand cupped her breast lightly, like it belonged there. Everything about him felt so right.

Even though she was plenty close enough, she scooted closer, just a touch, trying to meld her body to his. Her behind rubbed against him. Something hard pressed against her that hadn't been there a moment ago. She wiggled a little more.

"You gonna keep that up?" Matt asked. "Or would you like to settle down so I can go back to sleep?"

"Could you stop poking me with your...uh..."

"Stop rubbing your ass on him and he'll go back to sleep. Keep up what you're doing and I can't make any promises."

Trying to ignore the pressure on her behind, she focused on Matt's hand on her breast, right where it shouldn't be. Intending on nudging him to a safer location, she covered his hand with hers. He spread his fingers, just a little, and she found herself threading her fingers with his instead of pushing him away.

He kissed her neck lightly. Just enough to get her pulse going.

She shouldn't be here in bed with him. Except she didn't want to leave. She liked his lips on her neck. The hard knob pressing against her behind. His hand on her breast. Which made her realize she really had to get out of that bed.

Unaware of the turmoil inside her, he continued to caress her neck with his lips. It felt so good. So right.

His kisses on her neck deepened. All common sense left her. She needed to feel his lips on hers. She turned in his arms and fit her mouth to his. A rush of pleasure filled her when he slid his tongue between her lips. His hand moved down her back. In time, his fingers slid beneath the elastic of her pajama shorts and then her panties, each advancement slow enough to give her time to protest.

Above her head, the shadow of a tree branch caressed the canvas with a gentle morning breeze. She shifted away from Matt, just a bit, and guided his hand to her front. Safe. That's what she felt as he stroked the tender folds of skin.

Needing to feel him as well, she slid her hand beneath the elastic of his running pants. He pulled his lips from hers, and his dark eyes locked on to hers. "Abby." He shook his head just enough to say no, without saying the words. She read in his eyes his fear that he wasn't man enough. Oh, how wrong he was. She closed her fingers around him. He sighed and closed his eyes. Within seconds, he swelled and hardened.

Even though she'd had sex with Paul and Jovan, she'd done it because it'd been expected of her and not because she wanted it. But as Matt worked her to the edge of climax with his finger, she knew she needed to join her body with his. Even if it meant they'd only have this one time. She had to be one with him.

She moved his top leg behind him so she could roll him onto his back.

"What are you doing?"

"Shhh."

"Abby."

She ignored him and worked to roll him. As if he realized protesting would make no difference, he shifted his shoulders and plopped onto his back. She worked his running pants down over his erection and then wiggled herself out of her own clothes. The campground echoed with the sound of someone chopping wood. *Ker-thwack. Ker-thwack. Ker-thwack.* Keeping time with her pounding heart.

She positioned herself over him and they locked gazes. Without a word being spoken, she knew he loved her. The need to protect herself kicked in. She needed to end this. She needed to get out of this bed. Out of the camper. Out of his life.

Through the cloud of fear, she noticed his fingers pressing lightly against her hips. His touch felt so right. Despite her fears, being with him felt right. She focused on what she felt inside her heart. If even for only one day, she wanted to believe love was real.

She bore down and pushed until he was fully inside her. Their eyes stayed locked as she moved against him. Their minds as linked as their bodies, he said again, without moving his lips, that he loved her. She wanted to reject those words while embracing them at the same time. As long as he didn't say it out loud, she'd be fine.

I know you're scared, his touch said as he caressed her. *I won't hurt you.*

She wanted so badly to believe.

Trust me.

She leaned forward, placing her mouth on his, as much because she needed his kiss as to stop reading his thoughts. With her eyes closed, she concentrated on him filling her, moving her hips in an ever-increasing rhythm until she lost control and slid over the edge of ecstasy. Yet, even then, she kept moving against him...and the pressure built...until she wanted to scream.

His hands stopped moving. His fingertips dug into her. He pressed his head into the pillow and let out a low growl. She felt him throb inside her. No matter what he thought, he was a real man. All the way through. Reluctantly, she separated herself from him, but she refused to leave his arms. She settled onto his chest and closed her eyes.

"Abby?"

Please, don't say it. Don't say you love me.

"Thanks for last night."

Her mind stalled. He hadn't said he loved her? Why? They'd just made love. This was the perfect time for him to say it. But he hadn't. He'd said thanks. And not even thanks for the roll in the hay. Instead, he was thanking her for last night.

He brushed his fingers through her hair. "Abby?"

Now. Say it now. "Umm?"

"I..."

She held still. Waiting for the words she longed to hear. For the words she was afraid to hear.

"I wish I would have met you a long time ago."

She brought herself up onto her elbows and stared down at him. "Before you were opinionated and stubborn?"

"Before I was paralyzed."

She put her hand on his heart. "You're not paralyzed here." She moved her hand to his forehead. "Or here." She concentrated on the feel of his body next to hers, so strong, safe, and secure. "So what if your legs don't work.

You're perfect, just the way you are."

He turned his face away. She touched his cheek, the bristly growth of coarse hair prickling her fingertips as she brought his face forward. "I mean it, Matt. You're absolutely perfect."

For a moment, he was quiet. She could almost see the gears working inside his head as he worked to reject her words and then slowly grow to accept what she said.

"If I can get someone to pick me up, would you mind going back to Milwaukee alone?"

Alone. Without Matt. The beginning of the end.

"Dad said the group home will be done this week. I want to be there for the completion. It's something I feel I need to do. So can you manage hauling the camper back to Milwaukee on your own?"

Him, going home to Fuller Lake, to the family and job he loved. All of the things he needed. And she wasn't one of them.

CHAPTER TWENTY-SIX

With his head tipped back and rolled toward the side window, Matt watched the countryside roll by. He'd been "asleep" for the last hour. Feigning sleep to keep from talking. More to keep his father from gloating. *Knew you'd come back*, had been his father's greeting words. It had only gotten worse after that.

Beside him, his father tapped the steering wheel in tune to an old rock song wailing from the radio. Made Matt wish he really were asleep.

Mile by mile, familiar landmarks whizzed by. Thirty miles south of Fuller Lake was the farm that had a corn maze every fall. He'd had his first kiss there, with Emily Schaftner.

Eight miles later came the huge cement badger at the entrance to the petting zoo. He smiled as he remembered the goat that had nipped Brad right where a thirteen-year-old boy never wanted attention called to in public.

Ten more miles and they passed the go-kart track where he'd spent many a weekend as a kid pretending he was the next NASCAR champion.

Fifteen minutes later they passed the used car lot where Matt had bought his first car. Then the restaurant where he'd had his high school graduation party. When they passed the first house he'd helped remodel, he knew he was truly home.

Within five minutes, they crossed the distance from the southern city limits to the northern edge of town where the whole family lived, Brad two blocks east of their parents' and Matt's house four blocks north.

He frowned when they passed the road to his parents' house. Probably taking a detour to the grocery store. Instead, his father turned left onto Park Street. Toward his own house.

He didn't want to go there, yet he eagerly looked down the road, mentally picturing his house. "Forget the way, Dad?"

"Have a nice nap?"

Damn it, they couldn't go to his house. The idea of coming home was to cut himself free of his old life, not cement him to it. "Shouldn't we be getting home? If I know Ma, she's watching the clock, wondering where we are."

"Don't worry. We're right on time."

His house was just a block away now. He wished he was in a drivers-ed car with his own brake. He'd be stepping on it about now. Except that would require the use of his legs, and if he had that, going to his house would be no problem.

Without consciously doing so, he craned his neck. His heart sped up when he saw his neighborhood. And then, there it was. The beautiful Victorian home with the front porch and the gingerbread trim.

This moment felt all too familiar. Much like when he'd come home from rehab. But it was startlingly different because nothing in his life was the same. The hope was gone now.

His dad pulled into the driveway. Matt had barely grabbed hold of his wheelchair when his mother came running down the driveway. His door flung open. He was almost knocked sideways with the impact of his mother's hug.

"I can't help on the group home if I can't breathe." He tried to pry her fingers loose. Other than the death grip, he had to admit he wouldn't have wanted anything less from her.

Despite his complaint, she held him longer than normal. "I'm so glad you're home."

Home. He sighed as he looked at his house. May as well get it over with, he decided as he set up his chair. With more experience than he'd ever wished to have, he transferred into his wheelchair and then wheeled up the driveway, conscious that he was hurrying and powerless to control his eagerness.

In the kitchen, he paused, taking all of it in, like he was seeing the room for the first time yet seeing everything only as a long-time lover could. How could he ever have been eager to leave this place? This town? His family?

He moved through the house, inspecting every room. This house was a part of him. He hung his clasped hands on his neck and pictured Abby. Coming here had been a mistake. Just like he'd feared. Now that he was back, he didn't know if he could leave.

§

"Just like old times," Matt's father said the next morning as he pulled his Buick to a stop in the group home's parking lot.

Aware of the wheelchair behind his seat, Matt stared at Derrick's pickup on the other side of the lot. He'd spent a lot of time in that truck just like Derrick had spent a lot of time in Matt's Silverado.

A beat-up, once-red pickup pulled up beside his father's Buick, effectively blocking Matt's view. A barely-twenty-something kid Matt had never seen before climbed from behind the wheel and performed a surfer's wave at his father. The kid trotted off toward the nearly-completed group home that had been built without Matt's help.

"Yeah, just like old times," Matt answered.

"It's good to have you back."

This might not be just like old times, but his heart gave a couple of hard thumps at the thought of being back. A dizzying concept. One he wished could be lasting.

He needed to tell his father he wasn't staying. That he was only here to finish out the build.

His father pulled the door latch. The door opened a crack.

"Dad."

Holding the door handle, Carl Huntz looked at Matt with eyebrows raised.

Go ahead, tell him. Tell him you're never going to walk again. Tell him that construction's not a job you can do anymore. Tell him you only came back because you need to put this part of your life behind you.

Despite the curious wrinkles around his father's eyes, his dad looked happier than Matt could remember. How could he disappoint his father?

His father tipped his head and arched his eyebrows a bit further.

"It's good to be back."

His father's grin made Matt feel like a fraud. The big bear hug was even worse. Gripped in his father's powerful grasp, he said, "I can't work if I can't breathe, remember?"

"Sorry," his father said as he let go. "It's just that it feels like a lifetime you've been away. But you're back now, and things are going to be good." He nodded. "Things are going to be great."

Great, Matt thought as his father got out of the car and headed for the building. His dad was going to be crushed when he found out the truth.

Delaying the inevitable, Matt took his time putting the wheels on his chair. He hauled his ass into the chair and then slowly made his way across the yard that had been leveled smooth. Rolls of turf lay off to the side, waiting to be spread out.

He circled the building, checking things out. Huntz & Sons Construction had done a damn fine job. The contract for next year's group home build was already theirs, and his father had plenty of winter jobs lined up. As many as any of the larger construction crews in town. Matt had gotten his wish. Huntz & Sons had reached the big leagues.

"Yippee," he whispered. What good were wishes come true if he couldn't be a part of them?

He came around the corner of the building and stopped short of plowing into someone. Derrick. Standing close enough to sucker punch. Or hug.

Derrick stood perfectly still for three long seconds as the two ex-friends stared at each other. Finally, Derrick said, "You look good."

Matt took in Derrick's tired, bloodshot eyes, and the way his clothes hung on him. He wished he could say the same. "You look like shit."

Derrick smiled, the dimple piercing his cheek, and for a second he looked like the same guy Matt used to go fishing with, play basketball with, just sit quietly with. But then the smile vanished. He looked like a guy who slept way too little and worried way too much.

"You say that like you care," Derrick said.

"I do." Surprisingly, he did care. "Seriously, are you feeling okay?"

Derrick ran his hand through hair that looked like it'd thinned out in the last three months. "You don't really want to hear me whine about my problems."

"*Want to?* No. But..." He rubbed his hand over his mouth. Damn. Had he really been about to say that's what friends are for?

The skin around Derrick's eyes sagged. "I need to get back to work. My job's already hanging on a frayed line as it is."

"Like my dad would fire you."

Derrick raised one eyebrow. No words necessary to confirm it was true.

"I'm sorry," Matt said. And he was. Derrick was a damn good worker. A hard worker. And he'd been family.

Still planted where he'd been standing, Derrick rubbed his thin fingers across his forehead. He looked too exhausted to move, and Matt envisioned his friend's toothpick legs being too weak to hold him up.

"You're supposed to be mad at me, not nice. Mad, I can understand. Mad, I deserve." Derrick dropped his hand to his side. "I don't deserve your sympathy."

"No. You don't."

The sad eyes looked even sadder. Like he knew they were the proper words but not ones he wanted to hear. He nodded. "I know I'm not someone you want to be stuck working with. It's probably better for all of us if I quit, but I hope you don't mind if I wait until everything's done on the group home. I'd like to finish out this project."

Derrick *didn't* deserve his sympathy. Friends didn't *deserve* anything. And that, right there, was what being a friend was all about. Could he tell Derrick that? That friends care about one another because they're friends. Matt hung his hands on the back of his neck. His stomach flipped and his heart raced. Could he forgive? Forget? Just put it all behind them and move on?

As though the silence granted permission, Derrick nodded once. "I'll tell your dad on Friday that I'm quitting."

Your dad. Not *Pops* like Derrick had always called Matt's dad. Derrick was quitting more than just a job.

"Derrick," he called out to his friend's back.

Derrick stopped and turned around.

"You're right. You don't deserve my sympathy. You have it as a free gift, because that's how it works with friends."

Derrick's eyebrows tipped in toward his nose. Questioning. Puzzled. And then his eyebrows raised. "Seriously?"

"It might take some time before I'm ready to start telling you my darkest secrets, but yeah, we *are* friends."

It took Derrick less than two steps to clear the distance between them. Derrick reached out like he was going to hug Matt but then pulled back in an awkward moment. With a grin that brought out his dimple he shrugged. "What the hell."

In a flash, Derrick strangled Matt in his embrace. And it felt wonderful.

§

Abby walked into her mother's room to find her sitting at a table, stringing large beads onto a leather cord. Could this really be the same woman who seven months ago couldn't turn the page in a book?

Her mother looked up. Her content expression morphed into one of horror. She flopped her body over the pile of beads. "You can't see. Go away, out in the hall, just for a minute."

"Can't see what?" Abby asked, pretending she hadn't seen a thing.

Her mother waved her hand. "Just go. I'll call when it's safe."

Out in the hallway, Abby leaned against the wall.

She had so many reasons to be happy. Her mother was doing better than Abby could have ever imagined. Her mother moving into less restrictive housing was now a very believable concept. Below the surface, though, she was disappointed in herself. How could she, the physical therapist who'd gone to school to work with brain-injured patients, have not been able to help her mother?

She let her head tip back against the wall with a thump. She was letting her frustrations with her job color her judgment. Working with patients like her mother was a slow process. Much slower than helping someone learn to walk again after a hip replacement or knee surgery. There were days when she wished she were back at St. Luke's. The rewards of her job were more evident then.

"Okay," her mother called out. "You can come back in now."

Abby stepped back into her mother's room and almost laughed. An entire box of loose tissues covered the table like a blanket.

"Matt didn't come today." Her mother adjusted a tissue that'd been neatly lined up just a second ago.

"He went home to visit his family. Remember?"

"I miss him."

Fully aware of the emptiness inside her that only Matt could fill, she said, "I do too, Mom."

"Will he be back tomorrow?"

The question felt too much like the old one about her father. She put her hand in her pocket and crossed her fingers. The superstitious motion hadn't helped her as a child, but maybe that was because she hadn't wished hard enough. And God knows, she was wishing plenty now. "Not tomorrow, but he'll be back."

"Good. Because he promised to help me put the ends on—" She covered her mouth. "He's going to help me with something."

Abby crossed her arms over her stomach and prayed that soon it'd be Matt's arms around her. "He'll be back."

§

"Just like old times," Derrick said twelve hours later

as he pulled into Matt's driveway. He parked in front of the garage in the spot where Matt's Silverado used to sit and slid the gear stick into park. Some kind of rock music that both Derrick and Crystal loved played on the radio. Twin headlights illuminated the vinyl garage door panels, beyond which was a room filled with the toys Matt had found necessary to buy over the years, toys that no longer had a purpose in his life.

There was still a wheelchair tucked away behind his seat just like there'd been this morning. He hadn't done anything more than play gofer all day. And Derrick wasn't coming in for a cold bottle of beer because that would be just a little too weird, given the circumstances. But Matt nodded, anyhow, because this was the closest it'd felt in a long time. "Like old times."

"Pick you up in the morning?"

"Bright and early." Matt grabbed his wheelchair and hauled it over the seat. Rock music blared as Matt put the wheels on the chair. Beyond the lace curtains on Mrs. Mezmitz's darkened kitchen window, Matt knew his elderly neighbor was watching. He hauled his body into the chair and started to close the truck door when Derrick stopped him.

"Thanks for talking to your dad."

It had been easy telling his dad to stop being so hard on Derrick. If only it were as easy to tell his father he wasn't going to walk again. "You're a good worker, even if you do make a shitty friend at times."

Derrick laughed. Just enough light came from the dash for Matt to see the deep dimple in Derrick's cheek before it disappeared and the mood became serious again. "I'm sorry about what I did. I wish I could go back and change things."

Matt settled back in the wheelchair. "Why didn't you hook up with Crystal after I left?"

Derrick was silent for a moment, like he was weighing the benefits between a brush off and the truth. Then he sighed. "Truthfully, we tried. Even though you'd broken up with her, it still felt like we were cheating." He shook his head. "We just couldn't get past that."

"Do you still love her?"

"With all my heart."

Matt knew all too well what that felt like. He'd only been away from Abby for one day, but it felt like a lifetime. He'd hate to know what a real lifetime apart felt like. "Life's too short to not spend it with the people you love."

Derrick frowned and Matt shook his head and grinned. Now *this* felt like old times. "For being so smart, you can be darn stupid. If you love Crystal, you should be with her."

The furrows in Derrick's forehead deepened. "You're kidding, right?"

"You figure it out Mr. Class Valedictorian."

§

The beautiful weather from the weekend held throughout the week and Friday was no different. The hot sun seared Matt's arms, but it felt wonderful. Being outside was glorious. Working with the guys was a dream come true.

Matt wheeled over the brick path toward the raised flower bed where flats of red and pink flowers waited to be planted. He stopped sixty feet short of his destination and watched as Crystal dug her fingers into the soft dirt, with Derrick at her side. They looked good together. Happy. Exactly as Matt wanted. So why'd he have such a hard time making his arms move? His shoulder muscles were tighter than the fan belt on a brand new car and his stomach was tangled like a string of Christmas lights.

Derrick caught sight of Matt and waved, his dimple evident even from that distance. Crystal looked up, her head twisting to see who Derrick was greeting. She was stunningly gorgeous, even with dirt shadowing her face.

His eyes locked with hers. The knots in his stomach released their hold and his shoulders relaxed. She could have been a stranger. A beautiful one, but a stranger nonetheless. That's what he felt as he looked at her. No attachment. No anger. No love. Granted, there was a sense of loss for what could have been, but overpowering it was relief that "what could have been" hadn't happened.

He closed the distance. Looking at Crystal in her designer jeans, three-hundred dollar boots, and fashion T-Shirt filled him with a longing for Abby. Two more days and they'd be together again. All he had to do was break the news to his father that he'd never walk again.

"You're just as pretty as those flowers," he said.

"You look nice too, Matt."

He took two cans of soda from the pack hanging on his chair and held out the ice-cold Diet Pepsi to Crystal and then handed Derrick a Mountain Dew. "Dad thought you might be thirsty."

"Tell Pops thanks."

Crystal brushed dirt from the flowerbed rail and sat down. "You really do look good. It looks like you've mastered the chair."

"It was either that or stay in one place forever." He nodded toward the building. "Dad said he needs me for something." Probably a switch plate needs installing. Something even Kaylee could do. "Nice seeing you, Crystal."

"You too."

It had been nice seeing Crystal, putting their relationship fully in the past. He eyed the group home building as he wheeled toward it. He wished he could have been present for every step of its construction instead of just the beginning and the very end. That desire confirmed what he'd known all along. The construction part of his past was going to be the hardest part to cut himself free of. Construction was in his blood. The only way to fully get it out would be a full transfusion.

He pulled open the door leading into the lobby and then wheeled to the administrator's office where his father had set up a temporary command post. "At your service." He wheeled up to the desk made from a sheet of plywood stretched between two saw horses.

His father sat back on the folding chair, pulling away from the project binder. "You're planning on leaving as soon as this job is done, aren't you?"

So much for waiting another day or two to break the news. Matt looked at the jagged corner of the plywood sheet. Even though his dad had already cornered him, he couldn't do anything more than shrug.

"I'm hoping I can change your mind. I want you back as a full-time member of this crew."

He hung his hands on the back of his neck. If he could be productive, be something more than a gofer, he'd have a damn hard time saying no. But for as much as he loved being a part of the crew, the sad truth was that he wasn't all that helpful.

"I'd love to, Dad but— "

"I don't want to hear buts. If you can't give me a flat-out yes, I want you to at least take some time to think about it before you say no."

His father wouldn't be saying that if he knew what Matt knew. He needed to tell his dad that he wasn't going to walk again. No more stalling.

"Say you'll think about it. Seriously consider it."

His mouth dried up. He rubbed his tongue against the roof of his mouth, working up enough spit to talk. It took every ounce of self control he had to keep his eyes on his father. He unconsciously clasped his hands. "I'm not going to walk again, Dad. I've gotten back everything I'm going to." He shook his head. "I can't say I'll stay on when I know I can't do the work."

"The job I've got for you doesn't require any skills you need your legs for. I want you to take over our projects. Prioritize the work, assign the jobs, hunt out new projects and make the bids, order all the supplies, stuff like that."

His mind resisted what he was hearing. It wasn't possible his father was putting him in charge of the heart of the business. "But that's your job."

"And now I want it to be yours."

"But..." He covered his mouth as the offer swirled around inside his head. He lowered his hand to his chin. "You're trusting me with full responsibility for this company."

"Yes, I guess I am."

"I'm stunned. I don't know what to say."

"'Yes' would be nice."

"Well, then, hell—" The 'yes' fell from existence. If he took the job, what would that mean for him and Abby? He couldn't manage the projects from Milwaukee. He couldn't expect Abby to quit her dream job and move to Fuller Lake just so he could have his own dreams come true. A long-distance relationship couldn't last forever. And he didn't want a life that didn't include her. But this job was important.

Abby? Or the job? One or the other. But not both.

Shit.

Between a rock and a hard place took on a whole new meaning.

"Can I have a couple days to think about it?"

"Take all the time you need, as long as your answer comes from your heart."

But what if his heart wanted two things and he couldn't have both?

§

Abby sat on the end of the couch with her legs curled beneath her, the cordless phone on her lap, and her eyes on the clock. Matt had been calling every night at nine without fail. Ten minutes to go.

Her toes tapped with anticipation, but her stomach churned with dread. With each call, as he talked about his family and his job and Derrick, she heard the wistfulness in his tone. It was only a matter of time before he told her he wasn't coming back.

The phone rang and she jumped. With her heart thudding, she pushed the answer button. "Hello."

"I must have misdialed and got heaven because you sure sound like an angel," Matt said.

Her cheeks turned toasty and she couldn't erase her smile. "With talk like that, I wouldn't admit it even if this were a wrong number."

"The way I feel, it can't be wrong." There was no teasing nature to his voice.

She bit her lip as tears filled her eyes. How could

something so sweet be so painful to hear?

"Did you hang up?" he asked.

"No way, not without hearing about your day." *Tell me how much you hate it there. Tell me you're coming home.*

"I saw Crystal today."

Her stomach seized up. Crystal, the woman he'd planned on marrying. A man couldn't ever totally erase his feelings for his first love, especially someone as caring as Matt.

She had to work hard to keep her voice calm. "How was she?"

"Great. Beautiful, as always."

Beautiful. There was no way she could compete with beautiful.

"Dirty," he continued. "She was planting flowers. I never would have believed it if I hadn't seen it for myself. She looked happy."

Great, beautiful, and happy. What a dangerous combination. Abby's stomach twisted. She swallowed hard.

"A lot happier than I ever remember seeing her. I think her being with Derrick is a good thing. They make a nice couple."

How could she have forgotten Crystal was now with Derrick? The tension she'd been holding inside rushed outward in a sigh. Even with the reprieve, she still felt the cloud of heartbreak looming on the horizon like an approaching deadly storm. If it didn't come in the form of Crystal, it'd be something else. And it'd be soon. She could feel it, just like animals that reacted differently in response to brewing bad weather.

"My mother was asking about you," Abby said. "She misses you." *I miss you. So much.*

"Tell her I miss her, too." And then, he laughed. "Tell her I miss her chickendoodle cookies. Ma's a good cook, too good. I think I've probably put on ten pounds these last few days. But Ma could really learn a few things from your mom. Especially when it comes to cooking with horse feathers."

The lights shining from the apartment building across the street twinkled as her eyes filled with tears. She bit her lip and blinked. Why did he have to be so darned perfect?

"How was work?" she asked, feeling only a little guilty that she'd picked the one topic that pecked at his insecurities.

"Oh, man. What a day. Brad put a dead mouse in Chad's lunch box. I never saw a guy jump so high in my life. It was great."

She closed her eyes and chastised herself for having done such a proficient job in showing him he could still have the life he'd planned. "Sounds great."

"You okay, honey? You sound kind of down."

Honey. Why'd he have to torture her that way? "I think I'm getting a summer cold."

"I'm sorry. Wish I were there to take care of you. Make you chicken soup and all that."

"Me, too." *Come home, Matt. Come back to me. Please.*

"I could send Kaylee down to baby you. She's good medicine. At least, she made me feel better when I was in the hospital. I'll have her color you a picture. At the very least, it'll make you smile and you can't feel like crap when you're smiling."

"I'd like that." He'd talked about his mother, Brad, Derrick, and Crystal. About the only person he'd missed so far was his father.

"Something else happened at work today," he said.

"Does it involve any dead animals?"

"No."

Silence stretched between them, warning her that the time for joking was over. She wanted to hang up so he couldn't continue, but she didn't want to miss one second of their time together.

"Dad offered me a job."

She almost laughed at how she'd worked herself up to a near state of panic. "Your father's only spent how much of the last few months trying to get you to come back to work?"

"It's a good job, an important one. And it's something I can do. He wants me to be project manager. Basically, I'll be...I'd be running the company."

She pressed the phone tight to her ear and rocked forward and back. She'd just lost him.

"Abby?"

Her throat was tight, but she managed somehow to speak. "That's great, Matt. I'm happy for you."

"It is great." He didn't sound happy.

She hated hearing the troubled tone of his voice. This job really was great. And he deserved it. He should be celebrating instead of worrying. She stopped rocking and wiped her eyes. "You'll do a wonderful job, I know you will."

"Are you saying I should take the job?"

This was best all around. "You'd be a fool not to."

"I would, wouldn't I? Here's the thing." He paused. "Damn, this isn't how I wanted to do this."

Oh, God. He was going to say he loved her.

She longed to hear those words, but it'd only complicate matters. Before he could speak, she said, "Matt, take the job."

"If I do, what happens to us?"

Us. Him and her. Together. One unit.

She brushed away the tear before it had a chance to break free. "We'll still be friends. Always."

"I don't want to be friends. I love you."

The last three words echoed in her head. She wished she could permanently imprint them there so she could hear him say it over and over because after this phone call, she'd never hear it again. Her heart swelled and pressed against her breastbone and her throat tightened.

She hugged herself with her free arm and wished Matt were with her so she could see him one last time. "I'll always have you in my heart, Matt, but your place is with your family. Like you said, this is an important job. I want you to tell your father you accept his offer."

"Abby—"

"I have to go." As soon as she hung up, she opened

the line so he couldn't call back. With her arms wrapped tightly around herself, she hung her head and rocked on her knees while an unbearable pain ripped through her.

This is best for Matt. This is best for Matt. This is best for Matt.

Wiggling its way around the chant, the truth pushed through her thoughts.

She hadn't told him to take the job for him. She'd done it for herself. Because she was too scared to give love a chance. And now she'd lost Matt. Forever.

The impact of what she'd done hit her with full reality. No more smiles from Matt that melted her from the inside out. No more gentle touches that made contact with more than just her skin. No more conversations that required nothing more than a reading of his expression.

No more Matt.

Ever.

"Oh, God," she whispered. "What did I do?"

§

No matter what Abby had said, his taking the job wasn't what she wanted. And Matt wasn't so sure it was what he wanted, either. Too bad he wasn't still with Crystal, having to decide between her and the job. The choice would be easy. The job would win hands down.

The realization of that logic struck him dead on.

There was no way he could take the job. Not if it meant losing Abby.

He put his thumb over the "1" button to speed dial Abby. He paused when the motion sank in. The night Abby had taken him to meet her mother, he'd reprogrammed his parents' home number in the vacated speed-dial-five that had once held Crystal's number. Abby's number had landed in the number one slot where his parents' number had been. If he'd only paid attention, he would have known he loved her two months earlier.

He pushed the button and groaned when he heard the busy signal. Without hesitation, he pushed the "3" button. Another realization struck. He'd deleted Crystal's number as soon as he'd moved to Milwaukee. He hadn't gotten rid of Derrick's.

"Hey there," was Derrick's greeting.

"I need a favor."

"Anything, it's yours."

"I need a ride to Milwaukee. Tonight."

"Road trip. Cool. I'll be there in about ten minutes."

"Derrick," Matt said before his friend could hang up.

"Yeah?"

"Thanks."

After ending the call, he made the final one that was going to seal his future. When his father answered, he said, "Derrick might miss work tomorrow."

"You're his personal secretary now?"

"He's taking me back to Milwaukee."

The silence coming over the line told Matt he'd disappointed his father yet again, but this time he didn't care. He was doing what was best for him. Not what his father thought was best for him or what he felt was best for his family. This time he was putting his needs first.

"Dad, I appreciate the job offer, more than you'll ever know, but...well, when you asked me if anything was going on between me and Abby, I kind of lied. Not on purpose. I didn't know how I felt, but now I do. I love her. I'm sorry."

"Will being with her make you happy?"

"Yes." There was no need to think on his answer.

"Then there's nothing to be sorry about. The job's not going anywhere. It'll still be there when you're ready for it."

The reflection of headlights walked along the wall as a vehicle pulled into his driveway. Derrick. He needed to go. But first there was something he needed to know. "Did you only offer me that job because I can't do the other work anymore?"

"Do you really not know the answer?"

He stared hard at the corner of the glass coffee table. Little bits of his past that he'd overlooked his whole life filtered through his mind. His father claiming he was too busy to write up this bid or that bid and asking Matt to do it. Having Matt order the supplies for random projects. Why had he been so blind?

There was a knock on the kitchen door. Derrick, ready to go. Matt turned his chair away from the doorway, looking for a moment of privacy.

"Yeah, I think I do. But I've got to ask. If it'd been Brad who'd had the accident, would you have offered him this job?"

His father's laugh rang clear over the phone line. "That's what I love about you, your crazy sense of humor."

"Dad, thanks for trusting me."

"Even though I wish you weren't leaving again, I'm happy for you. Abby seems like a nice girl."

After knocking again, Derrick opened the back door. "Hey, Matt? You ready to ride?"

"Thanks, Dad. I've got to go." After a brief pause, he added, "I love you."

"Love you, too."

Matt wheeled to the kitchen. "Yeah, I'm ready."

"So what's in Milwaukee that requires a late-night ride?"

Matt grinned. "My destiny."

Derrick's dimple showed as he nodded. "Ah. She must be special."

"She is."

§

The clock on Derrick's stereo system glowed 1:28 when they pulled up in front of Abby's apartment building. Light shone from her living room window. Matt wasted no time in grabbing his chair from the rear passenger section of the truck. "I'd invite you in, but—"

"—two's company and three's a crowd. I understand. I'll be at your apartment. Give me a call if you need a ride."

Matt popped the wheels onto his chair and then made his transfer. He couldn't have wheeled up the sidewalk any faster had he had a rocket pack attached to his chair. "Please answer," he whispered as he pushed her doorbell. He pounded on the door too, for good measure.

There were no sounds of life inside the apartment, but Derrick's truck purred at the road. He pounded on the door again.

"Come on, answer."

He had to knock a third time before the door opened. Abby's eyes were red and her face was tear-streaked. Seeing her that way filled him with a pain he'd never felt before. Her hands shook as she pressed them to her mouth.

"Matt."

As much as he hated seeing evidence of her pain, it reassured him that he'd been right. She hadn't been serious when she'd told him to take the job. "I turned down Dad's offer."

"Matt. No."

He wheeled forward and closed the door. Derrick's truck finally pulled away.

Needing to touch her, to feel her, he put out his hand. Without hesitation, she put her palm to his. He gave her a slight pull, bringing her onto his lap. He nuzzled his nose in her hair and breathed deeply. She smelled like heaven. Her arms went around him.

"I love you," he whispered, her hair tickling his lips. Her arms stiffened and he felt her breathing still. She radiated fear, and he couldn't blame her. She'd had a pretty shitty past when it came to relationships.

With a finger to her chin, he lifted her head from his shoulder and locked his gaze on hers. "Do you trust me?"

Her answer was a very slight nod. He ached to be able to kiss away her fears, to instantly heal what hurt inside her. If there were a way to make her father and her prior boyfriends pay for what they'd done to her, Matt would have made sure it happened. She didn't deserve to be hurt the way she had. God willing though, he'd make up for what they'd done.

Without looking away, he said, "You once called me stubborn."

"And opinionated." Her voice quivered.

"Yeah, that too." He flashed a quick smile before turning

serious again. "I mean it, Abby. I love you. I want to share my life with you. And your mother, too." He brushed her cheek with his fingers. "I'm going to marry you, Abby. I'll wait, no matter how long it takes until you're ready. I'll be right here for you and nothing's going to change that."

A tear slid down her cheek.

"Will you marry me?"

She looked away. He could see her wrestling between her heart's desires and her brain's need for protection. He wished there was a way to prove right now that it wasn't just words, that his love was real. She'd see, though. If it took twenty years, he'd spend every second of those years showing her how much he loved her.

"You don't have to answer now, honey. Just promise you'll give me a chance."

She slid off his lap and turned away just enough to send a signal he didn't like. She was scared, that's all. Just trying to protect herself.

"Milwaukee isn't your home," she said. "Fuller Lake is. It's where your family is. Call your dad. Take the job."

He worked hard to keep himself passive when inside he was a jumbled up mess. He knew she loved him. What he wasn't sure about, though, was whether her love was stronger than her fears. "Fuller Lake is nothing but a dot on a map. My family will still be my family, whether I'm here or there. And the job may be one hell of an opportunity, but it'd be meaningless without you. I'm not going anywhere without you and your mom."

Still turned away, her arms slid around her waist in a hug while her head tipped back. He wanted nothing more than to pull her into his arms and protect her from everything horrible in the world. He held his ground only because he knew she needed space to work on whatever she was wrestling with inside her head.

His heart pounded at every pressure point, trying to make its great escape. She had to say yes. That was the only outcome he'd accept.

She lowered her arms, and he knew his wait was over. She didn't look at him. He shook his head, silently protesting the obvious.

"Fuller Lake is your home," she said. "It's your life."

No!

She turned and looked at him. "I want it to be my life, too."

The words hung precariously, like if he breathed too hard they'd blow away. His words tiptoed from his mouth. "And me? Do you want to be my wife?"

She nodded. Her mouth bent into her buy-these-gloves smile. "In a heartbeat."

He held out his arms and she came to him. She nestled on his lap and wrapped her arms around his neck. "I'm still scared, but I trust you."

The sweetest words he'd ever heard. He tightened his arms around her and smiled when she melted against him. "Know what our house is going to need?"

"Our house. I like that." She rubbed the back of his neck, tracing her finger over his scar. "What does *our* house need?"

"A big, floppy-eared dog. Named Fido. What do you say we go to the pound tomorrow and pick him out?"

"Sounds like a plan."

"No backing out." Not concerning Fido. And most certainly not concerning their relationship.

Her fingers stopped moving and she lifted her head from his shoulder. His breath stalled.

"Matt?"

He couldn't breathe.

"Do you think you could use your connections and get a room for Mom in the group home your dad just built?"

He let out the breath. "Honey, if I have to, I'll have him build a whole group home just for her."

She leaned close and brushed her lips against his. "I love you, Matthew Lucas Huntz."

He guided her lips back to his. Such sweet heaven her kiss was, filling his entire being. This life that he now had certainly wasn't what he'd ever planned, but with Abby in it, it sure was one heck of a life worth living.

The End.

ABOUT THE AUTHOR

Lorrie Kruse has always been drawn to books. She remembers the excitement when the Scholastic book pamphlets were handed out way back in grade school. She immediately started circling all of the books she wanted. Little did she know that one day she would write her own book. Being a creative person, it's only natural that her creativity would creep out in the form of writing.

Lorrie's reading interests have shifted over the years. Once she hit the teen years and moved past kids' stories, she moved on to horror stories. (Three cheers to Stephen King's wife for pulling his manuscript out of the garbage.) She's also been a fan of romance, medical mysteries, suspense. Some of her favorite authors are Janet Evanovich, Robert Crais, Harlan Coben, Jane Porter, and John Sandford.

Lorrie is many things besides a writer. By day she's a legal secretary (not to be confused with the illegal secretary of her evening hours). She's a wife (to a wonderful prince of a husband, Brian) and a mom (to a non-furry two-legged critter (Tyler) and a very furry four-legged critter (Token, an Alaskan husky). Lorrie rarely sits idle. If she's not doing one of the aforementioned activities, then she's probably making jewelry or crocheting another pair of socks (much to the dismay of her hubby who says why don't you just buy socks at Walmart). And, if there's a wayward teddy bear in need of a home, Lorrie's your go-to-gal, as long as that bear doesn't mind living in a log home in the country in often-chilly central Wisconsin.

Lorrie hopes you've enjoyed reading this book. She would love to hear from you. Her website is: lorriekruse.com or email her at lorriekruse@gmail.com.

Made in the USA
Lexington, KY
10 December 2015